AWARDS AND PRAISE

ISLANDS

Shortlisted, 2020 Miles Franklin Literary Award

'*Islands* is a riveting and brilliant portrait of a family in crisis.' *The Age*

'Frew has fashioned another heartbreaker . . . the scattered chronology plays with the tragic inevitability of damaged people hurting others. Just the tip of an iceberg of sadness is glimpsed, and the story is the more powerful for its restraint.' *Sydney Morning Herald*

'Frew's talent for descriptive prose and psychogeography is evident throughout . . . her experimentation makes *Islands* stand out, puncturing the narrative at key moments before exploding the notion of the Family Story. Her writing verges on the sublime.' *The Saturday Paper*

'Overwhelming . . . a deep and meditative piece of literature. As we watch the family unravel, we are all the time hoping that Anna will come back, that this catastrophe can be fixed . . . utterly engrossing.' *Australian Women's Weekly*

'In this multi-voiced story, Frew's outstanding ability to empathise with characters who are unable to empathise with each other shines through . . . a work of great compassion and insight.' *Books + Publishing*

'A beautiful study of sorrow that describes the disintegration of a family and the ongoing trauma of a disappearance.' *Readings*

'Frew's deceptively slow-burn tale of a teenage girl—adrift, bewildered, seeking solidity—moves inexorably to its climax, laying bare a certain darkness at the heart of the alternative lifestyle. But it's the tale of a survivor, too.' **Luke Davies, award-winning author of** *Candy*

'At this point it could be too early to call it, but I'm thinking this could end up on my top 10 books of the year list . . . Beautifully written, difficult to put down, hard not to feel the ache.' *Geelong Advertiser*

'In its exploration of maternal, sexual, unrequited and platonic relationships, *Hope Farm* is a finely calibrated study of love, loss and belonging.' **Thuy On,** *Sunday Age*

'[An] assured exploration of that awkward moment between childhood and the teenage years [as well as a] devastating critique of the treatment of unwed mothers in the '70s.' **Margot Lloyd,** *Adelaide Advertiser*

'Frew is a gifted writer, evidenced here by finely balanced observations and atmospheric description . . . Silver is poised at the beginning of adult understanding and Frew handles the challenge with deftness. Silver's insight and compassion are juxtaposed with naivety and the idealistic force of her first crushes.' **Ed Wright,** *Weekend Australian*

'Absorbing . . . A beautifully told story of courage and survival, *Hope Farm* is about growing up, belonging, and long-kept secrets.' **Carys Bray, author of** *A Song for Issy Bradley*

Peggy Frew's first novel, *House of Sticks*, won the Victorian Premier's Literary Award for an Unpublished Manuscript by an Emerging Victorian Writer, and was shortlisted for the UTS Glenda Adams Prize for New Writing. *Hope Farm*, her second novel, won the Barbara Jefferis Award, was shortlisted for the Stella Prize and the Miles Franklin Literary Award, and longlisted for the International Dublin Literary Award. Her third novel, *Islands*, was shortlisted for the Miles Franklin Literary Award. She has been published in *New Australian Stories 2*, *Kill Your Darlings*, *Meanjin* and *The Big Issue*. Peggy is also a member of the critically acclaimed and award-winning Melbourne band Art of Fighting. *Wildflowers* is her fourth novel.

wildflowers

PEGGY FREW

ALLEN&UNWIN
SYDNEY · MELBOURNE · AUCKLAND · LONDON

First published in 2022

Allen & Unwin
Cammeraygal Country
83 Alexander Street
Crows Nest NSW 2065
Australia
Phone: (61 2) 8425 0100
Email: info@allenandunwin.com
Web: www.allenandunwin.com

Allen & Unwin acknowledges the Traditional Owners of the Country on which we live and work. We pay our respects to all Aboriginal and Torres Strait Islander Elders, past and present.

 A catalogue record for this book is available from the National Library of Australia

ISBN 978 1 76106 692 4

Typeset in 12.7/17 pt Adobe Garamond Pro by Bookhouse, Sydney
Printed in Australia by McPherson's Printing Group

10 9 8 7 6 5 4 3 2 1

FOR TEGAN BENNETT DAYLIGHT

I.

WHEN THE PHONE CALLS STARTED Nina was surprised and wary. Then came dread, and not long after that a flattened and feeble anger. Nina stopped answering the calls, which were from her sister Amber, her other sister Meg, and from her mother, Gwen. She stopped answering the calls and she began to make a series of changes to herself, her life. She did not do this with any sort of control or intent. She did it like someone in a dream.

The first thing she did was put an end to the affairs. Such an old-fashioned word, *affairs*: a word for her parents' generation. But they had been old-fashioned, with all the trappings, all the clichés—flowers, champagne, hotel rooms, lingerie. You could, in 2014, still find men who were into that sort of thing. Steep little hills they were, affairs; when you lined them up end to end, as Nina had over the years, what you got was rhythm and structure. There had been one disruption to this pattern—Luke was his name—but that too was over.

The truth was that they had already been tapering off. Nina was getting older and men didn't look at her as often, or proposition her. She was only thirty-seven, but she'd always relied on a wispy kind of prettiness that, just in the past couple of years, seemed to have abandoned her, and while she understood that there were several things she might do about this, she had kept hoping she wouldn't have to. She wasn't sure if she was morally opposed to things like botox and fillers—even dyeing her hair, getting her eyelashes tinted—or just lazy. Either way, there was a resistance, and somehow it had all gradually slithered from something that she might consider one day to something that it was probably too late for.

There was also the matter of meeting men. In the past it had always just happened—they'd found her. There were things that she could do about this as well. She could figure out the right places to take herself—the right bars, at the right times. Or there was eHarmony or whatever, which she only knew about because her friend Sidney kept trying to make her go on it. But it had all seemed to require too much effort.

And then the calls had begun, and the messages left on her phone. Amber's: formal, solemn, solicitous, upsetting. Gwen's: tremulous, hope-filled, pitiful, infuriating. And Meg's: brisk, demanding, persistent, annoying.

Nina hadn't called any of them back. She'd had a man on the go at that time, one of the few that was still limping in every now and again, catching her eye, gamely offering his worn rag of a pick-up line. (Nina hated how cynical she'd become, but all the same it was hard not to be—twenty years and so many men and, honestly, there had been only one in all that time who had at any point surprised her, and that was Luke, and look where that ended up. An unkind word came to mind when she thought of these stragglers, these late limpers. It was *dregs*. But she supposed this, in all fairness, could also be applied to her.) One afternoon, this latest man had sent a text—*Tonight?*—and

Nina had deleted it without replying, and blocked him, and that was that.

She'd taken to lying on the couch in the front room late in the evening. She lay there and looked out the window at the street. The light wasn't on; nobody could see in. Not that Nina would care. Not caring was the most interesting part of this time of change, this dreamlike time. She had receded into some very quiet, very still inner zone, and from there she was watching herself no longer caring.

This was, strangely, accompanied by a sense of panic. It was the dreadful silent squirming kind—very familiar to Nina. The panic was there in her inner sanctum, the place she was looking out from. But she had come to realise that it was like a very small hurricane—almost ornamental—and if she kept still and did nothing, it just whirled away there beside her quite harmlessly.

Across the road was a huge vacant block surrounded by a high chain-link fence. Every now and then someone came and mowed it, but in between mowings the grass got long and sometimes sprays of little flowers appeared, pink, yellow, white—were they wildflowers, Nina wondered, or just flowering weeds? She wasn't sure what the difference was. Somehow people managed to dump things in the grass: broken bikes, prams, children's car seats. Nina didn't know how the people got these things over the fence. She didn't know why they bothered getting them over the fence; why not just dump them on the street? It seemed an odd distinction to make. Why was it any more polite, any less irresponsible, to chuck your rubbish into a fenced vacant block than to just leave it on the nature strip?

From the couch she couldn't see the grass or the piles of rubbish. She could just see the top of the fence and beyond that, in the distance, the lights of the city skyscrapers, and above it all the sky, which on this particular night was overcast, orangey grey. It was chilly and she pulled the blanket down and tried to throw it over herself without sitting up. She used her feet to grab the end and get it into place, undulating like a seal on a rocky beach. This was not in keeping with the tidiness of the room, its order, its tone, but who cared? There was no one to see her. Who cared even if someone was? The blanket was one her mother had given her, pale and darker blues in a chevron pattern. Gwen had got it at a sale. It was pilled now, but it looked all right folded over the back of the couch. The couch had cost a lot of money, and all Nina used it for was to lie on at night sometimes, by herself. She supposed that at least this meant the couch was still in very good condition. She could sell it. Perhaps she would.

She could rent this room out to someone. A housemate. Would that be a good idea? She wasn't sure. Probably not. She had lived alone for such a long time and had grown accustomed to certain freedoms, certain privacies.

What was it for, this room? This was one of the things she thought about on these nights. She didn't use it. When she brought men to the house she didn't bring them into this room. She should say 'used to bring'—when she used to bring men to the house.

It was like a sort of display, with the nice couch and the sideboard and the pictures on the wall. A showroom or a set, carefully curated to indicate—what? That this was a house. A home. Where—okay—where a family might live. A family with Nina plus another adult in it, and children, or at least pets.

But Nina was thirty-seven and she lived by herself. That hadn't happened for her—a family, a home. And it hadn't happened for them either, Amber and Meg, Nina's sisters. They didn't even have their own family anymore. A year and a half ago their father had died, and their mother had either turned into or been revealed to be a strange, faraway woman who didn't look anyone in the eye. And anyway, even before that, the three of them, Nina and her sisters . . . well, you could hardly call it a family.

It must be late. She didn't want to sleep here. She didn't want to fall into that habit; the couch would get worn out and also she didn't want the room to become too familiar. She liked the way it made her think, when she visited it. She liked the ideas it provided—selling the couch, getting a housemate; ideas that, even with their slightly narcotic edge of self-delusion, brought a stirring, a sense of direction, possibility.

Above the mantel was one of her father's paintings from the nineties. Aggressive slabs of puce and lurid yellow on a ground the colour of bandaids. Like most of his abstract work it made Nina think of infections, skin problems, inflammation, pus. Still, she was very fond of it. She would keep the painting, whatever else she did—or imagined doing—with the room.

She got up and walked down the hallway, which was getting harder to walk down because of all the boxes. In the kitchen she fried an egg and ate it from the pan, off the spatula, standing at the stove. She threw the empty eggshell out the window.

When she had washed the pan and spatula and put them back in the draining rack where she kept them (what was the point in drying them and putting them away in the cupboard and the drawer if she was just going to get them out again the next night?), she went into the backyard and picked a handful of rocket leaves from the row of dirt-filled polystyrene boxes that her landlady, Viv, had given her. The rocket took care of itself. Two years ago Nina had planted one punnet of seedlings from Bunnings (three dollars and ninety-five cents), which in no time gangled crazily out of control, breaking into starry white flowers. 'Bolted to seed,' Viv said. Nina thought she'd wasted her money, but once those plants died off new ones grew and they just kept on seeding and sowing themselves and there were always leaves to pick.

She ate the leaves—which were very peppery; they seemed to be getting more so with each crop—standing in the tiny concrete yard under the dirty and faintly luminous orange city clouds, and then she went back inside and brushed her teeth and went to her bedroom and got into the bed.

'What's going on here?' Sidney had said when she dropped over the week before, squeezing past the boxes in the hall. 'More boxes? You're not moving are you? You can't—you'll never find rent this cheap anywhere else. You'd have to go out to Reservoir.'

'I'm not moving,' Nina said. 'I just don't want all this stuff.'

Sidney peered into the bedroom. 'Wow,' she said, 'even the curtains.' Her voice echoed.

They sat in the kitchen. Sidney had brought a bottle of wine so Nina gave her the glass and drank from the coffee cup.

'Do you have any food?' Sidney said, and Nina fried her an egg.

Sidney watched as Nina disposed of the shell. Then she reopened the window and stuck her head out, leaning over the sink. 'That's quite a pile of eggshells you've got,' she said. 'Out there on the concrete.'

'I'll deal with them later.'

Sidney sat down. 'You could put them in the bin.' She looked around. 'Where is your bin?'

Nina was taking a plate and a fork from one of the boxes. 'I put it away.' She set the plate with the egg on it in front of Sidney. 'If you want greens there's rocket in the backyard.'

'I'm okay.'

'Thanks for the wine.'

'Ellis got it at some conference.'

Ellis was Sidney's husband. They both worked at the hospital where Nina worked. Ellis and Sidney were both doctors; Nina was in admin. Nina was extremely overqualified for her job. She had done other things, before, that she knew some people would think she was much better suited to. But she'd stopped doing those things.

Sidney indicated a stack of letters on the table. 'Did you see these? I brought them in. They were falling out of your letterbox.'

Nina shrugged.

Sidney picked one up and turned it over. 'Who's Amber Atkins? A relative, I'm assuming.'

'My sister.'

'I didn't know you had a sister. Why's she writing you all these letters?'

'She wants me to have a meeting with her. She's joined NA.'

Sidney turned sideways in her chair and stretched out one leg. She was wearing a grey pants suit and tan lace-up shoes with a small heel. 'These shoes cost four hundred dollars,' she said, circling her ankle, 'and they are the least comfortable shoes I've ever worn.' She sighed and tipped her head back. 'What kind of drugs?'

'Pardon?'

'What kind of drugs is she addicted to? Your sister.'
'Heroin. At first. Then she got off that. Then it was anything.'
'You all right?'
'I'm going through an interesting time.'

Nina woke early, in the navy pre-dawn. Without the curtains the room felt hard, but that was the whole idea. She got out of bed, straightened the quilt, and tipped the Salvos bag out onto it. A pair of tracksuit pants, dark blue poly-cotton with elastic at the ankles, and a long-sleeved t-shirt, light blue cotton with a crew neck, *Kennards* printed over the left breast. Grey socks that had belonged to someone called Archie McNamara, according to the sewn-on labels at the toes.

She took off what she was wearing, which was a pair of dark denim Oakley men's jeans that she'd had to roll up—although the bottoms had come unrolled during the night and now she was standing on them—and a brown flannel shirt that was a slim cut but long in the body, almost to her knees. The grey Explorer socks she'd still had on when she got into bed she found hiding under the covers like big exhausted cloth worms. All these—the jeans, flannel shirt and socks, which all smelled pretty bad—went into the Salvos bag.

One thing she hadn't packed away was her lingerie collection. It was in cardboard boxes but that was only because it always had been—Nina had hardly ever worn any of it. It filled two good-sized boxes. Sidney, when she saw, had said, 'Don't go lighting any matches in here, will you.' Nina told her that most of the lingerie was actually silk, which is not as flammable as polyester, but Sidney hadn't been listening. She'd taken a deep green bra out of one of the boxes. 'Can I have this?' she said. Nina said that she wanted to keep them all, sorry; with the system she was using they would only last a couple of months. 'What system?' Sidney wanted to know, but Nina didn't have the energy to explain.

The lingerie boxes were under the bed. Yesterday's set was a red lace bra with too-small cups that Nina's nipples had kept climbing out of and a purple G-string—which fitted all right, she supposed, if you consider what G-strings did to be fitting. Nina didn't; she found them very uncomfortable.

She couldn't remember who had given her any of these things. It had not been Luke; that was one of the ways in which he'd differed from the others.

The bra and G-string went into the 'worn' box, which was now three-quarters filled with musty, flaccid satin, silk and lace, mostly black and red (no imagination) but some pink and (God, why?) purple and a little bit of cream or blue. The green bra Sidney had admired was the only green thing. She pushed the box back under the bed.

She took new underwear from the 'unworn' box and put it on. Peach silk shortie things that gave her an alarming no-pants feeling and a black bra with a circle of tiny plastic fake pearls between the cups. She did the bra up as tightly as she could, which was too tight. Then the clothes. The tracksuit bottoms were probably one size too big and had large pockets that would be useful now that she no longer carried a handbag. The Kennards top fitted quite well. Over this she put on a knee-length anorak, forest green with a soft red tartan lining. It had been a good find, as it was warmer than it looked but not too heavy, and it had good pockets, some with zips. She had been wearing it for about two weeks and might keep it for longer if nothing better turned up. There were a number of small stains on the front but it smelled okay. Archie McNamara's socks went on next and then a pair of Dunlop Volleys that, like the anorak, were having quite a long run.

She didn't know what she looked like, because she'd put the mirror in the backyard, but she felt well covered, if somewhat wide through the thighs—especially once she'd put her keys and wallet and lanyard and glasses case in the pockets of the pants.

In the bathroom she washed her face and brushed her hair. She blew her nose on some toilet paper in case there was something unsightly hanging around in there. It was interesting to observe how far she was prepared to go with this not-caring. It would seem that she didn't want to go so far as to disgust anybody. The bathroom mirror was with the full-length one, both leaning against the wall outside, to the left of the back door. Viv might want them. Nina brushed her teeth.

Outside, in the diaphanous semi-dark, the prams and bikes hulked in black mounds behind the chain-link fence of the vacant block. The Salvos bag bumped like a Santa sack over Nina's shoulder.

When she reached the op shop she took out the worn clothes and put them into one of the collection bins. On the ground lay various boxes, a broken chair, a kid's bike and several garbage bags. Nina crouched and felt the nearest bag, which was soft, and then opened it, undoing the knot and taking care not to rip the plastic. She had become quite efficient at this process. The first two items—an atrophied pair of leggings and a sports bra reeking of perfume—indicated that the bag held the belongings of a young woman and was probably not worth persisting with. There were five bags in total: three cheap thin grey ones (the leggings-and-bra woman's) and two thicker orange ones, good-quality. Nina tried one of the orange ones. Better. There was a smell of eucalyptus wool wash and the first thing she pulled out was a fine linen shirt, pale pink (she thought; it was hard to see). Then there was a heavy knitted jumper, which she rejected as she had her anorak and it was September and the weather should soon be warming. The next thing was a pair of corduroy pants, not too large, and which appeared to be a dark brown. She was getting a picture of the former owner of these clothes—someone small, boyish, with spectacles, perhaps an academic. She put the cords and the shirt in her bag and rummaged further but didn't find any socks.

Was it unethical to take clothes that others had donated to a charity when she could afford to buy them—and could in fact afford to buy new clothes, like she used to do? But she was putting them back afterwards, once she'd worn them. And there was something important about this process, the crawling on the ground, the furtiveness, the discomfort, the lack of dignity—was *debasement* too strong a word? It was like the food, at work. She wasn't exactly stealing; nobody was being inconvenienced by her actions. The only person being inconvenienced was Nina herself.

A car came around the corner. Nina waddled on her haunches so that her back was to it. The car went by. The sky was getting lighter and more traffic was passing on the main road at the end of the street. She tied the orange bag up again and moved on.

Her morning tram rides could be difficult. Because she no longer used her phone (it was in the house somewhere, the battery flat; she hadn't put it in a box; hadn't made a decision about it yet), she no longer had anything to do. People ignored her now, or—depending on what she was wearing and how long she'd been wearing it for—actively avoided her, and so she found herself sitting quietly alone on those bright-lit early trams, sliding through the city, staring out into the glassy near-black. It was in this state—fractured, repetitive, rhythmic—that certain things might come upon her, certain spools, certain loops.

The dark room. The terrible smell.

Amber on the bed, on her side, her knees drawn up. The dirty soles of her feet. Blades of grass and streaks of mud on the mattress. Nina moving closer, the dust under her bare toes, thick and silky, her breath catching in her chest.

The tram passed Flinders Street Station and Nina sat inside it, a thirty-seven-year-old woman dressed in ill-fitting clothes from a garbage bag, with tears rolling down her chin and skimming the stained front of her anorak. The tight bra hurt. The undershorts, riding up, cut in.

The tram crossed the bridge, the dark water, and the park opened up to the left, and then the tram paused outside the Arts Centre and a man in the uniform of a security guard got on. His eyes accidentally met Nina's and there was a frozen moment in which he wore a horrified stare and she tried to send him a look that said, Don't worry, I'm actually okay. This involved trying to smile while tugging the cuff of her Kennards top down and wiping her nose with it. Then the man's face changed and Nina could see that he had realised that she was just a crazy person, and he sat down and took out his phone and the tram began to move again and Nina couldn't stop the smile now so she just left it and smiled wetly out the window at the sinister mobs of trees in the park, the flower clock, the cars with their tail-lights shallow red against the sunrise.

Because Nina's job was casual, and because she'd had it for four years now, since 2010, her boss, Ursula, didn't mind when she came in as long as she got thirty hours done each week. Nina rarely even saw Ursula; perhaps once a fortnight they might pass one another in a hallway, or wave across the cafeteria. Nina felt almost as if she worked for herself.

The hospital was always open. Overnight, at some point, they must close the main doors and only have the emergency entrance in operation, but when Nina arrived at any time between six and seven thirty on these early mornings the whole place was already lit up and the main doors whooshing grandly back and forth as people went in and out of them.

She walked past the smokers in their gowns and slippers, leaning on their frames or sitting in their wheelchairs, then up the ramp. Her Dunlop Volleys flapped a bit. They were better with the Explorers; Archie McNamara's socks were too thin. Under the tracksuit pants the seam of the satin shortie things seemed intent on bisecting her, and the lace trim on the too-tight bra was irritating the skin near her armpits.

Sometimes something broke through the not-caring, a small spurt. Perhaps it was the panic, the mini hurricane. Now it happened: a part of her mind made a sort of wailing sound, and flashed to an image of who she had been only a month ago, before the phone calls and Amber's letters, ascending the ramp in nice ankle boots and a skirt and top from Zara, clean tights, her hair blow-dried, her handbag over her shoulder, her comfortable cotton underwear not drawing any attention to itself. Another part of her mind tamped things back down. Shut up, it said. This is the whole idea.

There was something wonderful about the foyer of the hospital. Its air swirled with wafts of coffee and fried food from the cafeteria, the jellybean smell of the chemist, the watery green, slightly rotten one of the florist and a perpetual piney undercurrent of disinfectant. People walked through, rushing or slow, or sat at the cafeteria's tables, or waited at the lifts—surgeons and nurses in coloured smocks and pants, doctors in suits, patients in gowns or pyjamas with crutches or casts, trundling walkers or drips on wheeled stands. Outside the florist a man was talking into a smartphone on speaker; a metal brace caged his head, pins entering his neck and temples. 'Don't give her the dry food,' he said. 'She thinks she wants it but she doesn't.' Stethoscopes and lanyards dangled, sneaker squeaks echoed, pigeons got in through the courtyard doors and whirred onto tables.

The project Nina was working on today—and had been working on for the past eight or so months—involved taking boxes of old records out of the basement and scanning the records and then storing the scans on hard drives. It was mindless (Nina remembered her father's gentle forlorn chiding: 'All that study! All those degrees!'), and touching the sheets of dusty paper gave her chapped hands and she sometimes got headaches from the sound of the scanner, but she really didn't mind it. She could listen to music if she wanted to, or podcasts—well, she used to, before she stopped using her phone.

The podcasts had been art history ones mostly, recordings of lectures from obscure American or British universities, their sound quality often poor. There was something about these that made the time wash past, made the small windowless room with its fluorescent lights and drifting dust motes seem eternal, otherworldly. Perhaps the hiss-laden voices with their affectations of speech and their propensity for lengthy tangential rambles reminded Nina of her father and his friends, his art cronies, talking at night in the kitchen of her childhood home—a seemingly timeless undemanding background presence. A comfort.

(The wailing came again, in her mind. It had seemed timeless, that presence, but it had not been. Time had gone sliding ruthlessly on and left her father behind, before they'd had the chance to fix themselves as a family, to fix up all the mess. Shh, said Nina to herself. Enough of that.)

Now, without her phone, she just remembered the podcasts. It was amazing how much stayed in there, in her memory, and how repeating actions could bring it all out again. Fragments rose as she slipped the pages onto the glass, felt for the soft fit of corner into corner, lowered the lid, put her hand to the mouse.

Of all the Byzantine mosaics in Ravenna, the Theodora panel attracted the most attention.

Bonnard, the subtle master of pace, understands absolutely the way in which a scene is digested by the viewer.

Hypnotic and ambiguous, Millais's *Autumn Leaves* has no literary reference but is concerned with pure beauty, art for art's sake— what would become the creed of the Aesthetic Movement.

Today, before she started, Nina went to the kitchenette that was next door to Ursula's office and made a mug of tea and took four milk arrowroot biscuits from the large Tupperware container of Arnott's Family Assorted. This was not her usual habit; before she would have eaten breakfast at home, toast or muesli at the table, using a plate and a knife, or a bowl and a spoon. She would have used a cup and a teabag that would then have to be transferred to the bin, making drips. The bin would have gradually filled and then need emptying. The dishes and cutlery would require washing. Milk would have to be purchased from the supermarket, and bread, and butter, and muesli. Crumbs would accumulate, the table need wiping. All of this had never seemed onerous before, but now it did. Now it seemed impossible.

She wasn't sure that her status as a casual entitled her to these biscuits but she was very hungry, and she figured that nobody ever wanted the milk arrowroots and so they probably wouldn't be missed. She ate them one after another, bending over the sink. She put a lot of milk in the tea and drank it all down. There was an aftertaste of cheap lemon dishwashing liquid. She went back past Ursula's office, which was still dark, to the scanner room, her wedgie enduring, her skin at the edges of the bra hot and fizzing.

It wasn't long before she was hungry again but she made herself wait. At twelve thirty she logged out of the computer, locked the door of the scanner room and went along the corridor and down the stairs.

There was a lot of security to do with the files, which were patient records; she had to use a swipe card to enter the basement where the boxes were kept, and she was supposed to keep the scanner room locked whenever she left it. Nina herself had never been given any kind of security clearance—no background checks or anything like that—but in any case what could she do with the information in the files? She understood why it was confidential but at the same time it didn't seem especially useful in any nefarious sense. Pages of test results, imaging reports, lists of treatments.

Once she had recognised a name—Miranda Joy Martin—but then wasn't sure where from. Secondary school? A face came to her, of a thin girl with olive skin and light brown hair, braces on her teeth, but it might have been someone else. Nina had gone to a big school. The birthdate showed that Miranda Joy Martin was one year younger than Nina. The address was in a suburb not far from the school, which of course didn't prove anything—Miranda Joy Martin would be Nina's age now, and could have moved anywhere in the past twenty years.

Nina read the file, which showed that Miranda Joy Martin had been treated for something called papillary thyroid carcinoma with surgery and radioactive iodine therapy in October 2002 and was given the all-clear at a follow-up appointment two months later. Nina felt relieved that Miranda Joy Martin had not had something worse, that it had been a straightforward case with a successful outcome (some files went on for pages and pages and ended with the patient dying; while Nina didn't go out of her way to read them it was hard not to notice)—but then she wondered how she even knew this person, or if she ever had. Was Miranda Joy Martin the thin, braces girl?

Meg would know. Nina's sister Meg had known who everyone was at school, and somehow continued to know about what happened to them all, presumably through vigilant Facebook gleaning. Nina had not been prepared to call Meg and ask her. She and Meg were not really in contact.

Ahead of Nina, three nurses in pink scrubs descended, their voices echoing in the stairwell.

'I can't stand McAllister,' said one. 'He mutters. I'm like, Tweezers? Did he say tweezers? And then he does that sigh, like you're giving him the wrong thing on purpose.'

They reached the bottom and went swinging through the doors. Nina followed.

The cafeteria was frantic, the queues long, the tables filled, the talk dense, the rev of the juicers and the roars of the coffee machine strident. At the collection end of the hot-drinks counter the tall barista with bad posture sang out order numbers and set down cups with swooping motions, his white sleeves rolled to the elbows. Nina moved between tables, past the sandwich bar and the curved glass fronts of the bains-marie with their webs of condensation, past a basket of shiny yellow cling-wrapped muffins. She hovered near the juice line until she saw two women who looked like doctors—well dressed, lanyards—rise from a table by the far wall, and then she went to the table and slipped into one of its still-warm seats.

A small thin man with a moustache appeared, wheeling a trolley.

'Miss?' he said, indicating the plates on the table. 'Can I take these?'

Nina shook her head.

The man had already reached for the plates with his purple-gloved hands, and she had to put out her own hand to intercept him.

There was a pause, during which Nina picked up a half-eaten tuna sandwich and took a bite. Her anorak was bulging up around her chin.

'Sorry, miss, I thought it was old food.'

Nina, still chewing, shook her head again.

The man wheeled away.

Heading back upstairs, Nina passed Ursula, who was waiting in the line for sushi with Ros from one of the research offices.

'Do you want to grab a table, Ros, and—oh,' said Ursula. 'Nina. Hi. I didn't . . .'

Nina stopped and pulled up her tracksuit pants, which were sagging because of their loaded pockets.

Ursula and Ros watched.

'Hi, Nina,' said Ros in her honking voice.

'Hi, Ros.'

Ursula was now looking at Nina's Dunlop Volleys.

Ros's nails, long and fake and blue, tapped at the back of her phone case, which was black with a grid of diamantes.

'Next, please!' called the man behind the sushi counter.

'Oh, that's us,' said Ursula.

Later, Ursula came to the scanner room. She gave a little knock at the open door and then stepped in and pushed it almost closed behind her.

'Nina,' she said, fiddling with the buttons on her cardigan, a synthetic yellow cable knit. 'I, um . . . Is everything okay?'

Nina rotated her swivel chair in Ursula's direction.

'I just . . .' Ursula stepped nearer, then stepped back again, touched the doorhandle. 'I don't know you very well, I mean, even though I've worked with you for, what, four years, I still don't—I mean, you keep to yourself a bit and so this is awkward. But, are you okay?'

Nina took off her glasses and put them down on the desk. 'I'm okay.'

'Are you sure?'

'Yep.'

'Really?'

'I'm okay.'

'Well, okay then, if you're sure.'

When her shift was finished Nina left the hospital, crossed the busy road and went into the park. She cut through a row of tall trees to a vast open field of close-mowed grass. The spring afternoon was whirling with pollen and bright with leaves. Her hair spun wildly and her anorak ballooned. She walked until it seemed that she was in the middle and then she lay down on her back. Her pockets thunked to the ground. The shortie underpants felt like a clammy rope between her legs. The bra squeezed her ribs. Her armpits were burning. She brushed her fingers against the grass and then pushed them down against the cold rubbery soil. She stared up at the torn white-and-blue sky.

The last time she had seen Meg and Amber or spoken to either of them was at Christmas, nine months earlier. Nina's ancient, falling-apart lime green Corolla had sat uneasily behind Meg's grey Suzuki Swift (clean and no doubt up to date with services) on the street out the front of Gwen's new townhouse. Amber was not represented by a car, due to not owning one; Amber would have arrived with Meg, if the two of them were speaking, or else been collected by Gwen, driving carefully in her white Yaris.

The air between the three sisters was bruised, the chitchat stagey, and mostly carried out by Amber in one of her typically frenetic and short-lived social performances.

Amber's limbs twitched. Amber drank wine and more wine. Amber did nothing to help with the lunch. Nina tried to help but gave up in the face of Meg's efficiency. Meg did everything: the turkey, the potatoes, the cranberry jelly. Gwen, heedless as ever, unfolded a paper crown with papery-looking fingers.

'It's good to have everyone all together,' she said. Her voice seemed to have lost strength.

Amber pushed back her chair, took fistfuls of the tablecloth. Strange dimples appeared over her eyebrows. 'I miss Dad!' Her lips quivered. Her orange paper crown came off and swooned to the floor.

Meg reached for her arm but Amber yelled, 'Don't touch me!'

And Nina didn't want to but thought of the dark room. The terrible smell. The tie at Amber's wrists. Amber's unnatural, crooked body, her exposed throat.

After a few moments of loud muffled sobbing from Amber and stiff silence from everyone else, Gwen got up, in her own paper crown—purple—and went around the table to put one of her thin-skinned hands on Amber's bowed head, the dull blonde mess of her hair.

Nina kept her eyes on the window, the street outside, the two cars. This was not unusual, an episode such as this, at Christmas—or, indeed, at any other Atkins family occasion over the past five years. It did seem worse, though, because it was taking place in Gwen's new, grey, echoing townhouse, the ugliness of which—the *sadness* of which—was like an embodiment. And it was so much worse without Robert, who had been dead then for less than a year. Their father, so often dismissed or ignored. How deeply Nina had underestimated the power of his indomitable cheer, its endurance, the buoyancy it had provided.

❦

'Nina?'

It was Ursula in her yellow cardigan, her blouse and skirt and stockings, very white sneakers on her feet. The sun was behind her head; her face was dim; a spray of staticky hair trembled, haloed silver.

'It is you. Are you okay?'

Nina closed her eyes. 'Yes, thanks. I'm fine. I'm just enjoying the sun.'

The wind was making swishing sounds in Nina's ears, and the officious dinging of a tram on the road seemed far away.

'Well, yes,' said Ursula after a little while, 'it is nice. But the ground must be cold. You're shivering, did . . . did you know that?'

Nina didn't answer.

'Nina,' Ursula said, 'I think you'd better get up and go home. It'll be a lot colder soon.'

'Okay,' said Nina, without moving.

Then she felt Ursula come closer, kneel down and take her by the arm.

'Come on,' said Ursula.

Nina opened her eyes into a pewter blaze, ragged treetops, swinging sky. Then she was on her feet, a sudden chill rushing at her back.

'Oh,' she said, 'I am cold, you're right.'

'Where's your car? Is it in the car park?'

'No car.' Nina pointed. 'I catch the tram.'

They walked back over the grass towards the tram stop, Ursula holding Nina's arm.

'Will you be all right on the tram?'

'Oh yeah. I'll be fine.'

'Nina, do you need to take some time off? It's fine if you do.'

'Oh no. No, it's good for me to come to work.'

They reached the road and crossed to the stop. The tram was coming, tall and white between the creeping cars.

As it drew up, Ursula said, 'Someone called for you today. Your sister—Meg? She said she can't get through on your mobile. I left a note on your desk.'

'Thanks.' Nina climbed aboard and sat down in her damp pants. Through the window she could see Ursula frowning and looking in. Nina gave her a wave. It was meant to be grateful and reassuring but Nina wasn't sure it came out that way. There was only so much you could do with a wave.

In the coral spring-evening light the tram charged up St Kilda Road. Nina, swaying, found herself thinking of Meg's voice on the other end of a phone line. The sense of guilt that it had so often prompted—guilt, or persecution.

Nina remembered the North Carlton flat she was living in when Meg started calling and trying to convince her that they needed to do something about Amber. That had been five years ago, when Nina was in her early thirties. It had felt tired, that flat. Too many affairs had been conducted from within it. But it was tired for other reasons as well. Amber, mostly. Amber's shit. There was a difference between Amber and Amber's shit—Nina knew this but had to remind herself sometimes. Amber was a person, somewhere inside the shit. Amber was separate. Amber was in fact a victim of the shit as much as anyone else was. But also the shit caused her to do things that made it really hard not to hate her. The shit did seem to be inside her as well as around her. She was sort of like a zombie, being propelled. It was hard to think about. It got confusing.

In any case, it hadn't mattered where Nina lived or what she did: Amber's shit—or shit to do with Amber—always reached her.

She was almost at the chain-link fence of the vacant lot when she saw the grey Suzuki Swift parked outside her gate and the figure sitting in it, behind the steering wheel—tall, dark, big-shouldered, teacherly. Nina made a rapid about face and walked back the way she had come. When she got to the main road she went very slowly along the row of shops, looking in the windows.

Had Meg seen her? She wasn't sure; she hadn't been able to see Meg's eyes, just the shape of her behind the windscreen, under the streetlight.

It was night now. Most of the shops were closed; the only ones open were the Thai restaurant and the convenience store. Nina went into the Thai restaurant. There were two other customers in there, a man and a woman, both wearing leather jackets that they had not taken off, giving them a stiff and creaky appearance. They sat facing one another across a small table on which stood tall glasses of beer.

The waitress came out from the kitchen and gave Nina a startled look.

The leather couple turned.

'Takeaway?' said the waitress.

'No, thanks,' said Nina. 'I'd like to eat in, please.'

The waitress looked at Nina's sagging pants. Then she looked at the front of Nina's anorak, where the outward curve of the zipped-up zip gave the impression that the stains were being offered for inspection.

Nina undid the zip. The waitress watched. So did the leather people, who had not gone back to their beers.

'May I sit down?' said Nina, and then went to a table that was against the wall behind a large sideboard, where she would not be easily seen through the window.

The waitress, after a few moments, took a menu from the top of the sideboard and put it on the table before Nina. 'Any drinks?' she said.

'Beer, please.'

Nina did not usually drink beer, but the towering glasses on the leather people's table had made her want some.

The waitress went to the fridge by the kitchen door. She opened it with a glassy rattle.

Nina had walked past this restaurant countless times but never been in. There was nothing inside that she couldn't have predicted: boomy, glossy floorboards; walls painted a deep red; heavy tables and chairs in dark timber; a wall hanging of patterned silk; the cellophane-wrapped lollies in a bowl on the counter; the waitress in her black trousers and white shirt; the leather people, who were clearly regulars. Something about this predictability struck her as unbearably sad. A tear fell onto the menu and lay, beaded, on the laminated surface.

The waitress brought the beer and a paper coaster, green and white, with a picture of an elephant. The outside of the enormous glass was cloudy with condensation. When Nina lifted it the coaster came too. The beer did not taste the way it looked, which was malty and substantial—in fact it was watery. It felt quenching though, and the foam burst in her mouth with tiny fluffy pops.

'Ready to order?'

Nina set the beer down, wiped her lip and pointed at any old thing.

The waitress said something that Nina didn't understand, with an upward inflection.

Nina nodded. More tears were running down her face.

The waitress took the menu from her and went away. She came back and put a box of tissues on the table. Then she went away again.

Nina pulled out a tissue. She looked over at the leather people. They had stopped watching her and were busy with the food that had arrived on their table: a plate of noodles with shiny brown morsels of meat, slick stems of broccoli and discs of carrot; a whole fish on a large white oval platter; a bowl of rice. The two of them danced their hands back and forth like puppeteers from the serving platters and bowl to their individual plates, taking up spoons and then putting them down again, awkwardly manoeuvring chopsticks, sipping from their beers. Neither spoke.

There was pop music playing but it wasn't very loud. Nina could hear the creak of the leather people's jackets, the click of their plastic chopsticks, their chewing. She felt the thin beer sloshing in her empty stomach. The tears were not stopping and she mopped at them in a mechanical way, making a pile of used tissues in her lap.

Soon the waitress returned with a bowl containing flat-sided translucent noodles and a collection of glistening fried vegetables and prawns. Nina took up her chopsticks and began to eat, the hot, salty mouthfuls slipping down, her stomach lurching in readiness, her tears still running. She ate and cried until all of the food was gone, and then she drank the last of the beer. Her belly felt like a hard ball. For a long time she sat in a low slump, lifting a tissue to her face every now and then. Eventually the tears stopped.

When she looked up she saw that the leather people had gone. The waitress was rearranging the drinks in the fridge. Nina rose and approached the counter and the waitress shut the fridge, went to the cash register, printed out a docket and put it down in front of her. Nina paid with her credit card, tapping it to the machine. The waitress held her hand, palm up, out towards the bowl of lollies.

Nina took one and put it in her pocket. 'Thank you,' she said, her voice thick.

Turning, she noticed a scatter of small white objects on the floor near the table she'd been sitting at—her used tissues, fallen from her lap.

'Oh. I'm sorry.' She knelt, her full belly pushing against her thighs, but the waitress was there with a bright orange dustpan and brush. Squatting beside Nina, she whisked up the tissues.

'Thank you,' said Nina, and on the tail of the words a creamy burp came out.

The waitress sat back on her heels, knees wide in her slim black pants. She laughed, a trilling peal of laughter that shook her hair in its bun, and Nina found herself laughing too, croakily, soggily.

'I'm sorry about the crying,' she said. 'I don't really know why it's happening.'

'No worries,' said the waitress, in her Thai accent.

Nina was halfway back down her street when the Suzuki Swift drove past, then stopped, then reversed, its engine revving high and hard. Wobbling, it passed Nina again, its headlights shining in her eyes, and came to a halt. The window on the passenger side went down.

'Nina!' called Meg.

Nina kept walking.

The Suzuki reversed once more, wavering along the parked cars until it got to the space, still empty, outside Nina's house. The car backed into the space and just as Nina reached her gate the car door was flung open and Meg clambered out and ran, heavily, past Nina to stand on the path.

'What's *wrong* with you?' said Meg.

'Nothing,' said Nina.

'Then why are you hiding from me? Why don't you return my calls? Why did you try to run away from me just now?'

Nina didn't answer. She stood with her hands in her pockets, her full belly a quietly gurgling shield between her conscious mind and the silent miniature whirlwind of panic.

Meg sighed. 'I'm sorry. Can I just—I need to talk to you. Can we go inside?'

Nina shook her head.

'Really?' said Meg. 'Really? You're going to continue to punish me? Jesus, Nina, I made a *mistake*. And it was five years ago.'

'I'm not punishing you.'

It was dim on the path between the paling side fence and the long spindly arms of the overgrown rosebushes in the front yard. It was hard to see Meg's face.

'Okay, fine,' said Meg.

Nina drew her anorak closer around herself and folded her arms.

'Fine,' said Meg again. 'I'll just have to say it out here. So. You know that Amber has joined NA?'

'Yes.'

'But you haven't spoken with her.'

'No.'

'And you haven't spoken with Mum either, have you?'

'No.'

'Mum's got enough to worry about, without you going AWOL.'

'Sorry.'

'Well, I've told them you're really busy with work. And your phone's broken.'

'Okay. Thanks.'

Meg peered at her. 'What are you *wearing*?'

Nina shrugged.

'Are you all right, Neen?'

'Yes.'

'Well, listen. Mum and I need you to show up for this. Just call Amber back. Just let her talk to you. She's taken this step and she needs us.'

'Okay.' Nina edged around Meg. 'I'm going inside now.'

Meg watched as she put the key in the lock. 'It's not that hard, Nina. Just let her say what she needs to say.'

'Okay.' Nina went inside and closed the door.

II.

IT HAD TAKEN MEG A long time to convince Nina. Many lengthy phone calls. During these Nina had experienced a lot of trouble staying on the line. She walked around the flat she was living in then, the tired-feeling one in North Carlton, from the front door to the bedroom to the kitchen; she fingered the brown edges of the leaves of her ailing maidenhair fern, crumbling beige dust onto the windowsill; she lay across the end of the bed and raised her legs in the air.

'Are you even listening?' came Meg's voice, small but still stern.

With the cordless phone held loosely to her ear Nina ate half a packet of stale peanuts. She took everything out of the kitchen junk drawer and spread it on the bench to sort. She sprinkled bicarb of soda on the mouldy grout of the shower and then discovered she was out of regular vinegar so she got her laptop and furtively googled with one hand to see if she could use balsamic, careful to turn the volume down in case an email arrived and Meg heard the ping.

When Meg was finally finished with her hectoring and Nina had hung up and then taken a look at eBay and checked her mail again it would be ten thirty and she'd make some toast, which might mean dumping everything back off the bench and into the junk drawer, and then she'd go to bed and in the morning maybe find the bicarb in the shower and try to wash it away with plain water so that it left a chalky residue.

Meg just wore her down in the end. Nina couldn't come up with any other explanation. It went against her values, absolutely. It was illegal. It was unethical. It was likely to be dangerous. Most of all, it was very unlikely to *work*, as far as she could see—and that was what really mattered. 'You can't just barge in and fix someone,' she told Meg. 'Change has to come from the person themselves.'

It wasn't that she stopped believing this. She never did, not for one moment. But it was as if Meg ignored it so many times that it became invisible. Nina went on offering it up and Meg went on powering, train-like, right through it, again and again, and eventually Nina got tired.

So it went ahead. On a morning in the late autumn of 2009, Meg collected Nina from her flat in a taxi and they went on to the far northern suburbs, where they stopped outside the place where Amber was living—a unit, with a front window blinded by a hanging sheet and a bag of garbage lying like a corpse in the empty carport.

Meg got out and the car sprang up a little. Nina, watching from the far side of the back seat, saw her heavy shoulders, her white top and blue jeans that somehow, like anything worn by Meg, resembled a uniform. When had she got so big, Meg? So solid. A slab of a woman.

Meg hitched her jeans and set off up the path. She took small steps because the paving stones were uneven and bearded with weeds, and this made her look more muscular, meaty, like a bodybuilder constrained by her own heft. She rolled up the path and rapped on the door and it opened almost immediately, which was a surprise, and Amber came out carrying an overnight bag, with her hair stringy and her sunglasses on and her hipbones visible above the waistband of her jeans.

There was some sort of an embrace, inexpert, the bag getting in the way, and then they moved towards the taxi, and while Meg didn't actually take hold of Amber she did follow closely and her arms seemed to be slightly raised, as if in readiness. But Amber showed no sign of running.

('What if she asks questions?' Nina had said, on the phone.

'She won't,' said Meg. 'Not if we're paying.' And then: 'We just tell her we think she needs a little holiday.')

Amber was in now, beside Nina, with her smell of cigarettes fresh and stale and her croak of, 'Hey, Neen,' and her feathery, sideways kiss, and Meg was in too, cramming in last and pulling shut the door, and the driver said, 'Airport now?' and Meg said, 'Yes please,' and the car pulled away and there they were, filling the back seat as if in some macabre re-enactment of childhood family holidays.

Except that they were not children at all, they were adults, they were three grown women, and Nina was probably just freaking out—because that was what Nina did, what Nina had always done, freaked quietly and undetectably out while things went on happening around her—but as she looked down at their legs she thought that they could never have been children, sitting in the back seat of the family car. She thought that they could never have been so small, the three of them, to have taken up so little space—to have fitted with such ease into their shared realm of back seat and school shoes and kitchen stools and baths and bunk beds and night whispers and secret codes and eruptions of laughter and small, close meannesses, of pinches and hisses, of looks and private signals.

The car of their childhood: a Mitsubishi Sigma station wagon, maroon, with the little bottle of touch-up paint like liquid rubies in the glove box and the gearstick rising from its navy leather pouch that wrinkled as the gears were changed like something living, an animal sac. Here it comes, with them in it—the three girls, and their parents in the front—driving up a black road with pink dry soil either side, and olive trees, and grapevines. All day the sky has been huge, hard blue with ripped-up clouds, but now it's evening and everything has softened, deepened, the air is thicker and the daubs of sunlight on a corrugated-iron shed are buttery and gentle. A holiday, near the New South Wales border, inland. They are staying in a cabin on a working farm where the girls can swim in the river and Gwen and Robert can sit on camp stools and drink wine. They have been to the nearest town for supplies, which fill the boot in their rustling plastic bags—because this is a time when plastic bags are used freely, thoughtlessly, stuffed in airy bundles into bins and forgotten. This is a time of certainty, of only ever looking outwards; this is a time of feeling your family around you like banked earth.

Meg, ten, is the Good One, and Nina, nine, is the Forgetful One, and Amber, little Bam, only five, is the Wild One, a puppy, a seal cub, naked except for blue terry towelling shorts, rolling in the rosy dust, grime like red dye at her elbows and knees and in the creases of her soft, babyish neck.

'Oh, Bam,' says Gwen, lifting her littlest daughter out of the dust and kissing her fat cheek, passing a hand over her sticky face, her unbrushed hair. 'What are we going to do with you?'

And: 'Oh, Nina,' says Robert, kneeling to look under a bed for a lost book, which Nina really did just have in her hand as she went from the bedroom to the kitchen. 'Nina, Nina, Nina. What are we going to do with you?'

And: 'Oh, Meg,' say Gwen and Robert, when they are ushered into the small cabin kitchen to see the wildflowers picked and arranged in a jar, and the table set for dinner with napkins folded under the cutlery, and glasses, and a jug of water with lemon slices and ice cubes. 'What are we going to do with you?'

Nothing. Their parents will not do anything with them, Nina and Amber and Meg, because they have been classified already, these girls, identified and branded, and what Robert and Gwen really mean when they say, 'What are we going to do with you?' is in fact something more like, 'We might have made you but we have no idea how you turned out this way; you are beyond our control and all we can do is stand by and watch.'

And they feel the wonder of their parents, these girls, and it doesn't—yet—frighten them. To be wondered at, to be held up as a mystery, ineffable, to be gloried in—right now it's delicious; it's something you can get an appetite for. And so Meg smiles her diligent smile, and Nina smiles her bashful one, and little Amber opens her red lips and laughs, and her bright, wet, baby teeth shine.

But Nina was not in the maroon Sigma, and she was not trying to find a book in a rented cabin on a farm near a big brown river. And Meg was not fussing with ragged flowers in the wood-panelled kitchen and calling brassily, 'Don't come in yet!' And Amber was not little Bam, rolling in the dust in her blue shorts. Gwen and Robert were not there to gaze upon them and ask fondly, 'What are we going to do with you?'

Gwen and Robert were not there at all. They had distanced themselves. They were in their early sixties, and they were, you could feel it, *immensely relieved* to have at last been able to get back to their own lives.

('Hello, darling,' said Gwen's voice on Nina's voicemail. 'Just ringing to say have a lovely time in Noosa. Meg's told me all about it, sounds wonderful, and I'm so glad that you're all going together. Oh, sorry, did I say Noosa? It's not Noosa, is it?')

Gwen and Robert were not there, and Meg and Nina and Amber were three adults, no longer held by that close earth of childhood. They had dispersed into a wider world that had proved not to find especially wonderful their industriousness or forgetfulness or wildness. And that was enough of a heartbreak in itself, Nina thought, that what was once wonderful, whole and unquestioned—someone's helpless and endearing forgetful-ness; or someone else's sweet longing to be grown and of service; or another person's looseness and lushness and dusty, fleshy, laughing wildness—could have turned out to be not only not full of wonder but in fact an impediment.

('I used to find it charming,' a man once told Nina, 'you always being late. The way you'd fly in all breathless with your buttons done up wrong and something falling out of your bag. But I have to tell you, it wears off, that sort of charm.')

That was enough to break your heart. But then there was the inability to shed, to bust out. How could something as wispy and fluttering as forgetfulness prove to be so durable, so adhesive?

Nina glanced at her sisters, at Amber with her fallen-back head, her lax neck, her eyes closed behind her sunglasses, her pink bitten fingertips working—blindly, hungrily—at a loose thread on her sleeve, and at Meg there on the other side, big and firm and watchful, with her dark plain ponytail like a schoolgirl's, a netballer's, her stern face, her chin slightly raised, eyes on the road ahead as if she were the one controlling the car.

They were all stuck, it seemed to Nina; held to ransom by qualities that were once considered harmless and even charming but had somehow become undesirable. Nina's being forgetful had turned into being flaky, and Meg's being good to bossy. And Amber's wildness—well, it was hard to say if Amber's wildness had changed, really, or just increased as it found more to feed on.

Amber was certainly the most obviously, the most spectacularly, stuck. The effects of Amber's stuckness certainly radiated the furthest: they were, the whole family—in a surface, everyday way, and also deeper, in their deep selves—stained by it. Amber's wildness was, after all, the reason the three of them were there in that taxi.

Nina checked: Amber, it seemed, had fallen into an instant sleep, her raw-tipped fingers curled in her lap.

Then Nina remembered with a horrible and familiar jolt that she had forgotten to close and lock the kitchen window of her flat, and as she did so felt Meg dart a look at her, and Meg said, 'What is it?' and Nina said, 'Nothing,' and Meg said, 'Did you forget something?' and Nina said, 'No,' and Meg sighed and went back to supervising the driver, and Nina sighed and thought that, yes, they were all stuck, deeply and comprehensively stuck, each in the shell of what she had turned out to be, and none of them knew how to undo themselves, and she couldn't see how this idea of Meg's could possibly work.

('I'm not . . .' Nina had said on the phone.

'Not what?' said Meg, with irritation.

'I'm not sure.'

'About what?'

'Um,' said Nina, and tried to find the words, but couldn't.

'What's not to be sure about?' said Meg. 'We have to do something. We can't let her go on like this.'

'But . . .'

'Neen, she's our sister. Our *little sister.*' There were tears in Meg's voice. 'We have to *get her back.*')

The words might have come to Nina then, as the taxi sailed towards the airport in a drizzle, in a soft grey morning. Blinking into the pearly light, she experienced an unfogging of the brain, an opening bubble of clarity. Her misgivings, her hesitations, she saw, were to do with what it was to be siblings in childhood, when there were overlaps and mergings, and the three of you looked out from the same place. There were certain things, then, that you could do to each other. There were certain liberties that could be taken, boundaries crossed. But this was when you were children, before the separation, the hardening, the stuckness. When the idea of who you were—bossy, forgetful, wild—still seemed like a mantle, something you might suddenly decide to throw off, startling your parents.

Over the phone, Meg had talked about *standing firm* and *being clear.* Meg had even used the phrase *tough love.* But what did these words really mean? What shape would they take as actions?

The taxi glided to the right, changing lanes, and Nina watched water flicking up from the black tyres of the other cars and remembered Meg putting Amber on a bench in a cubbyhouse made of greenish treated-pine logs. An adventure playground: trailing peppercorn branches, the smell of possum, faded beer cans crushed into dirt; a railway line somewhere nearby—the weighty passage of trains, the moaning of their horns.

It's dark inside the cubbyhouse, and it smells like earwigs and wee. Meg puts Amber on the bench, lifting her onto it so that her legs hang and kick, her jeans rucked up to show shins red with cold. Amber's furious face, her wide mouth, tears glassing her eyes. Her beanie risen like the hat of a gnome. Her arms reaching. 'No! No!' she cries. And Meg's body blocks the entrance, Meg's pointing finger magically fixes Amber to the seat. 'You stay there,' says Meg. 'Don't you dare move.' No door to close, on the cubbyhouse, but Meg turns and exits the dark interior and Amber does not follow. And then later, when Meg fetches her out and says, 'Were you scared? Were you terrified?' Amber, her face flushed and proud, her eyelashes spiky and wet, says, 'No!' And Meg says, 'Of course you were.' And Amber's little fists go to her hips and she says, 'I was *not*.' And then there is a pause, the three of them standing there in a dim afternoon, under the trees. Nina's hands are gummy with peppercorn sap. She opens and closes them slowly, feeling the skin stick and pull and then release. Then Meg says, 'You're a good girl, Bam. You did as you were told.' And Meg drops to her knees and puts out her arms and Amber launches into them, and then Meg starts to tickle her, and soon Amber is on the ground, her beanie fallen off, leaves in her hair, her shoulders up so her neck disappears into her woolly jumper and her face looks perfectly round, flushed and dimpled, and her laughter is like the spray from a shaken can of soft drink.

Nina blinked herself back into the car, inhaled the dense synthetic smell of the yellow tree-shaped air freshener dangling from the rear-view mirror, felt her sisters there beside her.

It was gone again, her clarity. She had blurred once more into general misgivings.

43

What was in Amber's bag? This question, Nina realised, as they entered the departures hall and Meg marched directly to the check-in counters, had been circling for some time—since before Amber got into the taxi; since, in fact, well before the bag even appeared. This question had hung, a wavery strand, in the back of Nina's mind since Meg had confirmed that the trip was on, that Amber had agreed, that she, Meg, had purchased the tickets.

('How long for?' said Nina, over the phone.

'Three weeks,' said Meg.

'What? Three—'

'Yep. I reckon the first week things will seem okay—she'll go along with it. The second week the shit will hit the fan, and the third week will be for recovery and consolidation.'

Consolidation. Where did Meg get this stuff from?

'I don't know if I can take that much time off. My students . . .'

'Oh, come on, you're casual, aren't you? I've had to use all my leave—*and* a chunk of my savings. I could be going to bloody Bali, Neen, but I'm doing this.'

A disconcerted silence from Nina.

'Look, if we're going to do this thing, we need to do it properly. We need to put in the time. This has been the problem all along, that nobody has been willing to actually *be* with her, to really knuckle down and ride it out.'

'But Mum and Dad . . .'

'What? What did they do? They were *soft*, Nina, they never set any boundaries, they never stuck with any kind of *plan*.'

'How long did you tell Amber it's for?'

'A weekend.')

All along, behind the other half-formed worries, hovered this question: what was in Amber's bag? Bags, actually—she had two: the overnight one, which was a black canvas gym bag with a fat plastic zip and lettering on the side, mostly worn off, *South-*something *Club*, and her handbag, a shapeless tan leather tote, grey at the seams. What would happen when these two objects were placed on the conveyor belt and passed through the X-ray machine at security? A flashing red light, the brisk approach of uniformed figures? Or perhaps it would be a dog. Nina looked around for one. It would advance with officious, padding paws and a waving tail, and bark, or sit, or do whatever it was those dogs did to indicate a bust, and, again, uniforms would descend. 'Could you come with us, please, miss?' (Amber, even with her too-sharp cheekbones and untended hair, was at twenty-eight still a miss, Nina was fairly sure, whereas Meg, thirty-three, might already be a madam. Nina, thirty-two, also got miss, as well as love, darl and sweetheart, even from people who were younger than she was.)

Meg was back, all three boarding passes safely in the pocket of her shirt. 'Come on,' she said, and set off towards security, pulling her small navy wheelie bag.

Amber followed, and Nina came last, eyes on the bags hooked one over each of Amber's skinny arms.

What might be in them? Not heroin—not anymore. And not ice—Amber, thank God, didn't seem to have gone for ice. Pot? Maybe. Please don't let her be that stupid, thought Nina. It was most likely pills, prescription ones, but too many, from too many different doctors. Because as far as Nina knew this was what Amber mostly did nowadays: doctor-hopping, or script-shopping, or whatever it was called. This was where Amber's addiction had been shifted to, rehoused. She had left the hard realm of the downright criminal and moved into this misty nether region of the not-quite-legal—and in doing so smeared things in such a way that their parents (with that palpable and understandable but still infuriating relief) now referred to her as 'recovered'.

She was better than she had been, it was true. Hugely, vastly better. Gone were the days—days that threatened to never end—of stealing and track marks, of flecks of blood on the pale green tiles of Gwen and Robert's bathroom, of used syringes found on the kitchen bench, of ultimatums and the changing of locks, and of begging and concessions and weary hope and backsliding. Gone were the days of Amber in the second bedroom at Gwen and Robert's, the closed door and the dark cave beyond, littered with paraphernalia—zip-lock bags, spoons, lighters, crumples of aluminium foil—reeking of smoke and unwashed clothes.

Amber lived independently now. Amber had a job, of sorts, in a costume hire shop. She had, according to social media, some friends, although they seemed to change frequently and were never brought into the same orbit as her family. But was Amber actually recovered? She never had any money. She often didn't show up—to lunches, dinners, birthday parties, to the dental appointments Gwen booked for her. Their parents, Meg and Nina had gleaned, regularly paid Amber's rent and bills. And Amber drank too much, her skin was dull, she was too thin, her teeth were in bad shape, her hands trembled, the whites of her eyes were murky. When she did show up she was barely there—she was outside smoking; she was in the bathroom, with her bag; she needed to leave early.

('When was the last time you had an actual conversation with her?' Meg had demanded. 'When was the last time the two of you made eye contact?')

How did Nina and Meg know about the pills, the prescriptions? They didn't, not really. A lot was being surmised. From the glimpsed interior of the scuffed handbag—blister packs that had fled their paper sleeves, and rattling plastic vials; from Amber's sallowness and her tremors and her slurred and thickened demeanour; from overheard exchanges between Gwen and Robert. *She said she had to get a bus and then a train all the way to Box Hill to see a doctor. She said her regular doctor was booked up. She said she couldn't get an appointment with anyone closer.*

Amber was no longer what she had been: an agent of—or a senseless roaring portal to—chaos; she had softened into something less demanding, easier to be around. The dog that was her addiction had stopped leaping and snapping and tearing at everyone within reach and was lying in a corner, head on paws. What Amber was now, with her shitty rented unit and casual job and mysterious private life, this sallow, diluted, evasive, lukewarm Amber—this, it seemed (and probably only in comparison to how awful things had been before) was good enough for their parents. But it wasn't good enough for Meg. Meg wanted the dog out.

They joined the line for security screening. Meg tilted her head from side to side, did circles with her shoulders. She didn't turn around. She didn't look at Amber, or at Amber's bags. Was she not worried? Had she perhaps warned Amber earlier, over the phone? *You know we have to go through security at the airport. Don't do anything stupid.* Or did she have confidence in the natural justice of the situation, should something be discovered, should the alarm sound and the red light flash, the dog appear, the uniforms? Might this even be an acceptable alternative to her plan? Amber busted, the contents of her bags revealed, itemised, charges laid, an official measure of criminality, something to take hold of at last, for Meg to wave triumphantly in the faces of Nina, of their parents, of Amber herself: *You see? There is a problem, and it must be solved.*

Through the X-ray machine went Meg's carry-on wheelie bag, and then Meg's sturdy blue handbag in its tray. Meg walked through the metal detector. Amber's bags followed, haltingly, as if both bags and conveyor belt vibrated with something—anticipation, or culpability, or an awareness of Nina's damp-palmed gaze. The bags entered the machine, and Nina saw the impassive face of the woman at the monitor, her scanning eyes, and then the bags continued to move, and came out the other side.

'Excuse me,' said a voice from behind, and Nina realised that she was holding up the queue, standing rigid at the threshold of the metal detector, still clutching her own luggage.

'Bags on the belt, please, love,' said a small uniformed man with grey hair and a walkie-talkie.

'Sorry.' Nina backtracked, stepping on toes. 'Sorry.' She plonked everything onto the conveyor belt, her old leather overnight case (*Pack light*, ordered Meg, *so Bam won't get suspicious*) and her small canvas backpack—and a scrap of paper was somehow ejected from somewhere and drifted to the floor. 'Sorry,' said Nina, crouching, feeling her bum hit someone's shins.

On the far side of the tall electronic gateway with its red and green lights, Meg folded her arms and rolled her eyes. Beyond, Amber's tall figure receded, strolling past the snack bars.

On the plane Amber bought a drink. White wine, in a small green bottle. Nina, guiltily, bought a plastic bottle of water, which she promised herself she would refill and use for the rest of the trip. Meg didn't need to buy a drink; she had her stainless-steel flask.

Amber drank her wine quickly, then tried to order another one, but found that there was not enough cash in her wallet. Meg looked out the window. Nina pretended to read the in-flight magazine. She'd noticed the nuggety black credit-card machine that the attendant had been holding out for passengers to use, but the attendant did not show this machine to Amber, or mention it. He was in a hurry, or he thought Amber didn't need more wine so soon—whatever the case, he and his clinking trolley moved on, leaving Amber still making a slow, tremble-fingered pile of small change on her tray table.

'Oh, he's gone,' said Amber, looking up at last. Her eyelids were heavy. Before they boarded she had gone to the toilet, and then once they were on the plane she'd gone again, as soon as the seatbelt sign was off. She gathered up the coins and some dropped, soundlessly, to the carpeted floor. Nina bent and tried to find them, her head pounding with blood, but they'd rolled away, and when she sat up again she saw that Amber had nodded off, the wallet in her lap, its mouth unzipped.

Nina swallowed down on the metallic taste that came at times like this. It was extraordinary, really, the depth of this wellspring, this font of sorrow. You would think she'd have run out by now, been drained and wrung of every drop, but up it came, abundant and piercingly fresh. She leaned forward again so that Meg, on the far side of Amber, wouldn't notice her sniffing and wiping under her eyes with her sleeve.

How could this have happened? How could she have ended up this way, little Bam, with her round pink face and chubby legs? And later, her golden litheness, her quickness, her clarity? Amber at fourteen on the film set, in the olden-days costume, blue dress and bonnet, white apron, escaped wisps of hair at her temples, her gaze on the director, sharp and ready. *Poise*, was the word adults used, time and again. *Never seen a child with so much poise.* And it was amazing, the way she took shape on the stage or the set, as if her wildness was something she could pull in and hold, trembling, concentrated, an essence, a power, to be released as she chose: one grain at a time, fine and bright, in the smallest facial adjustments, the slide of her eyes or the softening of her lips; or in controlled streams, the circling of an arm, two fluid steps, fingers opening. And then she could erupt.

Nina remembered a high school production of *The Crucible* in which it seemed that everyone—cast and audience—was only marking time until Amber's entrance. The other players lurched through their lines like a PE class taking turns at throwing and catching a ball before at last making way, and there she was in a long plain nightdress, hair loose, limbs in electric spasms, her head thrown back, a shrieking white-gold revelation. Ripples moved through the crowd; drowsing fathers woke up; mothers put their hands to their chests and smiled the way mothers often did at Amber, in awe and fear.

Or did Nina only imagine the fear, later? No—it had been there. Concern, trepidation, like a layer of gauze over the gloss of their compliments. *She's amazing, she's wonderful, what a talent.*

Nina sat upright and looked past her sisters at the blue sky. It would be warm where they were going—somewhere near Cairns, exact location as yet undisclosed by Meg, manager of bookings, maker of plans.

Meg had the window seat. Meg's back was very straight. Her tray table held her purple water flask and a skeletal apple core. A paperback lay face down in her lap. She too was falling asleep, her head dropping, jerking back up, dropping again.

Nina, on the aisle, thought of her own drink bottle, which might be on her kitchen bench or at the bookshop or the university, or maybe even on a bus—and which, wherever it was, would not have fresh water in it.

Cairns was bright. Sunlight flashed on the fronds of the airport's palm trees. Nina stood near the baggage carousels while Meg filled in forms at the car hire desk and Amber smoked outside. The thud of landing, the freshness of the light, the *reality* of the place had pitched her misgivings into outright anxiousness. When would Amber be told the truth, the purpose of the trip? And what was actually supposed to happen? Why hadn't she, Nina—earlier, when she had a chance—pinned Meg down, got her to outline the exact plan?

The night before, late, Nina had found an article online entitled 'Why interventions fail'. The author was a man, an American, an ex-addict who now helped families get their loved ones into rehab. The man warned that poor organisation and a lack of conviction on the part of overly emotional relatives were the two main factors that contributed to a failed intervention. He proposed that a relative who felt they could not stay strong in the face of the manipulative and distressing behaviour the addict would certainly display once confronted should not attend, but leave proceedings to other, stronger, family members and a trained interventionist such as himself. This weak relative was encouraged to write a letter to the addict that could be read out during the intervention.

Nina, lying in bed, had scrolled through a list of directives— *Make sure bags are packed and ready*; *Decide beforehand who will accompany the addict to rehab; If the addict has not agreed within the first hour, you will need to bring out your ultimatum*—and then shut her laptop and tossed it onto a pile of clothes that lay on the floor, next to her half-packed overnight bag. She curled on her side and pulled the covers close around her neck. Shit, she thought. Did Meg know about all this? The interventions the man was writing about were ones in which an addict was confronted, talked into agreeing to rehab, and then conveyed—speedily, allowing as little time as possible for a change of heart—directly to a rehab facility and handed over to professionals, who would then undertake the actual rehabilitation. This was what was meant, generally, by the term 'intervention'—rehab was the end point. But this was not what Meg—okay, Nina and Meg; because Nina, by being there, was complicit—this was not what Nina and Meg had planned. In this situation, Nina and Meg would not really be performing an intervention. That part of the equation, the part in which Amber was confronted with 'tough love' and convinced that she needed to dry out, had been deleted. (Here the word *consent* materialised, and Nina's apprehension gave a further throb.) In this situation (more throbbing, and the word *illegal*), Meg and Nina would in fact be taking on the roles of the rehab staff, the detox people—who were, one would hope, qualified and experienced therapists and medics.

Meg's legs were like blue tree trunks at the car hire desk, her feet planted in their rubbery-looking shoes. Amber, outside, visible through the glass doors, leaned with one knee bent against a wall, her smoke fanning white-grey, her hair gold in the too-bright light.

Amber never went to rehab, although it was something Gwen spoke about—and tried to scrape together the funds for. Nina had a clear image of her mother standing in the back garden of the family home in Thornbury, arms folded, the fence behind her dark with recent rain. Amber not there, but her presence overwhelming. (Amber was so often not there. What was there instead were her wreckages, laid out like artworks: the left-behind syringe; the phone call regarding her failure to show up for work; the front door ajar, Gwen's ransacked handbag and emptied wallet on the sideboard.) Amber not there, and Gwen, her arms folded, her eyes tired, saying, 'She needs to go into some kind of clinic. But we can't afford it, even if we redraw on the mortgage—it's just so expensive.'

Nina was vague on the timeline, but rehab had been mentioned during Amber's heroin era without ever happening, and then somehow the murky and inexplicable transition took place—this had been about three years earlier, when Amber was twenty-five—the thing that their parents insisted on calling her 'recovery'.

'She just gave it up,' said Gwen. 'All by herself. She decided enough is enough.' And Robert: 'Bam was always like that. You couldn't get her to do anything until she was ready.' The old wonderment. *What are we going to do with you?*

Nina, lying in bed at one am, thought: I should call Meg. But she wasn't going to—Meg would be asleep in her own apartment, sensibly asleep in her sensible pyjamas, with her packed bags zipped and ready by the front door.

Amber swept back into the building, taking long strides over the tiles.

'Warm out there,' she announced. 'It's almost hot!' She grinned, nudged Nina with a pointy elbow. 'Hey. You're on holidays, remember?'

Nina gave a forced smile.

Beneath Amber's cigarette smell there was a mustiness, as if she hadn't washed her hair or clothes in a while. She leaned an arm on Nina's shoulder and crossed her ankles. Here we go, thought Nina. This was Amber's Casual Act. She did this, usually, when they were all together, at dinners or lunches, birthdays, Christmases—that is, when she actually showed up. There was the Casual Act, and then there was the Sidling Off: the smoking somewhere outside, around a corner, the vanishing into the bathroom. And after the Sidling Off was the Slipping Away. *Where's Bam? Did she leave? Oh—but I didn't see her go* . . . First, though, came the Casual Act, in which Amber flew in the door—always late—and then seemed to be everywhere at once: kissing, hugging, asking questions and not waiting for the answers, pouring drinks and clinking glasses and laughing and shaking back her hair.

('It's such a *performance*,' Meg had said to Nina, many times. 'Doesn't it drive you crazy?'

'I don't know. Maybe she's for real. Maybe she is happy to see everyone. Maybe she just, you know, peaks early, can't maintain it.'

'Oh, come off it, Nina.')

Performance or not, Amber's Casual Act didn't ever last long. One of the saddest things about it was seeing the faces of Gwen and Robert, how they lit up, like children at a fireworks display, and how lost they seemed afterwards, after the Sidling Off and the Slipping Away, when they became creased-looking and distracted—exhausted, cranky, disappointed children rising stiffly to their feet in the cold darkness among divots and scattered rubbish. That was pretty sad, Nina thought, but even sadder was the sight of Amber herself around the corner, pulling on her cigarette, elbow propped on folded arm, all the pink and dazzle shut down, her face empty and grey.

'Shall we?' Meg had the car keys, and led them through the doors, and they left the air-conditioning and the muggy warmth descended.

In the car, Meg, with efficiency that filled Nina with an enervating awareness of her own inefficiency, pressed buttons on the GPS. As they rolled through sunlight shattered by palm fronds a woman's voice, cool and mechanical, began to deliver directions—the first of which was, confusingly, *Proceed to the route.*

Meg, unruffled, proceeded somewhere, and then very quickly they were on a proper road, going fast, and there were open paddocks winking with sugar cane, and distant silos and then a billboard that they all yelped at because it showed a huge picture of a foetus alongside a picture of a young woman with her face in her hands, and some writing about life and God and mistakes and suffering, and none of them could believe it—Meg said, 'What the fuck?' and Nina in the back seat said, 'Oh my God,' and Amber just bawled like a cow, 'No-ooo!'

And just like that, the mood shifted: Meg made an executive decision on the windows and they were all suddenly down, and the air that leaped in from all sides was warm and soft and smelled of paddocks and hot sun. They passed a wire gate with a ute parked alongside and there was a farmer-looking man in a hat, spraying a hose, and the water arced into the sky and there was a dark ribbon of it running onto the road, which they swished through, and the hot-wet stony smell hit them and Amber said, 'Petrichor!' and Meg said, 'Oh! I haven't thought of that for *decades*!' and behind her sunglasses Nina's eyes overflowed with tears.

Petrichor: the smell of fresh rain on hot ground. Who brought it home, that word—which one of them? Nina couldn't remember, and she was not sure that she ever knew; it belonged to childhood, to their fused existence, when even the things you tried hardest to keep as your own were only tenuously so. *Petrichor.* One of their signature, show-off words, brought out to twirl and flash whenever there was someone new to impress: an indulgent semicircle of wine-softened adults at one of Robert's art openings; a hapless dinner party guest, stuck at the table while Gwen dealt with something over by the oven and Robert went into one of his space-staring lapses, his social energy gone already—glad probably, had he paid even that much attention, for the clamour of his daughters as it bore down on and filled an otherwise awkward pause.

Continue on State Route Forty-four for another sixty-eight kilometres, said their flat-voiced robot guide, and Meg had her right forearm resting on the sill of the open window, her elbow out in the hot light, and Amber in the passenger seat was illuminated in such a way that her pallor actually shone, and her hair glittered in the wind and she was laughing about something that Nina must have missed.

Nina was thinking that the other thing about petrichor, the word, was that while it was their tool for showing off, while they all loved it and used it in a performance of brilliance, of what precocious and dazzling girls they were, they also all loved it for its associations. The alchemy of weather: the swelling or slackening of barometric pressures, the clustering of particles, transactions of energy—transference, transformation, release. A late summer storm over the backyard, the ripple of thunder. Sheet lightning, green-edged clouds, water hurtling from the sky. Running out to stand in it, on the steaming concrete, chins dripping, clothes soaked, yelling—to each other, to their mother smiling in the doorway behind them, up into the crazy air—'*Petrichor!*'

And Nina wasn't thinking, consciously, that Meg's idea might just have some kind of a chance. She wasn't thinking that— she wasn't even thinking, she was just *being*, for a moment or two, in a state that she hadn't thought it was possible to be in ever again. It was gone, actually, the state—it had passed; it lasted from when they saw the billboard and all yelled out until perhaps twenty seconds after Amber said, 'Petrichor!', so probably less than one minute in total—but it was something that hadn't happened since Nina was, say, fifteen. The three of them, together, breathing the same air, electrified by something vast, something immeasurably bigger than they were; the three of them like their own cluster of molecules, united, bobbing and clinging in the great roiling synthesis of the world.

The rest of the drive was mellow, as if steeped in the afterglow of the petrichor moment. The road neared the coast, and the sea was there, off to the right, blue and glorious in the distance, but closer in a dirty sepia. Coconut palms, white sand. No people. Amber found a golden oldies station on the radio, and nobody complained or even actually minded when she threw her hair around and played air guitar to Cold Chisel and AC/DC. Eventually they left the coast again to enter more fields—fields and fields—of glossy thick-stemmed sugar cane. Mountains sat, lilac and ghostly, against the late sky. Small, high-walled, open-topped freight carriages the colour of rust waited on rust-coloured tracks, which carved away between shining walls of cane. Once they saw one moving, a miniature locomotive pulling a single little carriage, a mound of chopped green stems showing at the top. 'Oh, it's real!' said Amber. Meg hummed the opening to the song by the Go-Betweens. They stopped at a place selling ice cream made from local fruit, and ate ice cream for lunch, even Meg, even though it was not lunchtime but four thirty in the afternoon.

Something totally unexpected had happened. The exact thing Nina, just that morning, had thought impossible. They all seemed to—temporarily, because it had to be temporary; the spell would break, Nina knew that it must—have been unharnessed from something, their adult selves, their hard selves, the selves so extensively marked by the past ten years, by so much failure and resentment and disappointment. They seemed to have slipped, miraculously, out of the unasked-for matrix of their sisterly connections, which had got away from them so early, rising and locking into place, in which Nina was ineffective, and Meg bossy, and Amber a lost cause. It had all lifted. How extraordinary, thought Nina. They were still who they always had been, still those sisters, but on this afternoon, in this car, driving with the windows down between cane fields under a deepening sky with purple cut-out mountains in the distance, they were wearing it so lightly, their bossiness and flakiness and wildness; they were wearing it like they used to, like it was supple, slippery, not completely fixed. Like it could be taken off.

Amber had her shoes off, her feet on the dashboard, and Meg wasn't saying anything about what would happen were they to have a crash and the airbags go off, which would be for Amber's legs to be broken for sure; Meg was actually laughing— *laughing*—at something that Amber had just said.

I am not imagining this, thought Nina.

And: Meg, you're a genius.

And: My God, what is possible?

And, tears spurting: Amber, I love you.

They passed through Mossman, and it was only two streets really, it was gone before they got a proper look at it: a couple of flat-fronted shops, a pub, the inevitable concrete hulk of Woolworths, with its barren acres of parking. A little stone church and a stand of trees—very tall, majestic, sending a delicate canopy of frond-like branches out over the road—before a river, a bridge, a yellow sign warning of crocodiles, and then the cane fields again. Nina turned to look through the back window. What were those; were they flame trees? They were like nothing she'd seen before. They were so beautiful her heart felt seared.

'I'll drop you two at the house,' said Meg, 'and come back for supplies.'

'Can we get more of that ice cream?' said Amber. 'Will they have it at the supermarket, d'you reckon? Black sapote—I never knew there was such a thing. I want to taste it again.'

'I'll have a look,' said Meg.

'And wine, please,' said Amber. 'And maybe some beer?'

'Okay.'

'And cheese,' said Amber, 'and olives. And what'll we cook tonight? I could make a pasta. Can you get some salami, if they have it, spicy, and—'

Bon Jovi, playing on the stereo, was subjected to an abrupt fade. *In three hundred metres*, said the robot voice, *turn left*.

Meg slowed the car.

All those times, Meg, thought Nina. On the phone. Did it seem to you like I didn't care? Because I do care. I care so much. I think I care too much.

Can I do this? wondered Nina. Am I strong enough?

They bumped along a dirt track with cane to the right and tall, dense bush—rainforest, Nina supposed it was—to the left. At some point they crossed a narrow bridge spanning a small creek. Once or twice there were entrances to properties, wide metal gates with their own tracks winding off into the trees or cane—no buildings visible. Nina fell asleep for a while, and woke when the car stopped. Another gate, with a sign that said SWEETWATER. Meg heaved herself out of the driver's seat to swing it open and Nina, fuzzily, reached for her phone to check the time, tried to calculate. It had been over an hour since they left the main road. And they were not at the actual house yet.

Amber turned in the front seat and winked at Nina. 'Iso-*la*-tion,' she sang in an Ian Curtis voice, and Nina, breathless with guilt, made a dumb 'huh!' sound and looked out of the window.

It was getting late; the air was filling with blots of darkness, the sun gone. Meg turned on the headlights. The forest was on both sides now, and even with the windows closed they could hear it, the echoing yelps and shrieks of unfamiliar birds, the whirr of insects. The bugs were rampant; they hurtled in waves against the windscreen. This track was the same biscuit-coloured dirt as the last one, but rougher, narrower, squeezed by the growth either side. The radio had either lost signal or been turned off.

Nina was looking out at the dark flicker of trees, the dangles of vines, when all at once Meg cried, 'Whoa!' and the car slid to a halt and the three of them were pitched forward and then back in their seats.

A moment, and then a gasp from Amber.

'What?' Nina craned between the seats. 'What is it?'

Amber was flinging herself around, all hair and arms. 'Oh my God!' she squealed, like a teenager. 'Oh my God! Oh my God!'

'Shut up, Bam,' said Meg. 'It can't get you while you're in here.'

'What is it?' said Nina again. 'What can't get her? Should I lock the doors?'

Meg snorted, shook her head, put the car in reverse and rolled it back a few feet. She sighed like a fed-up schoolteacher. 'Can you see it now?'

Through the windscreen, down on the track in front of them, something was moving, oozing against the dirt. Something greeny yellow, unbelievably wide but then also long and surely much too big to in fact be a . . . Nina shivered. Phantom insects scurried up her legs. The thing paused in its oozing and turned its head, which was oddly small, and its eyes in the headlights were a dazzled, reflective white.

'Oh my God,' said Amber in a low, quavering voice. 'What is that? What *is that*?'

'Shh, Bam.' Meg put a hand on Amber's forearm. 'It's a python. It's harmless. I mean, unless it managed to wrap itself around you. But look, it's going so slowly, there's no way . . . Unless you'd, I don't know, fallen over and hurt yourself so badly that you couldn't—'

'Oh, shh, shh, Meg, shut *up*!' Amber covered her ears with her hands. She curved her spine and whimpered.

Meg gave a laugh that was short, dry, and perhaps a little bit cruel.

Nina couldn't take her eyes off the python, which was very, very gradually, with a sort of lapping motion—minute and fluid and really quite disturbing—completing its crossing, moving out of the glare of the car's lights and into the darkness of the undergrowth on the far side of the road.

Meg didn't wait for it to finish. Once it was most of the way across she put the car in gear and nimbly—with the others saying, 'Watch out!' and (still), 'Oh my God!'—skirted the snake's tail, straightened up and continued driving, not too fast, but not too slowly either.

Nina was reminded of studying for her driver's licence, which she hadn't managed to get until she was in her mid-twenties—the practice written tests with their various scenarios. *You are at a level crossing . . . When driving in fog . . . Heavy rain is falling . . .* The answer she remembered recurring, a refrain, a mantra. She could recall the exact wording: *A safe and legal speed.* In the darkness of the back seat she smiled. Meg's motto, she thought.

Meg proceeded at a safe and legal speed, and the track went on and on between its close walls of tree trunks and vines, and no more snakes appeared in the headlights. At last they swung around to the left and out into a cleared area perhaps the size of a football field—expanses of lawn with palm trees sticking up. It was completely night now, but the moon must have been there somewhere in the sky because there was light, faint and silvery. The pale track wound down a gentle slope to a two-storey building, white, pitch-roofed, with a towering darkness of forest beyond.

THE CRUCIBLE WAS WHEN AMBER was twelve or so, when she was really hitting her stride. And then there was *A Midsummer Night's Dream*, and *Oliver*.

Amber in the long white nightdress, hair wild and blazing under the lights; Amber in a crown of dark leaves and red berries, a green robe, slender bare arms, a half-smile, one eye slitted with mischief; Amber with a ragged crochet shawl knotted at her chest, dipping side to side and swishing her skirts, her plain, sweet singing voice, her perfect cockney accent, bawdy and lovely at once.

The mothers, afterwards, on the steps of the school hall. Gwen like a reluctant dignitary, dazedly absorbing the compliments, or comments, or warnings, whatever they were. The awe and fear.

'Extraordinary, never seen such talent.'

'She's something special—you know that, don't you?'

'Amazing.'

'Wonderful.'

'Such poise. A born actor.'

'A *force*.'

Amber in the background, up on the railing, face ghoulish with left-behind make-up, laughing like a maniac, hanging upside down.

Meg calling, 'Stop that, Amber, people can see your underpants.'

Nina at Gwen's elbow.

(Where was Robert? Ah, see, there he was, back inside the door by the table with the piles of programs. He had one in his hands and was leafing slowly through it like a historian all alone in a vast and dusty library, holes in his jumper, frayed threads crawling from the sleeves of his jacket.)

Amber swung. Meg tutted and folded her arms. Nina listened.

'Yes, yes,' murmured Gwen. 'Thank you, yes, very proud.' She shifted her weight and the shoulder of her coat brushed Nina's ear—because Nina was by this time almost as tall as Gwen. Meg was taller. They were grown, Meg and Nina, in their final years of secondary education. They were supposed to be nearing an exciting time—university, independence, adulthood—but Amber had come bursting into the school, down the bottom with all the other year sevens, blasting her talent and eclipsing everything.

'Is that Amber girl your sister?' people asked, apparently noticing Nina for the first time.

On the steps Gwen shifted again and murmured, 'Well, we'd better get these tired girls home.'

'She's magnificent,' said one of the mothers.

'She's just brilliant, Gwen,' said another, squeezing Gwen's arm.

'Oh. Thank you, ah . . .'

Gwen didn't know any of the mothers' names—she never did, and never had. Gwen was never behind the sausage sizzle at the fundraisers, or getting thanked by the principal in the newsletter for tireless work and enthusiasm, for giving generously of her time. Gwen, when they were younger and she'd collected them from school, hadn't stood chatting with the other parents but waited shyly, alone by the gate. This was strange because Gwen herself was a teacher and worked at a school—a special school for children who were 'handicapped' (that was the word used back then).

Nina had visited this school where Gwen worked, and found it frightening. The air was full of moans and gurgles and smelled of tinned spaghetti and wee, and the children were arranged about the place in their wheelchairs or, some of them, propped on gross-looking beanbags on the floor, and all seemed to be wearing ugly tracksuits with the pants pulled up too high.

'It's only because you're not used it,' Gwen said later, in the car. 'In our society we keep disabled people hidden away. But they're just people. Like you and me. That boy, Harley, in the green t-shirt, he dived into a pool at the shallow end—before that he could walk and use his arms, and he went to a regular school like you do. He's still got the same brain inside. It must be sad for him, being stuck in an institution.'

After this Nina stopped diving at the pool.

The mother who knew Gwen's name, but whose name Gwen obviously didn't know, was still there with them on the steps. She was short and round and had feathery hair dyed a pinkish orange. She said, 'You're going to have to do something with her, you know.'

'Sorry?' Gwen's large brown eyes with their downward-tilting lashes blinked rapidly.

'Get her into the industry,' said the mother. 'TV. Movies. Find an agent. All that.'

Gwen made an evasive motion with her head. She laughed, a breathy embarrassed titter. 'Oh, I don't think so,' she said quietly, quickly, and reached for her children.

Nina was there, ready, and Meg had pulled Amber down off the railing, and so Gwen's arms pulled them all into an interlinked unit, and they moved down past the orange-haired mother, past the other mothers, and, like one of those dogs you hear about that somehow know their owner is almost home, Robert appeared in their wake, stuffing the program into his jacket pocket and pushing up his glasses and calling cheerily, to no one in particular: 'Bye!'

So it wasn't Gwen who *did something with* Amber and her talent. And it certainly wasn't Robert. It was Amber herself who demanded, towards the end of year seven, to join after-school drama classes two days a week. They were run by a theatre company, and to join you had to do an audition, which Amber of course blitzed.

It wasn't clear—or at least Nina would not remember—how Amber found out about these classes. This might be where the blurriness began, the lack of clarity regarding who was in charge of Amber, how decisions concerning her were made. This—if anyone was to have a go at retrospective sense-making—might be chosen as the point at which her wildness, leaping out and finding no bounds, began to take off.

'She must be good at this acting thing,' Nina heard Gwen say to Robert one night.

'Of course she is.'

Robert was leaning on his elbows at the kitchen counter, reading the newspaper. Gwen was peeling apples to stew—cheap cooking apples she bought in sweaty plastic bags from the bargain table at the greengrocer's.

'Robert,' said Gwen, using the sharp end of the word, and Robert reared up and turned to face her.

'Oh,' he said. 'You mean *actually* good?'

'Yes.' Gwen dropped a twist of peel into the compost bucket.

'Well.' Robert took his glasses off. His eyes, to Nina, watching from the hallway, seemed loosened, bleary. 'Well, that's wonderful!' His lips, always red and shiny, pursed in a pleased smile. His cheeks bulged. He looked like a slightly unhinged adult cherub.

Gwen took up another apple. 'Yes,' she sighed, 'it is. It really is. But I don't know the first thing about the world of acting. I mean, I don't think we can stop her. And I s'pose it's an outlet for all her energy. I just feel a bit, I don't know, nervous about it all.'

'Nervous?' Robert laughed. 'You're a funny thing, aren't you?' He returned the glasses to his face so that his eyes were once more safely contained, and he yawned and stretched and his untucked shirt lifted to show the soft pouch of his belly with its dark furry hair, and then he went up behind Gwen and put his arms around her. 'Nervous,' he said again, in a quieter, chuckling voice, and Nina crept away.

One day, when Nina was in year eleven and Amber in year seven, just starting her drama classes, there was a whole-school assembly. Nina, filing into the hall, breathing the stale air, her throat thick with ready yawns, looked up into the rows of filled seats and saw Amber's face shining out, and was halted—the toes of the boy behind clipping her heels—by the realisation that what the mothers said was true. Her sister was extraordinary. Even just sitting there, not talking, not moving, she was luminous.

The boy behind Nina said, 'Come on,' and pushed her in the back, and Nina started walking again, twisting her neck to keep watching. The girl seated beside Amber had leaned in and was whispering to her. Amber's head tilted, her lips parted, her eyes got huge and bright. She's *acting*, thought Nina. Right here, sitting in assembly. Without even an audience.

But then Nina, shuffling into her own row, taking her own seat, saw that Amber did have an audience—she had the whispering girl, who leaned so greedily close.

How would that feel, Nina wondered, to have every single thing you did be so pleasing to others? To see that pleasure in their insatiable eyes as they drank you up?

Nobody had ever told Nina that she was beautiful. Gwen didn't comment on her daughters' looks at all. Robert was always saying that all three were 'just lovely'—but he also used that word to describe things like a garden hose or a block of butter. It was in the wider world that Nina had learned about beauty as it pertained to her. There, outside her home and family, it was clear that being beautiful was the most important thing, for a girl. It was what people noticed. And there, outside, Nina had learned that while nobody ever noticed Meg and everybody always noticed Amber, she, Nina, was—surprise, surprise—somewhere in the middle. Nina was noticed by older, quiet women who were well dressed in an understated way. And she was noticed by certain men and boys.

Here are some things that Nina, over the years, had observed or had happen to her:

Their aunt Alison, Gwen's sister, on a rare visit from Adelaide, drinking tea on the back porch with Gwen as, down on the grass, eight-year-old Meg dumped toddler Amber in and out of an inflatable pool by the armpits. Alison saying: 'She's a darling, isn't she, little Meg. Such a good girl. And I wouldn't worry, Gwennie, she might blossom. They sometimes do, those plain girls, later on.' Gwen, her lumpy-veined legs sticking out from her chair, crossed at the ankles, saying: 'Looks aren't everything, Al.'

Meg in year ten on the bus to school, with two boys seated behind her, whispering: 'Bush pig. Hey, bush pig, we can smell your bacon.' Meg's arms tight around her bag in her lap. Meg staring out the window.

In a cake shop with Robert on a Saturday, Amber aged nine in a dress from the dress-up box—emerald green velvet with gold stars and moons; a rip over one shoulder showing tender-looking skin—legs long and golden, hair aglow, the freckles standing out across her sweet, straight nose. The woman behind the counter—middle-aged, tubby, name tag: RHONDA—her flat brown eyes bright with moisture, reaching over the high glass counter with the silver claws of her tongs to proffer a pink-iced bun. (To Amber only. Nina aware of herself as a hazy column of drab colours on the periphery.) Saying: 'For you, my darling, darling child.'

At *The Crucible*, at *Oliver*, at *A Midsummer Night's Dream*, all the mothers, mother after mother: 'Exquisite!' 'Beautiful!' 'Beautiful, beautiful girl!' 'That hair!' 'Those eyes!' 'A heartbreaker!' 'Divine!' (A tiny sample of an uncountable number of such comments.)

In year five, at Kate Beade's boring birthday party, the lights switched off for a game of Murder in the Dark in Kate Beade's boring bedroom, and Hayden Marshall somehow finding Nina and stroking her hair, following her as she tried to move away, his hand foreign and insistent. The lights coming on again and Ben Anderson saying: 'Urgh, look, Marshall's patting his dog.' Hayden Marshall's face seeming to swell as it went redder and redder, his small round dark eyes blinking, his hand snatched behind him. Hayden Marshall saying: 'No I wasn't! I was not!' Kate Beade's mother calling them all out for icy poles, a stampede, but Hayden Marshall waiting, holding Nina there by the back of her t-shirt. Hayden Marshall flicking Nina, hard, on the earlobe, then pushing her ahead of him out the door.

At a party in a sculpture park, Nina and Meg coming around the corner of a hedge and a man in a crumply white suit and a straw hat standing there. Nina almost running into him. The man holding a drink in a bulbous glass—a pink drink with a slice of orange floating in it. His face far away and hard to see under his hat. Nina looking at the drink instead. The man's body tilting back from the knees, then forward again, as if in a strong wind. Nina saying: 'Sorry.' Meg still there, but the man not looking at her; the man looking at Nina. The man bending. His hand coming towards her. His two first fingers brownish near their tips, the nails flat and yellow. The smell of tar. The fingers touching Nina's chin. Quite roughly—the fingers shaking. Nina saying, again: 'Sorry.' The fingers letting go; the man's hand falling to his side. The orange slice doing a slow twirl in its round glass. The man saying: 'Oh, no,' his voice shaking too. 'Oh, don't be sorry. Please.' Taking a lilting step back, fanning his hand to the side. 'Please, go on your way. I think you'd better. Right now.' Meg running off, and Nina walking, quickly, past—and Nina not imagining, Nina hearing clearly, the man saying: 'Rose of all the world.'

In the bathroom, with the chair against the door, Nina stood before the mirror and examined her eyelids, which were quite long, with deep pockets where they went up under the wide curves of her brow bones. The eyebrows themselves were a nothing sort of colour—mostly you noticed the skin around them, which was white and smooth. Her actual eyeballs were quite big; her eyes were moony, Nina thought—they were pale grey and there was a lot of them. Her face in general was pale and smooth, and everything looked sort of soft and spaced out on it. Her hair was a very boring light brown, and it was fine and floss-like, and had some quite curly bits and other frizzy bits, and by the end of a day it would have lifted itself right out of any hair ties or clips that she might have put it into. She looked like a girl from a really old painting, basically—or from the illustrated Greek mythology book they had got at a garage sale, with *Sarah, Rosie and Bradley Henderson, 22 Hotham Street, Windsor* written in biro on the flyleaf. She did not look like Claudia Schiffer or Cindy Crawford. She was not bright and gold and pink and fresh like Amber. She did not dazzle.

Sometimes, looking in the bathroom mirror—before someone came along, usually Meg, and tried to barge in, wanting to know why the door wouldn't open—Nina took a sort of secret enjoyment in her own face. *Mysterious* was the word that hovered then, and shimmered. But other times Nina felt quite disgusted by that face, its pallor and softness, the orbs of its eyeballs, their grey jelly, the frizzles of hair at the temples. It seemed to her then that she—her face and her whole self—was not just colourless and ugly, but somehow infuriatingly weak, somehow deserving of punishment.

In those dark and turgid gilt-framed paintings she'd stood before so many times at the National Gallery, the girls and women were sometimes being—was it ravished or ravaged? Nina wasn't sure she knew the difference. *Debased*, anyway, that would do. Quite a few of them were being debased by big men or beasts. They were taken off their bases, or their bases were rubbed out by the men or beasts, and the women were helpless without them, white and floppy, often tipped upside down or to one side, their arms and hair dangling. This was what happened to girls with Nina's kind of face (and arms and legs and tummy and bum and little boobs with their palest, most old-fashioned strawberry-ice-cream nipples; even Nina's pubes were a mousy indistinct fuzz like in a painting of a maiden by a stream with her draped cloth falling open)—this was what happened to those girls, those cowering girls, out in the world. Nina knew it, and people like Hayden Marshall and the man in the white suit at the sculpture park knew it too. They saw her, her softness, and they wanted to get her off her base and do things to her.

MEG PARKED THE CAR AND switched off the lights and they all got out. The sky was blue-black, rich and clear, and there was the low, lopsided moon. And there, too, were incredible quantities of stars, thick and bright, spread everywhere, and going up in layers.

'It's so warm!' said Amber, holding out her arms.

The air was soft, with an edge of moisture. There was a slight breeze, but it was soupy, balmy. Somewhere a sound, muted, constant; Nina couldn't place it.

Meg used the torch on her phone and squatted by the stairs leading to the wide verandah of the second storey to retrieve some keys. She mounted the stairs and switched on a light. The mass of forest behind the house immediately loomed. Something flapped in the darkness; something screamed.

'What was that?' Amber had taken the steps two at a time and was huddled behind Meg, clutching her elbow.

'A bird, probably.' Meg was finding another light switch.

The verandah was very deep; a whole living area was set up on it: couches, a television, dining table and chairs. Open to it was a kitchen: slate floor, yellow laminex benchtops, shelving stacked with crockery. A sort of doorless antechamber housed a washing machine.

'Nice,' said Meg, picking up a mug, a creamy ceramic with speckles. 'These're handmade.' Setting it back in place she frowned at one of the lower shelves, tapped with a toe at a nest of dented saucepans. 'Crappy pots and pans, though.'

There were no internal doors: each room opened only to the verandah, which ran the full circumference of the building. Each room had its own lock, and Meg jangled the bunch of keys like a jailer as she led the way, unlocking and opening. A prickle of discomfort rose in Nina.

After the kitchen, around the first corner, was a bedroom. Louvred windows, rough white calico curtains, the same bare dark lacquered floorboards as the verandah, a double bed with white sheets and an orange Indian cotton quilt, a bookshelf, a chest of drawers. After that a second, identical room—same size, same shape, same bed, same furniture, blue quilt this time. Around the next corner—at the back of the house, close to the dense, black, noisy wall of forest—a bathroom. Basic: white tiles, shower cubicle, basin, toilet, white towels folded over a freestanding rack. More louvres, frosted this time. Moths and smaller, darker insects wavered in towards the white glare of the overhead globe. Meg flicked it off again.

'We'd better keep these doors closed,' she said, 'if we've got the lights on inside.'

They all stepped out onto the verandah and leaned on its railing, peering through the darkness towards the forest. It was so near, only metres away. Nina could smell it, a complex smell, fat with pulpy wood and earth, but also sharp, green, cool. She noticed that noise again, a susurrating, running on beneath the louder, more spacious cries of birds, or whatever they were (no

bird Nina had ever encountered made such hair-raising noises).
It was water, Nina realised, the sound—running water.

Meg, on cue, said, 'Can you hear that? There's a creek down
there. Really close. We can swim in it, apparently.'

Nina realised that she had forgotten to pack her bathers. In
fact, she didn't have any bathers to pack. The bikini she'd pulled
out of the depths of her underwear drawer, blue-and-white-
striped, had atrophied since she'd last worn it; held up to her
bedroom window it sagged, the white parts a tired beige, little
pockets of prolapsed fabric letting light through. She'd thrown
it in the bin and then forgotten to buy a new one.

Nina didn't say anything about this, or make a sound, but
Meg, like a bloody mind-reader, gave her a narrow look.

'Did you remember to pack your bathers, you two?' she said.

'Mm-hm,' said Nina indistinctly, bending to slap at an insect
on her calf.

Amber didn't answer. She'd gone quiet, and was moving
slowly. She'd stumbled a bit as they exited the bathroom. Her
handbag was over her shoulder; had she dipped into it as Meg
forged ahead with her bunch of keys and Nina traipsed heedlessly
along—popping something, slipping something in? Or had it
been earlier, in the car—maybe during the snake incident, under
the cover of all that thrashing about? Nina didn't know how
long it took for these things to take effect. She didn't even know
exactly what 'these things' were—what Amber was on—although
she assumed that they were prescription opioids.

Meg had noticed Amber's slowing down too. She puffed air
out loudly through her lips, and the words *disapproving horse*
appeared in Nina's mind.

'Shall we?' said Meg, with a bit more volume than necessary.

Amber's head lifted like that of a sleepwalker. 'Huh?'

Meg made her horse noise again and moved off around the next corner, keys at the ready.

'Oh, right,' said Amber, shambling after her.

The last side of the house had French doors that opened into a larger bedroom, with built-in wardrobes. This room had a vast bed—king-size—and bigger and wider banks of louvres than the other rooms. The bed was topped with a pristine white cotton quilt, which Amber suddenly launched herself onto, face down, laughing.

'Get off, Bam,' snapped Meg. 'You'll get the bedspread dirty.' She whacked, open-palmed, at Amber's blue-jeaned legs.

Amber didn't move. She kept laughing, a lazy, husky laugh that unravelled into a phlegmy smoker's cough. She turned her head to one side to let the cough out and took handfuls of the quilt. Then she rolled slowly over, drawing in her arms so that she was swathed in the fabric. She gave a last hack and lay still, eyes closed. 'I'm tired,' she whispered.

Nina and Meg stood one each side of the bed, their sister between them, her face like that of a dead person, her body like a dead person's body, wrapped in a shroud. In the darkness outside a cry erupted: *Wheep-wheep-wheep*. The door behind them was open and the insects were coming, moths pocking at the windows, whirling at the bare globe, black gnats zapping past Nina's ears, against her face, her arms, something tangling in the hair by her neck. A huge beetle, iridescent green, lit on Amber's unmoving form and began to crawl.

Dread came over Nina. She shivered, folded her arms, looked to Meg.

Meg's face had turned crimson. Her lips were pressed into two white lines, her eyes slitted. It was her Face of Fury, from childhood, and Nina automatically stepped back.

'Get *up*,' said Meg, taking hold of the quilt and tugging.

Amber's shrouded body slid towards the edge of the mattress. Pillows toppled.

'Get *up*,' said Meg again, in a choked voice. 'Amber!'

Amber hadn't opened her eyes. She was smiling gently, like someone having a dream. When Meg pulled again at the quilt her head joggled passively.

'What are you doing, Amber?' said Meg in that same thick voice. 'Did you take something? What did you take? What are you *on*?'

Amber murmured something indistinct. She was still smiling.

Meg gave one last tug, dragging Amber almost off the bed, then let go and crossed her arms, hands in armpits. She swayed, rising to her toes. She was almost dancing. Her teeth worked at her lips. Her voice dropped to a whisper. 'You can't keep doing this. We're not going to *let* you, are we, Neen?'

Nina, backed almost to the wall, said, 'Um.'

But it didn't matter; Meg wasn't listening to her. Meg had her gaze, her furious gaze, fixed on Amber. Meg's breathing was loud and rough. Meg was turning, very carefully, towards the door. Meg was saying, in a voice that was only just under control, 'I'm going to go and see if there's anything here we can have for dinner. It's too late to go back to the shops now. I'll go in the morning.' Meg was out on the verandah and walking away, her soft shoes making very faint peeping sounds, like a pair of sad ducklings.

'Bam?' whispered Nina.

No reply; Amber was asleep. Nina watched for a bit longer to make sure she was breathing. There was an abundance of insects now; the walls dotted with them, the light globe wreathed in spiralling bodies, the air full of their patter and tap and buzz and zip. Nina went to the light switch and turned it off. She stepped out onto the verandah, found a light there and put it on. Glancing back she saw, by the foot of the bed, Amber's handbag.

Heart thudding, she crept to pick it up. Out in the light again, out of sight of the bed, she opened it. A wallet, sunglasses, cigarettes, crumpled receipts. A doctor's prescription, yellow paper folded into its sleeve. Boxes of pills: OxyContin, Percocet, Endone. The pharmacists' labels: *PRESCRIPTION MEDICINE. Amber Elisabeth Atkins. Take ONE tablet morning and evening, after food. Take TWO tablets every six hours. Take ONE tablet every four hours as needed. Do not exceed more than THREE tablets in one twenty-four-hour period.* The red and orange stickers: *Warning, this medicine may cause drowsiness. Do not operate heavy machinery. Do not consume alcohol while taking this medicine.*

Nina returned the packets, took the bag back. She bent close to listen once more for Amber's quiet breathing. Inside her stomach there was a cold, weighty feeling. Why are you surprised? she thought. What did you expect?

Amber breathed on, the sound a barely there thread under the frantic insects, which were now battling their way back out, towards the verandah light.

'Plain pasta for dinner, I'm afraid,' said Meg. She shook salt onto her palm, dropped it into the steaming pot of water, bent to check the gas flame. 'But I did find some wine.' She tore open a packet of spaghetti, not looking at Nina. 'She asleep?'

'Yep.' Nina fiddled with the hem of her top. 'You okay?'

'Yeah. Sorry about before. I just—I get so *angry* with her.'

Nina took a deep breath. 'I've been thinking,' she said, 'and reading, doing a bit of research, and I wonder if this whole thing is a good idea. I mean, a detox is—it's a big deal. It's usually done in a clinic or whatever, by—'

'Oh no you don't.' Meg dumped the pasta in the pot and glanced at her watch. 'Nina, you've made a commitment. We're here now and we have to go ahead with it.' She seized a wooden spoon and stirred. 'We need to be very clear and very calm. And the two of us will have to stick together, to back each other up, because she's going to try every last trick in the book. She'll try to turn us against each other. She'll go for you first, because you're the soft one.' Her cheeks were flushed, her nose shiny, her eyes bright. 'We're going to need to be strong. Okay?'

Nina looked at the floor. 'But, I mean, just then in the bedroom . . . You're saying we need to be calm, but you kind of lost it, and it's only the first night, Amber hasn't even—'

'Yeah, look, sorry about that. It won't happen again.' Meg took three plates from a shelf, forks from a drawer. 'It's been a long day. Here,' she said. 'And here.' She reached for a bottle of red wine on the bench.

Nina took the plates and forks in one hand, the wine in the other, but she stayed where she was. 'Do we have to . . .' she said. 'I mean, isn't there some other—'

'Okay.' Meg sighed. 'I have to tell you something.'

NINA HAD GONE TO PRIMARY school with a boy called Angus Black. They were friends for a while, in a secret way, meeting near the sports equipment shed at recess and lunchtime. They played shameful imagination games, instigated by Angus. They pretended to be sister and brother, a witch and a wizard, students at a magical school. They made potions from dirt and water and crushed flowers. They were nearly the same age, but Nina was in the year above, young for her class.

Nina was clever, everyone knew. Her frayed exercise books— the pages of which were always coming loose and floating away from her—were crammed with handwriting that was urgent and prolific; her smudgy pencilled maths equations were almost always correct; in reading time she sat as still as a painting, immune to the bored wriggling of others, the whispers and farts, her elbow pinning a paperback to the desk, her fingers pressing red marks into her temple, her eyes racing, ravenous, over the pages.

Angus was not clever—at least, not academically. Nina saw one of his worksheets once: not only had he not answered any of the questions, he'd written *DUM BUM* and *POO HED* in the margins. He was forever sitting outside the principal's office, swinging his legs violently, the untied laces of his shoes flicking. He was small and freckled, with dull auburn hair; he reminded Nina of the sandy-whiskered gentleman from *Jemima Puddle-Duck*. His eyeteeth were prominent and as he stood thinking up his next idea he would run his tongue over them and flare his nostrils. Nina waited, taking pale blue petals from the flowers of a sticky-stemmed shrub that grew beside the fence and making darker blue lines in them with her thumbnail. When Angus was ready he rubbed his hands together, clapped them, and did a little jump in the air.

'Now,' he said. 'Watch out just there, okay, 'cos that's the quicksand. Now, we've gone on a camp, right, in the forest, and when the beasts come what we do is . . .'

Playing with Angus was like reading a book or watching a movie. You gave yourself over, you went somewhere else, and when the bell rang and it was time to stop you came unsteadily back, blinking.

'Don't play with that boy,' said Meg at dinner one night.

'What boy?' said Nina.

'Angus Black.'

Nina's face burned. 'I don't play with him.'

'Sarah B saw you at lunchtime,' said Meg, chewing. 'He's in year four. And you're in year five. And he's a boy. You shouldn't be playing with him.'

'Why not?' said Gwen in a muffled voice as she bent to pick up a tea towel that had come untied from around Amber's neck.

Robert wasn't there—he was at a late meeting at the university or at an art opening or something like that.

Nina used her fork to make patterns in her tomato sauce. Her stomach was heavy with mashed potato.

'Kangus Bwack,' said Amber.

'Shh!' Nina glared, and discovered tears, ready to fall. She held her eyes as wide and still as she could.

'I think it's silly, this idea of girls and boys not being able to play together,' said Gwen. 'What does it matter?'

Nobody answered. Nobody was listening to her.

Nina stared, desperately, fiercely, at Amber.

Meg finished her sausage and set her knife and fork together.

Amber put her head back and lowered her eyelids.

Gwen stood and began stacking dishes. 'As long as you get along and are kind,' she said, turning to the bench, 'I don't see why any child of any age, girl or boy, shouldn't be able to . . .'

'*Kangus Bwack*,' whispered Amber, and, 'SHUT UP!' yelled Nina, and the tears popped out, and her glass of water tipped over, and, 'Can't you get through a meal without spilling something?' sighed Meg, who had a napkin ready to stop the puddle before it ran off the edge of the table.

'. . . anyone they want to,' said Gwen, from the sink.

Nina did stop playing with Angus Black. Some of the girls in her class found out—popular girls who were not friends with Nina but nonetheless believed it to be their business—and they staged an intervention, appearing at the sports shed in a row, with their hands on their hips.

'I was just getting some flowers,' said Nina, seizing a gummy handful and stumbling away, past the toothy ginger blur that was Angus.

She returned to playtimes spent with Lizzie Miller and Kate Beade, her designated social equals, boring and nice. They were who she invited to her birthday party, where she opened their boring nice presents with sadness and guilt, and felt secretly relieved when Amber got into the lemonade and, after twirling on the swing, vomited all over Kate's dress, causing Kate to cry until her mother was summoned to come and get her, by which time the party was over anyway and Lizzie had to leave as well.

Still, Nina didn't pine over Angus Black; she forgot him quickly enough, falling back into books, daydreaming through lunchtimes on the climbing frame with Kate and Lizzie, whose voices batted like gentle moths, easily ignored.

It was Meg who announced that Angus Black had been expelled. By this time Meg wasn't at primary school anymore—she was at what Robert liked to call the 'big school'. One by one, when they got to year seven, the Atkins girls would move from their local state school to a private one that meant lengthy commutes on public transport. The fees for this school were paid by Robert's mother, who had apparently told Robert that if he chose to have entirely no ambition in life that was his funeral, but the poor children deserved at least a fighting chance.

The private school, with its large, well-maintained buildings and excess of resources, would be astonishing to Nina. For the whole six years she was there she would not stop looking back and forth between it and her family. Discovering, on her first day, just how odd, how *outside of things*, her parents were was like being hit with a large wet towel, and Nina never got over it. Even in year twelve she would arrive home and go out to sit alone in the backyard, pulling up blades of grass and looking at the cobwebs netted under the eaves of Robert's studio. What kind of a life, she would wonder, were they leading, her family? What kind of people were they, with their clapped-out car—a Volvo station wagon with no air-con and rips in the seats, which had replaced the maroon Sigma when Nina was twelve—and their unkempt house that was much too small for five people and so many books and artworks?

She ventured to discuss this with Meg, once.

'No one's *normal*,' Meg said, with authority. 'Not once you get to know them. Everyone's weird.' It was one of the truest things Meg would ever say. But it didn't, at the time, help.

So Meg was not at the primary school anymore when Angus Black got expelled from it, but she knew. Meg, the future organiser of reunions, the raiser of funds (for a classmate who got leukaemia; for the Leadbeater's possum; for an orphanage in Bangladesh), Meg the rememberer of birthdays, the maker of cards, the baker of cakes. Meg, who knew who was going out with whom, who had kissed whom. Meg, who would tell these things in the dark on a late weekend night or during holidays, in a serious whisper, allowing herself one or two giggles before turning over her pillow and pulling up the covers and settling down because she needed to get a good night's sleep. (And later, when she was in year twelve and Nina in year eleven and Amber in year seven, Meg, stern and solid in her white flannel PJs with the blue polka dots, would tell of who was having sex with or giving blow jobs to or being gone down on by whom, to Nina, who had already done some of these things herself and lived in terror of Meg's Finding Out, and to Amber, who might not have even been listening properly but chortled and thrashed her legs like an idiot, pretending—or perhaps not pretending—to fall out of bed.)

'Angus Black got kicked out of school,' said Meg.

They were in the car, all of them, parents in the front, girls in the back, the girls getting bigger now, knees clashing. Gwen was driving, as she usually did; Robert was in the passenger seat with an art dealer's catalogue, making rampant inky notes on the pages and pushing his glasses up his nose with the back of his hand.

'Angus who?' said Gwen, braking for a red light. They were on their way to the opening of a group show in which Robert had a painting. Collingwood, a summer evening, the streets busy with people, shops lit up, smells of overripe fruit and smoke and spit-roasted meat.

'Angus Black.' Meg, who always sat in the middle so as to have the best view out the front, turned to look at Nina.

Nina met her eyes. 'Oh,' said Nina. 'I'd forgotten about him.'

Meg gazed, assessing. Her face was so close Nina could see the little yellow dot in the green-grey iris of her right eye. Nina had forgotten about that too. Being this close—breathing each other's breath, staring into each other's eyes—belonged to another time; it felt simultaneously familiar and strange. It was what it would feel like to suck your thumb now, after so many years of not.

Nina looked past Meg and Amber, out the window.

'Listen to this,' said Robert, tapping the catalogue with his pen. *'Elegant and raw.'*

'He got expelled,' said Meg.

Nina looked into an open-fronted greengrocer's, at bunches of bananas in a clawed mound, the deep black mouth of a cut-open pawpaw. Meg's leg pressed against hers, Meg's hip, Meg's arm.

Gwen was reverse-parking, looking over her shoulder and past her daughters, one hand on the headrest of Robert's seat.

'How can the one painting be both those things?' said Robert.

'He was out of control,' said Meg.

Amber's arm shot up and her fingers covered their mother's eyes.

'Amber!' Gwen shook her head free. 'Don't do that while I'm driving the car! What are you thinking?'

'You just looked so funny with your face right there.'

Gwen eased the car the rest of the way into the parking space and pulled on the handbrake. 'Don't *ever* do that again, Bam,' she said.

But Amber was out already, trailing along the greengrocer's display, feeling all the fruit like a blind person.

Gwen had her hands back on the wheel, even though the engine was off. She was breathing deeply and slowly, which was a sign that she had Had Enough. Robert looked up from the catalogue and Nina saw his attention shift, like a camera clicking to the correct f-stop. He let the catalogue slide to the floor and put his hand on Gwen's thigh.

'Darling,' he said. 'You look delicious this evening.'

Gwen sighed, but then she smiled, and when he leaned towards her she turned to him and they kissed on the lips, a firm, neat kiss. Then they opened their doors and got out.

'They suspended him,' said Meg, undoing her seatbelt. 'Three times. And after that you get expelled.'

❧

Angus Black was forgotten all over again, and Nina was twenty-eight when Meg rang her to say that he had died.

'It's in the paper,' said Meg, 'and I'm sure it's him—the dates are right, and he had a brother called Karl, remember?'

Nina did not remember Karl. She remembered Angus, though; the memory was right there, as if it had been waiting to leap out at her. Angus, with his vulpine teeth, his flaring nostrils. What had become of him? How had he died?

'Drugs,' said Meg. 'For sure. Or suicide. If it was cancer or something it'd say *after a long illness.*'

Drugs. Was that what Angus Black had gone jumping into, after getting suspended and then expelled and then whatever came next? Had he turned into one of *those people*? Nina, sitting on the end of her bed, was accosted by images. They were not of Angus Black, though—they were of Amber. Amber, who was now twenty-four, out in the hard world, being a junkie. Waiting in a car park for her dealer, arms folded, pacing. Exiting a public toilet, slow and lithe, eyes pinned, skin pale, everything about her drawn, sucked inwards by the vacuum of her high. Nina knew that Amber did these kinds of things, was in these kinds of situations. Nina knew that strangers saw Amber and thought whatever you think when you see one of *those people*: How sad, or, How could you do that to yourself, or, Yuck, or, Get away from me. Nina got up off the bed. She pushed herself away from the images, as was her habit. She was living through her twenties as much as possible as if she did not have a younger sister.

It was a Saturday, and she had a ten am shift at the book-shop where she worked. She bought a newspaper on the way, and found the death notices.

BLACK, Angus Gregory, 1977–2005, much loved son of Don and Susan, brother to Karl. Rest in peace.

Outside the convenience store she folded the paper, awkward in the wind. The morning was clear and cold—late autumn, metallic sunlight, the sky pale and thin-seeming—and there were hardly any cars on the road. *Rest in peace.* You saw it so often in death notices and on gravestones, but it seemed to Nina that it might have special significance in the case of Angus Black, dying at twenty-eight. Had he needed peace, after whatever kind of life he'd lived? Those kicking legs, outside the principal's office, those flying laces. Suspended three times, then expelled. Or could 'rest in peace' be a plea from his family? Please leave us alone now. Don't haunt us.

Nina wedged the paper in her bag and went to the traffic lights. She had some things in her own life then that seemed important; she had not expected them, and she had not expected to feel so protective of them. One of these things was Luke. Peace seemed to Nina a precarious state, beyond the control of a person. This news of Angus Black shone at her in a white stab, like a mirror angled to the silver sun, and she did not want to look at it. There was already so much to guard against. Amber—there was already Amber to guard against. The lights changed and Nina set off at a half-run.

THE PASTA—DRESSED ONLY WITH salt and pepper and olive oil—was delicious. Nina hadn't realised she was so hungry. The wine was acidic but it was better than nothing. The hoots and yelps and witterings went on drifting out of the forest; the moon had lifted high above the palms; the breeze against Nina's ankles was slow and cool.

'Okay,' said Meg, setting down her glass. 'You know I didn't help, when she was at her worst. All those years, with the heroin. I had to stay away. For myself, for Dave, for . . . you know.'

Nina nodded.

'But I did see her every now and then.'

Christmases, birthdays. Their parents trying so hard. Amber absent or there only briefly. Meg and Dave holding hands on the couch, Meg's hair greasy, her skin with a kind of sheen to it, bumpy with hormonal rashes. Breasts straining at her shirt. She had been at the mercy of something then, and they'd all felt it—even Amber seemed to. Meg entered the room and everyone else made way.

'Well, one time she approached me. At Mum and Dad's. She followed me to the bathroom. She came in, while I was on the toilet, and stood there blocking the door so I couldn't get out.'

Nina stopped eating.

Meg poured them both more wine. 'I haven't told you, Neen, how I felt about her at that time. It wasn't just that I was preoccupied with my . . . stuff. It was more than that. I felt like she was toxic, you know—that she was poisoning me, and the—the pregnancies.' Meg put her head back, blinked. Her words were tight. 'When I saw her, when I *smelled* her, even her voice on the phone—it was all . . . it was just . . . unbearable.

'So she came into the bathroom and she sat down on the tiles with her back to the door and started crying, and she said, in this whisper, Meg, why won't you help me?' Meg wiped her eyes with the back of her hand. 'And I said, I can't give you any money. And she said, I don't want money. I want you to help me get clean.'

From the forest: *Wheep-wheep-wheep!*

Meg took a jagged breath. 'She said, Take me somewhere. Lock me in a room. And no matter what I say, what I do, don't let me out of there. She was on her knees, on the floor, holding on to my legs while I was sitting there on the dunny.' She gave a messy sobbing laugh. 'And what did I do? I wiped, and I got up, and I pulled up my pants and flushed the toilet and washed my hands and I walked out of the room and left her there. On the floor.'

Nina's hands went out across the table, and Meg's hands went into Nina's.

'It's not your fault,' said Nina. 'You had troubles of your own.'

Meg's nose dripped. Her teeth were bared. 'I wanted those babies so much,' she wailed.

Nina rubbed her thumbs over Meg's knuckles. She extracted one hand, found a tea towel and passed it over.

Meg wiped her face. 'Sorry.' She sat up straight. 'Not that it's an excuse, but I mean, I was actually kind of insane.' She glanced out over Nina's shoulder towards the lawn and the track they'd come in on. She squeezed her lips together and swallowed and tucked her hair behind her ears. But her fingers were shaking. The veneer seemed very thin. She leaned—almost lunged—to grab Nina's hands again. 'So do you see,' she said, in a low, intense voice, 'I owe her this. She asked me for help and *I didn't give it*. I have to make up for that now.'

Meg's grip was hot and moist. A speck of saliva had flown from her mouth onto Nina's cheek; Nina could feel it there, a cool pinprick. Shit, she thought, what have I got myself into?

Meg let her go, sat back again, sipped from her glass.

'Okay,' said Nina. 'Okay. So what's the plan? What do we do?'

Meg didn't answer. She was staring in an empty kind of way, not quite at Nina. The wine was nearly all gone, and Nina felt it dragging at her, too—the booze, the tiredness. Also, the ever-growing sense that she might well be the sanest person in this house, on this little island of cleared land, so far away from everything.

The breeze had dropped. For a few moments, the creatures in the forest went quiet, and there was only the murmur of insects and the creek. Nina could hear Meg's watch ticking. Nina was freaking out. It was a kind of squirm very deep inside. She didn't move, her breathing didn't change, she knew that there were no external signs, but the outer walls of her body felt very thick and numb, and everything else—Meg there across the table with her staring face, the kitchen, the couches, the bedroom around the corner with Amber sleeping in it—seemed distant and glassy, and then there was that tiny writhing, as if the whole of Nina had been shrunk and pressed into a very small worm that was bending itself uselessly this way and that.

She made a huge effort. 'What do we do?' she heard herself say again.

Meg stirred. 'Well. We confront her, first thing in the morning. Over breakfast. We say, You have a problem, and we are going to help you, and we're all going to stay here for as long as it takes. And then we ask her what she's got in her bags, what drugs. And we ask her to hand them over.'

'What if she won't?' said Nina's faraway voice.

'Um, yeah,' said Meg. 'It could get tricky then.'

'She needs to agree,' Nina heard herself say. 'We can't force her.'

Meg sighed. 'Oh, Neen. This is the thing. I think we'll have to. It's not her we're up against. It's not *her* that'll fight us. She's been taken over—she's not her real self.'

The worm bent. Nina tried to think. There was an idea there somewhere, half-formed, if only she could sharpen up and get a hold on it.

'I looked in her bag.' Where did that come from? Her hands felt heavy in her lap. 'Just before.'

Meg's eyebrows went up. 'Really?'

'Endone,' said Nina. 'And Oxy-something. And another one I can't remember.'

'Okay,' said Meg. 'Okay.' She drummed her fingers on the tabletop.

'I took them. I flushed them.'

Meg's fingers stopped. 'What?'

'I flushed them. All.'

Meg gave a bark of a laugh. 'Nina Atkins! Did you really?' Her eyes in the dim light were hard and sharp.

'Yep.'

'Wow.' Meg shook her head. 'I didn't see that coming. Well. Game on, I guess.' She got to her feet. 'In which case, we'd better get some sleep.'

Meg used the bathroom first, and while she was in there Nina tiptoed to the big bedroom, felt in Amber's bag and took out all the drugs. She collected her own overnight bag from the top of the stairs and went to the first of the two smaller bedrooms, where she opened the bag and stuffed the packages down under her clothes. She found her pyjamas and put them on.

'Bathroom's free,' called Meg.

'Thanks.'

Nina padded along the verandah, passing Meg, who was getting changed with the door open—flesh-toned bra, big white Cottontail undies; wide, pale haunches, bellybutton like a stunned eye gazing out between silky-looking rolls of stomach flab.

Poor Meg, with her matron's body, loosened and scarred but with no children to show for it. Poor Meg the Boss, the Organiser, the Fixer, with no children to marshal, to tidy, to kiss with a mother's smacking kisses. There had been a book in their shared shelf, in their shared childhood room with the bunk beds: *Little Mother Meg*. It had belonged to Gwen, from when she was a girl. Out of extreme boredom Nina read it one school holidays. She'd thought that it was going to be about a woman who was a mother but was also very, very small, even perhaps magically small like Mrs Pepperpot, and that this little mother would have adventures, like falling into one of her children's schoolbags and getting carried to school or riding a dog or whatever. The book was in fact about a teenager who was just busting to get married and have kids of her own, and Nina was filled with disappointment, and also revulsion. Who would want to give up their young body, their ability to move unhindered through the world? Look at Gwen, with her veiny legs and dimpled upper arms, so slow, so weighty. Her endless, boring preoccupations—eating vegetables, not scuffing your shoes, washing your hands, doing your spelling words; who would actually *choose* that tedium, that kind of slavery? Nina had always suspected that, unlike Little Mother Meg, Gwen had somehow ended up where she was by accident. She didn't seem to mind the slavery so much as to seem eternally surprised by it. ('How can three girls possibly make so much mess?' 'We're out of milk *again*?' 'When did this floor get so dirty?')

In the bathroom, a moth had fallen into the toilet bowl. It burred, waterlogged, on its back. Nina brushed her teeth and then walked along the verandah to the stairs and went down to the grass. The night had settled; the lawn was cool and dewy under her bare feet. She pulled down her pants and squatted and the grassy smell of her own urine was a comfort. Above her the building glimmered against the black jumble of forest.

Who was in charge of this house? Who would be in charge, over the coming days? Meg the matron, lying heavy in her bed? With her keys and her rules and her intentions?

Nina was tired. Her eyes felt dry. She blinked up at the dark verandah. There were other powers in all this—quieter ones, without rules. There was Amber, shrouded in the white bedspread. There was the way she'd foiled Meg, so soundlessly, slipping away like that into herself, into sleep. Unreachable.

AMBER ON DRUGS WAS NEVER really *there*. By 2009 she had not really been there for a good ten years, first because of heroin and then because of prescription drugs. Amber's addiction was a dense haze, a disturbance in the atmosphere surrounding her that sent anyone who approached glancing off into confusion. But when Nina tried to remember Amber *before* drugs (which she did sometimes, usually when drunk, at various periods throughout her life) there was not any more clarity, really. All she got was a closing door, a departing streak of limbs and hair.

Amber had not been lost then, at twelve, thirteen, fourteen, during her drama years. She'd been the young Amber still, wild in a way that was mostly glorious. And she had *been there*, physically, in the house with the rest of them. Yet in Nina's memory she was not there. Why was this? Had Amber the non-person, Amber the addict, superseded all other versions of Amber completely, erasing them not only in real life but also in memory?

There were memories, though, and they were clear. But they were wild themselves, outside of Nina's control. When they came forward, when they sharpened and resolved, it was not at her calling but of their own volition.

Here is one: 1993—when Amber was twelve and Nina sixteen. Amber returning from a role in a TV show. Filming in Aspendale, miles away, early in the mornings. The decisions, the permission, lost in the blur, but somehow Amber staying away for four nights with someone—another family? a teacher?—and returning electric with joy, dark circles under her eyes, hair matted with spray and eyebrows ridiculous with pencil that took days to wear off.

'I got a line!' she announced, standing in the middle of the living room, her bags and a flung jacket on the floor at her feet. She stilled herself and lifted her chin, then turned to the back door and pointed. 'Look!'

Everyone looked.

'What?' said Meg.

Amber threw herself backwards onto the couch, laughing. 'Nothing!' she said. 'That was my line! I had to point and say, "Look!"'

'That was it?' said Meg. 'It took four days just to say one word?'

'Oh no, so many other things happened.' Amber gave a lazy sigh. 'But it's hard to explain. You kind of had to be there.'

'Go on,' said Meg. 'Explain.'

Amber shook her head slowly, wearily. 'It's just too hard.'

Meg snorted, opened her mouth, seemed to think better of it, closed it again and folded her arms.

Nina and Gwen stood watching. (Robert was at work.)

Dreamily, Amber ran her fingers through the ends of her hair. Her lips pursed. She closed her eyes for a moment and her whole face was suffused with a rapturous sort of tension.

Then her eyes opened and she sat up straight, grinning, and leaned towards the armchair, which Meg was plonking herself into, and Amber's hands rose, fingers unfurling, and she licked her lips and said in a low voice: 'Well, first you have to get there when it's still dark and they have all these big trucks and there's a food table under this big tent thing and you can have anything you want, there's even pancakes, and Nutella and *Pop-Tarts*, they somehow have a toaster, and these huge container things with boiling water and you can make tea or coffee or *hot chocolate* and there's, oh God, just so much good food. And then there's the trailers, they're like the back part of trucks, there's a whole lot of them, they're like rooms, you go up little steps and they've got lights and furniture inside . . .'

Meg listened, her face very still, and Gwen and Nina stood at the edges and listened too, their eyes lowered, like eavesdroppers.

Another memory. Around the same time, '93. A Sunday morning. Nina going with Gwen to collect Amber from the house of a friend, probably someone from the drama group.

Plane trees, their splotchy grey and tan trunks, their nubby golden pompoms. Rows of parked cars. Low brick fences and, behind them, brick apartment buildings.

A stairwell, dark and cold. Dried brown plane tree leaves and a supermarket catalogue splayed on the landing, showing cuts of meat. Iron banisters with flaking black enamel paint and cobwebs.

The door to an upstairs apartment, white with a full-length frosted-glass panel through which were visible heaped dark low shapes.

A white oblong of a face through the glass. A voice. 'I'll get her.'

Gwen looking to Nina: a query—a plea, almost.

Nina: 'I really need to go.'

Gwen: 'Ah, Dianne? I'm sorry, could we . . . Would Nina be able to use your bathroom, please?'

Inside, a strangely defiant woman in a silk blouse, jeans with ironed creases, a full face of make-up. A hat? (This part unclear.)

A dim tunnel, lined with piles. Boxes and bags, overfilled and softly slumping. Stained cream carpet only just visible.

A cloud of op shop smell. Dust. Cheap paper. Stale BO and stale cigarette smoke and stale perfume. Foot sweat.

The living room. One wide window looking over the street, the plane tree branches. Enormous pieces of dark furniture, crammed in. Expensive things, stuck for some reason in the wrong house. In a corner, dusty faceted crystal shapes spilling over hoops of brass—a chandelier, piled on the floor. The smell of baked beans, sugary, unwholesome.

'No! No!' called voices from behind a closed door.

'Sophie,' barked the woman—Dianne—thumping with a fist that was laden with gold and diamonds. 'You come out of there right now! Right now!' Sagging, breathless. 'Or I will have to give you a *smack*.' This use of a childish word not at all funny.

Nina will not be able to recall the door opening, Amber and her friend emerging, how they got Amber to leave, any of that.

She will have an image of the bathroom. The door with a broken lock—ragged holes in the timber frame, as if the bolt had been forced, the screws torn out. Deep pink tiles, the air pink with reflected light. The smell of wet newspapers and mould. A dead orchid in a pot, the yellow tongues of its leaves.

She will remember the drive home. Amber in the back seat with her overnight bag beside her, humming and chewing the ends of her hair. Gwen playing Radio National, something boring about fruit bats, long scrapes of static. The smell of the flat there in the car; an ugly smell that must have been on Amber.

Driving up Punt Road, under the bridge, past the MCG, past brick fences and blank-fronted terrace houses.

Inside this memory is another memory. Images from a holiday: a long drive, a country town, a street of old square buildings and a small brown stumpy-legged dog that wriggled and wagged and bumped its head at their hands for pats. The three sisters, much younger, crouching, exclaiming, a tangle of stroking hands. The wet dab of the dog's nose, its velvet-rag ears pressed back, the strange rounding of its spine as it rose on its hind legs and licked and quivered and scrabbled at them. And then, against her bare shins, a fast blunt fleshy jabbing that went on for some time before Nina realised and looked properly and saw the blind pink penis straining, and she sprang up, hot and sick, with her hands held out in front of her, cold in the air where the dog's saliva was on them, and while Meg and Amber had made the same realisation and were doing the same thing—jumping up, backing away—Nina felt as if she were the only one coated in ugliness, in shame, and the sense of being unclean took a long time to dissipate.

Because she was only sixteen Nina didn't make any connection between the feeling of being humped by a strange dog and the feeling of being inside that flat with Dianne and her sea of possessions, her wrong furniture and her invisible daughter defying her from behind a door, and knowing that Amber was there too—had been there all night, away from the safety of her own family. Nina just felt set upon by that same shame and ugliness.

She glanced at Amber, and Amber caught her looking and grinned and then bulged her eyes and stuck her tongue down under her bottom lip and pushed it out, and Nina turned back

and gazed again at the grey buildings passing. Something new—
a sense of responsibility, as unwelcome and inexplicable as the
shame—settled on her. She looked at Gwen, who was driving
the way she always did, as if alone in the car, twitching her lips
or raising her eyebrows or smiling and cocking her head and
giving it a little shake as she listened to the voices on the radio.

'Who are those people, anyway?' said Nina.

Amber didn't answer. Nina didn't know if she'd even heard.

'I don't know about that,' said Gwen, but she was talking to
the radio.

What was happening? She was moving away, Amber—this was
what Nina would see when she looked back. Amber moving away
already, and Gwen and Robert just letting it happen.

She was too young, Nina would think. She was so young!
Why did nobody see that?

But also, back then, there was the formidable presence of
Amber herself, that young Amber, the force of her. And there
was no precedent. Gwen was not wild, and neither was Robert.
Meg and Nina certainly were not. So there could be no imagining
what wildness, unbridled, might do. Back then, as far as any of
them knew, Amber was always going to go on being the Amber
she'd always been: an explosion of a person, uncontainably light,
harmlessly, gorgeously free.

NINA HAD NOT EXPECTED TO sleep. There was a creature hidden somewhere near the ceiling of her room that kept chirping, and there were bugs too, invisibly going about their battings, and from outside there had been the determined calls of the *wheep-wheep* bird. And then there was the worry that Amber would wake up and find her bag raided, her stash gone.

So she lay anticipating crashes and shouts, and then suddenly the room was light and the night was over and she realised that she had slept—in fact slept right through, so deeply that when she first woke she didn't even know where she was. She saw the bookshelf, and her bag on the floor, and then she turned her head and saw on the wall very close to her face a small blue-and-green spider with long, hinged legs, hanging, still and venomous-looking, against the white-painted timber. She wriggled slowly away, then quickly got up.

The forest was very close on this side of the house. There was only a small strip of lawn in between, sparkling in the sunlight. The forest itself was extraordinarily busy with different kinds of interconnected plants. Nothing seemed to stand alone: between every tree, every branch, hung some kind of vine—strings of heart-shaped leaves; grey barbed-wire-looking things in multi-stranded garlands; flat ribbons, deep green, massed in dangling, shabby beards. The tree trunks were crowded with staghorns and moss.

Nina went along the verandah—past Meg's door, which was shut—and around the corner. From this side, the back of the house, the forest was further away; the view was more expansive, the sky visible. She could see a path, which must be the one to the creek, narrow, paved with irregular stones, pale against the dark earth. It sloped downwards, leading out of sight. Bordering it were banks of shiny crimson-mouthed bromeliads, their stems reptilian necks, their fringed gullets bright and wet-looking.

It wasn't hot, but it wasn't cool either. In her t-shirt and light pyjama pants Nina felt oddly held by the air—as if she couldn't quite locate the edges of herself against it. The word *temperate* came into her mind. Temperate, temper, temperance. She went closer to the railing. Off to the right stretched the lawn she'd seen last night, cropped close, its scattered palms elegant and clean-trunked. It went on, a gaping space, for perhaps three hundred metres, until the cluttered wall of forest turned to close it off.

The bird calls this morning were not the same as the ones from last night. The actual cries were different and there were more of them, but they were also mostly gentler and more frequent, so the effect was of a rippling blanket of sounds rather than the intermittent and abrupt screams that had taken place in the darkness. She saw a pigeon walking fatly on the lawn; she saw two tiny yellow birds—finches?—fluttering high in the branches of a tree to one side of the path; she saw a thick-beaked kingfisher squatted lower down. She saw—and she had to laugh and shake her head at the cliché, but also just in astonishment at the *excess* of this place, its brightness, its lushness, its casual, unending wondrousness—a giant blue butterfly. It came towards her in wobbling slow motion and then another, identical, butterfly emerged from the forest and the two of them rose together in a grand soft tumble before vanishing over the edge of the verandah roof.

Then something moved on the grass directly below. A blonde head appeared, white shoulders in a ratty pink tank top. Amber. She walked over the lawn to the mouth of the path, her body lengthening as Nina's perspective altered. She was wearing a pair of cut-off denim shorts and her legs were pitifully thin and white, a dark bruise on one thigh. Her steps were delicate, soundless. Her hair hung down her back.

Nina found herself reversing into the shelter of the verandah, near to the door of the bathroom, ready to duck and hide. What happened last night? Was there yelling, a scene—had she slept through it? How long did someone take to start withdrawing? What time was it now, and when would Amber be missing her next hit—if she wasn't already?

Amber didn't turn around. She walked on, evenly, silently. Between the crazy bromeliad hedges she went, under the tall dark trees, and her bare feet stepped from stone to stone and she moved down the slope and was gone.

Nina, her own feet also bare and noiseless, went along and around the next corner, so that she faced the side lawn. To her right, at the end of this stretch of verandah, were the stairs. The car was not there at the foot of them; Meg must have gone, driven to Mossman for supplies.

In the kitchen the wall clock said that it was eight forty-five. This seemed arbitrary. Nina didn't know what time they'd gone to bed last night, what time they'd arrived at the house, what time the sun had set. She put a hand to the nearest surface: the yellow benchtop. She felt unsteady, vague. For a moment the ridiculous idea occurred to her that she might have somehow in her sleep taken some of Amber's pills.

She went to the bathroom, where the toilet moth had vanished—flushed, presumably. Back in the living area she found her backpack, took out her phone. No messages. She tried to call Meg and realised that there was no reception; the row of bars at the top of the screen had vanished. No connection whatsoever. Wow, she thought. Nice work, Meg.

There didn't seem to be much point in getting dressed, so she descended the stairs in her pyjamas. The house, she saw now in daylight, had a ground floor with its own verandah. On this side were closed glass sliding doors, very dusty and layered with cobwebs, a contrast to the clean surfaces upstairs. The whole downstairs area was markedly different—the weatherboards grimy, the irregular sand-coloured paving stones unswept. Three broken outdoor chairs lay in a tipped-over stack, their white plastic stippled with black muck. There were patterns on the ground—the dirt shaped in rivulets as if blown in, wet, towards the house and then left to dry. There must have been a storm, and nothing done to clean up after it.

Nina peered through the door, and made out what looked like a half-built kitchen—benches, shelving, but instead of the oven, cooktop and fridge, empty cavities. On one bench was a yellow-and-black toolbox; an electric drill lay beside it, cord dangling. Everything—benches, floors, the toolbox and drill—was covered in thick dust. There were boxes on the floor. In one Nina could make out a pile of magazines and what she was almost certain were photo albums; another held rags or drop sheets, or perhaps folded bedding coated with grime; from another rose the bony neck and dirty, downturned hood of a white Planet lamp.

Nina put her face right up to the glass, cupped her hands either side. Beyond the kitchen there was a cane couch missing its cushions and a bed base covered in an incongruous ruffled pink valance, its mattress half off. Framed pictures leaned with their faces to a wall, showing torn brown paper and wire loops. At the foot of the bed lay one pillow, no pillowcase, stained in brown ovals large and dark enough to see even from this distance. Goosebumps came up on Nina's arms. She took the handle of the sliding door and gave a tug. It began to move, letting out a whiff of mildew. Nina pushed it closed again and walked away, trying not to hurry but wanting to.

She entered the creek path. Under her feet, the stepping stones were damp and cool and rough. The moist air got even closer.

It's just a half-renovated apartment, she told herself. Don't be silly. It's where they've dumped all the stuff they cleared out from upstairs. Still, her skin went on crawling. It was left-behind things, she thought, that were so unsettling. How they took on the appearance of artefacts or evidence. It was like a crime scene, that place, with the pillow on the floor, the skewed mattress—hapless objects, redolent of some broken-off action.

Then, further down the path and out of sight of the house, in a brown-green world of wet growth and tangles, she found herself thinking of Amber's vestiges, her heroin tableaux, back in the day—the speckles of blood on the yellow tiles of Gwen and Robert's kitchen; the evil shape of a dropped needle on the rug under the coffee table; the nest of blankets, clothes, tobacco, teaspoons in the den that was Amber's bedroom. These tableaux, she thought, these objects—they didn't just speak of the abjection and senselessness of the acts that they were remnants or by-products of; they spoke also, and perhaps more clearly, of the person who left them behind.

She felt sick now, stepping down the path. The forest breathed around her, flooded with sounds. It smelled rich and earthy.

Why would you leave them out for discovery, these vestiges, this evidence, these manifestations of shame? A cry for help? A genuine mistake, due to total fucked-upness, to being so wasted you couldn't even see the mess? Surely not. If you can remove yourself, get to your feet and walk away, then surely you can also wipe up the blood, pick up the needle. So it's not a lack of awareness, the absence of shame, that leads to this behaviour. It must in fact be the opposite—it must be that the person feels shame so deeply that they have lost any kind of a grip on it, any hope of getting it under control.

Oh, humans, humans! thought Nina. What is *wrong* with us? She made a sound, a small, rusty sob, and had to stop and wipe her face.

There was a splashing from further down, where she could glimpse the water between the trees, shining in the splintered light, slipping along its channel. Over near the far side there was a flash of pink.

She cleared her throat, called, 'Bam?'

The stepping stones had ended, and there was just a short, steep hill webbed with the huge ridges of tree roots, leaf mould between, ankle deep. She had to take the final descent in a clamber, hands and feet. The banks of the creek were high, the roots nearest the water clutching at sheer edges, and the water, running fast between clumps of rock, looked shallow—at least close in to where Nina stood, right at the brink, her toes curled over. It was perfectly clear, the sandy bottom visible, the submerged leaves and sticks.

The place brimmed with a particular energy—elevated, like water held just below boiling point. The sun came in shafts through holes in the high-up canopy. There was moss; there were insects making horizontal passages over the rushing surface; there were birds everywhere, stirring invisibly, calling their endless calls; there were smaller, woody roots that hung from high like bare brown wires, and dipped into the water. Wherever Nina looked something fluttered or zipped or scurried, something had just departed a slender branch and left it bouncing, something was making its tiny, laborious way through the gunk between two fallen twigs. Inside a curled leaf just next to where her hand rested on a branch a reddish-brown spider ravelled and unravelled its legs. And the water, the busy water, pouring ever onwards, creasing around rocks and pinching itself up where its currents converged.

Nina's despair was a mass in her chest. What was to be done? They'd thrown themselves into this place, the three of them, had brought all their bullshit along, like dust, like grime—what sort of alchemy was Meg expecting? It was wrong. Their problem, the thing they were concerned with, belonged inside: in buildings, in clinics, in places where rules existed and training had taken place—in places where, most of all, there were other people.

A rustle, a splash. She scanned the water, the rocks, the opposite bank. She took hold of the branch—away from the spider—and leaned out to look right and left.

'Bam?' she called.

Nothing. But where could she be? The forest on the other bank was dense; there were no signs of any paths through it, nor any other paths on this side, as far as she could see in either direction. The only way in or out was back the way Nina had come.

What was happening? Had she gone mad? There must be a path somewhere, out of sight. Or had Amber waded up- or downstream and around a bend?

'Bam?' she called again. 'Amber? Where are you?'

A bird made a glottal, mocking sound.

'Bam?' Nina stepped down and into the water, which was shockingly cold. She took two strides and then got up on a large flat-topped rock. Beyond this was a shallow trough, and then, nearer the far bank, another set of rocks, higher ones. Nina yanked her pyjama pants up to her knees and stepped in again, waded further.

The water suddenly was up to her thighs. The current was lightly dragging, insistent. She let go of her pants legs, which were soaked already, took two more big, searching steps across the soft, slimy bottom, seized hold of the next rock, began to haul herself onto it.

'Amber?' she called. 'Bam?'

It was darker over this side, the canopy thicker. From the far side of the rock something hissed. Nina froze, one knee out, toes in a hollow just above the waterline, arms overhead, fingers splayed on the warm, gritty surface.

The birds chittered and yelped, the insects clicked and buzzed, the trees creaked, the breezes ran in ribbons along the rushing surface of the water, something went *bob-bob, bob-bob*, and over all of this was the tremendous thumping of Nina's heart. She strained to hear. Had there been a hiss? Had she imagined it?

A plop, and there it was again, a low, dangerous, intentional hiss.

Slowly she began to lower her foot, slide herself back down.

And then all in a rush Amber shot up from the far side of the rocks, a pink-and-white ghoul, with long arms and long hands that seized Nina by the wrists.

'*Raaah!*' said Amber, and then broke into a hacking laugh. She rose, higher and higher—she was up on top of the rock, squatting, leaning back. Her cold fingers gripped tight, her full weight pulled at Nina's arms. Her hair streamed silver and green. Her shoulders were high, her ribs visible, her nipples hard studs under the pink top.

The rock banged and scraped at Nina's chest. She fought, twisting her wrists.

'Oh God, don't *do* that, Amber,' she cried in a small, tense voice. (The mantra of their family: *Don't do that, Amber*; *Stop that, Amber*; *That's enough, Amber*.)

Amber kept laughing, through chattering teeth.

'Why would you *do* that?' There was a film of sweat on Nina's upper lip. She tugged against Amber's grip.

Now Amber stopped laughing. But she didn't let go. She looked down, her eyes green in the murky light, her hair plastered to her skull. Her teeth clacked. Her open lips were rimmed with blue. Without expression she stared at Nina.

Nina yanked with her arms. Her wrists stung. 'Let go of me, please,' she said. There was a fizzing in her stomach. It's the drugs, she thought. She knows I took them.

Amber just stared.

'Let go!' Nina got a better footing and stepped back, wrenching her arms downwards, and Amber let go and gave a great, splay-legged leap and landed, sitting, in the water beside her sister.

A pause. The two of them breathing. Amber's lips were really quite blue, and her whole body was quaking. Her teeth sounded like a miniature hammer drill.

Nina, standing, the current flipping at her pants legs, said, 'Get up. It's too cold in the water.'

Amber went on sitting there. The water bulged at her back and gushed through at her armpits. Her white floating arms shook; her knees were up, her feet braced against the bottom. She stared at Nina.

'Get *up*,' said Nina again, and heard Meg's voice from the night before, from the bedroom. *Get up. What did you take? What are you* on? Nina tried to look past Amber's shaking, her blue tinge, to see what kind of state she was in underneath. Was she high? She was upright. She'd been remarkably strong, holding Nina's wrists. So she was certainly not wasted like she had been the night before. Of course she wasn't; it would have worn off ages ago. No, she must be the other way—jittery, agitated, pissed off. Maybe even delirious; Nina had no idea what withdrawal from pills looked like.

Amber hunkered in the water, staring and clattering, and Nina gave her another careful once-over. You'll live, she decided. There was a strange new chilly hatred inside her, and she wasn't sure if it was only for Amber, for her idiocy, her compulsive trouble-making. It might also be for Meg, for pulling this whole stupid stunt. It might even be for herself, for not saying no, for always being so weak, such a ditherer. Whoever it was for, it made her feel—for the first time in a long, long time—very clear and very calm. She bent and scooped a handful of water, put it to her lips, slurped it into her mouth. It was glorious, clean and quenching, and she took another handful, and then a third, bending low, almost tossing the water up towards her face.

She didn't look at Amber again. She turned and waded away from her, crossed back and climbed out and crawled with a surprising amount of dignity up the steep bank to the path, and then walked, the sodden legs of her pants swooshing, to the house.

HOW DO YOU KNOW WHEN someone is really lost? When a person has been changed by something—drugs, addiction—so much that they are no longer who they were before?

Amber's wildness was fundamental, and over an elastic span of time—one year, two, or three or five or even ten—it had met and twined and merged with addiction in one of those transformations that take place too gradually for the human mind to track. Nina could have chosen one of any number of events to mark as the turning point, the moment in which it seemed to her that the 'old' Amber was lost. There was the sighting of the first syringe, a slim dart, white and orange, between a skirting board and the old rose-patterned carpet at the house in Thornbury. The first sight of blood, on the yellow tiles. There was the first hospital trip: an early-morning phone call from Robert to the share house in which Nina was living, *Sorry to wake you, Neen, but something's happened.* The first time certain words were spoken. Gwen in the kitchen, tomatoes, parsley, a knife, no eye contact, *We think she's using heroin.* Meg outside Thresherman's holding a loaf of dark rye, the crinkle of its paper wrapping, its close musky smell as she grasped Nina's arm (pigeons, high sun,

Nina late for a lecture), *Wait, listen. She's an addict—you realise that?* Shocks, shifts, adjustments. But the moment one happened it was overtaken by the next—because addiction is shambolic and cascading as well as secretive, and on all fronts fundamentally resistant to the keeping of a sensible record.

There was an event that Nina would select and return to, and come to think of as significant, emblematic of deep change. This event did not include Amber directly. It was *about* Amber, as almost everything in the life of the Atkins family came to be—but Amber herself was not present for it. That was how it worked, Amber's addiction, its evil skill: it was everywhere but she herself—the *real* her—was hardly anywhere, and maybe even nowhere.

One afternoon in the year 2000, when Nina was twenty-three, she drove in her just-purchased second-hand lime green Corolla over to her parents' house in Thornbury. She went there to pick up a small bookshelf that Gwen and Robert no longer needed, which she would put in her new flat, the one in North Carlton that would come to feel exhausted by all of the affairs conducted from within it, and the kitchen window of which she would lurchingly remember she'd left open in the taxi on the way to the airport with Meg and Amber.

She let herself in.

'Who's that?' came Gwen's terse voice.

'Me—Nina.'

There was an unclear, relieved-sounding response.

Nina found Gwen in Amber's room. Amber was nineteen then. She had not, like her sisters, finished school and started university and moved out. Amber had stayed, as if camping, in the bedroom that had been all three girls', and turned it into a drug den.

Gwen was kneeling on the floor beside the bed—there was only one bed by then, a double, a futon; its mildewy smell was there alongside the smoke and staleness—wearing a pair of tight blue latex gloves like those worn by people in hospitals. One of the bedside drawers was open and Gwen was briskly, dispassionately, taking things out of it.

'Sorry, darling,' she said. 'I just have to do this while she's not here. Keep an ear out, will you?'

Nina stared.

Gwen had a small pile beside her on the floor: scraps of paper, cigarette lighters, crumples of foil. Nina saw the split square of an opened condom packet near the foot of the bed, a bra looped emptily on top of a heap of other clothes. A paperback copy of the first Harry Potter book on the bedside table.

There was a sort of pressure of knowing that Nina spent a great deal of energy keeping at bay, but even so, she understood that things were bad. She knew that Amber had become a junkie, that she stole and lied and took appalling risks. And she knew that Gwen and Robert were consumed by all of this, held to ransom, desperately dog paddling their way through the days, and at night retiring for inadequate spells of downtime with their inadequate props (their books, their crossword puzzles)—spells that at any moment might be broken by various demands (Amber trying to borrow more money; Amber threatening suicide should they not lend her money; Amber screaming over the phone at someone—a dealer, a boyfriend—and then slamming out of the house at two am; a phone call from the police; a summons to a hospital) and that in any case must be underlaid with such a pervasive and constant unease that lying in their bed with those books and puzzles probably felt like lying on a deflating lilo in the middle of a swamp.

Nina did know all of this, understood it to be the situation. And yet on that particular day, something about the sight of Gwen with her exhausted face and her blue-gloved hands going through Amber's things brought a new kind of cracking, stinging awareness. It had never occurred to Nina, in all her years living at home with Gwen and Robert, that her mother would violate her privacy. Her sisters, yes—nothing was truly safe from them—but not Gwen, with her quiet, sturdy morals, her awkward decency. Gwen would never pry. But here she was in her gloves, gathering up the lighters, the foil, the bits of paper, dropping them back in the bedside drawer, pushing the drawer closed, lifting the edge of the mattress to peer beneath it, lowering her head and shoulders to look under the bed, standing and going to the chest of drawers to rifle through its contents with a kind of seasoned efficiency, lifting clothes and shaking them, pushing one drawer shut with her hip, her hands already in the next.

The code by which her family operated was, in that moment, no longer what Nina had always believed it to be. Something very important had been let go, disregarded, ridden over. She gazed, horrified, at her mother. Did Gwen not realise what this meant— that it wasn't only Amber who was lost, changed, irrevocably damaged; that she, Gwen, had also been changed? By Amber, by Amber's shit. She, Gwen, had actually become *a different person*.

'When?' stammered Nina.

'Mm?' Gwen opened another drawer.

'When did all this *happen*?'

In 2008, three years after Angus Black's death and one year before the Sweetwater trip, Meg again delivered news of him, this time in an email headed *Angus Black* and containing only a link. The link was to a coroner's report on a government website. From this report Nina learned that Angus had died as a result of a fall down the staircase of a rooming house, and that the drugs found to be in his system at the time—prescription medications—combined with alcohol might have contributed to the fall. Prescription medications. Nina, despite herself, paid attention, because by then—since 2006—this was Amber's new world.

The inquest had been made and the findings delivered. Angus Black was gone, completely, had been gone for years. But Nina could not stop thinking about him, and about his parents—despite how bad this made her feel, how afraid. Unwillingly, she returned often to the coroner's report, a PDF of scanned pages which she had downloaded to her laptop.

Angus Black, the report said, had a long history of mental illness, drug addiction and alcoholism. Angus Black was found dead on the second-floor landing of a boarding house in East Melbourne at six forty-five am on Wednesday, 9 March 2005. He had been dead for at least four hours. His neck was broken. His clothes had vomit on them, and vomit was also found in his room, which was on the third floor. Also found in his room were various medications—oxycodone, lamotrigine, nitrazepam, oxazepam—as well as between thirty and forty empty port bottles, two-litre flagons that sold for less than ten dollars each.

The death of Angus Black was reported to the coroner by the Royal Melbourne Hospital, where his body had been taken from the boarding house by paramedics. The coroner's investigation was originally concluded without inquest, finding that he had died as a result of the injuries he suffered through falling down the stairs. Angus Black's parents, Don and Susan Black, 'questioned the adequacy' of this investigation and 'raised concerns' regarding the medical management of their son by a number of doctors, drawing particular attention to 'the prescribing methods of the medications nitrazepam and oxazepam' and the way in which these medications may have contributed to their son's death.

And so the investigation was reopened, because of Don and Susan Black, who believed, presumably, that the drugs might have been the cause—that their son might have fallen because of his intoxicated state, or that their son might have died even if he hadn't fallen, because of his intoxication. There was the vomit, in the room. There was the fact that Angus Black had left the room sometime in the middle of the night and begun to go downstairs. Was he looking for help? Because, perhaps, he realised that he'd taken too much, gone too far?

Don and Susan Black believed that their son had access to fatal doses and combinations of extremely addictive prescription medicines—narcotics; opioids—and they wanted to know how it was that he came to be in possession of these. They wanted to expose the flaws in the medical system that allowed such access, so that the system could be overhauled and events such as the death of their son be less likely to occur in the future to other people's sons, and to other people's daughters, and also to other people like them, Don and Susan Black—parents, carers.

Was that what they believed, Don and Susan Black—that it was the fault of the doctors? Was that what they wanted— attention brought to the holes in the system, to the problems with the issuing of prescription narcotics? Nina had no way of knowing. The true motives of Don and Susan Black were not in the coroner's report. The coroner's report only stated that Don and Susan Black wanted the methods of the doctors who prescribed opioids to their son to be examined, from which it could be inferred that they wanted these doctors to be held to account. To, perhaps, be blamed.

But it wasn't the doctors who made Angus Black take all those drugs, and drink all that booze, and wipe himself out. Angus Black—surely, given his history—wasn't a hapless victim of an error on the part of a prescribing doctor. Angus Black had, the report said, visited numerous doctors, asking for different kinds of benzodiazepines, asking for the highest possible doses. It was Angus Black who went around collecting all these medications, and it was Angus Black who took them, in dangerous quantities and in dangerous combinations, and washed them down with six-dollar port.

Angus Black was someone living at the edge of safety, someone who in his consumption of mind-altering substances was seeking—what?—escape, ease, distraction, refuge? Peace?

Don't ask why the drugs, Nina once heard a psychologist say on the radio. *Ask why the pain.*

Also not in the coroner's report were the things that Don and Susan Black might have said to each other inside their mock Tudor house in Kew, behind the willow tree, behind the gold-and-pink brocade curtains, at the end of the day of the hearing. What wasn't in the report were the things that they might have thought privately, separately, after the long day in the court-house—in their outdated bathroom with its pink tiles and frosted shower screen; in their bed with its heavy timber frame, in their bedroom with its walls painted an eighties powder blue.

Nina didn't actually know what Don and Susan Black's bedroom or bathroom looked like, but she did know about the mock Tudor house—in need of a coat of paint, flanked by a side garage with sagging timber doors—and the willow tree in the front yard, behind a new-looking timber fence that did not match the house. She knew because she had gone there, driven to Kew, to the address listed in the White Pages online, and got out of her car and stood across the road on an early winter's day, the thin sun milky on the flaking white face of the house, on the—really, there was no other word for it—weeping branches of the willow. She didn't see Don or Susan Black. There was a car in the driveway, an old green Peugeot, but the curtains of the house were drawn, downstairs and up (Nina imagined that they were gold and pink; in reality she could only see their off-white vinyl backing) and nobody came out while Nina was standing there across the road.

Another thing not in the coroner's report was what Don and Susan Black might have said and thought in private once the inquest was over and years had passed and their son was still dead.

Don't ask why the drugs. Ask why the pain.

Don and Susan Black, Nina was sure, believed that what they were doing was a service to their community, was in the interest of the general public; that in having the inquest reopened and in bringing to account the doctors who prescribed opioids to their son and in drawing attention to the problem of 'script-shopping', they may have been able to prevent what happened to them from happening to others. To people like Amber and Meg and Nina and Gwen and Robert. They believed this, Nina was sure, but she didn't think that it was their true motive. Nina thought that Don and Susan Black were, when it came right down to it, simply raging blindly at the world for taking their son away from them. They were looking for someone to blame, perhaps, but also they were looking for an explanation for something that was inexplicable. *Injuries sustained from a fall* would never be enough. *Accidental overdose* would not either. *Suicide. Homicide,* even. None of these would have been enough; nothing could ever adequately explain to them their son's death, because it wasn't the circumstances surrounding it that they needed explained, it was the basic, cold, hard, shitty and permanent and absolutely unacceptable *fact* of it. Of Angus Black being gone forever, but also of his life—the life that he'd lost—having been the kind of life that it was. It wasn't the twenty-eight-year-old Angus Black whose face was prematurely worn and who smelled of old BO and whose teeth were rotten, and who made his way from GP to GP, his scripts stuffed into the pockets of his dirty pants, who visited one pharmacy and then another, waiting for trains, scratching his sores, who stopped at the bottle shop for another flagon of port before mounting the stairs of the boarding house— it wasn't this Angus Black that his parents railed against the world for taking away. It was little nine-year-old sandy-ginger Angus Black, in his school shorts, with his fresh skin and his child's smell, musty, chalky, sweet and blameless, rubbing his hands together and jumping in the air, running his pink tongue across his teeth and flaring his nostrils and saying, 'Now!'

Nina was thirty-one when all this was happening. Still working her casual jobs at the bookshop, the university, the art gallery. She was a young thirty-one, with her flakiness, her forgetfulness; she had been seeing Luke, who was married, since she was twenty-four. She had never travelled overseas, or lived in a different city. She understood, in a deep part of herself, that she didn't know a whole lot about the world.

There was one thing that she did know, very well. She knew that people—like Gwen and Robert and, presumably, like Don and Susan Black—were actually contaminated by the shit they were enmeshed in, the shit that was the lives of their fucked-up kids, and that those people then became unappealing to others, to the outside world. She knew this from observing her parents.

Nina—at this stage, anyway—believed herself to be only slightly contaminated. She had the privilege of being allowed to, mostly, stay away. Immature as she might be, she was able to recognise that the kind of suffering her parents underwent as they struggled in the swampy orbit of Amber and her dysfunction was something that she, Nina, was blessedly immune to, exempt from. She knew this with relief, but also with guilt, which was of course a contamination of its own.

What she didn't know, and what she would really like to know—were she to drive again to the mock Tudor house in Kew, to get out of her car and go in through the newish timber gate, to brush by the willow tree and ring the doorbell and ring again and knock and knock until Don or Susan Black at last opened the door, with his or her stricken and unsatisfied and preoccupied face, and said, 'Yes?'—what Nina would really like to know from Don or Susan Black was, Did you have hope, still? At the end, before you knew it was the end, did you believe that he might yet change, Angus, that he was not lost to you already, not already a lost cause?

Because the coroner's report—the report itself and also the fact of the reopening of the investigation—didn't answer that question either.

NINA SHOWERED, RINSED HER WET pyjamas and wrung them out, then draped them over the railing of the verandah. Dressed, her wet hair dripping down her neck, her skin still damp or perhaps damp already from the humid air—nothing felt distinct in this place, nothing separate—she sat on the bed (after checking that the toxic-looking spider had gone). Her stomach gurgled. When, she wondered, would Meg be back with food?

She looked around the room. It was beautiful, with its clean white walls, its calico curtains, the parallels of its louvred windows. The bookshelf was inviting—Colette, Toni Morrison, Siri Hustvedt. She could love this place, this isolation, if she were here for a different reason. A holiday. Alone. She hadn't had a holiday on her own since . . . well, she'd never had a holiday on her own.

A couple of times men had taken her away for a night or a weekend—these were men before Luke. Luke could never do such a thing. But even if he did, Nina knew, it would be the same. It would be on his terms.

Stop, she told herself. Think about something else. She pinched the skin of her upper thigh.

She considered her overnight bag. She knelt and pushed her hands into it, into the mess of clothes, worming her fingers between layers of cotton and denim, feeling buttons and seams and openings, and then the bottom of the bag, the grainy wrong side of its leather. She glanced at the door, got up and closed it, sat on the floor with her back to it and pulled the bag closer, feeling again, in up to her elbows. She couldn't find the boxes, the packets of pills. She started taking things out. She tried to be systematic, lifting one item at a time, making a pile, but in the end she upturned the bag and let everything out in a sloppy heap which she then spread with her hands like a kid levelling a sandcastle. They were not there. She checked again by putting all the clothes back into the bag, one item at a time. Definitely gone.

'Okay,' she said out loud. 'Okay.'

Amber had got them. She must have come in during the night while Nina, stupid Nina, was so unsuspectingly and deeply asleep. Amber at the creek, her hard cold grip on Nina's wrists, her green stare, knowing, accusatory. Nina shoved the bag away. She thought of the night—the dark night, filled with the cries from the forest and the movements everywhere, the legs and wings of insects grazing walls and windows with tiny whispers, the chirping creature up on the ceiling doing who knows what, perhaps silently lowering itself somehow, crawling vertically or abseiling from a thread, the blue-green spider stepping its legs out and in, bobbing its sinister body. The doorhandle turning, the door inching open, Amber a black shape crawling over the floor to the bag. Nina's whole back felt cold; a shiver started at the base of her neck and fanned out and down.

Why hadn't she just flushed the pills, like she told Meg? Because she never did anything properly? Because she was a ditherer, a half-doer, an imprecise person whose actions left a grey smudge like pencilled letters erased and rewritten too many times? She groaned.

Again she looked at the bag. Maybe it wasn't just her flakiness that made her keep them—maybe she'd meant to return them to Amber, behind Meg's back? As a way of undermining Meg, as a protest at Meg's bossiness, at the fact that she, Nina, had been railroaded into this thing, made an accessory. She'd never really agreed. She'd never wanted to do it. She still didn't. It was a crazy idea. Something of the cool strength she'd felt earlier, walking away from Amber in the creek, returned. When Meg got back she'd tell her. *I'm out*, she'd say. *Drive me to the airport.*

Then she heard the car, the car door closing, Meg at the steps, her heavy ascent, Meg calling, 'Hello?'

She went around to the living area. Meg was in the kitchen, heaving bags of groceries onto the bench. She turned, saw Nina, took her by the arm and pulled her into the adjoining space where the washing machine stood, so the two of them were crammed, hot and close, in the semi-dark.

'Have you seen her yet?' whispered Meg.

Nina whispered too—she couldn't help it. 'Yeah. Down at the creek.'

'And how does she seem?'

'I don't know. Angry?'

There was a noise from the verandah and they sprang back out into the kitchen.

'Bam?' called Meg.

Amber appeared in the doorway. She was still in her wet clothes, her hair in rat's tails, her limbs speckled with black silt, her tank top and cut-offs sagging. A leaf, oval, bright green, cleaved to the skin of her throat. Her hands fluttered by her sides as if she were shaking away something fine and gauzy—cobwebs, or hair from a brush.

'Give them back,' she said.

'Bam.' Meg went towards her.

'You can't just go through someone's stuff,' said Amber, 'and take things.'

'Let's sit down.' Meg gestured beyond Amber to the table and chairs. 'Let's talk.'

'No!' Amber stayed in the doorway. 'Just give me my stuff!' She was shouting now, very loudly; her voice slammed around the small room. Her face was red, her eyes big and dark. 'This is *not fair*!' she shouted. 'You can't do this to me! I need those pills! They're prescription!'

'Calm down,' said Meg, her hands raised. She kept stepping forward, slowly and quietly. She was wearing wide-legged cotton pants, navy blue, creased under the bum from the morning's drive. 'Amber,' she said, 'the pills are all gone. You've got to understand, we're doing this—'

'Take me home,' said Amber in a hard, tight voice. 'I want to go home.'

'We—'

'Take me back to Cairns then. I'll stay in a hotel until tomorrow night.'

'We're not flying back tomorrow night. None of us is going anywhere.'

Amber stared.

Meg took another step towards her. 'I know it's hard for you to accept, but we're all going to stay here until you feel okay without the pills.'

Amber hurled herself sideways, towards the wall, the row of knives, jagged on their magnetic holder. She had one, its big blade flashed—and there was Meg's dumb pink hand thrusting itself out.

'Oof!' said Meg.

Nobody moved.

Meg frowned, as if annoyed or offended by the glove of blood that reached to her elbow, by the blood on the floor, the blood running down the wall in a raised trickle. She shuffled backwards. Leaning against the sink, she held her hand high, the blood-glove shining.

Amber let go of the knife and it clanged to the floor.

The hush ripped open and the noise, again, exploded.

'Ah, fuck, fuck!' yelled Amber. Her hands went to her hair, then the sides of her face. 'Look what you made me do!'

'Amber,' said Meg. 'Amber, calm—'

'Give them to me! Give me my stuff!'

'You have a problem—'

'I need those pills!'

'And we are going to—'

'You can't take them!'

(Nina was speaking too, had at last mustered her voice. 'But, Amber,' Nina was saying, 'don't you have them?')

'It's going to be hard work, but we will see this thing—'

'I hate you, I hate you, I hate you!'

('Amber, don't you have your pills? Didn't you—')

'Amber, we are all going to stay here in this place for as long as—'

('But, Amber, I thought you took them back. I thought—')

'Get away from me!'

Amber whirled, slipping on the blood. Her skinny leg angled out and her knee met the wall, bang, and her hands darted towards the floor like she might do a tumble, a handstand, a cartwheel—but then she was up, skittering across the verandah to the stairs, and gone.

AMBER DURING HER DRAMA YEARS—at thirteen, fourteen, fifteen—was, at home, the golden wraith that would come to live so elusively in Nina's memory. She lost jumpers, socks, hairbrushes, forgot her lunch, slept through her alarm, failed to turn up to an after-school dentist's appointment, left one shoe behind at a sports carnival, went to bed without brushing her teeth, misplaced textbooks, fell asleep at the kitchen table over homework due weeks earlier, and was usually the last to leave the house when rushing (late) to school, regularly neglecting to lock or even close the front door behind her. But on stages, in wings, in make-up chairs and rehearsals and on sets and before cameras she was *there*. Away from her family, facing outwards, she hummed with narrowed energy. She executed every action so cleanly, so sweetly, so *absolutely*, that Robert was moved in a rare moment of attention to observe that his youngest daughter was 'like a laser'.

Come back, come back, Nina would, later, plead from inside her mind, through the bright glancing avenues of memory, to the flicker of her sister. If only Amber would come back, then everything would be changed—the whole story of their family.

By doing what she did—by moving away—Amber, it came to seem to Nina, had caused something to come undone for all of them. Because if she was able to just drift off like that, and nothing drew her back and held her in place, then what was holding any of them in place?

Or could it be that Nina was blaming something on Amber that was not her fault? Was Nina trying to invent an explanation for something that might just be inexplicable: her own recurring lostness?

During Amber's drama years Meg and Nina both started university—Meg studying physiotherapy, Nina an arts degree—and, as young people were quite easily able to do in those days, they moved out of home. Meg shared a townhouse in the outer northeastern suburbs with one housemate. It was a short bike ride to her campus. Nina lived in the inner north, in a five-bedroom Victorian terrace with a revolving cast of tenants, cracks in the walls and marijuana plants growing inside a thicket of bamboo in the backyard.

Meg, away from home, did just what her tactless aunt Alison had so long ago suggested she might: she blossomed. Her sternness waned, and a kind of sunny vitality appeared in its place. Her need to do things for others seemed to change in tone—become gentler, less performative—and she began doing more things for herself. She cut her hair to above her shoulders, revealing the elegant length of her neck. She swam regularly at an outdoor pool; to protect against the chlorine she used a body oil from a health food shop, which smelled of sweet orange, and gave her suntanned arms and legs a dusky sheen. She wore loose cotton clothing and leather sandals and sometimes a kerchief tied around her head. In winter she wore Blundstone boots and jeans like a farmer, and flannel shirts, and heavy knitted jumpers in dark blue or cream. Her skin was very clear and smooth, her hands strong, the short nails pinkish and lustrous. She had a casual job in a health food shop and jars of dried lentils and beans stood on the windowsill over the sink in the kitchen of her house, glowing like earthy treasures in the morning light.

Nina, on the other hand, seemed to go through a process of un-becoming. Perhaps it started with her lack of certainty about what it was she wanted to do after school—the reason she'd ended up enrolling in arts, which she found easy and mostly boring. Another contributing factor was probably the group house, which she had found via a sign in the window of a bookshop: *Fitzroy. Small room. No rules. Bring your pets, bring your lovers, bring your good vibes.*

When Nina rang the number a croaky-voiced girl who didn't give her name said, 'Oh yeah, the room? Oh yeah, when can you move in?' When Nina said that she didn't mind, the girl said, 'Well, now? Now's good for us.' When Nina said that now was fine, the girl said, 'Hang on,' and put the phone down, and Nina heard her yell, 'Hey, Tania, wait a sec, you still got that key? Give it.' Then she picked up the phone again and said, 'Yeah, come tomorrow. And don't forget the bond.'

Nina hung up and was deluged with regret. She stared at the address she'd written on the message pad. It was February 1994, and her classes started in two weeks. Robert and Gwen weren't saying that she had to move out but it was just what everyone did. She already had a casual job at a sandwich shop in the city and money saved up. Meg had moved out the year before and now came for dinner once a fortnight with her radiant skin and serene face and a bean stew in an op shop casserole dish. Nina had seen where she lived, the townhouse, which had exposed brick walls and brown carpets and aluminium window frames and was dark, but which Meg and her housemate had made nice with pot plants and rugs and lamps and (maybe this was the housemate, who was studying midwifery) cheap framed posters of Anne Geddes prints that caused Robert to look as if he was trying to identify an unpleasant smell.

How had Meg done it—made a good place for herself? How was it that she, Nina, had managed to almost certainly fuck things up with just one phone call? She hadn't seen the house. She hadn't met the people. And yet she'd somehow agreed to move in and start paying rent as soon as possible. Plus the bond, whatever that was.

It did not for one moment occur to Nina that she could simply fail to show up at the house the next afternoon—something she would one day look back on and laugh about with a kind of rueful affection for her former self.

After a while she heard the back door open and Robert come into the kitchen from his studio. She went through to find him lumping peanut butter into the groove of a stick of celery. He took a jar of sultanas from the pantry and used the tips of his fingers to drop them onto the peanut butter, his lips bunched in concentration. Then he took a knife and cut the stick in half and presented one of the halves to Nina. They stood together, crunching.

When Robert had finished he burped gently. 'Pardon me,' he said. Then he peered into Nina's face. 'You all right?'

Nina sighed. There was peanut butter on the backs of her teeth. 'Yeah,' she said, falsely. Then, 'Dad, how much is a bond, usually? For a share house?'

'One month's rent, I'd say,' said Robert, licking his fingers. 'Why? You got a place?'

'I guess so.'

'Well that's wonderful!'

The house wasn't wonderful—but it wasn't terrible either. It was just a big dirty loose party house with people coming and going at all hours, where you wouldn't want to leave anything valuable in plain sight. It smelled of coffee and mildew and weed, and if you walked on the carpets without shoes the soles of your feet went black, and any food left in the kitchen would almost certainly be gone the next day, no matter what it was.

Her housemates were all older than Nina, all artists or musicians (or claimed to be, anyway), and while they weren't unfriendly they certainly didn't make overtures. The biggest problem, though, was that from the moment she moved in Nina was overcome by a terrible and enduring shyness, and she went on to spend most of her time hiding. In her room with the door closed, she lay in bed reading and eating sticks of chewy licorice from the university wholefoods co-op, tiptoeing out to the bathroom or the kitchen when nobody else was around. The only upside to this situation was that, so as to get out of the house as much as possible, she attended all her lectures and tutorials and got high distinctions for everything without even trying very hard.

She found herself catching the tram to Thornbury one or two afternoons a week, and staying for dinner. Returning to Fitzroy she felt a loneliness that was so paralysing she was certain others could sense it, and she kept her face hidden by crooking her arm on the sill of the window and sinking her chin into it. The harsh-lit tram slid down Smith Street, past rows of shops, closed and dark.

Towards the end of secondary school Nina had fallen in with two girls: Pip and Hannah. The three-way friendship was offhand and teasing, based on a mutual braininess and a dislike of almost everyone else. Hannah was dumpy and fair—the milkmaid, Amber called her—and Pip had black hair and clear grey eyes in a broad pretty face.

'Thank God that's over,' said Hannah after their year twelve graduation ceremony. She was wearing her blazer draped over her head, the empty sleeves like pendulous animal ears.

'What now?' said Nina. When she was with Hannah and Pip she used a particular voice, flat and slightly grating. The dry-ice voice, she called it in her mind.

'What now right now?' said Pip in a similar voice.

'What now forever?' said Nina.

They were standing outside the Dallas Brooks Hall in East Melbourne, where the event had taken place, waiting for their parents to find them. It was December, but a chilly night. Overhead the branches of giant oaks shifted, and the city sky was orange-grey and shallow.

Hannah twirled a blazer sleeve and stuck out one hip. 'Ahm gonna do mah ney-als,' she said, in the simpering voice they used to parody Chelsea Roberts and Serena Taylor-Johnson, who were the worst of the popular girls.

'Ahm gonna ride mah exercise bike,' said Nina.

'Ahm gonna eat ice cream and then ahm gonna make mahself puke,' said Pip.

Gwen and Robert appeared then, smiling in their usual stunned fashion, and Nina waved at her friends and said, in the dry-ice voice, 'Oh well, see ya.'

They met a few times over the summer, but continuing to ridicule Chelsea Roberts and Serena Taylor-Johnson without any longer seeing them or having any idea of what they were up to began to seem pathetic.

'We're giving those bitches way too much of our time,' said Pip.

The trouble was that there wasn't much else for them to do together. Hating others appeared to be all they had. This was of course not true—but the rules of the friendship had been in place for some time and pertained, rigidly it would seem, to the world of school. Outside of that context the three of them floundered.

When Nina was much older and thought back to Hannah and Pip, she did wonder if what might have made the difference was, when the moment had come to say goodbye outside the Dallas Brooks Hall, for her to have stayed in character as one of the popular girls and flung her arms around Pip and Hannah and squealed, 'Oh my God, I love you so much!' Maybe if some expression of real attachment, appreciation—okay, love—had been possible, no matter how stupid and ironic its delivery, there might have been something to fashion an ongoing connection out of. But it hadn't happened.

The last time all three of them got together they'd tried to burn Pip's shiny-paged VCE textbooks in the barbecue pit at Hannah's parents'. (Hannah was keeping her books to sell and Gwen had taken Nina's and put them away in case Amber could use them.) The book-burning was an anticlimactic affair of wasted matches and grudging thin strands of toxic green smoke. 'Get the pages open, there's not enough oxygen!' 'Rip the whole thing up—just rip it to pieces!' 'Fucker won't rip. It's goddamn indestructible!' 'Aah, my eyes, this smoke smells like melted wigs!' Nina would come to view this event as an appropriate metaphor for the decline of the friendship.

Hannah deferred her course (journalism) and spent her time working as many shifts as possible in an ice-cream shop and at a telemarketing company, saving to go overseas. She was living at home, and never wanted to do anything in case it cost money. Eventually Nina stopped calling her.

Pip was studying law but not at the same university as Nina. She had moved into a group house in Carnegie—the other side of town—where Nina visited her once, in late March. Pip made tea, which they drank sitting on the floor either side of a low table scarred with spilled candle wax.

'So my course is extremely uninteresting,' said Nina in the dry-ice voice.

'Bummer,' said Pip. 'I'm actually really into mine.'

This was confusing; Nina was almost certain that Pip was not being sarcastic.

There was a lengthy pause. Neither seemed to know where to go from there, and Nina, who when not at uni or visiting Gwen and Robert seemed to do nothing but lie on her bed staring in deep misery at cobwebs as thick as pantyhose, suddenly realised that she might be about to cry. She jumped to her feet and said, 'I've just remembered something; I'd better go.'

'Oh, okay,' said Pip. 'Are you—' But Nina had bolted.

On the front path one of Pip's housemates stood holding an armload of long-stemmed basil from the ad hoc herb beds that had been chopped into the lawn.

'Here,' said the housemate, selecting a handful and thrusting it at Nina, and Nina sat on the train back across the river in a cloud of warm ripe aniseed, desolation in her chest, the wrenched roots of the plants spilling crumbles of dirt onto her jeans.

That was the last time she saw Pip, who went on to become a very successful human rights lawyer. Years later she would sometimes appear on television, still with her doll-like face and speaking, funnily enough, in a kind of adult version of the dry-ice voice—which, Nina concluded, must have been her real voice all along.

At university, while everyone else seemed, like iron filings in a primary school experiment, to be busily creating new formations—joining, splitting, rearranging—Nina maintained an aura of clear space, ignoring invitations to icebreakers and clubs, slipping from rooms as soon as classes were over and withdrawing to sheltered corners of the library. Hunched between the grey laminex desk partitions she ate enormous dry chocolate-chip cookies purchased with her staff discount from the city sandwich shop, sprinkling the pages of her books with crumbs. Even once she'd finished her studies, she sat, temple propped on fist, throat chocked with sweetness, drawing in her notebooks—sketches so light as to be barely visible: flowers, trees, horses, the Lady of Shalott in her boat with her hair and sleeves and skirts and haunted eyes.

In her room at the party house she read and read. Tennyson, Blake, Coleridge. Katherine Mansfield. She read Carson

McCullers and Jean Rhys and felt that strange lonely longing for an unlived past. She read Hemingway and Jack Kerouac and F. Scott Fitzgerald and Cormac McCarthy and wished that she were a man, and felt even lonelier.

She fluttered between a kind of helpless romanticism—a delicate and passive yearning for nothing and no one specific, just for beauty—and the sense that if only she could force her way out of her shyness, her wanness, her *caution*, she might find that she harboured something clever and bold, some kind of gritty bravado. Lying on her bed, she practised a look that was frank and assured but not unfriendly.

Escaping the house's evening swell—people coming and going, the phone ringing, the noisy making of plans, smells of onions frying and cigarettes and pot—she walked the streets and looked through windows at lit-up scenes.

She saw a group of girls her own age dancing in boots and short skirts and ripped stockings, safety pins in their ears, their soft bellies showing as they lifted their arms, their voices fanning into hard and joyous discord as they yelled, 'I don't wanna . . . I don't think so.'

She saw a woman in an armchair watching television, legs outstretched, bare feet crossed at the ankles, her shoes and socks on the floor to one side, a seal-like black dog crouched, licking between her toes with gentle thoroughness.

She saw a room filled with people seated at small tables playing mahjong, not a single one of them speaking, the only sounds the rattle of the tiles and, from somewhere further inside the building, high wavery music.

She saw a man leaning on a mantelpiece with his head down and one hand in the air swivelling at the wrist in a mad jitter while jazz blasted and a small child dressed only in a t-shirt dived into the lap of a green couch.

Back in her room she wrote things down and then ripped the pages from the notebook and tore them into shreds and hid them under the carpet where it had come up in a corner.

An empty fountain at night is the saddest thing.

The hot sun and the open blue, the smell of city trees and even a piece of silver paper blazing on the footpath, all this now is my youth and I wish I could own it.

Jasmine, I breathe you, sliding and rich. Bluestone. Fences. Streetlights in the rain. Is there comfort to be had in these outside things, that stand day and night and are ignored and abused and still smile their secret smiles? Let me in.

Somewhere in her heart she recognised the unoriginality of her angst, its mawkishness. Was this where the shyness came from—embarrassment at her tender and wordy passions, their newborn wobbliness, the trace marks they bore? There were students in her poetry tutorial who spoke unabashedly of the beauty of language, whose voices when they volunteered to read aloud trembled not from fear but with ardour, who, when the tutor said something like, *It's the word 'kindness', isn't it, that tells us something more about Wright's ponies,* smiled ecstatic smiles and nodded slow and deep. There was even one boy with a buzzcut and a round ruddy face and small gold hoops in each ear, dressed always in the same dirty pink shirt and black jeans and leather waistcoat, who would rise unbidden to his feet and hold up his hands, and quote Dylan Thomas, the tears bulging in his eyes. Nina was appalled by these displays, but she tried to be fair, to recognise that the passion that was so publicly expressed by these people was no different from the passion that she so privately, so furtively, let out of her own self and then destroyed all evidence of.

She was not like them, the talkers, the spouters of verse, the ready smilers, the open worshippers. There was something holding her back. And it might have been that she was just taking her time, preparing herself for a belated entry, that when she was ready she would wear that expression she'd been practising out into the world, and—perhaps quavering a little with nerves the first time—offer to read in class, or begin to nod and smile. This might have happened. But something went awry.

'SHIT,' SAID MEG, LEANING OVER the sink. The tea towel she'd wrapped around her hand looked almost black, and shone, and sagged, and dripped.

'Are you okay?' Nina stepped closer but tried not to look. 'How bad is it?'

Meg sighed, as if being bothered with unnecessary questions. 'It's pretty bad,' she said, 'but if I can get the bleeding to stop I'll be all right.'

Blood was starting to pool in the bottom of the sink. There was a metallic smell that made Nina's throat contract.

'Another cloth.' Meg pointed with her elbow at the drawer. Nina fumbled.

'Come *on*, Nina.'

'Sorry, sorry.'

'Shit.' Meg wound the new cloth around the old one. Her free hand was unsteady and a moustache of sweat had formed under her nose.

Nina got a third tea towel from the drawer and Meg took it and arranged it, clamped down with her other, shaking, hand on the big oblong bundle of scarlet-soaked blue-and-white gingham. She was taking long, slow, intentional breaths.

'I'll be okay in a minute,' she said.

A bright glob of blood had landed on Nina's knuckle. Its glossy meniscus quivered. She wanted to shake it off, wipe it off, to shove Meg aside and run the tap and wash it off—she could not stand it. A whimper came out.

'Here.' Meg offered a clear corner of tea towel and Nina, her face averted, scrubbed at her skin with it.

'Sorry.'

'It's all right. You were never good with blood.' Meg's voice sounded normal again. She tipped her head from side to side, examining the bundle. 'I think it's stopped,' she said. 'But you're going to have to take me to a hospital.'

❦

They left the mess—the blood in the sink, the blood on the floor, the knife lying there. They left the groceries in their bags on the bench.

With shaking legs and shaking hands, apologising, Nina guided the car jerkily up the yellowish track.

Meg manoeuvred her roll of tea towels, got a finger on the button and put her window down. As they bumped away from the house she stuck her head out and yelled: 'Amber, if you can hear me, we're going to the hospital. We'll be back later. We can talk then. I know you're scared, but everything's going to be okay.'

No reply—only the purling of the forest.

They reached the bend in the track and Nina steered the car around and into the shade. 'I can't believe she stabbed you.'

'Really? I can believe it.' Meg was sitting slightly forward, the bloody mitt cradled in her lap, gripped by her free hand.

'Yeah, actually, I can too.'

They jolted along in the watery light, the tree trunks flickering on either side.

'I wonder where she went?' said Meg. 'Maybe we'll see her walking along the road.'

'What, trying to escape?'

'Yeah.'

'But it would take ages to get out of here on foot. Hours and hours. You'd be crazy to try that. You'd need to take supplies— water, at least.'

'Amber's pretty crazy.' Meg gave a small dry croak of a laugh. 'But she might not want to risk running into any wildlife. She was really scared of that snake.'

'Yeah. She was *terrified*.' Nina found herself laughing too— high, taut, dangerous laughter. She cut it off, pulled it in. 'But if we do see her? What do we do?'

'Lock the doors. Do it now; you might as well.'

Nina found the central locking button and pressed it.

'We put the window down enough to tell her that we're going to hospital and we'll be back,' said Meg. 'And she'd better not try to walk out of here because it's way too far and she might die of dehydration or get eaten by a python.'

Neither of them laughed this time. The funniness, if there had been any, was gone from the image of Amber in the front seat, spasming in terror, calling in her hysterical, young-girl's voice, *Oh my God! Oh my God!*

They continued along the track in an atmosphere of tense watchfulness. Nina stared so hard as they rounded each bend that her eyes began to smart. Her hands were weak on the wheel.

Her mouth was dry. But Amber didn't appear—the track just kept revealing itself, stretch by stretch, winding and rutted and bare of everything but weeds and twigs.

'We need to keep her there,' said Meg. 'At the house. If she gets away, if she gets into Mossman, or makes contact with other people, we'll lose her.'

'What do you think she'd do?'

Meg shrugged. 'Get to Cairns, to the airport, get a ticket, go home. Assuming she was smart enough to take her wallet.'

'Would she have enough money to buy a ticket? Or does she have a credit card?'

'Don't know. She shouldn't have a credit card but maybe she does—banks'll give them to anyone.'

'Or I guess she'd—'

Meg finished the sentence: 'Call Mum and Dad, yep.'

They reached the gate and Nina got them through it, jumping in and out, her heart racing. She slammed the edge of her hand down on the lock button again, wiped her sweaty palms on her dress and sent the car bouncing on.

'Or . . .' Meg's voice was grim.

'Or what?'

'She'd just find the nearest drugs. Try a doctor's surgery in whichever town she makes it to. Or buy off the street.'

'Really? You can buy drugs on the street in these tiny towns?'

Meg's face was pale and damp-looking, strands of hair sticking to her forehead. She sighed. 'Oh, Nina.'

'But, I mean, there are hardly any people.'

'Neen, there are always drugs, okay? Always. And there are always people doing terrible things to each other.'

Now that they were through the gate, one side of the road had opened onto cane fields. The green feathery tops glittered.

The sky was bright and clear. Nina squinted; her sunglasses were in her bag, on the back seat. Her throat was dry and a headache was beginning to sizzle at the edges of her vision.

Eventually Meg said, 'There's no way she'd have got this far,' and Nina dropped her shoulders slightly.

They passed cane field after cane field, the gates to other properties. They rushed up and over the little bridge.

'What are the chances,' said Meg, 'of us getting the only holiday rental in the whole world with a sharp knife?'

Nina laughed, a real laugh this time. She glanced at her sister. 'How are you feeling?'

'Okay. It's hurting now, but the bleeding's definitely stopped.'

At Mossman Nina pulled over and, pecking inexpertly at the screen under Meg's concise but brittle tutelage, used Meg's smartphone to search for a hospital.

'Now click "search",' said Meg.

Out of whiteness the screen assembled its boxes of text, its blue links. 'Amazing!' said Nina. 'Here it is. It's on Hospital Street.'

'Great. Now, see if there's a link to a map.'

'Um . . .'

'There it is—see? Click there. No, there. *There*, Nina!'

'Sorry, sorry. Here we go. It's . . . just up the road.'

'Great. Let's go.' Meg shifted under her seatbelt. 'Thank God there's a local one. I wouldn't fancy driving all the way to Cairns. I really need some painkillers.'

Nina, who had been about to pull back out onto the road, cancelled the indicator. 'Oh.'

'What?' Meg didn't look at her. She was breathing loudly and slowly, and jiggling one of her knees. 'Come on, let's go—can't you talk and drive at the same time?'

Nina put the indicator on again and swung out onto the road in a too-fast arc.

'Oof,' said Meg. 'Take it easy.'

'Sorry.' Nina overcorrected, braking hard. 'I'm not used to this car.'

They passed the shops, and a school—tin-roofed buildings, verdant trees, chain-link fences—and Nina found the turn-off and they reached the hospital. It was old and lovely: low, white, spreading buildings, arched windows and columns. Palms like a row of windmills.

'Wow,' said Meg. 'What do you call this? Spanish Mission? And jeez, it's huge.'

'Looks like a sanatorium,' said Nina. 'Like something out of a Katherine Mansfield story.'

'Who?' Meg was already working her way up from her seat.

Nina dashed around to help. Meg's arm was moist; Nina could feel the muscles under their sheath of flesh. 'Meg,' she said.

'Mm?' Meg didn't stop walking.

Nina scurried to keep up. 'I just—when you mentioned painkillers before it reminded me. Amber's got her pills. I don't know what she was talking about. She got them back—she must've snuck in during the night and taken them from my bag.'

Meg's steps were ginger, her upper body very stiff.

'I, um, I didn't actually flush them,' said Nina. 'I'm sorry.'

They reached the entrance and their reflections appeared in the glass: Meg's taut with pain, grim-faced and pale; Nina's sweaty, wispy, pink and guilty.

'I'm sorry,' said Nina again, trying and failing to get to the doors before Meg.

Meg yanked a door open. She sighed deeply and turned her eyes, glazed with suffering, on her sister. 'I know you didn't,' she said. 'I knew you were fibbing when you told me last night. *I* took them. From your bag, while you were in the bathroom. *I* flushed them.'

She gave Nina a good couple of seconds more of a look that wasn't reproachful, just burdened and weary—a look that said, I have long known that if I want a job done properly I have to do it myself. And then she hitched her handbag, containing her Medicare card and so on—which even in the melee she of course had remembered to bring—over the shoulder of her good arm and lugged her bloodstained tea-towelled fist through the door and towards the triage desk.

Nina followed, but not all the way to the desk, where Meg was already speaking with a nurse. Instead she slumped into the nearest row of plastic chairs. Further along sat an older woman: white hair under a yellow beanie, knitted vest, shapeless floral dress; stick-like bare legs crossed at the ankle, a pink line of sole where skin met rubber thongs. In the facing row was a young man: baggy shorts, thongs, Tupac t-shirt. He thumbed a smartphone. The woman just sat.

Fibbing. What kind of person used that word?

Nina's mouth was parched; her head pounded. She was hungry and thirsty and she felt like a chastened child, and actually right now what she really wanted to do was to run straight back out the doors and drive off and leave Meg here. Drive straight to Cairns and get on a plane and go home.

Meg didn't need her. Meg could handle things. She wouldn't even be fazed by being left without a car. With her freshly stitched and bandaged hand she'd calmly walk out and somehow get back to the rental property and (literally) single-handedly deal with Amber. She'd give her tough love and boundaries and cook her good food and endure her tantrums and fend off her crazed attacks . . .

Nina stared down at the floor.

That knife, how quick it was. Amber's pale fury, her lunge, the exploding of all of their voices into that close room.

But still. But still. Nina attempted to smooth out the narrative. That . . . incident (stabbing!) . . . was an aberration. Meg had dropped her guard. She wanted to go through with this stupid thing and so she bloody well could, without Nina. Back at the house, without her, Meg would sensibly, systematically, with care, safely and legally . . .

She gave up, put her elbows on her knees and dropped her face into her hands. What was she thinking? Meg couldn't handle Amber on her own. Nobody could. But all indications were that Meg was not going to back down. She was still talking about her stupid plan as if it were not completely batshit crazy. Which meant that the two of them—Meg and Amber—would, if left alone, destroy each other. And so Nina's role now seemed to be to somehow find a way to defuse the whole situation. To get them all packed up and back home. How the fuck was she going to do that? Tears were seeping out onto her fingers. She breathed for a while until they stopped, then wiped her face.

When she looked up she saw that Meg had vanished into some inner sanctum. Other than that nothing had changed. The woman sat, not looking at Nina. The man tended to his phone. Through the windows the sky dazzled, the palms tilted their fronds.

SO MUCH CAN BE SET into place during a person's first love affair—or sex affair, as it could more accurately be termed in Nina's case, there being no love involved. Dreadful risks may be taken, exquisite vulnerabilities offered up and misunderstood or brutally exploited. More than anything, associations may be made, and habits formed. It was Nina's anthropology tutor who was responsible for her induction into the world of sex, and while it's likely that no further exposition is required, here it is anyway.

He was older—by a good ten years. He asked her to come and see him. He sat behind his desk and offered her a cup of coffee.

Nina, taken by surprise, stammered something in the affirmative.

While he went to get the coffee she looked around. The desk and chairs were drab and industrial. There were no pictures on the walls, and hardly anything in the metal bookcase that seemed to lean slightly outward at its top. There were the set texts and a handful of other books, one of them *Microsoft Office for Dummies*, bunched at the end of one shelf, and on another shelf messy piles of papers, which Nina assumed were people's essays. The rest of the shelves were empty. Outside the window, framed by concrete walls that rose out of sight, was a small garden bed containing tanbark and one tree fern stump, tall and brown and completely leafless.

The tutor returned and put a polystyrene cup of black coffee on the desk in front of Nina. It steamed. He sat back down in his chair and sipped his own drink, which was in a mug with a picture of Garfield dressed as Santa on it, and *HO HO HO!* in large red letters.

Dutifully, Nina appraised him. She could not have predicted what was to come, but still she found herself trying to find something in him to appreciate. She didn't know why she did this—it just seemed to be a part of the deal, perhaps because of the coffee. She knew that he hadn't asked her to see him because she was in trouble; her marks were about as high as they could be. She didn't mind anthropology. She didn't see what kind of a future it had as a study, since it seemed fundamentally flawed and even admitted that itself (Nina had got full marks for her essay on cultural relativism)—although she quite enjoyed watching the films every Friday, sitting in the dark theatre, safely invisible. The tutorials were boring, and she'd never before now given the tutor a second thought. Making an effort, she noted that he had a soft-looking body with long arms and legs and sloping shoulders, and quite thin brown hair down to his collar. His face was shiny and his cheeks and mouth had a mournful, downward droop. His eyes were quite nice, she finally decided. Hazel, with clear whites. He was wearing his usual blue jeans and an open-necked shirt that was too formal to go with the jeans—a businessman's shirt, blue-and-white striped, a blue that clashed with the jeans—and his green corduroy jacket was hung over the back of his chair. She'd noticed, when he left the room, how the jacket's collar had been squashed into a wrong fold by his back and this had stirred in her an odd pity.

He sipped his coffee and asked why, when her written work was so exceptional, she didn't speak in class. He said that in his opinion it was a great pity that she did not contribute in this way. He allowed a long silence before he said, 'There's something special about you.' And then he wiped his mouth with his hand in a hasty, regretful gesture and said, 'I do apologise, that was most unprofessional.' But he didn't look sorry.

Nina understood that something illicit was being entered into—that he had opened the door to it—and, not knowing what to say or do, she reached for her own cup of coffee. Her fingers hit the white foam rim and the cup flipped and the hot brown liquid ran quickly towards her. She jumped up just before it fell onto her legs. It spattered her feet instead, and the carpet, which was the kind with squares of slightly differing ugly shades of grey. Helplessly she bent and retrieved the cup, now empty, and set it back on the desk.

'Oh dear,' said the tutor, but not angrily. He got up and came around to Nina's side of the desk and looked down at the mess.

'I'm so sorry,' said Nina at last.

The tutor moved closer to her. Nina could smell something bitter, like the smell from the Chinese medicine clinic near her parents' house. His jeans had pushed-out knee shapes at the knees. His tan shoes were so scuffed that the toes had turned white.

'I'm sure you can find a way to make it up to me,' he said, before stepping aside to let her out.

Nina walked, quickly, all the way back to the party house. She found the kitchen empty of people and a wine cask that was, miraculously, not completely empty of wine, and she drank a glass of cheap thick acidic shiraz, and then she had a shower and washed her hair.

'Yuck, yuck, yuck,' she whispered to herself, closing the door to her room. She tried to imagine telling Pip or Hannah about what had happened, in the dry-ice voice. And then he came up really close and he said, I'm sure you can find a way to make it up to me. And he smelled gross. It didn't help much. She went to bed—without dinner, because now someone else had come home and was doing something in the kitchen—where, strangely, she found herself hearing in her mind his voice saying, *There's something special about you.*

Nina never loved the tutor. She was never, not for one moment, attracted to him. But she began to think about him. The odd sense of almost maternal pity that the crumpled collar of his jacket had prompted kept reappearing. Little instances of dishevelment set it off: a loose button on the cuff of another of his too-formal shirts; something—cappuccino froth?—on the bridge of his long nose; a fat green line of whiteboard marker up the side of his thumb. This pity welled inside her like some kind of secret fluid, abundant and disgraceful.

Often she told herself the night before that she would skip the class. If she didn't see him, didn't feel the pity, then she might not lie in bed thinking of him. But she always went.

At some point she realised that she was making sure to save her nicer clothes for the days when she had the anthropology tutorial, and was timing the washing of her hair so that it would be clean but not too fluffy.

In class the tutor began to ask her questions.

'Can we think of other rituals along these lines? Nina?'

'What kind of status does a young man gain from this initiation, Nina?'

'Any further thoughts on this distinction by the Azande between human error and witchcraft? Nina?'

Before this, the tutor had never called on a particular person to answer a question. He would just ask it and somebody would offer a response—usually one of the two or three most outgoing members of the class. When he began to call on Nina, she, after stammering and blushing her way through her answers, would covertly cast around for the reactions of her classmates. Could they know that something was happening between herself and the tutor? Was Nina somehow illuminated by both her own self-consciousness and this new beam of attention he was directing at her? She felt as if she was—she felt incandescent. But if the other students did notice they didn't show it.

In addition to addressing her directly with the questions, the tutor, Nina was certain, looked at her more often. And when he said, 'If anyone needs to come and see me outside of class you know my door's always open,' he was, no doubt about it, staring right at her.

There's something special about you.

There was. Nina knew. (Or thought she knew.) It was the thing that had brought Hayden Marshall to her in the darkness of Kate Beade's bedroom, and the thing that had made the yellow fingers of the man in the white suit in the sculpture garden tremble, and the thing that had been sniffed out in her by the boys at high school who had—on camp, at parties, once under the stairs opposite her locker in year ten—come pushing into her with their hands and their tongues, and then let go as roughly and moved away. It was not a good thing but it did seem to be special, and Nina understood it to be both intrinsic and shameful.

Is it strange, then, that it was Nina who made the next move in this affair with the tutor, her first sex affair? Not really. Later she would learn to wait for the men to come to her, that this allowed her some power of her own, however ghastly. But back then—seventeen, sick with loneliness, so absolutely in thrall to the myth of her shameful specialness that she was blind to the abundance of other options, other possibilities, and wishing above all else to somehow blast her way out of misery—she found herself, one Wednesday evening, tapping on the door of the tutor's office.

He didn't ask why she'd come. He said seriously, quietly, looking at his watch, 'Can you meet me in an hour?' He wrote something on a sticky note and gave it to her and sent her back out into the corridor. Behind him, Nina could see, the carpet tiles were still marked with brown splodges from her spilled coffee.

On the little yellow note was an address. She knew the street. It wasn't far away. She walked there and found a single-storey, single-fronted terrace, painted brown, with snake-necked arum lilies overrunning its tiny front yard. She walked past because she was much too early—she went on without stopping, as if she had somewhere else to go. It was not yet dark, a warm dry evening in early April. The wind blew grit into her sandals and her eyes. She reached a strip of parkland that was bisected by a bike path and was nearly run down by a woman cyclist in a red business suit and sneakers who didn't ring her bell or call out but only swooped around Nina and pumped on.

For some time she mooned about beside the path. She didn't own a watch and so had to guess at when an hour might have passed. She was intolerably nervous. The wind had made her eyes water and she was worried that her mascara might have run; she wet her forefingers with spit and wiped under her eyes, which made the skin there pull tight.

When she knocked on the door it was very gently. Perhaps she was hoping that he wouldn't be there. But he was, and he took her straight into the bedroom, the first room, which had the blind down over the window that would have looked onto the arums, the street. He left the light off and shut the door and it became very dark. Nina banged her shin on the edge of the bed. She wished that she was drunk—that she'd had the foresight to organise something, a miniature gin from the bottle shop, where she would have been asked to show her ID, as she always was. She thought of Jean Rhys's heroines, with their booze and their slippery, cynical love affairs, their lonely bravado.

The tutor might have been nervous as well. Clumsily he removed her clothes, whispering, 'Sorry,' when he bumped the side of her face. He didn't kiss her, which was a relief. The Chinese herb smell was strong on the bedsheets, as well as a floral soap scent that summoned in Nina a fierce longing for the sheets of her home in Thornbury, washed by Gwen with eucalyptus laundry powder that came in a four-kilo tub, and dried stiff on the line in the sun.

Nina allowed him to arrange her on the bed and then lay waiting as he did things with a condom, sitting with his back turned, his sloping shoulders visible in the light from the edges of the blind, his underpants still round his thighs. Her nose twitched. These would be her lasting impressions of this first time: the smells of him and his bed, acrid herbs and synthetic flowers, the medical smell of the condom, and the smell of her own dry saliva from under her eyes.

He had lube, something she would never have thought of, but which she would understand later to be a blessing, and when he at last took his underpants the rest of the way off and turned and got on top of her with his sheathed and lubricated penis there was the sense of a barrier, which helped. It hurt when it went in, and then it was all right. Nina, trying to muster a Jean Rhys kind of jaded acceptance, had to keep batting away the word *probe*.

The tutor held his upper body high, his arms straight. He was, Nina saw when she opened her eyes for a moment, staring over the top of her head in a strained, almost despairing fashion.

'It's okay,' she found herself whispering.

The tutor grimaced and she understood that she wasn't to speak. She half-closed her eyes—her vision had adjusted by now, and she could see quite well—and watched as he laboured, the flesh of his soft chest jiggling, his small belly hanging. He went down on one elbow to free his hand and touched her hair, then her breasts, and she willed her nipples to harden and was relieved when they did. She looked at her own thighs spread either side of his hips. She looked pretty good. I am having sex, she thought. Experimentally, she put her hands to the tutor's shoulders, but his skin felt spongy and foreign and she took them away again.

She began to imagine being touched by another hand—a hand belonging to another man, who she could not see at all, who was only an impression, a hardness of body and darkness of hair. She closed her eyes completely and felt the presence of this man who she couldn't see but who was looking at her with great intensity, looking and touching, skimming her breasts with a flat palm, dipping a finger between her legs. They were on different sheets,

Nina and this unseeable man, in a different room. Where they were it was flooded with light and smelled of sunshine. She saw the man's hand touching her—she was seeing what he saw, and when he pulled back to watch as she stroked herself, her fingers wet, the wet hair curling, she felt his interest, his fascination. She watched herself spread her legs; she was bright and open, full and wet. She was outside of herself—she was the man. With his hand she reached. She watched his brown-skinned, delicate fingers meet her own fingers, slip in beside them.

The tutor's breathing changed and he gave two last jerky wriggles before collapsing for a moment onto his elbows. Then he slid out of Nina and resumed his sitting position on the edge of the bed. He reached to a tissue box on the bedside table and made small, intimate movements in his lap. There was a balloon-ey soft snap and she saw him lower the condom into a nest of tissues.

Nina lay, sticky and swollen, her fantasy still gauzy and bright at the edges of her mind. She let her knees fall to the side. All of her earlier nerves had vanished. There was a kind of languor in her body—a feeling of potential, adult and mysterious—that, like something illuminated very faintly in an otherwise complete blackness, could only be glimpsed indirectly. If only the tutor wasn't there she would be able to make herself come in about three seconds. She almost did it; one hand moved up between her thighs. But the tutor was getting to his feet, dressing, and then with a familiar-smelling rush of air her clothes were plopped onto the mattress right beside her face.

He didn't touch or kiss or even look at her, and at the front door he said, his head down, 'You know we can't be doing this,' and she nodded and went past the arums and down the street.

THEY RETURNED TO THE HOUSE in the early evening. The only thing Nina had eaten all day was a packet of chips from one of the hospital's vending machines. She'd drunk water-cooler water from a plastic cup, so cold it hurt her teeth, but she was thirsty again. Meg, her hand and wrist neatly encased in fresh gauze and suspended in a snow-white sling at her chest (six stitches; missed a tendon by millimetres), slept through the whole drive back, her seat reclined, her legs wide.

When they got to the gate with the SWEETWATER sign Nina peered out in all possible directions. What if Amber appeared? What if she had the knife? Meg slept on. Nina, scrambling, got the car through the gate, then relocked the doors.

She eased down the last stretch of track, across the grass. The white house stood against the forest, its verandahs dim and guarded-seeming.

Nina turned off the engine, yanked up the handbrake, peered again. No sign of Amber.

Meg snorted herself awake. 'Pardon?'

'I didn't say anything.'

'Oh.' Meg drew herself upright, made a hissing sound.

'You okay?'

'Yeah. I probably need more painkillers.' She checked her watch, then took a packet of pills from her bag, popped one from its blister as if she'd only ever done such a thing with one hand, and swallowed it dry. Then, reaching across, she took the keys from Nina's hand. 'I'd better hold on to these.' She put them in her pocket.

A quick check of the rooms revealed no Amber. There was, however, one of her signature wreckages: in the kitchen the shopping bags lay plundered, two on the bench, two on the floor. Across the dark tiles a spray of carrots, onions, potatoes, apples and tomatoes, their colours rich in the grainy evening light. A Dutch painting, Nina thought. *Fallen Groceries*. The knife was still there, and the blood.

Meg picked up the knife and, wielding the dish brush one-handed, washed it and swished out the sink. Nina, gagging, used a dry tea towel to soak up the blood, then a wet soapy one to wipe the tiles, and tossed both cloths, along with the already soaked ones from the sink, into the washing machine.

Then Meg approached the bags. She rustled through them, clucking her tongue. 'She's taken the wine. Four bottles. Little sneak. And the bread. And the cheese and the crackers and the bananas. Some of the dips, I think.' She reached into the final bag. 'And my fruit loaf! And my butter!' Her shoulders slumped. She made a face at Nina, a woe-is-me face, silly, exaggerated, but there were tears in her eyes.

(Meg at fifteen, sixteen, under the blanket on the brown couch in Thornbury, her cups of tea, her plates, her crusts, oozes of honey. A textbook and highlighter. Crumbs on her shirt.)

Nina opened the two-litre bottle of milk and recoiled.

'It'll all be off,' said Meg. 'All the dairy.'

Nina tipped things down the drain, spooned things into the bin, head back, breathing shallowly. The dark room filled with a rancid, vinegary stink.

Meg put on some lights.

'You sit down,' said Nina. 'I'll make dinner.'

And Meg, surprisingly, acceded, padding out to one of the couches.

Nina boiled eggs, opened a can of kidney beans, sliced cucumber and tomato, found a packet of water crackers, filled glasses of water. She arranged everything on the table. She would have liked to drink some wine, but even the dregs of last night's was gone, the bottle taken from the fridge, where Nina was certain she saw Meg put it. A large, flat helplessness descended. In the face of such entrenched abjection, what hope could there possibly be?

'It's ready,' she said, but Meg was asleep on her back with her knees up, her sling gleaming.

Nina went to the top of the steps. 'Amber?' she called. 'Dinner.'

No reply. Out in the darkness things rustled. Something croaked. Nina shivered and retreated.

She left Meg to sleep and sat, her back to the kitchen with its weak light, facing the barely visible lawn and the very faint curving line of the track. The stars were lavish, the crowns of the palms a row of huge, watchful heads against the deep green-black.

She bolted her food, willing Meg to wake up. Between mouthfuls she whispered to herself.

'Okay, so, tomorrow morning we call to Amber that we're leaving. We're going back to Melbourne, and we're going to forget about everything that happened here.'

Wheep-wheep-wheep!

'And then Amber will come and we'll all pack up and get in the car.'

Ba-rou! Ba-rou!

'I'll drive.'

A violent snore from Meg.

Nina inhaled a bit of bean and had a coughing fit. She recovered, wiped her eyes. 'I'm sorry, Meg,' she whispered, 'but it's just not going to work. People are getting hurt. It's dangerous and it's not going to work and we need to just call it off and get out of here.'

A crashing from the forest—something big moving through the undergrowth. Nina held her breath. Her heart pounded. Something gave a strident bray. What was it? A wild goat? A *donkey*? Or could it be Amber, trying to freak them out? The call came again, and a series of rich snorts followed by more crashing. It couldn't be Amber. Even she couldn't make noises like that.

Where was Amber then—was she nearby, listening too? Nina thought of her in the car, her panicked writing. She jumped to her feet.

'Meg,' she said in a moderately loud voice.

No response.

Nina went nearer. Meg's mouth was open, her chin sunk into her neck. Nina reached to touch her shoulder, but the way Meg's chest rose and fell seemed so forlorn that she changed her mind.

She went to the steps again. 'Amber?' she called. 'You okay out there? Want some dinner?' She began a reluctant descent. The lights in the kitchen and over the dining area were low and brownish, but the ones on the exterior of the house, including at the top of the steps, were very bright and white—floodlights, really. Under this blasting, bug-laced illumination the metal treads shone, the blades of grass that had been tracked onto them a lurid green. Below, the blackness looked almost solid.

At the bottom Nina went to the furthest edge of the apron of light. 'Amber?' she called again. 'We don't have to talk about anything.' She turned slowly, scanning. 'Tomorrow we're going home, okay?' Like it had the night before, the air was turning cool and moist; under Nina's hand the post at the bottom of the stairs had a wet skin. She wiped her fingers on her dress.

Was Amber waiting, perhaps, for Nina and Meg to go to bed, before she slunk in? Or was she drunk and already passed out somewhere? She wouldn't be in the forest, surely, no matter how impaired her judgement—not with the python and that other thing smashing around and neighing. Nina stared out over the lawn, and then towards the back of the house, the dim shapes of the stepping stones leading to the bromeliads, the creek path. The downstairs verandah, the sideways pile of plastic chairs and—her heart lurched—the wide glass windows and sliding door of the downstairs apartment, unlit and opaque, faintly reflective. Of course. That's where she was.

She went back up the steps, lingered hopefully for a while beside the fast-asleep Meg, then reluctantly found her bag. Her phone was almost out of charge, the battery symbol showing only a single thin red segment. She took it downstairs and over to the sliding door, then lit up its screen and shone it outwards. In the phone's thin blue glow she saw that the door was completely closed. She gave it an experimental tug: locked. So Amber was in there—she must be; the door had been open that morning. Nina knocked, and called. Through the glass she could see the creepy boxes, the bench, the toolbox, the drill. There were fresh footprints in the fur of dust on the floor. But the light didn't reach the room beyond, where the cane couch was, the mattress, the pictures leaning against the wall. Nina rapped and called a while longer, and then the phone went dead just as the thing in the forest started up again, and she whirled around and blundered to the steps and clanged her way up them once more, skittering past Meg to the other couch, where she huddled for a while.

What now? Amber was there, downstairs. Drunk and asleep, presumably. But also she was angry, and she had stabbed Meg in the hand this morning. Who knew what she was capable of?

After a while Nina got the Indian quilts from the twin bedrooms, put one over Meg and lay on the facing couch under the other. Then she got up again, went into the kitchen and took a big knife, and lay back down with it. Then, once more, she rose. She returned the knife and rifled through the kitchen drawers. She found a pen and a stapled sheaf of A4 paper with printed pages from a website on them—*Daintree Attractions*. She tore off a sheet, turned it over, and wrote in large, clear letters: *AMBER WE ARE GOING HOME ASAP IN THE MORNING. NO INTERVENTION, NO DETOX, FORGET ALL THAT. I PROMISE. NINA.*

She carried one of the dining chairs to the top of the steps and placed it facing outwards, blocking the way. She propped the piece of paper on it so that Amber, coming up, would see the writing. Then she switched off all the lights and curled on the couch with the quilt up to her chin.

THE NEXT WEEK, IN CLASS, the tutor ignored Nina. He did not look at her, and he did not call on her to answer questions. She sat in a kind of numb horror, writing nothing in her notebook, oblivious to the discussion. As the class went on and drew nearer to its end her heart began to pound. Look at me, she begged, inside her mind. Just once. But he didn't, and when the time was up and everyone rose she stayed in her seat because her legs felt very heavy and perhaps even unusable.

The tutor, who had put his papers away quickly, departed in the middle of the group, and Nina was left alone. The room seemed to be making faint clicking sounds, like a cooling heater. There was a feeling of extraordinary slowness—as if she might remain there for a very long time, months, a solitary reptilian creature, blinking into space—but then the door banged open and two boys came in and dropped their backpacks onto a table.

'You new?' said one of them to Nina, pulling out a chair. When Nina didn't answer he shrugged and turned to his friend. 'I slept for fifteen hours last night,' he said, 'and I could go back for more.'

A girl came in, and then another, and then three more boys and another girl. They all looked at Nina.

At last she stood, holding on to the edge of the table.

'Are you all right?' someone said.

'Yes,' Nina heard herself reply. 'I've just got the wrong room.'

Somebody laughed, and somebody else said, 'Shut up, it's easy enough to do; I've done it myself.'

And Nina got her legs to walk to the door and out, and to the library. She sat there until it was dark, leaned forward between the partitions of a desk, resting her head on her unopened rucksack.

After some time, possibly hours, she went to the bathroom and looked at herself in the mirror. She had a lipstick in her bag, which she had bought at Myer, mostly for its name—Cleopatra—which reminded her of the painting at the National Gallery of the queen with her broad, defiant, somehow Spanish-looking face, something careless and modern in the way she leaned back in her chair, dropping the pearl into the glass. The lipstick was a matt crimson and smelled adult and dangerous and Nina had never actually worn it. Now she put it on, badly, so that her mouth looked lopsided and crude—but before she could fix it someone came in and off she scurried with her head down.

In the dark her heavy legs took her through the university and out into the streets, where impatient lines of cars inched past the Italian restaurants and the streetlights were fluttering on, orange and cool. A herd of people waited at the ticket booth for the cinema; hard bunches of red and white and yellow roses stood in buckets outside a greengrocer's; pigeons sank their heads into their fat necks and curled their red claws; 'Ah!' said an old man to Nina—a waiter from one of the restaurants, his apron tied over his black pants, his hair slicked—'*la bella ragazza!*'

Nina walked on, and came to the brown terrace house with the arum lilies. She stood across the road and waited, and after a while the tutor appeared, riding a mountain bike, lime green, with aggressively knobbly tyres and a great many gears. He stopped outside the house and dismounted. Nina stepped forward, to the edge of the gutter. The tutor took a bunch of keys from his pocket, opened the door of the house and, still wearing his yellow bike helmet, wheeled the bike in. The door closed.

Nina stood. A little while later the door opened again and the tutor, now without the helmet, his head down, made a gesture and Nina crossed the road and went in past him.

Things proceeded in a very similar fashion to the last time. The differences this time were that the tutor was not as gentle or as nervous-seeming, and did not apologise when he bumped Nina while removing her clothes, and that Nina did not this time withdraw into a fantasy but instead watched as he probed her, and it was the actual, not imagined, sight of her breasts as he pushed them together and ran his palm over them, her nipples puckering and stiffening under his fingers, the flesh of her thighs forced out by his, the smoothness of her skin—it was watching herself, seeing herself, that brought a tiny bead of pleasure that was only just beginning to swell when he finished and pulled out. Just like last time, he ministered to his lap with tissues and then got up and into his clothes before gathering hers into a bundle and dropping them on the bed beside her.

At the door he said, 'Don't come here again.'

She didn't go again. She finished the anthropology unit without attending any more tutorials and still managed to get a distinction. Once or twice she saw the tutor on campus, and on these occasions she made sure to keep a blank face, as if there were no connection between them—and as far as she could tell he did the same.

WHEN SHE WOKE UP NOTHING had changed. Meg was sleeping on the couch opposite. The chair was at the top of the stairs. It was very early, the morning not yet fully come, the light filmy, and Nina realised that it was a sound that had woken her. She lay still, listening. It was the thing, the creature—there it went again, grunting and making heavy, branch-shaking movements.

'What *is* that?' Nina exclaimed, sitting upright.

'Hmm?' Meg stretched and her feet emerged from the end of the quilt. Her toes spread. 'Ouch.' With care she turned on her side and blinked at Nina. 'I don't remember falling asleep.'

'Yeah, you crashed.'

Meg indicated the quilt. 'I gather you did this.'

'Yep.'

'Thanks.'

The thing in the forest had stopped and Nina couldn't be bothered telling Meg about it, couldn't be bothered with being dismissed, disbelieved, accused of having too much of an imagination. Instead, she leaned towards her sister and whispered: 'She's in the downstairs bit. She's locked herself in there. It's a kind of work site—a half-finished renovation.'

'How is she? Did you talk to her?'

Nina shook her head. 'I didn't see her but I'm sure she's in there. I looked in yesterday morning and the door wasn't locked, but last night it was. It's a sliding door, locks from the inside.'

Meg raised her eyebrows.

'So.' Nina swung her feet to the floorboards. 'I reckon let's get all packed up and start putting things in the car, and hopefully she'll see us and come out.'

'Packed up?'

'Yeah. Should we try to ring and book a flight, do you think, or just turn up at the airport?'

Meg rolled onto her back again and looked up at the ceiling.

'Meg?'

No answer.

'Meg. You can't seriously—'

'Nina . . .'

'Are you crazy? We need to get out of here. We need to call this thing off.'

The greyness was lifting from the air. Beyond Meg, beyond the verandah, the shaggy heads of the palms were emerging, deep green. Something made a peeping sound in the canopy at the side of the house; something else whistled; another thing went *gah-gah-wheet*.

'Meg.' Nina felt an uncharacteristic determination. There was nothing blurry, nothing imprecise about this situation—for once she was certain. 'Look at you. You've been badly injured. We can't stay. Something worse might happen.'

Meg lay still.

'Well, I can't be a part of this.' Nina stood, went to the railing. 'I'm sorry, I gave you the wrong impression because I'm just not good at saying what I think, but from the beginning I never wanted to—'

'You go, then.' Meg's voice was quiet.

Nina turned. 'What?'

'You go. I'll drive you to Cairns and then I'll come back.'

'I can't leave you here with her. I mean, how—'

'Amber won't hurt me again.' Meg sounded very calm, and also sort of ridiculous, pompously noble, like a nun or a saint in an old movie.

Nina snorted. She couldn't help herself. 'Of course she will. This kind of thing—this is how . . .' She stepped nearer, lowered her voice. 'This is how people get *killed.*'

'Don't be so dramatic. She's my sister.'

'I'm not being dramatic! Don't you read the news? People kill their sisters all the time, over drugs. People kill their sisters and their brothers and their parents.'

Meg eased herself into a sitting position. Most of her hair had slipped out of its ponytail; she raked it back, one-handed. 'Well,' she said, 'we're stuck then. We can't agree.'

'No. We can't.'

'You can't force me to leave.'

Nina looked at Meg's pants, her pocket with the car key in it. If only she'd been smart enough to take the key while Meg was asleep. She could have got Amber in the car and surely then Meg would have had to come with them. That was the solution. If she could get Amber out of there, then the whole thing was over.

Meg put her hand to her pocket.

Nina returned to the railing, looked out over the wet lawn. The morning had revealed itself to be overcast, low-skied and heavy, the palm fronds dismal in the gluey light. Could they overpower Meg, she and Amber? In theory it would be easy, with

Meg's injury, but the idea of it, of taking her on—of getting physical, of using *force*—filled Nina with panic. Her hands turned weak and useless just at the thought.

Meg stumped around, first to the bathroom and then the kitchen. 'Cup of tea?' she called.

Nina, not answering, went herself to the bathroom and saw in the bin the opened boxes of aspirin and Endone and their emptied blister packs. There was a biscuity smell that must be from Meg's urine and Nina felt a wave of revulsion belonging to childhood, at her big sister's physicality, the oblivious and clumsy closeness of her, the smell of her breath.

When she went back Meg was pouring steaming water into a teapot. She used the fingers of her bad hand to put on the pot's lid and winced.

'Did you just flush all your painkillers?'

Meg set the kettle down. 'Yep.'

'What for? Won't you need them?'

'I'm being fair.'

A surge of meanness rose. 'You sure?' said Nina. 'You sure it's about being fair?'

'Yes I'm sure,' snapped Meg. She carried the teapot to the table, brushing past. She smelled of BO and stale hospital disinfectant.

Nina stayed where she was, so Meg had to brush past again on her way back into the kitchen. 'You sure it's not just so Amber can't get hold of them?'

Meg put her good palm flat on the bench. Her shoulders sagged. 'Look,' she said, 'we're both hungry, okay? We need food. A cup of tea and something to eat, and then let's talk.'

Nina didn't reply. She wasn't hungry, although she hadn't eaten much of the crappy dinner she'd prepared the night before. She didn't even feel sorry for Meg, who must be really hungry, not having eaten since—when? The day before yesterday, unless the hospital gave her something. Nina folded her arms. She didn't offer to help as Meg found some bread in the freezer, painstakingly undid the plastic bag and dropped two slices into the toaster.

Meg made four slices of toast and put them on two plates, then carried the plates, one at a time, past Nina to the table.

'I don't want any,' said Nina.

Meg didn't reply.

'Stop being a martyr,' said Nina.

Laboriously Meg carried cups, knives, Vegemite and, from the fridge, an almost empty pot of suspect-looking strawberry jam to the table, not looking at Nina. Then she sat and began trying, one-handed, to dig Vegemite out of the jar with the tip of a knife. The jar slid away, into the teapot. Meg dropped the knife and put her face in her hand. 'Oh, won't you just stop?' she wailed. 'You're so mean. You've always been so mean to me. What did I ever do to you?'

Feeling returned to Nina with a stab. She unfolded her arms. 'I'm—'

'Just leave me alone,' said Meg. 'You're so cruel. You could never understand what I'm trying to do here.' She took her hand from her face and banged herself on the chest with it. 'It's out of love, it's all out of love, but a person like you could never see that.'

Nina experienced a kind of vertigo. It was the feeling of someone who has discovered that she took something too far. 'What—what . . .'

Meg's face was wet and raw. She waved her hand. 'Oh, you know, all those times with Amber—that first breakdown, after the film shoot, when she was so young . . . where were you then? Not *helping*. Looking on, all cold and snooty, like what I was doing was some kind of dumb work, something for a stupid person, for, I don't know, a *mother* to do. You think it's beneath you, don't you, to *care*? But you know what's really sad? What's really sad is that you don't know what you're missing out on. It's the most important thing in this world, to care for another person.' Her lips were fat with crying. 'It's all we've got.'

In the doorway, Nina faltered. Defences swirled and then evaporated. 'I was,' she said, and, 'But,' and, 'I didn't . . .'

Meg sat and cried messily, her hands in her lap.

Nina went over. She stood beside Meg at the table and reached for the knife. She slid Meg's plate closer and spread Vegemite on the two pieces of toast. She poured the tea—strong now—into Meg's cup. Then she went into the kitchen and found a clean tea towel and offered it to Meg.

Meg took it. Wiped her face.

Nina sat down. She poured tea for herself.

The whites of Meg's eyes flashed as she tore at the crusts with her teeth. She hiccuped and sobbed. When the last of the toast was gone she looked down at her plate.

'This is what they gave me,' she said, 'after the last baby. After the labour. Vegemite toast and tea. Except with butter and milk. I was so hungry I ate it all, and Dave . . .' Her voice veered. She wet her lips. 'Dave was holding the baby.' Her eyes flicked to Nina. 'They let you hold them for a while you know, to say goodbye.'

Nina nodded. She did not know. She had not been there, or asked Meg about any of this—at the time or later.

'Anyway, Dave looked at me as if to say, How can you *eat*? And the thing is, that was our whole problem—there was this part of me that was like an animal, wanting, you know, to be pregnant and to give birth and make milk, and that was what had taken us to that point. Even when Dave said, Maybe this isn't going to work out, maybe we could stop trying, maybe we could be okay without this, just the two of us—even then I could not let up. And we were sitting there in that hospital room with this dead baby, so small you could see all the veins through his skin. His little head was like a . . .' She whispered: 'Like a cricket ball.'

'Oh, Meg,' said Nina, tears springing from her own eyes.

'And Dave was looking at me and I was this animal, this beast, that had just roared and sweated and pushed out this baby with all this blood and gunk, you know, and now I was hungry, I had to eat.' She glanced at Nina again. 'I mean, I was also crying, I'd been crying the whole time. The midwife kept whispering to me, Put your grief aside for now, you've got a job to do. But I cried through the whole labour and then I cried all over the poor baby. I was scared to wipe my tears off his tiny face. His skin looked so thin.'

Nina's own tears streamed.

Meg sighed. 'It wasn't just that moment, you know, me bolting down toast in the same room as a dead baby.' She gave a wry laugh. 'We'd worn ourselves out. It was over. I think we'd both known from when they told us that he—that last one—wasn't going to make it. But still. That's what wore us both out—my . . . my *hunger*. My need for things. Like babies. Like a family.' She sighed again, long and slow. Then she looked directly at Nina. 'I know what I can be like.'

Nina smiled wetly.

'But I also know that some of what I want, Neen, it's *good*. It *matters*. It's the . . . the *going about it* that I have trouble with. I get too, I don't know, I get like a, like . . . What do I get like?'

'Like a train?'

173

'I was going to say bull. But I'll take train. Train's actually a bit nicer.'

☙

The note was gone from the chair. Nina felt a small jolt of confusion (Amber? Had she come up in the night?), but then saw it, shifted by the breeze, lying off to one side, at the edge of the verandah boards. She moved the chair from the top of the stairs and she and Meg descended.

I'll just say it, thought Nina, before Meg gets a chance. I'll just say, Do you want to go home, Amber? And then when she says yes, I'll say, Two against one. Give me the keys, Meg.

The door to the downstairs apartment stood open. They stepped into the dank kitchen area and blinked and called out, but there was no reply. They went towards the inner room and Nina saw the bed with the mattress back in place, and flung across it a sheet with a print of pale blue flowers and one large fresh wine stain. On the floor lay several empty wine bottles (already? Could she have drunk that much?), an opened tub of dip with two dead bugs in it, flaccid overheated cheeses still in their plastic, Meg's butter oozing, rancid, from its foil, the fruit loaf unopened, spoiled in the heat.

Amber was not there. The room smelled fumy, volatile, of microbes at work, of decomposition and booze.

They went back upstairs.

☙

The morning passed. Their stand-off regarding leaving remained unaddressed. Nina made more toast. Above the forest the sky was even lower. The air felt thick. Great streamers of white cloud slurred through the tops of the trees.

Nina showered and put on clean clothes. She helped tie a plastic bag over Meg's hand and arm so that she could do the same. Meg flinched. She was pale again, her breathing careful. Neither of them mentioned the thrown-away painkillers. Neither of them mentioned Amber, but they were both listening. Meg kept the car key with her at all times.

Later, from the couch, her bandaged hand on a pillow like an offering, Meg looked up and said, 'Hey, Neen, that stuff I said before about you not helping—I can't point the finger, you know. I didn't help Amber all that time when I was with Dave, trying for the babies. I don't know what your reasons were, but I'm sure you had them.'

Nina felt her chin wobble. Had there been reasons? Did she have reasons now, for always being such a flake, so—still—lost? Or was this some basic flaw in her personality? Was this just *her*?

'You were only young,' said Meg.

'Yeah, but you were only a year older!' A tear crept from Nina's left eye. What made a person capable of such kindness, and another so unaware of her lack of it?

'Just . . . don't feel bad, okay?' said Meg.

It began to rain, the thickest, hardest rain Nina had ever seen. It turned on like a giant shower, fast and full, and Nina ran to whip yesterday's washed tea towels from the verandah railing, and drag the chair further in. The note to Amber went whooshing off under the rail. Nina couldn't see where it landed—she could barely even see the ground through the dense screen of falling water.

The rain turned the afternoon pale grey, hemmed the house and blurred the lawn to a green waver, the forest to vague darkness. The verandah felt close and damp. The nearest palm trees were just visible; their leaves bounced with a kind of hysterical endurance.

'Guess we won't be seeing Amber anytime soon,' said Meg. She couldn't keep still. Up and down she walked, making a tuneless half-whistle between clenched teeth.

It was the pain, Nina knew. Two or three times she almost offered to have a look for some Panadol, but each time she stopped. She wasn't sure how such an offer would be received.

Nina's legs itched with bites. She glugged down glass after glass of water and her stomach swelled. She felt soaked, softened, as if she could split. She'd fetched a book from her room—*The Well* by Elizabeth Jolley—but couldn't get past the first page.

Meg settled at last and read, or at least appeared to, holding her fantasy paperback up one-handed, lowering it to her lap to arduously turn the pages.

The hours inched by. The rain thundered without pause.

At some stage they ate more toast, and then at around six pm Meg insisted on cooking—boiling rice in one of the shitty saucepans, frying onions cut by Nina (not to Meg's satisfaction: 'Diced, I said'), sprinkling cumin, salt, pepper. It was nearly dark and they put on the lights; their sepia weakness turned the kitchen and verandah into cave-like spaces, small and rounded and lined with shadows. They sat over their bowls with their heads and shoulders bowed, as if the air or the hammering noise had actual weight. Under Nina's elbows the table was sticky.

Then the electricity went out. They found a torch in the kitchen, and candles, a box of matches, and they were fussing with these in the watery gloom when Amber climbed the stairs and emerged from the silver veil of rain.

Nina and Meg stood to attention.

A silhouette against the torrent, Amber lifted her arms and pushed back her dripping hair. She came to the table. Nina could see her face—leached of colour, filled with misery. Amber put her hands, which were trembling, on the back of a chair. She turned her eyes on Meg.

They all spoke at once.

'How're you feeling?' said Meg.

'Amber, we can—' said Nina.

'Let's do it,' said Amber.

AMBER WAS FOURTEEN WHEN THE film shoot happened—her first and only feature film. She didn't look fourteen. Adolescence had not settled or slowed her body as much as it had Nina's and Meg's; she looked like a twelve-year-old still, only tall, her curves barely there.

'I've made it!' Amber flounced around the dining table, shimmying her hands up and down. 'Big time! Big time! Want me to peel the potatoes, Mum? Talk to my agent!' Laughing deliriously she draped her arms around Gwen's neck and sagged at the knees.

'Oh, you'll still be doing the potatoes, my dear,' said Gwen. 'Don't get too far ahead of yourself.' But she was smiling. She lifted one hand and very gently, almost uncertainly, stroked the burnished mass of Amber's unbrushed hair.

Nina, over for one of her frequent dinners, freshly upended by the sex affair with the tutor, felt the onset of self-pitying tears. What had she got so wrong? How was it that everyone else knew what it was they loved to do—or, if not loved, were at least satisfied with, like Gwen and her disabled kids, her bushwalking, or

Meg and her anatomy textbooks and swimming and lentils? She went into the bathroom and stood for a while with her back to the door, swiping at her eyes.

❦

They went out to the set, Gwen and Robert and Meg and Nina, over a weekend. It was hours away, in the country near Wangaratta. Amber was already there, had been gone a week, under the care of a producer or someone—Nina was not privy to the arrangements.

Gwen drove them in the Volvo, Robert in the front passenger seat, pointing out trees, Meg and Nina in the back.

Flat yellow paddocks, giant dead silver trees, wire fences. An unsealed road, a tract of billowing bush, holiday cabins. People everywhere, in baseball caps and many-pocketed, many-zippered jackets. Trucks, jeeps, a small crane, folding chairs, a chugging generator, fat orange and grey power cables laid out across the dusty ground. The buzzing of flies, the blaring of megaphone announcements. Standing in line for paper-plate meals in the dense air of a marquee. Amber under lights calling, 'Mother! Mother!' with her arms flung out.

On the afternoon of the first day they sat on the grass in front of the food marquee—Nina and Meg and Gwen and Robert— and watched as, further down a slope, beyond two cameras, Amber ran out of a small timber hut and into the arms of a woman in a drab brown dress and grey bonnet. Amber ran into the woman's arms at least ten times, and each one looked very similar to the last, Robert whispered. Then finally that stopped, and they got to see five or six repetitions of the woman being dragged away by some men in uniforms and Amber crying.

A call came through the megaphone—'Break!'—and the cast and crew began to straggle up towards them. The Atkinses stood and, not knowing what else to do, remained standing like an awkward welcoming committee by the marquee's entrance.

Between the taller figures Amber wove, in a blue dress and a white pinafore, her hair in plaits under the dark bonnet, narrow lace-up boots neatly tied.

'What's wrong with her face?' said Meg.

'It must be make-up,' said Gwen.

Amber tipped back her head, her eyes with their drawn-on slashes of eyebrow thrown deeply into shadow, and Nina was struck by how long and skinny her sister's neck was. Amber's shins between the full skirt and the boots were narrow and childlike. She looked remarkably young.

Then, bizarrely, there came another Amber. She appeared from behind two heavyset men, a thin blonde girl in exactly the same dress and pinafore, her hair in exactly the same plaits. This girl—who wasn't Amber, of course; who moved not with Amber's composure but with a darting sort of action, as if escaping something—came out from behind the men and flitted at Amber, catching her hand.

'What . . .?' said Meg.

Robert made a squeak of delight and clapped his hands together.

Amber came striding with this other girl (slightly smaller, Nina could see now, with a brittle sort of thinness and a smaller face) hurrying along beside her, almost skipping to keep up.

When they had almost arrived a cry came from behind them, and Nina saw that the girl, the Amber copy, had indeed escaped—from a slim woman in a wilted-looking pink dress and a large hat who was coming after them at a jog, calling, 'Emily! Emily!'

Amber glanced back but the copy—Emily—only increased her speed. She was ahead now, pulling Amber with her, and she almost pulled Amber right past the welcoming committee of Amber's family and into the marquee, and was only prevented from doing so by Meg stepping forward like a human roadblock and Amber at the last moment veering towards Gwen and throwing her free arm—the one not held by Emily—around her.

The woman in the pink dress, clutching her hat, almost fell on top of them.

'Emily!' she said, her voice breathy and short. 'I *asked* you *please* to wait until I—'

'There's two of you!' announced Robert.

Amber hung on her mother. She was in the throes of a huge yawn; her neck and shoulders trembled with it.

'Hello,' said Gwen, in her fast and awkward social voice, 'I'm Gwen, Amber's mother, and this is Robert, her father—'

'Come on, Ambie,' said Emily. She had a cartoon voice, sweet, high, clear. 'Let's get some *yummies*.' She tilted her head and smiled.

'—and Meg, and Nina,' said Gwen.

'Emily's mother,' said the pink woman faintly. 'Sue.'

Emily was watching Amber, still holding her hand, swinging their joined arms in a quick, relentless back-and-forth that made Nina want to step in and slap her hand away.

Nina tried to see Amber's face. *Ambie?* Surely even Amber, the most mercurial and indiscriminate of friend-makers, would not go for this.

'Is . . .' said Robert. 'Are you . . . *twins?*'

Sue gave him a funny look.

'In the movie, he means,' said Meg. 'He knows his actual daughter in real life is not a twin.'

Gwen's laugh sounded like some sort of gasp.

Emily was whispering to Amber. Nina caught the words 'Coco Pops'. She also saw the way in which Amber was leaning in to Gwen, like a much younger child, a tired child, overwhelmed. Nina saw how, when Emily moved nearer to whisper, before Amber lifted her head and popped her eyes and licked her lips in a kind of lightbulb performance of avarice, Amber actually pulled away from her, nearer to Gwen, and for a second Amber's whole body went limp.

A moment, a kind of rattled hush. There existed—Nina would be certain that she didn't imagine it—a tension between Amber and Emily and Sue. It was tightly compacted and felt as if it had been building for some time.

'Coco Pops,' said Emily in that bubblegum voice, and swung Amber's hand higher.

'Coco Pops!' said Amber, and launched herself off Gwen.

The two of them hurtled into the marquee and Sue, droopingly, followed.

'Rude,' said Meg.

At the cabin that night, Gwen made a chicken stew with white rice. They'd left Amber at the set along with all the other cast and crew, still going. Big floodlights were blaring down, and Nina, walking away, had turned and seen Amber sitting on a log in front of a real, burning, campfire, sipping—sipping and sipping and sipping—from a tin mug that was not full of tea from the (probably empty) billy hanging over the flames but with Coca-Cola from a two-litre bottle held by an assistant.

'They're going late,' said Meg, with her mouth full.

'Yes,' said Gwen. 'They must still have a lot to get through.'

'Did anyone say what time they'd be back?'

'I don't know. Whenever they're finished, I suppose.'

'Where's she been staying?'

'With someone called Ruth. She's a producer or something.'

'*Are* they twins?' said Robert. 'In the film?'

'No, said Meg, 'she's a stand-in, that other girl. That's what someone told me. She's like the fake Amber.'

Silent eating for a while, and then Meg snorted and said in a stupid voice, '*Ambie*, let's get some *yummies*.'

Gwen looked blank but Robert, for once, was tuned in.

'Meg,' he said, 'it's not her fault, that poor girl. She's one of those types.'

'What types?'

'Oh, you know,' said Robert. 'A pleaser.'

❀

The second day was hotter. They sweated and waved away the flies. Robert dozed. Meg had brought her paperback, and read it. Gwen sat in her sunglasses and bushwalking hat.

Crew members kept returning to the marquee for drinks.

'You guys are keen,' a rangy guy in black jeans said, and winked at Nina. Beads of water glistened in the stubble on his face. Nina felt herself flush.

Amber appeared every now and then, with Emily, the two of them closely attended by Sue, in another pink outfit, who even when not hurrying had a flapping look about her.

Meg, after sitting in a brooding fashion for some time, shuffled nearer to Gwen.

'Mum, why isn't Bam staying with us, in our cabin?'

'Oh, well, I s'pose she's settled where she is. We don't want to inconvenience anyone.'

Meg's voice was only just quiet enough. 'But we've come to spend time with her.'

'Well, yes, I suppose so.'

'What about this morning? We could've seen her then, made sure she had a proper breakfast. We don't even know which cabin she's in. Or who this Ruth person is.'

'I know, I know.' Gwen's whisper was limp. 'I know what you're saying, but they've obviously got a whole system here and I don't think we can come along and—'

'Mum, she's only fourteen.'

Down by the hut a blonde girl—it wasn't clear which one— ran across a corner of the set, causing a light stand to teeter. Sue hovered and feinted like a giant pink mosquito, arms outstretched.

'Oh goodness,' said Gwen, and then, 'I feel as if I should be helping her. Sue, I mean.'

But she didn't. What would she do, go walking down onto the set? As she had said, there was a system, and their place in it was, apparently, here by the marquee.

The morning wore on. Emily did a lot of 'standing in', a brave little figure out in the sun.

'Poor kid,' whispered Robert.

'*Emily's* mum gets to go down there,' whispered Meg to Gwen.

There was no answer to give to this. Meg was simply pointing out what they all knew: that they, the Atkins parents, had somehow set themselves up to be uninvolved, with a consequent lack of agency. Like they always did—like they had at the girls' schools. And, like always, Gwen and Robert didn't seem to mind this; in fact, seemed to prefer it.

*

After lunch—sandwiches—Nina and Meg and Gwen and Robert had put their paper plates in the bin and were settling back into their watching positions when Amber came running from around the corner of the marquee.

Emily, as if on cue, popped out of the marquee's entrance.

Amber halted in a spurt of dust. 'Guess what?' Her eyes, as far as Nina could tell, were on Meg.

Meg frowned and looked away.

'What?' said Robert.

'The director just talked with me, and he wants me to do another film!'

'Oh,' said Gwen in a cautious tone. 'Well done, darling.'

A moment of weird silence, in which Nina realised that Sue was also there, standing behind Emily. There was again that sense of compacted strain between Amber, Emily and Sue.

Amber's chest heaved. Her face was radiant. 'He said any film he does, he wants me in it!' She was not looking to Meg now but casting around. She turned to Emily, and faltered.

Emily stood, arms dangling, mouth slightly open—a picture of forlornness. But then she seemed to regain her composure. She dashed forward and took Amber's arm. 'Oh, *Ambie*, well *done!*' she said in her bubblegum voice. 'That's *amazing*! I'm so *happy* for you!' She clung to Amber, almost panting with effort.

It was such falsity—such bad acting—that Nina couldn't bear to go on watching. She looked past the two girls to Sue.

Nina had not yet had the opportunity nor the inclination to observe Sue closely. There had only been an impression: hectic, kinetic and pink. Now she had a proper look. The resemblance to Emily was strong—a tense thinness and a sort of attenuated prettiness, a *pert* face. This face was now strangely frozen. If poor Emily's figure, moments earlier, had embodied forlornness, then Sue's face—despite or perhaps because of its rigidity—was now an expression of pure rage.

There was something white in Sue's hand. It was a paper plate. It shook. She advanced on her daughter with staring eyes.

'Emily,' she said, in a terrible voice, 'I have *spoken to you* about this many times and yet you simply *do not seem to hear me.*'

Silence. Emily, her own face stiff, glanced at Amber.

Everyone watched the paper plate trembling between Sue's fingers, almost touching Emily's chest.

'When you finish your lunch, *Emily,* I expect you to put your rubbish *in the bin.*'

Emily took the plate. She let go of Amber and walked to the bin.

'And now,' said Sue in that same voice, 'because of you, we are *late.*' Her dress that day was a darker pink. Sweat had made magenta ovals under her arms. She directed her frozen face at Gwen. 'Sorry,' she said in a grinding voice, then turned and began to walk down to the set, her movements jerky, her hat bobbling.

Emily followed in a sort of affectless march, with Amber drifting behind.

'Golly gosh,' whispered Robert.

THEY SAT, THE THREE OF them, without speaking. Nina had lit a candle and propped it in a mug. The box of matches lay on the table with the heavy torch and more candles—the candles were a pinkish-red, as if belonging to a cookbook from the seventies, alongside chequered tablecloths and straw-basketed bottles of chianti.

Meg had served rice for Amber, who'd raised a trembling forkful to her lips but eaten no more. Meg had brought Amber a glass of water, but this had been ignored.

Nina, keenly aware of the importance of this moment—a crystallisation, a momentary three-part alignment; what could they do with it?—felt the old panic swimming in her, the vagueness, and resisted, breathed, willed herself to stay sharp.

Meg was also striving, bearing down on herself, on her pushiness, her need—Nina could see it there in the loaded stillness of her body.

And Amber? Amber quaked. She licked and bit at her lips. On her chin were speckles of something dark red. Wine? Vomit? Amber's eyes were on the candle flame. She rocked slightly, back and forth. Every now and then, sighing as if nauseated, she made as if to rise from her chair before resettling, returning to the rocking.

Nina tried to focus, to consider. None of them could go anywhere right now. Driving in this rain would be almost impossible—and where would they go? To the airport, which would be closed by the time they got there? Did this mean, then, that now was not the time to voice once more her opposition to Meg—to explain that they must forget about the detox and all leave, as soon as possible?

Amber gave one of her rattling coughs. She looked at her sisters, wild-eyed, like she'd only just noticed that they were there. She said, as if for the first time: 'Let's do it.' Then, as if to clarify: 'I agree.'

She couldn't have drunk all that wine. Hadn't Meg said that there were four bottles? It had been—what—a day and a half since the knife incident, since Amber stole the groceries. Four bottles in thirty-six hours. Nina watched her sister. Yeah, she must have drunk it all. Drunk and slept and drunk and slept, alone in that dust-filled room, or wandering out in the forest, wherever she'd been when Nina and Meg went down to find her, before the rain. Had she even had access to water? Were the pipes connected down there? Nina tried to remember if she'd seen taps in that kitchen, through the sliding door. She leaned across and pushed the water glass nearer to Amber.

'Come on.' Amber's voice was harsh. 'What's the plan then?' She turned to Meg. 'How long? How many days?' Then she laughed, a sudden cackle. 'Hurry up, before I change my mind.'

'Well,' said Meg, 'what do you think the plan should be?'

Amber laughed again. She stopped rocking back and forth and commenced swaying from side to side. She rubbed her nose, flicked at her hair, worked her lips. She was in some kind of state—drunk still, or feverish. Could this be withdrawal from the pills? Her face, even though she kept laughing, was hard and pained-looking.

'Bam?' said Meg carefully. 'What do you think?'

Amber's mouth twisted. 'I don't know! Fuck! *I* don't know—isn't that up to you?' She hunched, dropped her face to her hands. Her voice became high and feeble, 'I don't know,' she said. 'I don't know, I don't know, I dunno, I dunno I dunno I dunno I dunno . . .' Her shoulders heaved. Then she pulled herself upright again and bared her teeth in a ghoulish grin. 'Tell you what, though,' she said, loud now, loud and slurring. 'You'd better lock me up tight and you'd better shut me away for a fuck of a long time because I am telling you, you pair of *psychos*, that you have *no idea* what you're up against.'

Meg sat very still. Was she holding back? Or was she genuinely at a loss?

'Do you think,' Amber croaked, 'that I haven't tried a hundred times to beat this?' She tossed her head and made a hollow hooting sound. Then her chin puckered. Her voice fell and thickened. 'But why would *you* want to do it?' she said, staring not at either sister but down at the table. 'Why would you *bother*?'

Meg glanced at Nina. 'Because we love you, Bam. Because we want to help you. Because we know that this is not the real you. We want to help you get back to being the real you.'

Amber kept her eyes down. A pause, and then, whispering: 'Can you remember that person?'

'Yes,' said Meg decisively. 'We can.'

The rain drummed. They sat in the weak circle of candlelight. Amber shook her head, wiped her face.

Meg leaned forward. 'Trust me. She's there. The real you. We just need to get the drugs out of the way and then you'll see. I promise.'

Amber sighed. She looked up and around, out at the dark, saturated night. 'What time is it?'

Meg checked her watch. 'Twenty to eight.'

Amber started to sway again. She folded her arms, then unfolded them. She still wasn't looking at Meg or Nina. 'So we'll start tomorrow?'

Meg didn't answer.

'I just need to sleep,' said Amber. 'I just need to get through tonight. If I can't sleep I'm going to go insane. I mean it. I need something. Just for tonight.' She glanced at Meg. 'Help me.'

'We don't have anything,' said Meg. 'I flushed all your pills. And I just flushed my own, the painkillers from the hospital. And you took all the wine.'

Amber lurched to her feet. 'Fuck.' She clutched at her chest. 'Jesus Christ. I can't do this. I can't do this.' Her breathing was loud and ragged.

'It's all right.' Meg got up too. 'Slow, deep breaths. You're okay. You're okay.'

'No! No!' Amber wheeled. She rushed to the railing and leaned out into the watery darkness.

'Just breathe,' said Meg. 'Slow, deep breaths.'

Amber stumbled back towards the table. 'I can't!' she gasped. 'I can't!' She hurtled to the kitchen entrance, then stopped and turned with her back to the wall. She slid into a crouch, arms over her head. 'Meg!' she cried. 'Meg! I don't want to hurt you!'

Meg went to her. Awkwardly, she got down on her knees and Amber collapsed into her lap.

Nina stood up. Now was the time. Now she must speak. Before any further damage could be done. Maybe if they got in the car they could drive at a crawl to Mossman and find a chemist, or go to the bottle shop. Get through tonight, and then in the morning they could leave.

'Meg,' said Nina.

But Amber's head lifted. She was saying something, urgently, quietly, to Meg. She had her hands clasped and held out in front of her.

Then Meg nodded and they rose, holding on to each other, and very quickly they moved past Nina, and Meg snatched the torch from the table, and then they were at the steps and the white torchlight swung up and caught the long wet slashes of rain falling, falling, and then it swung down again and the steps clanged and the black closed over and they were gone.

ON THE SECOND NIGHT, THERE was a party to celebrate the end of the shoot. Trestle tables appeared, and lavish quantities of dazzling food: slivers of jewel-pink salmon, filaments of dill, oysters, prawns, tumbles of lemon wedges, fat dark field mushrooms, cured meats in soft bright folds, drizzles of golden oil, great padded oblongs of Turkish bread.

'Fancy,' said Robert, swirling a glass of pale champagne, something green already caught between his teeth.

Gwen, misjudging the situation, had brought the leftover stew. She set it on a far corner of one of the tables and then moved quickly away from it.

The night air was dry and cool. The black hillside looked stamped against the navy sky and over it a round yellow moon rose, grand and prop-like.

Nina stood at one of the tables dropping greasy black mushrooms onto a paper plate. She had drunk two glasses of champagne already, quite fast, and there was a fizzy lightness to her head, her neck and shoulders. She watched as Amber appeared on the far side of the tables, on a slope of grass, sauntering, hands in pockets. Her hair was still in its plaits but loose bits had come out, gently framing her thin but still-sweet, still-glowing and, with its curves of eyes and eyebrows dark with left-behind make-up, uncharacteristically serene face.

A woman approached Amber, one of the film people—perhaps someone important, since she had on a blouse and a tailored jacket over her jeans—and spoke eagerly, smilingly, nodding and shaking her head. Nina didn't need to hear to know what she was saying. (*Amazing! Wonderful! Such talent! Such poise!*) What was interesting—what set a twirl of pure interest rising inside Nina—was Amber's response. There was no shrugging, no dipping of the head, no performance of modesty. But neither did Amber behave like the Amber who Nina knew—untethered, elusive, on the verge of absence. She stood listening, clear and straight, her hands still in her pockets, her eyes steady on the woman's face. Her expression was attentive, welcoming. When the woman had finished Amber took her turn, speaking only for a few moments. She did not twist her hands or chew the ends of her hair or look off into the distance; she did not mumble or squirm; she addressed the woman directly and calmly, and the woman, before turning and walking properly away, actually made two or three steps backwards, like a bumbling, reverent subject.

Just as had happened that day at the school assembly when Nina saw Amber as a stranger might—saw just how luminous, how captivating she was—all of the clutter of sisterhood was magically cleared away and, from her booze-softened vantage point, Nina felt, quite simply, awe. It really was amazing—*Amber* was amazing, the tremendous welling power of her charisma.

Amber strolled on. Nina scooped salad onto her plate, took up a plastic fork. As she began to move—not quite steadily—towards the drinks table, she caught sight of a pale figure standing under a low shrubby tree. It was Emily. Her arms were clenched in an odd cross high over her chest, and her small face was transformed, swollen and buckled with—what? Anger? Pain? Nina halted, stumbling a bit. Emily too had been watching— she was watching Amber still, her whole body fixedly attuned to Amber's lithe progress across the grass.

Later Nina would return to this moment and it would seem to her that, drunkenly, in an unexpected and profound lunge, she had perceived some things, based on this observed moment of private anguish and on Sue's earlier tirade, which had ostensibly been about Emily failing to put her rubbish in the bin but of course was really about Emily failing to do something else. Nina would imagine that she'd understood something she prob-ably never could: what it was to have a parent with unmeetable expectations. She would imagine that she knew what it was like to never be good enough. To never please. And how unjust it felt to behold Amber, who was so pleasing to everyone, and who was like that not only without trying but without even caring very much whether she was or was not.

Nina would imagine that, standing there in the smell of cooked mushroom with a grease-soaked paper plate bending in her hand, she'd felt the weight of Emily's inability to please her mother and the injustice of being punished for this inability. She'd imagine she felt Emily's miserable outrage, and then the savage desire to blame, the cruel urge to redirect.

But it did not happen, this lunge. Nina, later, made it up. It could have happened, or some of it anyway, but it didn't—because Nina did not let it. It would have been too ugly, and too sad. She put Emily's agonised face out of her mind and went to get another drink.

She found a spot on the periphery, in the lee of a cabin, and sat on a stump with her paper plate and her third glass of champagne. She swung her head back to look up at the moon and the rich not-quite-black of the sky. She saw Meg laughing by the fire with a group of women in baseball caps. She saw Gwen standing awkwardly at the brink of a circle of people and skipped her eyes away, not wanting to witness more of her mother's social helplessness. She saw Emily and then Amber climb through the wire fence that led to the sweet-smelling paddocks and go running, their twin blonde heads glimmering over the glimmering dry grass.

It must have been the booze, and being in the country—she felt, like a drug kicking in, her perennial sadness take on a soaring quality. It was majestic and tenuous. She sat very still.

After a while the tall man in the black jeans walked with slow purpose towards her, and she put down her plate and her empty glass and got to her feet.

They went around the cabins and down and then back up the gravel road. He took a stubby of beer from the pocket of his jacket and offered her some—it was warm. He talked about the films he'd worked on, the stars he'd met. 'Sam Neill,' he said. 'Top bloke.' Nina tried to listen but kept being distracted by the moon, the clean air, the hugeness of the sky, the buzzing of alcohol in her veins.

Eventually they went up into the bush, and at the foot of one of the white-trunked trees he took off his jacket and spread it on the ground. They sat facing one another, very close, and Nina's soaring feeling was still there, buoyed by the beer, but when he began to take off her clothes there was a sort of downward slip, a flagging, and she knew that it wouldn't be very different from what had happened with the tutor. There was an inevitability to her disappointment; she had failed before, at this, and she would fail again now. His breath smelled of meat. His stubble hurt her chin. His tongue felt cold.

'I might go back,' he said, afterwards.

'Okay.'

He drew his arm out from under her, kissed her on the temple. 'You all right? Did you . . . you know, did you have a good time?'

'Yeah, of course.'

'You're sweet.' He kissed her again and stood, did up his jeans, stretched his arms over his head. 'Well, nice meeting you.'

'You too.'

He bent and she thought he was going to kiss her again, which she didn't want, but then saw that he was trying to get his jacket out from under her.

'Oh, sorry.' She shifted to one side.

He shook the jacket. 'You coming?'

'I might just go back to the cabin.'

'Really?' In the dark she couldn't see his face, just his tall shape standing over her. 'You don't need to be embarrassed,' he said. 'They won't have missed us. And I won't tell anyone, I promise.'

'It's not that. I'm just a bit tired.'

'You sure?'

'Yeah.'

Together they tramped back down the hill, and at the gate, the tideline of the bush, parted ways with a brief and clunky embrace. Nina went to the cabin, which was empty. She walked restlessly about the place and then she went into the bunkroom and locked the door and lay down and undid her jeans and pressed out a small, sore, sad orgasm.

She woke up to someone rattling the doorhandle.

'Who's in there?' demanded Meg's voice through the thin timber. 'Amber?'

Nina got up and opened the door.

'Oh, it's you. When did you come in? I searched this room before and it was empty.' Her eyes were making a brisk assessment. 'What are you doing sleeping in your clothes?'

'I didn't mean to fall asleep.' Nina's mouth was dry. Her temples throbbed. 'What's going on?'

Meg sighed. 'We can't find Bam.' She strode to the kitchen.

Nina followed. The wall clock showed that it was past midnight.

'And for a while,' said Meg, 'we couldn't find that other girl.' She ran water into the kettle. 'Emily. Her weirdo mum had a fit.'

Gwen came in. 'Oh, Nina, there you are,' she said. Her cheeks were pink. 'Have you seen Amber?'

'She'll be hiding still,' said Meg with authority. 'Thinking it's a joke.'

Gwen sat down.

'I saw them go through the fence,' said Nina. 'Ages ago. Near the barbecue—the fence into the paddock there.'

'Tea, Mum?' Meg put teabags into mugs. 'Yeah, Emily said they were playing hide-and-seek and Amber hid somewhere and just couldn't be found. But that was hours ago.'

'There might be a dam,' said Gwen in alarm. She spread her fingers on the surface of the table. 'We should get back out and keep looking.'

'Just a quick break,' said Meg. 'We're getting tired.' She poured out the hot water and put a hand on Gwen's shoulder. 'Don't worry about dams. Amber's a good swimmer, Mum. She'll be fine, I'm sure. She can be an idiot, but she's got an excellent sense of self-preservation.'

Nina's head was still thick. She joined Gwen at the table and Meg put a mug of tea in front of her. The three of them sat for a while without speaking. The fluorescent light was very cold and very bright. Outside, voices called, near and far-off. Through the double window over the sink Nina could see that the moon had moved higher and lost its yellow—now it was as glaring and chilly as the fluorescent tube. Beneath the moon, through the darkness, torch beams passed, wavering, frail.

For hours they searched. There were not enough torches to go around so Nina wandered where she could see by the moon, calling and staring into the shadows. Passing one of the other cabins she saw through the open door Sue sitting on a couch with her arms around a blanket-wrapped Emily.

At one point she came face to face with the black-jeans guy.

'She'll be okay,' he said. 'She can't have gone far.'

'Thanks.' Nina went around him and kept looking.

It got cold. The fire under the barbecue had ebbed to a mound of ash, grey and soft orange. The food lay abandoned on the tables, paper plates in ghostly discs on the dark ground.

At last someone said, 'We'd better call the cops.'

'Yes, it's probably a good idea,' murmured Robert, twin white moons reflecting in his glasses lenses.

'Where's the nearest police station, does anyone know?'

'What time is it?'

'Nearly three thirty.'

They were having this discussion—ten or so of the film people, plus Robert, Meg, Nina and Gwen—between the cabins and the picnic area, when they saw a baseball-capped woman bringing Amber across the paddock.

'Go on,' somebody said, and Gwen and Robert stumbled forward.

They met at the fence. The woman had her arm around Amber and was rubbing at her, and Amber was very passive, her head down, her hair, mostly escaped from its plaits, hanging over her face. Her clothes in the torchlight—a pair of red corduroy pants and a pink t-shirt—were dirty, the t-shirt covered in rust-coloured marks.

'She's really cold,' said the woman. 'We need to get her warm, quick, blankets or something.'

'I'll bring some,' called Meg, already running back towards the cabins.

It was a struggle to get Amber through the fence. Nina stood to the side. In the overlapping circles of torch beams she saw her parents, bent-kneed, their arms out like farmers delivering a calf. She saw Amber's white fingers gripping the wire, gripping Gwen's wrists, and Amber's white face moving, Amber's eyes staring blankly, shallow and green, right into the light. Her legs got tangled and Gwen and Robert lifted her clear, and then she sank to the ground at their feet.

Meg was there with the blankets and they wrapped her up and Robert carried her, a roll of green and blue tartan with a pair of very thin, pale, dangling shins at one end and at the other, shining in the torchlight, floating out with the rhythm of Robert's steps, strands of hair like the threads of a broken spider's web.

They passed the rest of the searchers and Gwen said, 'Thank you so much, she's okay, we'll just go in and get her warmed up,' and the group, with murmurs and a flutter of torches, dispersed.

They passed the doorway where Sue and Emily stood silently.

'Wait,' someone called. It was the baseball-capped woman.

Their parents had gone inside, Gwen holding Amber's knees as Robert manoeuvred her through the cabin door, but Meg and Nina turned at the bottom step.

'Thank you,' said Meg, taking the woman's hand. 'We can't tell you how grateful we are.'

The woman shook her head. 'It's fine,' she said. 'But listen. When I found her, she was in a car. A wreck. Right down there, miles away, near the next property. She was in the boot, locked in. I heard her banging.'

Inside the cabin there was the sound of running water and Gwen's voice, soothing.

'In the boot?' said Meg.

'Yeah. It was an old sedan, rusted out, but the boot still shut I guess.'

There was a long pause.

'I thought you should know. She must've been in there for a long time. She was hysterical when I got her out. Totally frantic.'

Amber wouldn't or couldn't say what had happened. Not that night in the bath, her fingers bloodless on the rim, her face on her knees, the skin of her back mottled white and fierce fresh pink, with Gwen kneeling beside her speaking quietly and a bank of steam overhead. Not later as she lay in the bottom bunk wearing Meg's pyjamas, her hair dried and brushed, extra blankets piled on her, Robert and Gwen taking it in turns to sit on the chair they'd brought in from the kitchen, in the smells of warm milk and rubbery hot-water bottle. Not later still—early morning, light at the top of the plasticky curtains—when she woke screaming and Meg shot down the ladder from the top bunk and took hold of her, saying, 'Bam, Bam, it's okay.' Nor would she speak as that morning went on and she wouldn't get up, but lay curled with her face to the wall.

Meg had told Gwen and Robert about the baseball-capped woman, what she'd said about the car.

'What happened, darling?' said Gwen to Amber. 'Did you get in there to hide and it closed on you?'

'Didn't you realise that it would lock?' said Robert.

It was Meg—in the Volvo, as they rolled over the gravel with Amber still in pyjamas between her sisters in the back seat, under a blanket, her lips pale, her breath sour, having refused breakfast, purple circles beneath her eyes, her hair limp, her fists clenched; as they began to pass the other cabins and Sue and Emily, who were putting bags into the boot of a yellow Nissan, and who turned and watched with inscrutable faces; as Robert and Gwen waved at Sue and Emily with gestures of reassurance—it was Meg who said, tersely and quite loudly, 'Amber, you have to tell us: was it her? Did Emily shut you in the boot?'

Even then, Amber couldn't say. She just stared, and shook.

NINA STOOD AT THE TOP of the stairs. The rain banged down on the metal treads. The candle she held barely made a dint in the blackness. She returned to where her bag lay on the floor beside one of the couches and took out her phone, but she already knew its battery was flat.

In the kitchen, in the unsteady bowl of candlelight, she searched through the drawers but couldn't find another torch. She stood stupidly in the doorway, hot wax running onto her fingers. From beyond the just-visible line of the verandah railings the darkness pressed.

At the table she put a second candle in the mug and lit it, her skin prickling, thinking of those cave divers who lose their light and their bearings and can't tell up from down, and who flail and die in a helpless panic.

She pulled out a chair and sat. What to do? Amber and Meg were downstairs, presumably, in the half-finished apartment. They hadn't taken the car; she would have heard it, wouldn't she, over the rain—the doors slamming, the engine? Or would she? But where would they go, and why would they leave her?

No, they were downstairs. Nina ran her fingers through her hair, which was fuzzy from the humidity.

Amber's hands held out like an offering, her wrists together, her urgent, low voice. Meg's nod. Nina shivered. She thought of Meg, two nights ago—could it really only have been two nights?—leaning across the table, her feverish face. *She said, Take me somewhere. Lock me in a room. And no matter what I say, what I do, don't let me out of there.*

'Fuck,' said Nina aloud, and got up.

The rain drenched her immediately. She went down the steps with one hand on the wet metal rail and the other blindly raking the air. Raindrops ran into her eyes and mouth and off the tip of her nose. When she reached the bottom she jarred her spine taking a non-existent step. Too scared to let go of the rail, she turned to her left and blinked and stared. Yes, a light—very weak, a submerged flicker, but there, she was certain.

As well as the endless pelting of the rain there were rushing sounds, and a gurgling. Somewhere nearby water was flowing— from the gutters, downpipes? She shifted her feet on the soggy grass. Was she standing in water? She couldn't tell. Fingertips still on the rail she took a step towards the glint of light but didn't go any further. It was too risky. She couldn't recall what was there on the porch, if there were any steps or some kind of lip where the grass ended and the paving began. And what was making that gurgling sound? Maybe there was a drain—with or without a cover. She needed a torch. Turning with care, she groped for the bottom step, cracked her shin on it, gave a forlorn mew, and made her sodden, slippery way back up.

She took one of the candles to the bathroom and dried herself off with the remaining towel; the ones she and Meg had used earlier, left hung over the balcony railing, were dripping. In the mirror, in the slanted weak light, she was hollow-eyed, hair pasted to her scalp, ears jutting. She wondered what time it was. She shuffled back to the living area, sat at the table and waited. The clammy air had cooled, and after a while she got up and went to one of the couches and lay down and pulled up the quilt. In the smudgy cave of candlelight she closed her eyes. The rain clattered on and on and she lurched into sleep.

NOBODY KNEW HOW TO HANDLE Amber, after the film shoot and the car-boot disaster. They took her home and she went to bed and went on refusing to speak.

Gwen took her cups of tea and bowls of soft foods—porridge, soup, yoghurt with honey and sliced banana; the kinds of things the Atkins girls had eaten as babies. Amber ate some but not much. Gwen gave her hot-water bottles and glasses of cordial (which the Atkins girls had never been allowed)—lemon barley and Ribena. Gwen sat and rubbed Amber's thin arm as Amber lay facing the wall.

Robert drifted in and out. He sat in the chair by the bunk like someone in a waiting room, with a sort of forced calm. He hummed tunes, and sang sometimes, songs by Van Morrison or The Beatles. He gazed around at the room—which was now just Amber's, but still had all the beds, the set of bunks and the single, Meg and Nina having each purchased cheap second-hand double beds on leaving home. Like a visitor at a museum, he gazed at Meg's old bed, which—under a heap of Amber's shucked-off clothes—had been left neatly made; he examined the rucked rag rug that lay over the old cream-and-pink rose-patterned carpet, and the cheap pine chest of drawers with its officious label made long ago, Meg's writing, pencil on paper, stuck with dog-eared tape: *AMBER*; he peered at Amber's River Phoenix poster. He, too, stroked the thin arm, the thin shoulder. He kissed Amber's unwashed hair.

Nina, on one of her visits, went into the room and had a reaction to the smell, which was close and peculiar, sickly sweet but also slightly rancid. Amber appeared to be asleep, her back turned. Nina went out again, her stomach churning.

There was a worried conference taking place in the kitchen.

'I just can't take any more time off work,' said Gwen. 'Robyn's on maternity leave and they haven't found anyone to replace Liz yet, and . . .'

'I can stay home a bit more, if you like,' said Robert. 'But anyway, she'll be all right, She doesn't need someone with her every moment.'

'But leaving her alone . . .'

'Give her a bit longer,' said Robert. 'Another few days and she'll be jumping up out of that bed, you wait. This is Amber we're talking about.'

But Amber did not jump up, or talk, or do anything other than lie there.

Nina was visiting again, two evenings later, when Meg marched in and announced that too much time had passed and that this wasn't a good situation and that something needed to be done about it.

Gwen was in her work clothes, Robert in his painting clothes. They sat at the table with mugs of tea. Meg stood. The late sun shone in her hair and on her brown skin. Her strong arms were folded. Nina was off to one side, on the couch.

'I'm going to take her,' said Meg.

'What, to your place?' said Gwen.

'She needs better care than this. She needs someone with her during the daytimes. She needs to get up and moving.'

'But what about your classes?' said Robert.

'I can get the notes from a friend.'

'Really?'

'Dad, have you ever known me to miss an assessment? To get a bad mark?'

Robert grinned. 'Never!' he said, as if for the first time considering this fact and finding it amazing. 'It's true!' He turned to Gwen and raised his hands, palms up.

Gwen's closed lips made a sharp, pulsing movement. She fiddled at the handle of her mug. 'I don't know . . .'

'Look,' said Meg, 'I can give her what she needs. I'm available. It's the best option.'

'I don't like the idea of her being here alone all day while I'm at work,' said Gwen, sighing.

'Let me help,' said Meg.

❧

And so Amber went to Meg's, and stayed there for—a week? Two? Three?—Nina didn't keep track; Nina wasn't paying attention; Nina was busy having her second (or third, if you counted the black-jeans guy) sex affair, with one of her housemates: a DJ, apparently, although he never seemed to get any gigs at actual venues. He had surprised her late one night in the kitchen when she thought nobody was around and, before she could sneak back to her room, kissed her with a dry and chemical-tasting mouth. He was clearly high, shuffling his expensive sneakers on the lino floor and making bopping movements as if there was music playing, even though there wasn't. He didn't even speak to Nina before he kissed her. They had never spoken before; for a long time she wasn't sure if he knew that she was one of his housemates and not some random visitor.

In theory this affair should have had a better chance of success than the one with the tutor. Neither party was in a position of authority, officially speaking, and there were no laws being broken. But some kind of pattern had already been set, and in its tone and dynamics, in the currents of dominance and control that ran through it, the whole business was strongly tainted by what had come before. Nina found herself again being arranged on a mattress and subjected to an unceremonious probing by a latex-encased penis—although with the DJ there was no lube, and she was always left chafed and sore.

He did have a few more moves than the tutor, and he was slightly more attentive, but still the only pleasure she managed to work up was again through seeing her own body have things done to it. And like before, this pleasure was slow to develop and would really only be getting started when the DJ (after announcing repeatedly in a terse voice that he was going to) came. He did not dismiss her as the tutor had done—at least, he did not get up and toss her clothes at her and usher her from the room; he dismissed her instead by rolling over and falling fast asleep and staying asleep until well into the next day, by which time Nina—having lectures to attend or a shift at the sandwich shop, or simply because she had lain sleepless beside him for hours worrying about how he would react when he woke and found her still there—would have crept from his room.

(Unlike the tutor, with his ready box of tissues and upright, fastidious lap-tending, the DJ lazily removed his condoms while already half asleep, his face sunk into the pillow; Nina when she got up might find one adhered to her skin somewhere, or on the floor under her bare foot, cold and squishy.)

He was in charge. Nina felt no sense of entitlement. She made herself available to him with a soft, abased readiness—waiting in the kitchen, lingering near the entrance to his room—and sometimes he took what she was offering and other times not. And yet there was pleasure in it for her somewhere, crepuscular, perverse and separate—privately hers. She felt herself now to be an adult woman with a secret life. The thrill of this she carried around with her, on the streets, at university, at work as she spread margarine on rye and reached with a gloved hand to unstick the topmost square from a yellow tower of sliced cheese. Looking into the faces of office workers as they spoke their orders, she thought of herself naked and opened and being entered by the DJ and got wet between the legs and her knees almost buckled. Her arousal was a nebulous twining thing that hid in the folds of these elliptical associations—she felt more turned on while making sandwiches and imagining being fucked by the DJ than while actually being fucked by him. Yet still it lived, and over time she learned to nourish it and to improve her access to it—to more efficiently dissolve herself into the place where it would come billowing into action—and eventually to become literate in its perverse looping logic. At work, at university, alone in her room, she would go over things he had done to her that at the time felt nothing more than uncomfortable while holding open with part of her mind a portal to that diaphanous half-world, and the things he had done would be put through some kind of magic filter and imbued with eroticism and then slipped away to some warm and invisible place, ready for later use. It wasn't long before she was capable of squeezing out a brief blip of an orgasm while being fucked by the DJ via a ready and waiting fantasy of being fucked by the DJ in a slightly different way.

So Amber went to Meg's, and from Nina's preoccupied and marginal viewpoint the crisis was over. At some stage—although Nina would never be able to say exactly when it was—Amber returned to Thornbury, out of bed, eating, drinking and talking.

Something Nina did recall was Meg's fury upon discovering that, once back at school, Amber had returned to the drama group.

'But she wasn't to do that,' said Meg, standing over Gwen as she unloaded her work backpack—Tupperware lunchbox with a slick of salad dressing, ball of cling wrap, apple core. 'She'd agreed to quit.'

'Well,' said Gwen, zipping up the backpack and hanging it on a peg, 'she does love it.' Her eyes were twitchy, apologetic.

Meg made a violent sound of frustration. 'Oh God, *Mum*! She was traumatised! She's fragile. It's too much for her, that world. The competition. The people. We should be avoiding triggers.'

'Darling, I know. I know you said that, and you're probably right, but I just'—Gwen glanced towards the hallway and lowered her voice—'I can't lock her up.'

Slowly, pityingly, Meg shook her head, and Nina waited for her to say something put-upon, something like, I did all that work and you can't even manage one simple task. It was extraordinary, Nina thought, how Meg had this in her, this anger that was both incredulous and resigned—a mother's anger. But where had she learned it? Gwen wasn't like that.

Meg said nothing, only sighed with deep meaning.

This was on a Thursday evening, and soon the slamming front door announced Amber's arrival, home from drama. She went straight to her bedroom.

Meg banged about the kitchen, reheating her eggplant moussaka and making hummus with the chickpeas she'd brought, pre-soaked, in a container. Gwen, relegated to salads, veered away from her. In the richly spiced air there was exactly zero conviviality.

After a while Meg snapped, 'Doesn't she come and say hello, when she gets home?'

'Of course she does. She's probably just tired today, after drama.'

Meg sighed again, loudly, and chopped angrily. She gripped a wedge of lemon between her strong brown fingers and the juice spurted. When the table was set and all the food laid out, she wiped her hands and left the room.

She returned with a tearful Amber, whom she put in a chair and whose plate she piled with food. Meg took Amber's wrist and, with infinite gentleness, drew her hand away from her face, the chewed, wet cuff of her school jumper from her mouth. She cut a piece of moussaka and lifted it on a fork to Amber's lips. Amber's eyes, green with tears, met Meg's, and Meg nodded, and Amber took the food.

'Good girl,' murmured Meg.

Gwen and Nina averted their eyes. (Robert, despite having been called numerous times, had yet to come in from his studio.)

Then Meg said, in a voice that was firm but low, and—this struck Nina full in the chest—warmly, wholly loving, 'Go on.'

Amber put back her shoulders and gazed with trembling resolve at Gwen. Thinly, she said, 'I'm not going to drama anymore.'

Gwen spoke then but Nina didn't hear it—she was in a state, having a freak-out, brought on by that note of love in Meg's voice. In that moment Nina was absolutely convinced that nobody would ever speak to her like that. Her body seemed to be dissolving and she stared helplessly out from it as her mother said something to her sister and her other sister looked on and her father walked in and sat down, all of them completely solid and real, none of them noticing that she was not.

And then Meg met Dave, and here was a new phase in the life of the Atkins family, which Nina's memory would log as a series of dinners at the Thornbury house. At the centre of these dinners were the young couple, vital, steadily assured, filled with the earnest energy of a certain kind of early adulthood—left-wing, educated, socially conscious. They spoke of permaculture, the student union, of Kennett selling off state schools, of Srebrenica, the civil war in Somalia, of their planned trip to South America as volunteers for an NGO that was building health clinics. Meg had gone on blossoming and become almost queenly; Dave, lanky, with thick dark hair and a high colour, was attentive—adoring, even—sitting forward to listen when Meg spoke, his lips parted and moving slightly as if in silent agreement.

'Aren't they wonderful?' said Robert, right in front of them, hands clasped under his chin, eyes bright behind his glasses— and, after they'd left, rhetorically and with deep satisfaction, 'Those two. The world belongs to them, doesn't it?'

Later, Nina would have no memory of Amber being at these dinners. But she must have been—at least at some of them. What part did she play, then, if Meg and Dave were the central focus, taking up all the light? Did Amber drift in and out, excusing herself as soon as the meal was over, going off to her room? Was she in the hallway, on the phone, slouched on the seat by the telephone table, legs up, bare toes spread against the old brown-and-cream wallpaper?

She would have been on the phone to one of her drama friends—because she had gone back to drama, gone back on her promise. There was, as far as Nina knew (Gwen told her some things), outrage at this from Meg, and a fresh promise, which was then broken, followed by more outrage and more promises and more breakages—until Meg, not giving up, because Meg did not give up, changed her approach, saying that Amber would 'have to learn the hard way'.

Nina did remember Amber's bedroom, a site of total chaos: piles of clothing, the floor buried, books and papers strewn. Looking back, she would wonder if this was a warning of or a precursor to Amber's future—her drug den, her trail of debris. But how could you tell? How could you identify the point at which normal adolescent untidiness becomes dysfunction? There was not—as far as Nina could recall—any evidence of drug use back then. Just a messy bedroom. Just an elusive, flighty teenager.

Amber was in year ten, then year eleven. She was still disorganised, forgetful, distracted and frequently late, and she was not doing well at school. Every now and then she proved herself capable of creative output that bordered on the transcendental: an abstract painting of wispy pink shapes that seemed to hover, hauntingly delicate, over a daubed white background; a comedy script in which the pushy saleswoman at an upmarket boutique convinces a hapless wealthy shopper to spend thousands of dollars on an outfit made entirely out of newspapers. For a media studies class she made a video of herself on a beach in the late evening, walking into the water fully clothed. This she then edited to run backwards in slow motion, boosting the treble of the stretched-out sound so that an uneasy hiss ran the length of her slow emergence from the lilac water, broken by weird, distorted seagull cries. The video was pronounced extraordinary by Amber's teacher, who added that Amber almost certainly had a brilliant future as a filmmaker should she want one. But these projects were blips, exceptions: by and large she was only just passing most of her subjects.

Despite the promise of the director, she had not got any more screen roles since the ill-fated shoot, only parts in stage plays put on by the school and the drama group. She still did the occasional audition, which she would talk about in a feverish, abstracted way—struggling, when questioned, to produce relevant details such as the name of the production or the date of the audition.

She asked Nina to help her run her lines for one of these, and Nina was shocked by how badly Amber did—fluffing words, recalling them out of order—and by how flustered she became when this happened.

'Sorry!' cried Amber, writhing in the middle of the living room, tugging at her hair. 'Sorry! Sorry! Oh God, I'll never get it!'

'Yes you will,' said Nina.

But when they tried again and Nina ventured to correct her on something Amber flew into a rage, snatched back the script, and stormed off.

So no luck at any of those auditions—but then came one success, a walk-on part in a TV production, no lines.

'Absolutely not,' said Meg. 'She's doing VCE now—she needs to focus on school.'

'I don't see how I can stop her,' said Gwen, blinking agitatedly.

'Of course you can. You're in charge.'

But Meg and Dave were going overseas—this exchange took place at yet another Thornbury dinner, the farewell dinner, Meg and Dave showing Robert maps in a well-thumbed copy of the Lonely Planet guide to South America, Amber (as far as Nina would be able to recall) not present, Meg upbraiding Gwen in the kitchen while the two of them heaped raspberries into a scallop-edged tin lined with shortcrust pastry.

'Just put your foot down.' Meg sliced a vanilla pod lengthways. 'See?' she said. 'How much richer the smell is, when you use the real thing?'

Gwen straightened from checking the oven, her cheeks flushed. She leaned over the sticky pod and inhaled, eyes closed, smiling.

'See what I mean?' said Meg. And in the sweet air of that kitchen with her mother beside her, her mother's arm against hers, it's possible that Meg chose for once not to press, not to hound. It's possible that Meg chose—not only for herself but for Gwen too, and Robert and Nina, and Dave, even for Amber—a leave-taking that was unburdened, free of strain.

Whatever the reason, no more was said about the TV role.

NINA WOKE TO A DREADFUL sound. An exhausted sighing wail, ghostly, almost singsong. She opened her eyes. It was day, murky flat light, and there was a strangeness in the air, an absence. Had she been dreaming? Above her, on a rafter, a little cream-coloured gecko spread the pads of its toes, its jewel eyes serene.

She got up from the couch and went to the railing. The rain had stopped—that's what had changed. The sky was still close and grey, but there was no rain falling, and its din had been replaced by sliding ribbons of noise: busy, muffled rushings and sharp drips and trickles. Everywhere—on leaves, trunks, branches, across the stretches of lawn—shone horizontal gashes of silvery light.

Then the sound came again. It floated up from below, hollow and despairing.

'Oh God,' said Nina aloud, and made for the stairs. But Meg was coming up them—grim-faced, pale-faced Meg, with bluish marks under her eyes and her sling no longer dazzling white but smudged and grubby, her bare feet caked with mud, the wet cuffs of her pants flapping.

They met halfway. Meg's eyes were pink-rimmed. She shook her head in a warning. 'Leave her,' she said. 'She wants to be left.'

The sound again—this time it started high and keening and then plunged, almost to a growl.

'Meg.'

'She wants to be left.' Meg's voice was snapping, final. 'She *asked* me to do this.'

'Do what?' Nina heard herself say, although she was pretty sure she knew what the answer was, and also that she didn't want to hear it.

'Let's have a cup of tea,' said Meg. 'The power's back on.'

'Do what?' Nina repeated, a coldness in her stomach. It would seem that she needed it to be spoken.

'Come on.' Meg moved up a step.

'Do *what*?' Nina stayed where she was, and so now they were uncomfortably near, Meg's head level with Nina's chest.

'Confine her,' said Meg, no longer looking at Nina but speaking to her chest.

'*Confine* her?'

Meg didn't respond. She had her free hand on one rail, blocking Nina.

Again the moans.

'She's okay. She's actually okay—she just needs to vocalise. She's not calling for help or anything. She's hydrated and she's as comfortable as is possible and—'

'In what way have you *confined* her?'

'I've restrained her.' Meg looked up now. 'Because she asked me to. Because it's what she needs. Because I am *helping* her.'

'Jesus fucking Christ.' Nina gave a broken, disbelieving laugh. 'You've tied her up? Like an *animal*? And she's making these noises, like, like a cow giving birth—and you're trying to tell me that she's "actually okay"?' She laughed again, and then she sobbed.

'Come on.' Meg's hand was on her arm. Meg's warm bulk was there, turning her, guiding her. Meg's arm was around her and the two of them were up the stairs again and then Nina was back on the couch and Meg was pulling up the quilt.

'I know it's hard,' said Meg. 'I know.' She was crying too, her mouth bending at the corners, tears falling onto her sling. She plopped down for a moment, squashing Nina's legs. 'Ah, jeez,' she said, and closed her eyes and breathed very slowly and deeply, and this reminded Nina of Gwen—of Gwen having one of her Moments in the hallway after dispatching a surprise dinner guest of Robert's—and Nina was set upon once again by the fog of her old weakness, her uncertainty.

Amber's wails had stopped. Nina, her head against the cushion, fought the paralysis. She blinked her eyes and pulled her legs out from under Meg, swung them round and stood.

Meg gave her a brief, considering look. Then she nodded. 'Go.'

'Go?'

'Take the car. Have you got any money? Find a motel. Stay away from here for three days. Then come back. Things'll be better by then. She'll have turned the corner.'

Nina looked down at her sister, her blotchy face, her rumpled clothes, the dirty sling against her chest. 'I don't think I can—'

'Please. This is how you can help. This is what you can do to contribute.'

'But what if something goes wrong? There's no phone reception. You've only got one working hand. What if you need help?'

'We'll be okay. I promise. We've got enough food.'

'I can't.'

'Neen. Please. You have to. I need you to—I can't make this work with you here.'

218

Nina's head was aching. She went to the kitchen and filled a cup with water and drank it down.

Meg came in, took the bread from the freezer and put slices into the toaster.

Nina filled the kettle and switched it on, and then the two of them leaned at opposite benches.

Nina tried again. 'But, Meg, it's not about me leaving you to do this. I don't think you *should* be doing this. If I leave, it's as if I'm condoning you tying Amber up and—'

'Oh God, Nina.' Meg raised her free hand, palm up. 'What did you think you were agreeing to in the first place? What did you think you were *condoning* in coming here?'

'I don't . . .'

'What—you thought Amber would just hand over all her pills and the three of us would go for some walks and play Scrabble and drink tea for a couple of weeks and then go home?' Meg shook her head. 'Honestly? You honestly thought it wouldn't end up a big horrible abject mess?'

'I . . .'

'Look. I've thought long and hard about this. I know that it will probably change things. Relationships.'

'Yours and Amber's, you mean?'

'Yes. But mine and yours as well. I'm well aware that the two of you may be very angry with me for some time. Possibly for a long time. There's a role that must be played for this to work. For Amber to be shown what she is capable of. I'm prepared to play that role. Even if she hates me forever. Even if you do, too.'

The toast came up, and before Meg could do her martyr act with the Vegemite and one hand, Nina intercepted her. When she'd finished scraping the black stuff onto the dry surfaces, she offered the plate and Meg took it and went out, and downstairs.

Nina put two more slices into the toaster and, like a sudden overflow, the idea of leaving spilled into her consciousness and then filled it completely. She could be away from here, from her sisters, from the awfulness of what was taking place. She could be in a clean room, with an air conditioner. She could have a shower and change her clothes. She could go to a cafe and order food that wasn't butterless toast and Vegemite, or gluggy rice and onions. She could drink *coffee*.

Maybe—could Meg be right? Could Amber need this? To be shown something, to be forced into some understanding of herself?

And anyway, what, really, could she, Nina, do—here, now—to change things? In order to get down there and untie Amber she would have to physically accost Meg. She would have to push her over, fight her—hurt her. There was a spasm in her throat at the thought.

So. If she left, what then? She could get help. She could go to the police. But what would that mean? Meg getting arrested? Or committed? Both of them, her unhinged sisters, being sectioned? Nina began applying Vegemite to the next pieces of toast. A harsh smile came to her face, then immediately went away again, and—oh God, would she never run out of tears?—she fell into a hunched, screw-faced, miserable sobbing, the knife dropping to the benchtop.

She gave in to it, for a while. Then she sighed and sniffed and lifted the hem of her dress to wipe her face, and retrieved the knife and continued scraping.

She could call home—Gwen and Robert. But the idea negated itself immediately. The happiness in Gwen's voice on Nina's voicemail, the day before they left—the *relief* in her voice, at the thought of her three daughters enjoying a weekend away together, out in the world (in Noosa, wherever), being independent adults. The way they were supposed to be. How could she, Nina, puncture this newfound buoyancy? How could she drag her parents back down? They were not a part of this. They, relieved and deluded, had chosen the word 'recovered' for Amber—for themselves—and were holding on to it for dear life. And you couldn't blame them. They'd done their time.

What if she got help from someone else, not the police? What if she went to the nearest property and explained that it was a kind of domestic situation, nothing truly serious, but more than she could handle on her own? She stood, knife in hand, and pictured herself knocking at a door, or stumbling across a cane field, flagging down a tractor-riding farmer. Nina Atkins, pale and sweaty, mud on the hem of her dress, hair a crazy frizz: Sorry to bother you, but I'm staying on the property next door and one of my sisters has tied the other one up . . .

She laughed out loud.

'What?' Meg was back. She had the plate of toast and it was untouched.

Silence, still, from downstairs.

'Nothing. How is she?'

Meg went to the sink. 'She's okay.'

Nina didn't want to find out more—she didn't want to know. But she couldn't help herself; she was propelled by vicious stabs of guilt. 'She didn't eat any?'

'She'll be okay,' said Meg. 'She's drinking water. It's hard for her to keep anything down.'

Nina stood there, staring at her sister's back, and fought the invisible internal churning. She couldn't be paralysed. She had to *do* something. She was the only person in this situation who could make a difference. And she couldn't hurt Meg. So it had to be plan B—get help.

'All right,' she said. 'I'll go. But I can't take the car. I think you should have it, in case of an emergency.'

Meg turned.

'If you can drop me at the main road I'll hitch from there.'

Meg wiped her good hand on her pants. 'Okay.'

Nina went to her room and put some changes of underwear in her backpack, went to the bathroom and took her vanity bag. Amber's toothbrush was there beside the basin, a cheap red plastic one with blown-out bristles; Amber's toothpaste was the cheapest brand, squeezed in the middle as if by a child. Nina's heart throbbed. She rushed away from the guilty feeling, back out to the living area, where she took her wallet and her dead phone from her handbag and put them in the backpack too. In the kitchen she added, carefully, blade down, one of the large knives.

Meg was waiting by the stairs. She handed Nina her purple metal bottle, heavy with water. 'Ready?'

'Yep.'

They went down and got in the car, and Meg started the engine and made a slow experimental one-handed turn over the lawn, and then there was a sliding feeling and Meg said, 'Shit, we're bogged,' and stamped on the accelerator, and there was a slippery whizz and a gliding, and then they leaped forward onto the claggy track. They passed under a languid tree—a tropical fruit tree, perhaps (yes, there were buds of some kind, weird yellowy blisters on straw-like stems)—and a spray of water went flashing onto the windscreen, and Nina was pretty sure that she was doing the wrong thing—that a stronger person, a *better* person, would never have let the situation get this far out of hand—but she honestly couldn't see that there was any other option at this stage, and a kind of soaring horror entered her, and she wanted to seize Meg by the shoulder and kiss her, and say, 'I'm sorry, I love you,' because she didn't know what was coming next but she did know that whatever it was, this—now—was a point of rupture.

AMBER'S ROLE IN THE TV show did not go well. Nina found this out from Gwen, over the phone.

'I'm not sure what happened,' said Gwen. 'She came home early, in a state. She won't tell me anything; all she'll say is that she couldn't get it right.'

'But wasn't it just a walk-on part?' Nina was in the hallway at the party house, squatting on the floor. There had, when she'd first moved in, been a phone table and a stool to sit on, but they'd since vanished.

'Yes. No lines at all. I just can't imagine what could've . . .'

'Did you tell Meg?'

'No.'

'You wouldn't want to worry her,' said Nina quickly. 'Not when they're about to leave.'

'No, I wouldn't.'

Gwen sounded despondent, and Nina felt a stirring of responsibility. Who was going to help their mother with Meg away? Gwen did so much and Robert wasn't very helpful, and Amber was so . . . Nina got to her feet, the phone cord stretching.

'But, look, she's all right really,' Gwen was saying. 'She seemed to bounce back pretty fast. She's been going to school and everything.'

After they hung up Nina remained standing in the hallway for a while. It was a Sunday morning and her housemates were all either sleeping or had not yet come home. She went to the back door and let herself through to the courtyard. The late summer air was heavy; the flat leaves of the bamboo stood motionless.

She tried to think about Amber, about Gwen and Robert and what was going on over there in her so-called family. But she found that she was only able to think about herself.

It had been almost two years since her sex affair with the anthropology tutor. The DJ was long gone. Nina had, to some extent, changed. She had started to come out of her bedroom more often. She had sat in the kitchen and drunk wine with her housemates, had joined in conversations, had gone out to see bands, to parties, danced in bars, sang karaoke. There had been four—no, five—other sex affairs. She was, at last, making her belated entry. And yet she was, still, dogged by a sense of aloneness.

The tremulous romanticism by which she'd been so strongly affected upon first leaving her family—which she'd always felt, but which in the lonesome splendour of her cobwebbed room and with the aid of her poetry classes had crystalised from a homely, unexamined presence into something not unlike a calling—this had not receded. It was melancholy, that's exactly what it was: a sadness that was exquisite. She was kind of addicted to it. And she found that she couldn't—simply could not—reveal this aspect of herself to anyone.

Drunk, in the dark, in bed, she would sometimes whisper into the neck of whoever she was lying with, 'Help me.' But she would whisper it so softly that the other person wouldn't hear.

I am so afraid, she wrote on the back of the door of a toilet stall in the Student Union building, a grey-lead mumble of a message, right down low in a corner.

Nina did not know why she needed help, nor what form that help might take. And she didn't know what she was so afraid of. Was it, she wondered, the hugeness of her melancholy, its unknowable strength? (*Beautiful sorrow*, someone called it, during a tutorial on Keats.) Was she afraid that it would undo her? That it would actually burst her?

In one of her notebooks she wrote, *The past, as described by Tennyson: Dear, sweet, deep, and wild.*

She wrote, *Mono no aware: 'the pathos of things' (Japanese, Heian, 18th century).*

She wrote, *Lacrimae rerum: 'tears of things' (Virgil,* The Aeneid*).*

She wrote, *Apple blossom, cherry blossom, winter sun, a rainbow.*

She glued into the back of a notebook a photograph of herself and Amber and Meg on that long-ago riverside farmstay. Ten, nine and five, standing in tall blonde grass with brown water behind and a scorching blueness of sky above. Their glaring youth, the fierce loveliness of their child bodies. Below this image she copied lines from Tennyson: *So sad, so fresh, the days that are no more.*

She wrote (and then tore out and destroyed), *Have I always felt old, and so achingly sad?*

How deeply, how vividly she felt this melancholy! How strongly she was moved to do something with it! (But what?) And how uselessly unoriginal this desire was! Hadn't it all been covered already, centuries ago, in so many paintings and in the pages of so many books? And what was wrong with her, anyway, that she was, at the age of twenty, so hung up on the glorious sadness of the brevity of life? Didn't she need to *live* life first, before she started to mourn for it?

There was a strange, guilty pride in these lonely thoughts and feelings. They had become both a refuge and an indulgence. When she dipped into them she was in a way removing herself from the world. It was a circular activity: she went inside her mind to a place that she did not want to share, and what she did in there was think about not being able to share it. Will I? Won't I? Should I? *Can* I? You could measure out a whole life—or stave off the actual living of it—trundling these considerations round and round.

On this still and thick morning, in this yard that smelled of concrete and ants, she stood, dipping, trundling.

Was everyone else walking around being invisibly ravaged by these unshareable thoughts? Did it not become impossible? Was this how people went mad?

And what about true intimacy—this thing that seemed to Nina more and more theoretical as time went on; this thing that was so absent from her sex affairs. Was true intimacy the revealing of this intensity of feeling to another person? And was this something that she really wanted? And how did you *do* it?

She considered the boy from her first-year poetry class, the spouter of Dylan Thomas in his grubby pink shirt and leather waistcoat. Regularly, publicly, this boy burst himself with beautiful sorrow. Shared his intensity of feeling. And still seemed to go on living.

But wasn't it a performance, that kind of bursting—moist, unsolicited quoting of poetry in a public place? There had been something stagey about it. It was, in fact, extremely stagey. And it was a sort of indiscriminate sharing, almost an infliction. But wasn't it all a performance—writing a poem, a song, and printing it, or singing it? Painting a painting and hanging it on a wall?

A tram passed, away beyond the high brick back wall, its bell sounding, dull in the syrupy air. Nina was overcome by a roiling upsurge of irritation. It was unbearable—she could not bear herself. 'Oh *God*,' she said aloud. 'Nina! What do you *want*?'

It was Meg she went to, about the trundling and dipping, the existential distress and confusion about intimacy. Nina didn't plan this, not rationally, but she did take certain actions. She rang Meg and asked if they could have one last dinner, just the two of them, before Meg left for South America. Then, on the afternoon of the appointed evening, Nina bought a bottle of nine-dollar merlot and drank nearly all of it, sitting on her bed with her shoes on and the blind down, under the yellow wash of her low-wattage bedside light, writing feverishly in a notebook.

She would be reminded of this the following day when she woke up wearing a pair of pyjamas, which was strange because while she did own one pair—given to her by Gwen—she never wore them. Then she remembered that Meg had brought her home, and realised that it must have been Meg who found the pyjamas in the back of a drawer and helped her into them and into bed. She saw the full glass of water on the bedside table, which she drank all in one go, then got up and half-ran to the bathroom to vomit. It was on the way back that she saw the notebook, closed and neatly placed on her desk, which was not where she'd left it.

But before that, Nina had somehow made her way through an unseasonably windy and cold March night to the Vegie Bar, got the door open and swayed over to the table where Meg was already sitting.

'Oh dear,' said Meg.

Nina fell into a chair without taking off her jacket or undoing its buttons. Her bag somehow flew under the next table.

Meg got up and retrieved the bag. 'Sorry,' she said to the people whose table it was under. 'She's my sister.'

Then Meg sat and listened while Nina said all kinds of things, none of which Nina would be able to remember, apart from one, which was, mortifyingly, 'When you and Dave started having sex, was it horrible?'

Thinking about it the next morning, Nina was pretty sure that Meg didn't answer this, because she also remembered that while she was saying it the waitress was putting down their vegie burgers, and just after she said it someone nearby who was not Meg laughed in an involuntary, choking way.

Meg rang the next afternoon, in the middle of Nina's hangover. 'It wasn't horrible,' she said. 'But it was sort of embarrassing and weird. And it certainly wasn't *good*. But it gets better and better. It took ages actually before I even had an orgasm, and now I have them all the time. What we've ended up finding works best is—'

'Okay, okay,' said Nina. 'Thanks, that's enough.'

'There's no *magic* to it, is what I'm saying,' said Meg. 'I mean, of course there's attraction and romance and all that stuff, but also it's two people working together—'

'Okay, thanks, you can stop now.'

Working together. Only Meg could make sex sound like something you did in the Girl Guides.

A small, stiff silence.

'Anyway, sorry about last night and thanks for dinner, and have a good trip,' said Nina.

'That's okay,' said Meg, sounding injured and formal. 'It was my pleasure. And I will. See you in three months.'

'Oh shit—wait. Don't . . . Can we just say goodbye nicely?'

A noisy sigh. 'I was only trying to help you.'

'I know! I'm sorry!'

'I was only trying to answer the questions you asked me last night, loudly, in a restaurant full of people who were listening.'

'I said I'm sorry!'

'Grow up, Nina. You're not special. Sex can be awkward, and everyone feels sad sometimes.'

'I didn't *say* I was special.'

'It's what you think.'

Then Nina accused Meg of reading the notebook she'd been writing in, and Meg said that it had been hard not to given it was right there on Nina's pillow, but she'd only glanced at it, and that had only been the pages that were open, and anyway she'd done so while putting Nina to bed after escorting her home, Nina who was so drunk she'd tried, while they were still sitting at the table at the Vegie Bar, to put lipstick on without a mirror. And Nina said, 'Please tell me I didn't.' And Meg laughed and said, 'Don't worry, you'd forgotten to take the lid off.'

After that they were able to say goodbye nicely, and did so, and hung up.

❧

Later, eating fish and chips in the tiny park around the corner, Nina admitted to herself that Meg probably really had only glanced at the pages of the notebook that were right there, open, for her to see. Bloody Meg and her morals. She admitted to herself also that Meg, in sharing her repulsively wholesome thoughts on sex and nearly describing some actual physical details, had only been trying to help. And that it would be admirable to do anything even remotely kind for someone who'd made you come out for dinner at short notice two nights before you were due to leave on a three-month trip and then showed up exceedingly drunk and asked embarrassing loud questions and didn't pay for anything and then had to be helped home and into bed.

But Nina, lying on the grass with salty lips, squinting against the sun's glare on the bone-white paper and the pile of steamy yellow food before her, could not quite believe that she was not special. That she was ordinary, like Meg, who *worked together* with Dave when they had sex and who felt sad sometimes. It still seemed to Nina that Meg was over there with all the other people in the world and she, Nina, was here, alone, drenched in aloneness and specialness. Why did she believe this? Why was this easier to believe?

Meg wrote boring, righteous aerograms, from Paraguay, from Ecuador and Peru, which Nina skimmed. Bus rides, mosquitoes, a lost bag that was found, *phew!!!*, some kind of worm that could burrow *into your skin, don't worry, we don't have them—we're pretty sure anyway!!!!*, jungle, machetes, *this team of volunteers is AMAZING*, blisters, calluses, digging trenches, *these kids have nothing but they're so happy*, the third wall of a schoolhouse built, *this experience is changing me in so many ways, thinking so much, our parents just told us we were wonderful all the time but they never <u>expected</u> anything* (Nina skimmed slower), *you and me and Bam have had barely any guidance, wisdom from elders* (Nina paused to roll her eyes up to the ceiling), *a lot of big feelings, all*

this stuff coming out, I cry every night in our tent but so glad I have Dave, so sweet and loving (Nina rolled her eyes again but out of habit more than anything), *no wonder Bam is so lost, when I have children I am going to make sure to nurture them properly, I will never forget these lessons.*

Nina yawned and skimmed and absorbed the comfort of Meg's words like a cat lying in the sun. She let the aerograms with their rudely torn seals fall between her bed and the wall. She went to her classes, and joined in the big cheap dinners that got cooked in the party house kitchen whenever someone had a bout of domestic enthusiasm, and went to parties and to the pub with her classmates. She continued to sleep with the two boys she was sleeping with at the time—Dave (another Dave; it was a bit weird) the engineer, who never called her but was sometimes just there at the end of a night with too much wax in his hair and a soft grin, and Richie the law student, who called punctually every second Wednesday evening and asked Nina out to see a band on the Friday, and who quite sweetly always had clean sheets on his bed when they went back to his shared flat, and the dirty sheets in a pile that they tripped over sneaking into his room in the dark.

Nina's sexuality went on being a mystical realm of dim looping associations and buried illusions that accommodated her partners while asking almost nothing of them, and true intimacy still seemed to her an impossible ideal. She continued to spend a lot of time glorying in the splendour of her private melancholy, dipping into her secret self, trundling her solipsism round and round, but more and more often this was something that she did distractedly, habitually, like someone tending to a vine that has yielded the best of its fruit and is beginning to fade.

Most significantly, Nina found herself beset by a jangling urge to *make* something. She began to collect from op shops books of a certain type: old and large, with musty covers that were usually of faded red cloth, and pages filled with lists and coloured illustrations. *The Big Book of Did You Know? Animal Kingdoms. Life Among the Incas. Creatures of the Deep.* Back in her room she opened the curtains and the window. She cleared her desk and set out a pile of these books, her metal ruler, a large and sharp pair of scissors stolen from Thornbury, an untouched travel set of watercolours given to her by Robert years earlier. She took an A3 pad of stiff white art paper and cracked it open to the first page.

Nina—despite spending so much time thinking about herself—did not directly notice any of these changes. She did not recognise the part Meg's letters might have played in them. She was only twenty still, and possibly at the height of her flakiness, and this muddling towards self-improvement felt just that: muddled. As if by some external control, the thought What is wrong with you? made regular appearances, along with You are stupid, You are ugly and You deserve to suffer. But if you were to have been there, if you were to have seen Nina walking down Gertrude Street on a weekday afternoon in 1997, in her flannel shirt and jeans, her Doc Martens, her straw-coloured knapsack from the army surplus overfilled with books from the op shop, her soft brown hair flying back in fine curls from her round pale forehead, her moony eyes dreamily preoccupied behind a pair of white plastic sunglasses, you might venture to think that this was a young woman who had found herself a place in the world.

AS NINA GOT OUT OF the car Meg grabbed her wrist. 'I've changed my mind,' she said. 'I don't think you should hitch. It's not safe.'

Nina unzipped the top of her backpack and showed Meg the knife.

'Oh,' said Meg. 'Right.' She squeezed Nina's wrist. Then she landed a hard kiss on her knuckles. 'Oh God,' she said. 'Okay. Okay then. Do you want me to wait with you?'

'You should get back.'

'Okay. See you in three days.'

Nina stood for some time beside the main road, sweating. Brown puddles shone on either side of the tarmac. Every leaf on every branch glittered. The clouds had lifted and the early sky was pale and clear. Across the road the tasselled cane spired, tender green.

Eventually a car came, a station wagon, and Nina put out her thumb and it slowed, splashing, and stopped. She got in the back.

The driver was a stocky man wearing a broken-crowned straw hat and a dirty blue shirt. Beside him in the passenger seat was a very old woman in jeans and a pink top. Her scalp showed through her white hair. She had on a large pair of sunglasses. She didn't turn around.

'What're you doing out here?' said the man, pushing the car up through the gears. He was looking at Nina in the rear-view mirror.

'Oh, I was—I've been staying at this place and . . . My, my friend dropped me here. I just need to get to a town, please.'

'Mossman all right then?'

'Yes, please.'

'Rightio.'

He seemed harmless enough. And the presence of the woman was reassuring. Nina had been holding her backpack in her lap, her fingers on its zip; now she relaxed her hold, slid the bag to the seat beside her.

There was a smell she recognised—what was it? A complicated food smell, cardboardy, stony, but rich also. She looked behind her. The back of the wagon was filled with boxes. Through the holes cut into the tops of them Nina could see dull yellow-grey skins, reptilian, curved.

'Melons?'

'Yep.'

'You grow them?'

'Yep.'

'Any good?'

The woman spoke. 'Us locals like them,' she said, in a quiet, indistinct and dismissive voice, and Nina felt reproved.

They bore on, ripping through sheets of water, joggling over potholes. They crossed the humpbacked bridge and Nina saw how high the creek was below, the streaming dark masses of it rushing crossways. A teetering giddiness hit her and she clutched at the door.

'You right, love?' said the man.

Nina wiped at her upper lip. 'Oh. Yeah. Sorry. I'm fine.' She swallowed and took a deep breath, forced her hands together in her lap.

The skin on the old woman's arm—which rested on the lid of the storage unit behind the gearstick, right in Nina's eye line—was like loose plush fabric, pale and powdery, falling into tucks at the elbow. It quivered with each bump of the car.

The man lit a cigarette and its dry hard smell came to Nina and she welcomed it, took it slowly through her nose. Her heart began to steady. Cigarette-related memories came in a series of bright quick exposures. A daytime backyard party, Nina very small, looking up at a man—grey hair, green jacket, a daisy behind one of his ears—whose large expert fingers did things with paper, filters, curling brown tobacco, and then the pop of the match, the sibilant first draw, the fascination of smoke from nostrils. Outside the milk bar in Thornbury, a low orange car, black seats, an arm along the sill of the opened window, a woman's arm, flabby and tanned, a black t-shirt, sunglasses, brassy hair, ash flicking to the pavement. Deanna Murphy deep in some trees after dark on a school camp, her dirty bent fingers, her sunburned nose in the yellow flare of a lighter. Amber in the backyard of the Thornbury house halfway through a family lunch, ashing mechanically into Gwen's herb pots. Amber arriving at a dinner, late, smoke on her like gauze, issuing theatrical embraces with evasive eyes. Amber in her room at eighteen, during the heroin years, Gwen tapping on the door, calling, *No smoking inside, please, Bam.* Amber walking past the open front window in a black jumper with holes in it, her hair limp, her colourless lips yanking at a cigarette, pacing the yard, waiting for someone: a boyfriend, a dealer . . . Amber, Amber, Amber—yes, Amber, thoughts of Amber, up they came with the kick of the smoke, fast and sore and multitudinous—but (Nina squeezed her hands) surely there was more, surely she, Nina, had something for herself!

Outside the 7-Eleven near her old flat, rushing for the bus on a rainy spring morning, the mouth of a laneway, paling fences, someone's left-behind smoke sliding under the woody branches of an overhanging fig tree. Inside bars when you could smoke in bars, tables wet with slopped beer, the damp of the bar mat, green hanging lights over pool tables. Dancing in bars, dancing at parties, how it felt—oh, precious thing!—to be just one dancing body in a group of dancing bodies. Walking home from the bus stop after work on a Thursday, thinking of Luke, their evening ahead, passing a bar, people smoking outside, streetlights coming on, seeming to float, black shapes of cars and buildings against a tender pink sky. Tying her coat outside a shop window, a woman in a headscarf against a wall, the tough quick wink of her dark eye, her salute to Nina, the smell of the cigarette between the woman's short, strong fingers and the smell of coffee from an open cafe door, the smell of pastries, the smell of a wet winter road . . .

Nina looked out at the cane fields, the purple mountains, the washed-clean sky. She had existed beyond this moment in the car with the melons and the man's eyes in the mirror and the old woman's arm. She, Nina, had existed beyond the white house, the verandah and the dark kitchen and the forest and the terrible apartment below, where Amber moaned and wailed in the dusty fetid air. There was more to her—surely there was more.

In Mossman there were a few stalls set up outside the stone church, in the dappled shade of the huge and graceful trees. Tables had been erected; plastic chairs were occupied by large women in loose bright dresses. Close now, Nina saw that the trunks and branches of the trees were covered in green fur— other plants, small, somewhere between ferns and mosses, with long fringes of thready roots. Spots of sun leaped back and forth across the brilliant tablecloths, the cellophane-wrapped packages of coconut ice, the white and baby-blue teddy bears stuck, stiff-armed, into small wicker baskets. A headache slipped behind Nina's eyes.

The melon farmer and his sour companion had a table waiting for them—the woman went directly to the chair behind it and sat, inscrutable in her sunglasses; the man lugged boxes and opened them, produced a white plastic chopping board and a large knife, sliced a melon and arranged the slices on a green enamel plate with his large, work-blackened fingers.

'Can—can I help?' ventured Nina, but he didn't respond. Perhaps he hadn't heard her.

Nina moved away from them, in particular from the stern and impenetrable lenses of the woman's sunglasses. She stood under the woolly lower branches of one of the trees and drank the last of Meg's bottle of water. Her bladder throbbed. Her headache was layered, glassy.

There were only ten or so people outside the church—and perhaps five of those were vendors. Not one of them had once looked directly at Nina, but when she walked away, across the road and towards the hooded facade of the enormous pub, she imagined that she could feel many eyes following.

She passed, on the other side of the road, a petrol station and a cafe, both with the name Raintrees. Were they raintrees then, those trees? Such a beautiful name, and they were beautiful, Nina found them beautiful still in their grace, the elegant reach of those long branches, but the clinging mossy ferny stuff had unnerved her. She thought of the childhood visit to the Victorian country town with its chalky and dark brown colours—a chilly memory with Vermeer-like clarity—and the humping dog, the soft nap of its ears, the realisation, the stepping back, the ugly and muddy sense of betrayal, of foolishness, of shame.

At the far end of the front bar of the pub, two men in shorts and singlets sat looking up at a television screen. They glanced at Nina for only a moment. Nina followed the LADIES sign and went to the toilet, which was clean and cool, and then she went back and waited at the other end of the bar, drinking water from a plastic pot glass, until a woman appeared and took forty dollars in cash from her for one night in a single room.

She felt saturated with exhaustion. The pain in her head moved in skating waves and she dropped below it into sleep. She slept and woke and slept and woke, lying on the bed in her clothes, and then it was late in the day.

The room had thin walls, painted a silvery blue. There were the smells of air-freshening spray, which made her throat prickle, and bulk laundry detergent and old cigarette smoke and—from the big kitchen she'd glimpsed downstairs, presumably—the soaked-in smell of thousands of past lardy meals. Despair pinned her to the bed. From the window that opened onto the balcony a curtain puffed in. It was made from a strange synthetic crimson fabric, like a cape worn by a child in a school play.

What was she supposed to do? Her mind made useless weak gnawing motions.

The air outside was dimming. Orange lights were coming on. Below her the pub shifted its energy, gathered itself for the evening. Voices began to sound, doors to open and close; somewhere there commenced the humming of a machine.

Get up.

She heaved herself like a recuperating patient from the bed to the small upright chair in the corner and sat looking past the ballooning curtain at the curved back of a white plastic garden seat that was on the balcony, and the mauve and green and peach of the sky beyond. At least the headache had passed. In the street below someone called out what sounded like, 'Mitchell, ya fucken arse rat.'

Nina folded herself over her thighs and reached for her sandals.

She sat in the dining room, alone at a table for two, her mouth flooding at the smells of hot grease and salt. There were three other groups, all families and clearly tourists. Unlike the locals at the market they did not hesitate to glance openly at Nina, and smile, some of them. They were all busy with things—a Japanese father and son leaned together over the bright oblong of a smartphone; a pair of middle-aged women, too far away for Nina to hear what language they were speaking but whom she decided for some reason were Germans, took turns reading aloud from sightseeing pamphlets while the three adolescents with them sat, heads down, their thumbs flickering over the keypads of their phones; on the third and last table a woman whose appearance suggested no particular nationality to Nina peered at the small display of a digital camera, jerking it sideways each time a large-eared boy of about ten, leaning into her, made a grab for it. Across from them an older woman read a newspaper.

Nina wished that she'd brought down a book, then remembered that she hadn't packed one. Then she remembered that she still needed to charge her phone. What messages might be on it? Would Gwen or Robert have realised that all three of their daughters, while on their 'holiday', had inexplicably gone off-grid? This was difficult to know. If Gwen's message was anything to go by, there was no expectation of contact. *Dad and I'll look forward to hearing all about it when you get back.* But that was how things were between Nina and her parents; she couldn't speculate as to what the situation might be for Amber or for Meg. She assumed that Amber would be the one whom Gwen and Robert called most often, to check on her. And Meg was probably the one who called them, to check on them. It was possible that over the past few days they'd tried to call at least one daughter and failed to get through, and were worried. Should she do something about this? Call them? But what would she say? She'd either have to lie—which she wasn't sure she could manage—or get them involved.

At this, her swimming, weak feeling made an appearance. *Infirm* was the word for it; she felt infirm. She cast around for distractions. A blackboard on the wall near the stairs was inscribed with a curly *Welcome!* and, under that, *$10 parma Tuesday's, kid's meal's half price Fri and Sat.* The appearance of the dour teenaged waitress was a relief. Nina ordered the fish. She sat looking down at her hands for a while. The strange awareness came to her that she didn't know what day it was. She got up and went to the toilet, passing the table with the newspaper-reading woman, but didn't get a good enough look to see the date.

In the bathroom with its square deco tiles the colour of old bone knife-handles she forced herself to think. It'd been a Friday when they left Melbourne—which felt like an aeon ago—and so Saturday had been the day of the stabbing, the trip to hospital, and then Sunday—yesterday—was the rain and Amber reappearing and then running off again downstairs with Meg, and so today was Monday. Monday, 18 May. Only four days had passed. Nina stood up and flushed, and from between the glass slats of the high narrow louvred window a breath of warm air came down, and the scent of muddy river banks.

The fish arrived. It was battered, with chips and a coil of viscous tartare. Nina realised that she had been supposed to order salad or greens separately. It was too late; the waitress plonked down the plate and strode away, her t-shirt straining, the gap between it and her black leggings showing a band of young and marbly flesh. Nina surrendered and ate the food. It was oily and hot and filling.

When she'd finished she paid and went out into the street, which was empty. The silty river air moved in bands over the black road. Fixed above the door behind her was a bug zapper, its light sizzling blue; every now and then an insect exploded itself on it with loud violence.

She went into the front bar. It was full of men. Some ignored her; others stared. As she crossed the room there seemed to be a palpable change in the atmosphere: a general tightening of awareness, almost a bristling. On a high screen muscled male forms ran and leaped over lurid grass. By the pool table there was a bellow of rude laughter. Nina felt, more strongly than at any other time in her life, the tremendous and unjust responsibility put onto a woman by a roomful of men.

She ordered a glass of white wine and sat at a small table too close to the television to watch it without craning her neck ridiculously. This was a mistake; she had nothing to do, nowhere to look. In desperation she got out her wallet and pretended to sort through the sheaf of receipts it held, some of them so old they were falling apart. Her hands were shaking. Was she imagining it, this sense of simmering threat? Dreadful thoughts came into her mind. This isn't some wine bar in North Carlton, you idiot. This isn't a gallery opening or a book launch.

She kept her head down. She gulped at the yellow wine, which scoured her throat. A hum started at the base of her skull. Savagely she shoved the receipts back into her wallet. What did she want? A man to obliterate her? Was that why she'd come in here like a fool, alone in her thin cotton dress with her bare city legs and her soft arms and her nipples standing out like two miniature terrified headlights? Did she want to go to the next level—past the moment of the dangling maiden in the painting, the gripping of flesh in powerful arms? Did she want a man to finish her off at last?

Something fell away, a curtain of delusion, and she saw that all along she'd been barely dabbling—that her affairs had always been safe; that somehow, despite feeling like a helpless object, she had never allowed herself to be truly debased. She did not know what that felt like. Disregarded, forsaken, used—these she knew. But she did not know debasement. She did not know violence.

'Excuse me,' said a voice, and Nina lurched to her feet, bumping the table. For long moments the empty wineglass hung at an impossible angle until a man's hand appeared, square and freckled, with blunt wide nails, and caught it, set it safely upright.

Nina saw blue work pants, a collared synthetic t-shirt of the kind worn by tradies and council workers. She saw a young, friendly and confused face, an eyebrow piercing, ginger hair. The man was holding out a slip of paper—one of her receipts. 'You dropped this.'

She snatched it, muttered, 'Thanks,' and rushed from the room, skidding in her sandals as she swung the heavy door, knocking an elbow. Were they laughing, behind her? Were they shaking their heads at the craziness of women? Was the ginger-haired guy dropping his gaze and blushing as another man, in a low voice, said something foul?

She ran, jangling with fear, up the empty stairs and along the empty corridor and into her room. She checked that the door was locked. It seemed very insubstantial, that door—as thin as cardboard, the lock a tinny button on the round aluminium knob. She put the chair against it. Tangling herself in the curtain, she closed and locked the window. She took the knife from her bag and sat on the bed holding it.

Amber had asked Meg to tie her up.

Amber had agreed to being tied up.

Had she?

How could you tell?

Why, thought Nina, didn't I ask Meg for the details? What exactly did Amber agree to? Being tied up for three full days? For Meg to ignore all pleas, all threats, all terrible moans and wails?

But if Amber had agreed. If there was an agreement . . .

What if it worked?

A motorbike passed, down in the street. From the direction of the river came the shriek of a bird. The knife handle was sweaty.

What if Amber wouldn't eat or drink? What if she refused even water?

Could someone die, in three days, without water?

Would Meg force water into her—tip it down her throat?

How could you—how could Meg—tend to someone who was fighting, who was wailing, whose wrists and ankles were rubbing raw under their ties, who begged you to undo the ties, who sobbed, 'Please, please, I've changed my mind'? How could you grip the chin of this person (your sister, your little sister) in your fingers and put a cup to the blistered lips and slosh out water against the side-to-side jerking, the resistance?

No—a revision. Meg couldn't hold Amber's chin with one hand while forcing water into her mouth with the other. Meg only had one hand.

Would she do it while Amber was asleep? Wet the corner of a clean cloth, perhaps, and squeeze drops between Amber's dry, parted lips?

Was she sleeping, Amber? Could she sleep?

Oh God, don't forget to give her water, Meg!

Meg would not forget. Meg would never forget.

How do you, with only one hand, sponge piss and shit off someone's (your little sister's) skinny white thighs, someone's (your sister's!) buttocks, someone's (Amber's!) private parts, her genitals, her anus?

Should I, thought Nina, go back?

The red curtain hung as if made of lead. Her fingers on the knife were cramping; she changed hands.

But what, thought Nina, can I do? I'm not useful, I can't help. I don't have Meg's strength.

She sat with her back to the wall, her neck stiffening, changing the knife from hand to hand. She was too afraid to leave the room and go down the hall to the toilet, and after a while she urinated into the plastic rubbish bin. The air in the room was a dark orangey blue. Every now and then the voices of men rose from the street below—men leaving the front bar, men driving or walking away into the night. The building went into a deeper quiet. She fell asleep and jumped awake to the scream of the river bird. The knife was beside her on top of the covers. The tightness in her neck felt electric. She lay down, put the knife on the bedside table, and rode the waves of sucking sleep and jerking, rigid wakefulness until a copper disc of sun showed through the crimson curtain and the burr of a vacuum cleaner rose from a lower floor.

NINA FINISHED HER BACHELOR'S DEGREE with honours and, since there didn't seem to be anything better to do with her time, went on to do a master's. Compulsively, and with no ambition whatsoever, she continued to make art, filling cardboard boxes with stiff collages and wavery watercolours, and notebooks with sketches and poetry. These she did not speak of, and showed to nobody. On a regular basis she racked herself with the fraught intensity of a new sex affair and then was filled with an exhausted relief when it burned itself out. She turned twenty-two, then twenty-three. Her melancholy was at times as sharp and sweet as ever, but not always—more often now it had a dragging, almost chore-like quality.

Visits to Thornbury, to Robert and Gwen, had changed.

'Now,' said Robert, leaning close, eyes round behind his glasses, hands clasped, 'how *are* you?'

And Nina experienced a kind of haste, an urgency, to account for herself, how busy she was, all of the things she was studying, reading, the films she'd watched, exhibitions she'd been to. She became mired in detail; she went on and on. One evening, after dinner, she found herself describing a documentary she'd seen about young men competing for college basketball scholarships in America. There was only Robert listening—Gwen was washing the dishes and neither Meg nor Amber was there (off getting pregnant; off getting drugs). She was bored, telling him—she had no interest in basketball, the doco had gone for close to three hours, and she had been bored watching it—but it just kept coming out, her description, filling the room, filling the time with Robert and the space between them. 'And then the other guy, whose name I can't remember,' she said, 'he went to Boston, he had to raise all the money for it.' There was a jammed feeling in her head, a pressure, but on she went. 'And the first game, he fell and hurt his knee.' Her voice in her own ears was loud and irritating. She looked over and saw that Robert was asleep.

There was, of course, Amber somewhere—everywhere—in this. Amber and heroin, because heroin was happening now. Doors were kept closed. Gwen, fast-blinking, seemed always to be listening for something. Robert asked so earnestly how Nina was but then before she even began to answer he sagged back into the couch cushions with his eyes closed.

Nina did not understand her own behaviour, this new talkativeness, this bluster. She did not recognise that what she was doing was a response to Robert's weariness and Gwen's fearful vigilance. She was just compelled to do it, to perform something, an assurance, a cover-up, a distraction. It did not come naturally to her. It made her feel wrung out and faintly angry. She visited her parents less and less often.

Away from her family, though, she went on almost thriving. She had years earlier left the sandwich place and got the jobs at the bookshop and the gallery. She was able to recognise that she was getting too old for the party house, and moved out of it and into the one-bedroom flat. The men who she had sex affairs with were getting older and wealthier. She was now in the realm of lingerie and hotel rooms, which at times made her feel mature and mysterious and at others more helpless and lost than ever before.

A job came up, at the university. Tutoring undergraduates. It was nearly the end of first semester, a sapphire of a cloudless Melbourne winter day. Brassy cold sunlight hit the glass doors at the end of the corridor. Nina, standing at the noticeboard, felt an unexpected resolve come over her.

She went further into the building, around a corner. There was the smell of instant coffee, of packet soup and photocopiers. She knew he was gone—he'd left the university years before. She knew that, but still.

The door was open. Nobody was in the room. There were the grey carpet tiles, the same ones. There was the brown stain. There were the desk and shelves—probably the same ones, although who knew. The shelves had more books on them now. A pot plant stood on the corner of the desk nearest the window, a low nest of strappy leaves out of which stuck, as if bashfully proud, stems of little, hard-looking flowers. Beside the computer lay a pair of glasses with heavy black frames. Nina inhaled. Potting mix. A woman's perfume—citrusy, light. Pencil shavings.

She got the job. In her first class a brash girl with green dreadlocks and a big, pierced nose volunteered to read one of Elizabeth Barrett Browning's 'Sonnets from the Portuguese'. The girl, with her precarious bravado, started off too quickly, steamrolling the first stanzas, giving honky emphasis to odd words. She stumbled at '*sepulchral*', grimaced, flushed, bore on. Someone yawned.

Nina looked around the room. There were only eight students, but together they seemed a mass. A sallow, plump girl did not appear to be listening at all but instead regarded with sideways bitterness the dreadlocked girl's fake-fur coat, her low-cut top, her high, tight cleavage. Two boys sat as if waiting for a bus. Another person, with dyed-black hair and a great deal of silver jewellery, met Nina's eyes with an undiagnosable blankness. Nina imagined that she could sense agendas, complexities: youthful pride, comparisons, jockeying. Shit, she thought, I can't handle these people.

But then her eyes fell on a pale, thickset boy with ginger hair and acne scars who was leaning forward, elbows on knees, not looking at the dreadlocked girl but listening, hard, his lips parted.

By now the girl had steadied. She'd slowed. She was noticing the words. '*And how the red wild sparkles*,' she read, and the consonants popped and thudded.

A tension ebbed. Something else came into the room, an eddying interest, a potential. The ginger boy closed his eyes, raised his rapt face. The bus-stop boys blinked and turned their heads.

Thank God, thought Nina.

'. . . *those laurels*,' read the girl, who had forgotten to be self-important,

O My beloved, will not shield thee so,
That none of all the fires shall scorch and shred
The hair beneath. Stand further off then! Go.

A hush. Slowly, the ginger boy opened his eyes. The dreadlocked girl lowered her book, looked to Nina, grinned.

The sallow girl twisted in her seat. 'I love that poem,' she blurted. 'I've read it before.'

Nobody responded. The bus-stop boys were looking at Nina. The ginger boy's face shone with blissful readiness. The dreadlocked girl had gone back to the words on the page and was silently moving her lips.

'I love that poem,' said the other girl again, muttering this time, and frowning into her lap.

She was retreating. The bus-stop boys wouldn't wait for long.

'What,' said Nina, trying to catch her gaze, 'do you love about it?'

The sallow girl squinted at the ceiling. Her voice was raw and proud. 'I love how it's beautiful, but it's kind of . . . dangerous, too.'

A dreadful, gaping moment. Nina's heart banged. Would they all just leave her there, hanging? Would someone *laugh*?

And then: 'Yes!' the ginger boy burst out. 'That's exactly it!'

Nina understood then that this was going to work—this class, and others, in the future.

And later, back at her flat, having fallen straight into bed, buzzing, she understood something else. She thought of the sallow girl, her twisting, her muttering and frowning—the difficulty, the *ugliness* it took, for some people to come forward. It was so difficult, for some people, so ugly—and it was also possible.

The affair with Luke was no different from any of the others, in the beginning. They met at the gallery, which was where Nina met a lot of men. She worked there two afternoons a week sitting the exhibitions, and she worked the opening nights, pouring drinks and washing glasses. Luke was there at one of the openings. He was like any of the others, smiling, watching, asking her some inane question through the blizzard of shouted conversations as she refilled his drink. At the end, when almost everyone was gone, he came back and wanted to know when she knocked off, and she suggested he wait at a bar around the corner. She put away the last of the glasses and fixed her hair in the mirror above the sink, and then went out through the wide white room, waving goodbye to her boss, Wendy, who was leaning at the desk in her big purple-framed glasses, the artist drunk and happy beside her. Nina went to the bar and Luke was waiting. They had three drinks each and then they went to her place and had sex, and then he left. And, as she suspected he probably would, he turned up at the gallery the next week to say awkwardly that he'd like to see her again, and she gave him her number but he didn't give her his.

This was all fairly normal. Nina went into it wearing her usual cloak of self-delusion. It was remarkable how many of the men actually said to her, just as the anthropology tutor had all those years ago, *There's something special about you.* Those exact words. It was also remarkable how good this now made Nina feel. She had long since left behind the dreadful, lonely revulsion of that first time, when she'd imagined telling Hannah or Pip and laughing—aghast, incredulous. Now, despite having gained a comprehensive understanding of just how untrue the statement was, Nina received it with guilty, covert eagerness and squirrelled it away. The thrill she got from it—at the time, hearing it said, and also later, replaying it in her mind—was grubby and tenuous and lonely, but it was a thrill nonetheless.

Luke called her once a week and arranged for them to meet on a Thursday or Friday evening. At first they met at a bar, but before long he began coming directly to her flat with a bottle of wine. When they had sex it was very similar to all the other times. Nina put herself into certain positions, certain poses, and watched herself through lowered eyelashes. She paid little attention to Luke's body, allowing into focus only the parts of it that touched or penetrated hers. In her mind she went to where her pleasure lived, to swim in semi-darkness through its fluid, illogical layers, riding currents that might open into oblique, capricious orgasms, so liminal and arbitrary that they seemed fortunate, gift-like.

Luke was not slick. He did not give Nina flowers or lingerie. He did not book rooms at fancy hotels. The wine he brought to her flat was cheap. At first Nina felt some irritation at this—she had become accustomed to certain gestures, certain formalities, and even if she didn't like the things men gave her (and she rarely did) she felt entitled to them. They were a part of the deal. Luke didn't seem to understand what the deal was. He seemed to think that all he had to do was show up, as if there was enough value in them just being together, having sex. And in a way there was—it was enough, just, for Nina to have him want her. She wasn't sure if it was insulting that he dispensed with the illusions of gifts and hotel rooms and fantastical promises, or a welcome respite from the emptiness, the falseness, of these.

The other thing that was different about Luke in those early months was simply that he didn't put an end to things. He did not make himself any more available, but neither did he go away. He kept on calling, kept on turning up on those Thursday or Friday evenings with his crappy wine. Nina waited for the inevitable fade—the waning calls, the diminishment of time, attention, lust—but it didn't happen. There was a tension building, though, and at around the ten-week mark Luke, lying in Nina's bed one Thursday night, began to cry.

Ah, thought Nina. Of course. The signs had all been there. He didn't give her his number. He barely spoke about his own life. Nina didn't even know where he lived, which suburb—and something had prevented her from asking.

There had been one other affair before Luke in which the man had turned out to be married. The night that man cried was the last night Nina saw him. The crying had been preceded by a wholehearted abandonment to the physical, by the most frantic, the most desperate, needy sex, and by wordless heartfelt embraces laden with a sense of finality. (Tick, she thought, lying next to Luke.) And then, later—after the crying—had come the talking.

Luke cried for a short while into Nina's hair, snuffling and apologising, and then he untangled his body from hers and said, 'Can we talk about something?'

Here we go, thought Nina. Out loud she said, 'Of course,' trying not to sigh.

'I'm . . .'

'Married?'

'I'm so sorry I didn't tell you. I thought it would scare you off, and I—'

'Don't worry about it.'

As if he had prepared this speech, Luke went on. 'I've been married for ten years. Since I was twenty-five.'

This was very much on track. The other man, on that final night, had talked about his marriage. He had told Nina how long he'd been married and the names of his children and their ages—and probably some other things about them too, but Nina hadn't been listening. The man had cried again, a bit, with a kind of deliciousness, a luxury, telling her how much he loved the children. And then that man had said that he 'couldn't keep doing this'. He'd risen from this last session, his face wet and bright, brimming—Nina could see it—with a renewed energy, a freshness, a clarity. He even said thank you, his moist eyes lit with thoughtless, overflowing bonhomie. And then he left, and Nina felt like a rag.

But Nina was distracted from this bleak reminiscence. Married at twenty-five—that was out of the ordinary. Twenty-five was very young; it was not much older than Nina was, and despite the cynical and experienced persona she adopted when with men Nina was aware of her own youth, her immaturity. For the first time she felt a small amount of genuine interest in Luke.

'Twenty-five?' she said. 'That's young.'

'We'd only just started going out, and she got pregnant. Sarah, her name is.' (This was new; the other man had not told Nina the name of his wife.) 'She's—wonderful. A wonderful person. But we'd never have stayed together if it wasn't for the kids.'

Nina's curiosity slid away again. It was the same old story, just with an earlier starting point.

Luke continued. 'We've got two kids. Skye, she's the older one, the baby we got married for. And Millie is our second daughter, and she's profoundly disabled. She has global disabilities, cognitive and motor. Do you want me to explain what that means, in her case?'

Nina snapped back to attention. 'Oh,' she said. 'Okay. Yes.'

He wasn't crying anymore. Nina couldn't see his face in the darkness, but he sounded calmly determined. He had planned what he was going to say, she was sure of it.

'Well,' he said, 'Millie can't speak, or walk, or move at all. She can hear, but we don't know how much she understands. She does react—she smiles, she cries. She's like a newborn baby, really, in this body that just keeps growing.'

'How old is she now?'

'She's seven.'

'And can she . . . Will she ever . . .?'

'No. She'll always need this much care. She has a tracheostomy, a tube in her throat. One of us has to sleep in the room with her every night in case it gets blocked.'

'Oh.' Nina's cynical, Jean Rhys persona had been whisked away like a bandaid and she felt young and selfish and keenly aware of the fact that she had not so far in her life known any sort of deep suffering. 'That must be . . .'

'It's really not that bad,' said Luke. 'Sarah and I get along really well, and we love the girls, and our values are the same, when it comes to Millie and what we want for her. But we don't have sex. We rarely even touch. We're like cousins or some-thing. We work together, doing this job of raising a family. I will never'—his voice lost its steadiness for a moment—'do anything to hurt Sarah or the girls. Never. But I'm so lonely. You might not believe me, but I haven't done this before. That first night, when I asked you what time you finished, I didn't even know I was going to do that.'

'I believe you.' This was true. She had no real reason for believing him, but she did.

'Look. Nina.' He shifted higher on the pillows, turned towards her. She could see his outline against the drawn blind, his shoulder, his head. 'I—'

'I know.' She tried to summon her old persona, the anodyne receiver of endings, easily accepting, disengaged. She could pretty much do it in her sleep, and she was fairly sure that her voice sounded right. But the unsettled, abraded feeling was still there. She was glad for the darkness.

'Really?' He gave a small, embarrassed-sounding laugh. 'What do you know?'

'That you can't do this anymore. That you have to stop seeing me.'

There was a pause. Nina began to feel irritated. Come on, she thought. Get on with it.

'Actually,' Luke said quietly, 'that wasn't what I was going to say. I don't want to stop seeing you. I was going to say that I want to keep seeing you. If that's what you want. But I need to be clear. I won't change my life with Sarah and the girls. This would be, you know, just a sex thing.' He clicked his tongue, reached for her hand under the sheet. 'That sounds terrible, sorry. I didn't mean it to sound that way. I really like you. It would be more than sex. For me, anyway. It already is. But it could only ever be this much *time*, one night a week.'

Nina was receding into one of her freak-outs. Her ears got hot and her head thickened, and Luke seemed to shrink and shoot off into the distance. This had never happened before. Nobody (as far as Nina knew) had ever wanted to go on seeing her. Nobody (as far as she could recall) had ever brought up the matter of what she might or might not want.

'Just to be clear. I would not expect any commitment from you. In terms of seeing other people or whatever.' He squeezed her hand. 'Are you okay? I'm sorry, is this upsetting you?'

'No,' said Nina faintly, reflexively.

'Do you want to think about it?' He got out of the bed and went into the kitchen–living area of the flat. He switched the light on. After a minute he switched it off again and came back. He sat on the edge of the bed and began to get dressed. 'I've written down my number for you,' he said. 'It's my number at work, my direct line.'

Nina lay, numb and speechless.

When he had finished with his clothes Luke stood up. 'One more thing,' he said. 'This is okay with Sarah. She actually suggested it. She said, Do what you have to do, just be discreet.'

'She suggested it?' Nina's voice sounded rusty.

'Not—not *you* specifically. Just in general. There was a time when, you know, I'd want to be physical and she didn't want it and it was making us both unhappy. It was hard for her, I could tell, but she did suggest it.'

After he left, Nina waited for the numbness to lift, and then she put on the light and sat up in bed and finished the wine that was still in her glass on the bedside table. She pushed back the sheet and looked down at herself, arranged her legs to their best effect, touched the skin over her stomach. She tweaked up her nipples. She ran her fingers through her hair. It was only ten o'clock. She got up and put on her robe, went to the kitchen to make some toast. On the bench, on the back of an unopened electricity bill, was Luke's name and number. His writing was stupid, big and clumsy; he'd written his name all in capitals. Nina ripped the envelope open and pulled out the bill. She dropped the empty envelope into the bin.

Two days later she took it out again and called him.

SHE SAT AT A PLASTIC table outside Raintrees Cafe, her backpack at her feet, drinking a bad coffee in a tall glass with a metal handle that dug into her fingers. Before her a nibbled danish lay on a plate, its yolk of apricot crazily bright. It had been twenty-four hours since she'd stood on the verge of the brown muddy road and watched Meg drive back towards the property.

Sweetwater. Named for the creek, presumably. But the water in that creek, while clear and pure and cold, was not sweet—it had been, if anything, slightly stony, mineral. Nina licked her lips, tasting floury custard. 'Sweetwater' made her think first of dewdrops, of the petals of a rose, or the dark spear-shaped leaves and intensely scented small tight buds of a daphne bush, dripping after rain. Delicate, pretty things that belonged to nature. But then, as she took another sip of weak burnt coffee, less wholesome associations began to arise. Sweetmeats. What *were* they? Offal? Was she imagining that? An illustration, greyscale, crosshatched: a Dickensian scene, a cobbled marketplace, barrows of produce, milk in barrels, live poultry in wicker cages, a fat, aproned vendor with a tray. She stopped there, unable to picture the actual sweetmeats. Or: lolly water. Viscous chemical syrup that dilated the pupils and flushed the cheeks and rotted the teeth of children. Unwholesome things to eat and drink, things that were bad for you, that made you sick. Or—here came another iteration, another riff—potions, nectars, ambrosia. A vial held to the lips of a reclining invalid, a fading waif, or clutched by a mad-eyed seeker of visions, an opium-eater.

Nina shifted in her seat, looked out from under the tin overhang of the cafe's verandah at the saturated colours of the late Mossman morning. The sky was deeply blue, the sunlight flooding and yellow. The roads and buildings seemed to only just be holding back the growth—everywhere vegetation banked and reached and loomed, pressing, insistent, glaringly green. Even here the birds and insects kept up their eternal droning. Further on from Nina, just before the bridge, a ute had pulled over; a skinny-legged man in thongs and shorts leaned against it, his arms folded over a small belly, his face hidden by a cap and sunglasses. Along the far footpath walked, haltingly, a small cluster of tourists in clean, colourful clothing.

She had not come up with a plan. Last night's terror had receded but she felt fogged and listless, at the mercy of great, jaw-cracking yawns. The more she tried to rouse herself, to take action, the further she seemed to sink into apathy. She had left the hotel at ten without paying for a second night, even though she did not know of anywhere else in the town to stay. She had not made any attempt to get hold of a charger for her mobile, or used a payphone to contact her parents. The only person she had spoken to in fifteen hours was the woman behind the counter of the cafe. This woman, tall, with a craggy face and thin black hair pulled into a plastic butterfly clip, had treated Nina with the same sort of indirectness as the people at the market the day before, not making eye contact, not acknowledging Nina's order, and accepting Nina's money with an accidental-seeming movement of her hand, as if brushing away some crumbs. Nina, going outside to take her seat, had wondered if her breakfast would even arrive—and indeed, when it did, the woman put it down in front of her as if only momentarily relieving herself of it, as if once she'd finished clearing plates from the other tables she might come back again and take it away.

Nina took a bite of danish, and flakes fluttered to her lap, and left grease spots when she tried to brush them off. An incommensurate amount of anger rose. You are stupid, she thought. You are ugly. You deserve to suffer.

These thoughts weren't new, of course. They were very familiar. They had appeared on countless occasions. On the doorstep of the anthropology tutor's brown-painted house. On the empty tram looking out at the closed shops of Smith Street. In the cobwebby bedroom of the party house. In the bedroom of her tired flat.

Shut up, Nina thought. This is not about you—you're supposed to be thinking of Amber, and Meg, and what to do.

She got up, and began to walk. There was nowhere to go. Past the church and the bridge was just the grey road that led north, through cane fields and past tracts of forest; in the other direction was the pub, the school, a few other shops, and then a stretch of houses that led to, just visible in the distance, the giant harsh rectangle of Woolworths. Beneath her apathy, her sluggishness, there was the sense of a great emptiness, a gaping void. It was terrifying. Nobody was going to come. Nobody was going to approach her and tell her what to do.

A little further on from the cafe, in the direction of the bridge, was a bench. She went and sat on it. There was no shade, and within moments she was sweating. She wiped at her upper lip and squinted at the ground. Cracks in the pavement. Weeds. A throbbing was starting in her temples.

Okay, so it was down to her. She was the only person in the world who knew what was going on, what Meg had done.

She had forgotten to bring her sunglasses; she put her elbows on her knees and made a visor with her hands to shield her eyes.

She had two basic choices: undermine Meg, or go along with her plan.

How could she undermine Meg?

Call Gwen and Robert.

Go to the cops.

Go to the hospital?

Go back. Hitch and walk. Hide and watch. Wait for Meg to go upstairs and then sneak in and free Amber, get her out of the room. Stand with Amber beside the car. Two against one.

What if she went along with Meg's plan?

Three days. That meant staying here tonight and then tomorrow night. And then going back. That was the deal.

Then what? The worst would be over, Meg had said. But assuming the worst really was over, what was supposed to come next? The 'consolidation'? The days of yoga and Scrabble and walks, of herbal tea and nutritious meals, the three of them together?

What transformation was supposed to be taking place during these three days? What sort of a person was Amber supposed to turn into, to be, once untied? Subdued, gentle, obliging? But Amber had never been gentle or obliging—Amber who rolled in the red dust in her blue shorts, chubby and wild; Amber who put her hand over Gwen's eyes as Gwen reverse-parked the car; Amber who rubbed the wet flesh of strawberries onto her face and gazed off humming in the middle of conversations and vanished from family dinners and 'fell' loudly out of her bunk, cackling, after lights out when they were supposed to be quiet. She had been subdued, Nina supposed, after the car-boot episode, when she wouldn't speak or get out of bed. She'd been subdued then, and gentle (although not obliging). But surely nobody had thought that a good or healthy version of Amber.

That breakdown—because that's what it was, a breakdown— had been brought on by imprisonment, confinement. Amber was locked in the boot and left there, alone, for hours. Meg knew this. Meg had been the one to hold this event up, to draw attention to it—Meg had been the one to use the word 'trauma'. And yet here she was, intentionally bringing about the same situation. Locking Amber up. Ignoring her pleas.

Nina remembered Meg putting Amber in that cubbyhouse, in that long-ago winter-time park, drab green, smelling of possums and peppercorn tree sap. She remembered Meg's words after- wards, when she knelt and held out her arms. *You're a good girl, Bam. You did as you were told.* She remembered Meg in the kitchen at the Thornbury house when Amber was lying mute in the bedroom—Meg, tall and stern, her arms folded: *I'm going to take her.*

Meg took Amber then, when Amber was subdued and gentle—when she was weak and traumatised—and did what to her? Moulded her, trained her, to 'do as she was told', to 'be a good girl'?

She's not, thought Nina, going to turn into the person you want, Meg. Even if she gets clean.

What did a clean Amber even look like? Could such a person exist?

Meg, the night before last, in the candlelight, under the din of the rain: *We want to help you get back to being the real you.*

And Amber with her lowered gaze, her barely there whisper: *Can you remember that person?*

Who was the 'real' Amber, and when had she been lost? At eighteen, when the heroin started in earnest? At fourteen, when she had the breakdown?

What did Meg really think lay at the end of this whole process? After the imprisonment, the ignoring of pleas, after the eventual release, the rebuilding, the 'consolidation'. Amber cured? Docile, transformed? Who exactly did Meg think would emerge from the ashes of Amber's detox?

Amber sitting on the metal steps in the white sun, in clean clothes, her body easy, settled, her face calm. Her skin clear, the veins in her forearms no longer ropy and damaged, her scars erased. Not the 'real' Amber, the 'old' Amber, whoever that was, but a new Amber. A different person.

The pounding in Nina's head increased. She felt nauseous.

But Amber had recovered, all those years ago, when she'd gone to Meg's. She'd got up, and eaten, and started to speak. That had been under Meg's care, with Meg's help. And—if Meg was to be believed—Amber had asked for it again, that help, once she'd become a thin-faced junkie. She'd knelt on the bathroom floor, holding Meg by the legs, and begged. *Take me somewhere. Lock me in a room. And no matter what I say, what I do, don't let me out of there.*

Was Amber herself enslaved to this all-or-nothing fantasy of transformation? Of course she was—wouldn't that lie somewhere at the heart of her addiction, her shame-laden hopelessness: the idea that the person she was, the junkie, the liar, the thief, would, in order to change, to recover, need to become a completely different person?

Were they all—Meg, Nina, Amber too—like Angus Black's parents, mourning and longing for a chimera, a symbol of unrecoverable purity?

Under the sun, under the visor of her hands, to the queasy rhythm of her own overheated pulse, Nina at last came to a half-grasped realisation. There was no 'real' Amber—no Amber from 'before'. There was only Amber now. There was Amber laughing in the car on that first day when they drove from Cairns up the coast. There was Amber exclaiming over the warm air as they got out of the car in that velvet early dark, with the stars in layers and the carpet of lawn deepest green-black. This Amber, with her grey teeth and hard face, with her trembling hands and her scars, was capable of lightness. This Amber was able to laugh and to feel the air, to do these things unguardedly, openly, beside her sisters. In the car Meg had been laughing too. Meg and Amber laughing in the front and Nina in the back hiding secret tears of hope behind her sunglasses. They had been close then, the three of them, together in that moment of lightness, and the Amber who was there, an equal third, had not been clean.

Nina got up from the bench and moved clumsily, dark spots spangling her vision, towards a fence, trees, shade. She waited for her eyes to clear, looking down towards the bridge, the raintrees (or whatever they were), their canopies hooked over the horizon of the dark road.

It's softness we need, she thought, standing unsteadily by the fence. All of us.

Could they be drawn out, these moments of closeness? Could they be encouraged somehow, softly? And could that be enough, that closeness, those moments? The opposite of force. Proximity. Just that.

But getting on the plane, the three of them, and driving between the fields of cane with the purple mountains and the black road and the arc of water from the farmer's hose, the horrible billboard and the sunny air—all of that was what had brought about the closeness. And all of that was founded on Meg's deception of Amber, her lack of trust. *We just tell her we think she needs a little holiday.*

Still, Amber had come. She had agreed to come away with them for a weekend. What if they'd actually done that, the three of them together? No goal, no plan. No lies, no covert checking of bags. Just a weekend away on which Amber could be grey-skinned and ill and sneak whatever she needed into her body and fall asleep selfishly and be a pain and a disappointment—and also laugh and play air guitar and tell Meg jokes as they drove and taste black sapote and feel the supple night air. What might have happened on that trip? What reserves of acceptance might Nina and Meg have surprised themselves with? What near, small possibilities might Amber have glimpsed?

Nina was still very hot. Her head was still pounding. She needed a drink of water but she'd forgotten to fill Meg's flask before leaving the hotel. She could see, across the street, two figures—tourists, in glaring clothes and hats. They were, it seemed, watching her. She kept them blurry, at the edge of her vision. She unzipped her backpack and pretended to rummage inside it.

Her thoughts ran on with a kind of molten abandon. But hadn't Gwen and Robert taken Amber on weekends away? Hadn't Gwen and Robert practised proximity, acceptance, softness, for all those years in their home while Amber came and went from her stinking den, never obliging, never gentle, but always difficult, wild, impossible?

The people over the road were definitely watching her. Nina took out her phone and looked at its blank screen. She pressed the keys as if composing a text.

(Had it been acceptance? What about Gwen in her blue gloves going through the drawers in Amber's bedroom? What about the clinic Gwen spoke of, the detox program they couldn't afford?)

Was nothing clear, untainted? Nina's hands were shaking.

Amber hadn't died. She hadn't gone to jail. She could have done. And even if she traded it for something else, she had quit heroin.

The people were coming over. They were on Nina's side of the road now, stepping up onto the nature strip, crossing the pavement. Nina still had not looked properly at them—they were just shapes, one white and blue, one green and orange. She turned, still clicking keys on her phone, and stumbled along the fence back the way she'd come, towards the cafe, her feet catching in the shaggy grass.

'Hel-loo?' one of the people called. 'Are you all-a-right?'

Nina tried to say something but her voice didn't work. She half-turned and smiled and nodded and then waved, accidentally throwing her phone as she did so. It landed on the other side of the fence.

'Op-la!' said the person.

Nina, dumbly, went on smiling, waving and nodding. Then she went nearer to the fence and, kneeling, stuck her arm between its wires and retrieved the phone.

The people were about her age, perhaps Italian. Their appearance was expensive and clean; they were travellers, not backpackers. They remained standing a couple of metres away while Nina knelt and reached between the wires, and when she got up again and gave them another smile and wave they smiled and waved back, and then stayed there watching as she walked away.

She returned to the cafe, and then she passed it and went on down the street, on the footpath now, until she was opposite the pub again. The hot river of thought had stopped. She felt empty, defeated. It was an impossible situation. Nothing would work. Nothing could fix Amber, or repair the damage that all of them had suffered. Nothing that anyone had ever tried had come to anything, and Meg was an idiot to think that by pure force of will she would be the one to perform the miracle.

She crossed the road and entered the pub. She'd do what Meg had asked—stay away for three days. And then she'd go back, and she knew exactly what she would find. Meg would have failed. Amber would not be cured. Nina knew. She knew, she knew, she knew.

Yet in the night, in the dark, she woke to find it there, like a callus or a tic: stubborn, heedless, helpless hope.

IN THE EARLY WEEKS AND months of their now official and ongoing affair—their commitment, you might say—when she was apart from Luke, which was almost all the time, Nina thought about him more than she had ever thought about anyone. His words echoed in her mind: *It would be more than sex. It already is.* Particular details preoccupied her. His voice in the darkness, his smell (he smelled like cedar, but not too strong; he smelled clean, nice), the feeling of his upper arm against hers, his hip against hers, the warmth of his skin. She was assailed by flashing images of his thick dark eyebrows, the faint dent at the end of his nose, the chickenpox scars over one cheekbone and above one of his nipples. His nipples: small and flat and browny pink. Other details would evade her, and this was bothersome. The exact colour of his eyes—were they brown or hazel? She would try to remember to notice, the next time.

These preoccupations brought on a strange and frightening feeling: tender, questing, beyond her control. She found herself thinking back to the anthropology tutor, her initiation, all those years ago, and comparing. It was the uncontrollable noticing, the logging of details, that reminded her. With the tutor, the details Nina had been unable to stop noticing were vulnerable ones, even foolish (the whiteboard marker on his thumb; the cappuccino froth on his nose), and called up that dreadful swelling pity, almost motherly, repulsive. This was very different. With Luke there was no pity. There was no sense of duty. When Nina thought back to the tutor, to that ugly office with its carpet tiles, the spilled coffee and the sense of being propelled into something—some set of predetermined, unwanted actions (studying him as he drank from his Garfield mug, endeavouring to find something, anything, attractive)—the word that came to mind was *appeasement*. Somehow, with little in the way of direct communication, the tutor had made Nina—or Nina had made herself—seem indebted to him, an accomplice in the preservation of his dignity. Nothing like that hid in the folds of Nina's interest in Luke. She did not feel repulsed by her thoughts of him. They made her feel tremulous and uncertain, but not disgusted, not oppressed.

It was as if, with the tutor, Nina had been given a role to play, and only in the absence of any other offer had she taken it and limped reluctantly onto the stage. It had been a way in—to the world of adults, the world of sex—and she'd accepted it because she had believed that there were no other options. And it was no use ruminating on the foolishness or tragedy of this—it was just what had happened, and Nina was still a person, not undamaged, but not ruined either. She had a sexuality, and while it had been marked and shaped by what happened with the tutor (and the DJ, and the guy from the film shoot, and the friend of a friend of one of her housemates at the party house, and the guy who filled in once for the delivery driver at the gallery, and the guy at the bookshop's Christmas party, and all those other guys), it was still, more than anything, hers. Within the fields of this sexuality—where Nina had always played a passive role, making do with whatever she was given, even by her own subconscious—there nonetheless existed flickering, unknowable energies. It was a bent world she'd built for herself, private and constrained, reachable only via odd angles, tricks of perception, but it was hers, it was part of her, inextricable, perverse and precious. And it was not, contrary to what she had believed right up until Luke made his proposition, finite.

Nina had not imagined that such a thing was possible, but here was another stage, another arena into which she might step, wearing a different costume, playing a different part—where she might even, perhaps, improvise. The irony was not lost on her that it was only once a man was direct and honest with her about his lack of availability that she became attracted to him. But perhaps it was these new and firm constraints that somehow shifted her view and allowed her to consider other ways of being with someone.

Time went on—six months, nine, a year—and Luke just kept on showing up. It didn't matter what Nina did. Shower, wax, shave, dress with care, apply make-up, perfume, wear heels, light candles. Leave the ugly kitchen fluorescent light on, wear her ratty pyjamas and Explorer socks, not shave, not wax, not wear make-up, not brush her teeth. Luke showed up, and whether they had sex or not—because times came when they didn't— always they lay together and talked; always Luke was kind, affectionate, deeply interested in her. And he delighted in her. Every time. He kept coming back, and he kept finding her delightful. Even when the familiarity grew, and Nina's resentments appeared and began to calcify. It meant a lot to Nina, that delight. At the time she just felt it, loved it, thrived on it; much, much later she would see how much it changed her, what it allowed. Later she would see, too, what it meant for her future: what she might find with someone other than Luke.

At some point she realised that when they had sex she wasn't always outside her own body, looking at it, or away in a fantasy in which she watched someone else do something else to her. At some point she realised that there were things to be had if she stayed there in the room with Luke, inside herself, looking out. The mechanics of things became very absorbing, very specific. At some point she started looking into his eyes.

(She told Luke about Meg's Girl Guide advice, about *working together* at sex, and they laughed, and then Nina put her hands to her face in horror and said, 'Oh no! That's what *we're* doing, isn't it?' And they laughed even more, and then Nina said, 'Come here, and put your finger just—there. I need to stop thinking about my sister.')

Nina and Luke talked about almost everything. Films. Books. Stories from adolescence, from childhood. Sarah, Skye and Millie. Luke's parents. His brother. His job at the Centre for Adult Education. Nina's students. Poetry. Amber and Meg. Gwen and Robert. Nina's men from before: the tutor, the DJ, the others— the cycle of fatalistic disappointment she'd felt locked into. The only thing they didn't talk about was whether or not Nina was seeing anyone else at the same time as Luke. There was something in this that was to do with equality, with maintaining a balance—the other men Nina might or might not be sleeping with were the counterweight to Sarah and the children.

In fact Nina was not, for a long time, interested in other men. Which is not to say that other men were not there, paying her attention. But it was easy to turn them down—she did it distractedly, laughingly. She was preoccupied with Luke. Luke just went on being very interesting to her.

Their time together was not always pleasant. It could be boring, unfulfilling, anticlimactic. Sometimes they argued. Sometimes one or the other of them was unreasonable. But there was something about the way in which they met, its prescribed nature, its containment and regularity, that enabled them to resolve things, to endure together whatever difficulties arose. No matter what happened—if they fought, if Luke was needy or Nina distant—they never cut corners on their three hours. Nina never told Luke to leave; Luke never stormed out. They might, after a blow-up, lie side by side without speaking until it was time for Luke to go, when they'd bid each other a cold and formal farewell—but the next week he would be back, and then they'd talk about what had happened, and apologise and make up. Strangely, given its trappings of illicitness, its limited nature and the secrecy it required, the relationship came to feel, to Nina, profoundly safe.

In the early years their disagreements were seemingly inchoate, small, inarticulate dramas that rose quickly and collapsed just as fast. Beneath these, however, simmered larger troubles, the kinds of troubles Nina never anticipated because they were so embarrassingly unoriginal. (Nina did still, at times, think of herself as special.)

Here's an example. This was about three years in. A Thursday night. Thursday had come to be their regular night, although Luke did occasionally change it to Wednesday, for reasons they didn't discuss, but which Nina presumed were to do with Sarah and the kids. Luke arrived at six, his usual hour.

'I'm starving,' he said, taking down the glasses and opening the wine.

'Well there's nothing much to eat.'

This was not uncommon. Nina, who was now twenty-seven, still lived mostly on toast and canned soup, making a salad when she felt like she wasn't getting enough greens. But because Luke always brought the wine she felt obliged to supply some kind of food, and the effort she put into this varied wildly. Sometimes she made a special trip to the markets for soft blue cheese and fresh figs, or prawns, or Lebanese spinach pies she heated in the oven and squeezed lemon juice over; other times it was half a packet of stale Captain's Table biscuits and tasty cheese gone hard at the edges, or carrot sticks and Vita-Weats with peanut butter.

Luke poured the wine and sighed.

Nina wrenched open the fridge. 'Okay,' she said, 'there's some haloumi . . . wait—oh yuck, no, that's gone off . . . or there's a bit of yoghurt.' She closed the fridge and picked up her glass. 'Help yourself. I'm happy with wine.'

Luke turned his glass in sullen circles on the benchtop. 'Maybe I should run out and grab something.'

It was winter, dark already. Nina's flat smelled like wet laundry. The windows needed a wash; through them, between pale branches, was the furry orange glow of a streetlight.

'Oh, come on,' said Nina, 'don't do that. It's cold. And you'll use up all our time.'

Luke opened a cupboard. 'I have to eat something.' He took down a small can of tuna.

Nina put her wine on the coffee table and flopped onto the couch.

'I'm sorry I didn't have a hot meal waiting for you, my lord. And your pipe and slippers.' Her tone was light, but as she said the words she realised that they wouldn't be taken well. Then again, perhaps it was not entirely unintentional, her needling of him. There were things that were not being said: that she'd like, just once, to go *out* with him, to dinner, to a movie; that she found it annoying that he expected her to provide food, every time, when all he brought were those cheap bottles of plonk that he probably got in some bulk deal and had boxes of in his garage; that she wished he'd bring her flowers (such a cliché, but still, who else was ever going to buy them for her?); that she couldn't say it but she fantasised sometimes about them going away together for a weekend. These small, unspoken desires stacked themselves into a silent tower and at the top was the big one, the most unspeakable, unallowable want: that she'd like to spend more time with him.

That's what was going on inside Nina's mind. What was going on inside Luke's was an unknown. Perhaps he reflected—as he opened the can of tuna, found a crust of bread and put it in the toaster—on similar matters, on what he imagined Nina might wish for, on what he felt he was depriving her of. Or perhaps he reflected on what he himself was missing out on—perhaps after three years he had discovered that his loneliness had not been cured by this arrangement with Nina, that what he really craved was a full life with one woman, not two incomplete lives with two women. Perhaps, sensing Nina's ruminations, her tower of unspoken wishes (and the fact that the wishes were beginning to turn into resentments), he was beginning to rethink the whole situation—to consider escape, retreat.

None of these things did they discuss. They sat in silence—Nina on the couch with her glass of wine, Luke at the tiny table with his plate of canned tuna on a toasted heel of bread. To Nina, flaky Nina, the affair and its lastingness had simply sprung up and surprised her; resentment, frustration, the idea of wanting *more*, had not been an expectation. Who knew what Luke might have expected or anticipated? There had been no provision in his original offer for Nina to want more, but that didn't stop her from doing so.

Luke ate his crappy dinner and they both drank the crappy wine, and resentments hardened in silence. But also, after he finished eating, Luke came to sit beside Nina on the couch, and together they looked through a catalogue of a recent exhibition at Wendy's gallery, discussing the artwork, and then Nina touched his hair and said that she liked his new haircut, and they kissed and moved nearer, and then they lay down. This happened, and afterwards they talked, their bodies close. And it would seem that it was possible to want more, to feel resentful, to question one's commitment, and at the same time to enjoy being, right now, with someone—a particular person, the same person that the resentment, the wanting more, the questioning all pertained to. It would seem that these things could exist simultaneously, that they did not cancel each other out.

On a bus, Nina overheard two women who looked to be around her age talking about their five-year plans—'assistant manager by the end of next year'; 'trip to Paris for my thirtieth'—and felt completely bewildered. Nina, who was then twenty-eight and had been with Luke for more than four years, sometimes wondered if she should break things off, but never wondered what the future might hold. Perhaps this short-sightedness on her part was one of the main reasons the affair lasted for such an astonishingly long time. Occasionally, though, due to a random event in the outside world, her myopic perceptions would be—unpleasantly, shockingly—expanded.

One night in that same year—2005—she went to dinner at Gwen and Robert's. Nina walked from the train station through an evening sharp with springtime. The pavements were dark and wet, the street trees bright with new growth, the sky a liquid silver.

Meg was at this dinner, in the early weeks of her second or perhaps third pregnancy, awesome in her hormonal swollenness. Dave was there too of course, full of ruddy, anxious good cheer. Amber (still on heroin) was supposed to be there but did not show.

During the meal Gwen said, 'We lost a student this week, at work. Very sad. He'd been in hospital—an infection, from his tracheostomy. But still. He was such a sweet boy. We all loved him.'

Robert, Dave and Nina all made small sounds of concern or sympathy.

Meg, sober, matronly, leaned forward. 'How old was he?'

'Eighteen.'

'Is that normal, for someone with a tracheostomy?'

Meg spoke the word with concision; Nina, even though she knew what it meant—from Luke, from talk of Millie—had forgotten it already, as she always did.

'Yes,' said Gwen. 'In the end an infection comes along that just can't be treated. It must be so hard for the families, knowing it's going to happen sooner or later, but not exactly when.'

'How horrible.' Meg sighed, shiny with pregnancy, laden with the exquisite and personal burden of her recent pain as well as with new, fraught hope. This only increased the queenliness of her bearing; even Gwen seemed to bow before it, to lay down her own sadness.

There was a respectful sort of pause before first Robert and then Dave took up their cutlery again.

'I think,' said Gwen, in a more philosophical tone, 'that what the parents often struggle with afterwards is the guilt. It's a tremendous strain to care for a child with a tracheostomy, even if the family has some kind of respite. The child can't be left alone for a moment. Someone has to sleep with them, usually one of the parents. So when they do go there's finally this freedom. The parents can do all these things they've been held back from. But it's because their child has died. Just imagine how you'd feel.' She too, at last, picked up her fork.

Meg sat a little longer, gazing into space. After a few moments Dave stopped eating and took her hand. She turned to him, blinking, and he kissed her cheek, looked questioningly into her eyes. She smiled, and then the two of them went back to their food.

Robert watched this interaction with open, moist admiration, hands clasped under his chin. Gwen gave it one shy glance.

Meanwhile Nina sat with her ears buzzing and a chill spreading down her back. Why had Luke never told her about this? That the situation with Millie was not forever? She went into a spin of speculation. Perhaps it felt wrong for him to make plans based on the assumption of the death of his child. Perhaps it was just too difficult, beyond countenancing, to even consider Millie's death in the first place. Or perhaps Luke did not plan to leave Sarah no matter what happened.

Here was what set Luke furthest apart from the men that had come before him: he had (after a very short period of non-disclosure) been upfront about his situation, and he'd made no false promises. Falsity had been the calling card of so many of the others. (*There's something special about you.*) But Luke was, apparently, so determined not to make any false promises that he would not discuss the future of the relationship in any way at all. There was a kind of coldness to this that made Nina feel cheated. Even if it had been purely in fantastical terms, other men had spoken liberally of the future. *If only we could go somewhere, just the two of us—another city, another country. We could start a new life, away from all this.* How many times Nina had heard that. And yet—she thought, inside her buzzing head, her hands numb in her lap, her plate of mushroom risotto cooling in front of her—at least there had been some warmth to those bullshit promises, those ridiculous fantasies. They were not sensible or realistic, but they were heartfelt, even if only during the moment of their being said. They had felt, strangely, *generous*.

Other things happened to shock Nina out of her vagueness. At the bookshop she overheard an older woman, a customer, say to her friend: 'Well *he* died, and a month later this woman shows up and says, "I was his mistress."'

'What did she want? Money?'

'No! She just wanted to meet them all; she felt as if that was the right thing to do. I don't know what she expected, but of course Pam shut the door in her face.'

'Good on her.'

'Yes, I suppose so. But it'd been going on for twenty years apparently. She must have loved him as well. It's just awful, the whole situation. Awful for everyone.'

'Not for him! He had his cake and ate it too!'

They moved away, still talking. Nina stood behind the counter, a horrified flush rising from her neck to her face.

'You right, Nina?' said Dan, her boss.

'Yep.' Nina went back, with trembling fingers, to filling in a remainders form.

The night before this Luke had told her it was nearly Skye's fourteenth birthday and asked what Nina thought he should give her, and Nina had recommended a CD, *The Miseducation of Lauryn Hill*, because she knew—because Luke had told her—that Skye was into music. And Nina had felt excited about Skye getting that album, and she'd wondered what Skye would think of it—and then she'd remembered that she would never meet Skye or talk to her.

Around the same time Meg rang up one evening and said in a barging voice, 'Nina, I have to ask you something. Mum and Dad are worried. Are you okay? Do you have someone? You know, a partner. I'm sorry to just come out and ask you like this, but you're so secretive I don't think there's any other way to do it.'

Nina, who'd thought it was going to be Luke on the phone, again felt the dreadful flush.

'I'm okay,' she said, after a while.

'More information, please.'

'I have someone, and I'm okay.'

'Oh,' said Meg, and Nina could hear her greedy curiosity. 'Who is it?'

'I don't want to talk about it.'

'Is it a woman? Because that's fine, you know. Mum and Dad, all of us, we're fine with that.'

'It's not a woman. It's a man.'

'How long have you been going out?'

'Oh, a while.' Nina stared helplessly through the window of her flat, at the branches of the tree. She could feel a weakness coming into her voice. Even her hand felt heavy, as if it might drop the phone.

'Well, how long is that?' said Meg. 'A month? A week? A year?'

Nina didn't answer.

'What's going on, Neen?' said Meg. 'Don't tell me he's married.'

Nina hung up the phone.

Immediately it rang again and she walked away from it, into the bedroom.

She sat on the bed while the phone kept on ringing, and kept on ringing, over and over.

At last she went and picked it up.

'If you keep hassling me about this,' she said, 'or tell Mum and Dad, I will stop talking to all of you.'

'But, Nina,' said Meg.

'Did you hear me?'

'But Nina.'

'I mean it.'

Nina hung up and Meg didn't ring back, and when they saw one another next Meg didn't say anything, although she gave Nina a pleading look, which Nina ignored. Meg did this—the pleading look—every now and then for a few years, but she never said anything.

When Luke heard about Meg's idea to take Amber away and trick her into doing a detox, he was flatly disapproving.

'Surely you're not even considering it,' he said.

'Of course not,' said Nina. And then, after a pause: 'But it's, you know, it's complicated. And nothing else has worked. And Mum and Dad just seem to have given up.'

'It's wrong,' said Luke, with finality.

Nina did not raise the matter with him again, even while Meg was calling her about it almost every day, even when she began to sense that she was losing traction, that Meg was going to win. This process took a number of weeks, and during that time Nina began an affair with another man—the first since she'd started seeing Luke.

When she went with her sisters on the trip to Far North Queensland Nina did not tell Luke the details. In fact she lied, and told him that she was going on a holiday with her parents.

And when she came back nothing was the same. Nina was filled with a sick anger that aimed itself at Luke. How dare he make such a severe judgement about the attempted detox? Luke didn't know Amber. He didn't know Meg. He didn't know what it was like to live with an addict in the family.

It had been wrong, Meg's plan. Of course it had. Nina knew that. She'd known it at the beginning, she'd known it all along, and she still knew it. But what about Meg at the table on the verandah, with the tropical rain crashing down outside, her furious, wet face, her fist thumping her chest as she said, *It's out of love*? The plan itself had been wrong, but what about the impulse behind it?

Luke thought that life could be lived with hard rules. And Nina had thought so too. But now she wasn't so sure. They had come unaligned, the two of them. A faltering had begun.

Nina tried to change some things. She moved house from the flat to Viv's place—which she found advertised by a hand-written note on a board outside a wholefoods shop—with its lanky rosebushes and peeling weatherboards, its view of the vacant block and the city skyline. She bought the outrageously expensive new couch.

These things didn't work. The faltering turned into a shutting-down.

She answered the phone to Luke, she returned his texts, she continued to have him over for their weekly assignations, but she was remote, unresponsive.

'Are you okay?' said Luke, and, 'Are you mad at me?' and, 'What have I done?'

Nina did not answer, and did not answer. She let him into her house with a limp, subdued affect. She sat like a zombie on the new couch while he poured the wine and laid out the food (which he had started bringing). She responded to his attempts at conversation absently, almost indulgently. When they had sex she reverted to her old tricks of watching herself through her eyelashes, making herself a lump of meat, a dumb body that things were being done to. Sometimes accidental-seeming pleasure would wash in, but not often—the many-layered, dim recesses of that elusive world had, it seemed, been closed off.

Luke stopped asking her what was wrong. He sighed often, and became more needy, wanting to hold Nina more tightly after sex, to press his face into the back of her neck, to touch her hair. When it was time for him to get up, get dressed and leave, there was reluctance in his manner, and often as he bent to kiss Nina, who was still lying in the bed, he paused as if about to speak, but then didn't.

Nina grew colder and colder. A helplessness descended—her old sense of failure. The affair she'd started with the other man before she went on the trip with Meg and Amber came to an end; a different other man came along, and she started an affair with him. The new man gave her some lingerie (it wasn't bad, navy silk, and almost fitted) and she wore it for Luke, who said, 'These are nice,' with what Nina took to be morose acceptance. This didn't make her feel any better. Nothing did.

At this time, too, she gave away her jobs at the bookshop and the gallery. She stopped tutoring. She stopped writing, and making art. She got the job at the hospital.

It was a relief when Luke said that he thought they should break up. Nina, coming almost full circle, accepted this news without surprise.

'It's just not working,' said Luke.

Nina nodded.

'But it did work, for so long,' said Luke. 'What happened?' He made a grab for one of Nina's hands. 'Did you meet someone else? Is that it?'

Nina let him take her hand. She gave him a genuinely sad smile. 'We agreed not to talk about that,' she said. 'Remember? That was one of our rules.'

ON THE MORNING OF THE appointed day she got a ride with some tourists driving in a rental van to Cape Tribulation. She'd asked them the night before, made herself go up to their table in the bistro. This was after spending two days wandering up and down the main street, eating at Raintrees Cafe (where the waitress continued to barely acknowledge her) and in the bistro (where the other waitress did the same) and lying on the bed in the hotel room. She only had the one dress and it was creased and musty. Sometimes the dumb hope would ambush her with its sliding, guilty comfort, but mostly she felt stiff, dull, unreal. It was as if in submitting to Meg's plan and her own expectation of failure she'd been brought down under something weighty and thick, and all her turmoil, the agony of decision, the striving for thought had thinned, and risen, and departed.

The tourists were a couple from New Zealand, younger than Nina, tattooed and pierced. They did not appear to be thrown by a thirty-something woman wearing a dress badly in need of a wash approaching as they ate their parmas and soft carrots and peas and salt-speckled fat yellow chips, and asking in a creaky voice if they might be driving north the next day. She'd explained that she needed to go some distance from the main road and offered to pay them to make the detour, and they'd nodded pleasantly.

'Forty bucks?' said one to the other.

'I reckon,' said the other, although it sounded to Nina like *rickin*.

Their van had an image spray-painted on its side, a Rastafarian duck (or goose? A bird, anyway, with brown dreadlocks and a green, red, yellow and black knitted cap) reclining amid billowing clouds of white smoke.

'Sorry about the van,' said one of the men. 'We didn't know it would have that picture on it.'

Nina got in the back, which smelled like camping gear and a piney, not unpleasant, deodorant or moisturiser.

It was early and the street was quiet. Nina had forgone Raintrees for a muesli bar purchased on one of her walks to the supermarket. Her gums were sore. She tried to remember the last time she'd eaten fresh vegetables. They crossed the bridge near the church; in the trees each side of the water there were threads of mist.

'We're going zip-lining today,' said the man who'd apologised for the image on the van. It sounded like *zup-leaning*.

'Oh,' said Nina. And then, once she'd realised what he'd said: 'Oh, wow.'

They didn't ask her where she was going with her little backpack and dirty dress, so far down a back road north of Mossman. They didn't ask her a single thing about herself. The man in the passenger seat had an iPod plugged into the van's stereo; he turned the little wheel with his large brown thumb and deep, slow hip-hop came welling up out of the speakers, the rapper's voice like syrup, the spaces between the fat pulses of kick drum elastic, sultry. It made Nina think of sex, and she looked out at the mountains and—although they did not put this on her, although they were polite, respectful, kind—she felt embarrassed by her age and gender, by the fact that she held no interest for them.

Then she recognised the bridge, and not long after that the turn-off, and she said in her rusty voice, 'Here's the turn, thanks,' and then they were under the trees and it was dark, the morning above still overcast, and Nina was waking up now, feeling more real, and the dread began to form, hard in her gut.

When she came down the slope she could see Meg sitting on the metal steps, a distant dark-haired figure, and she wanted nothing more than to turn and run up the biscuit-coloured track to the gate and jump back in the van. But they'd gone, the cheerful New Zealanders, they'd waved through the windscreen and made a big U-turn and gone swaying away, the thud of their music spreading, blurring, falling under the fog of insect noise.

So she kept walking. Meg had seen her and stood up, and as Nina approached she took in Meg's dirty clothes and lank hair, the soiled sling. Her white, defeated face. Meg turned and went up the steps, and by the time Nina reached the car she was back down again with something in her hand. She came towards Nina without meeting her eyes. She held out the object, which flashed metal in the light: a pair of kitchen scissors.

The room was dark. The smell was terrible. Amber was lying on her side, her knees up. In the air just over her ankles there was a thin blind trembling, a snake's-tongue of black plastic: the end of a cable tie. The soles of her feet were dirty. Her legs, moving back and forth together in their bind, had left blades of grass and streaks of mud in a rough wide curve on the mattress. There were other marks too, higher up, either side of Amber's hips, dreadful, foul-smelling stains. The instep of one of Amber's feet rested in the arch of the other in a gentle dovetail that spoke so brokenly of normal sleep, normal rest, the normal small comforts sought by a body that Nina, approaching, felt her breath catch.

The tie at Amber's wrists was tighter, and a third tie was looped through it and around the middle bar of the bedhead. Her body was crooked, unnatural, her torso angled to accommodate the tied hands, her head back, her throat exposed.

Nina stepped nearer. She had taken off her sandals at the door and the dust under her bare toes was velvety, clinging. Her eyes were getting used to the lack of light.

On the floor by the bed was a yellow bucket, wet inside as if recently rinsed, and a pile of folded kitchen cloths. Beside these was a pillow. There was no pillow under Amber's head. The sheets, top and bottom, had been worked into a crumple at the foot of the mattress, along with a towel. These, Meg's gestures of care, which Nina could picture so clearly—Meg's hands placing the pillow, drawing smooth the sheets, spreading the towel like a mother preparing to change a baby's nappy—Amber had managed to undo, to reject. I will not be a part of this pretence, the pillow and sheets said. Or, more simply: Fuck you.

Nina thought of hunger strikes, of mouths sewn shut. Acts of defiance so reduced, so compressed, that they are almost unbearable to witness. She thought about the expression *rock bottom*. A hard and dark place, very deep, that only comes into existence when named by the person who's in it—or who was in it, but has now pushed off, rebounded, and is able to safely look back and down.

Amber breathed. Her feet adjusted themselves. Tears sprang into Nina's eyes. See? she pleaded, automatically, to Meg in her head. You can't force rock bottom on someone.

Nina put her fingers to Amber's bare calf. Warm, damp. Stubble, grime. Amber smelled not like sweat but like ammonia, like burnt things, like short-circuited electrics. She didn't move when Nina touched her. She was awake, though—Nina could tell.

Nina worked the blade of the scissors with care between the taut strand of plastic and the clammy, reddened skin of Amber's ankle. The snip was loud. The cable tie flung itself undone.

Amber lay still. Her eyes, Nina could see now, were open, but she didn't move her head. She gazed at what was in front of her—what she must have been gazing at for every waking hour of the past three days: a dim expanse of wall, the backs of framed pictures leaning, their wires rusted and loose; a box on the floor with what might be a curtain heaped in it, flocked paisley, orange and brown, furred with dust.

Nina put the scissor blade under the evil cinching line of plastic where it crossed the little elongated oval of space just below Amber's pressed-together wrists, between Amber's forearms, which looked so yellow in this light, so sickly, their veins sunken and greenish. The blades closed, the tie popped, and Amber, like an exposed insect, drew her knees closer to her chest, covered her head with her arms. An upward surge of dust motes. The gape of the severed ties. Amber breathed long shuddering breaths and Nina was appalled all over again.

'I'm sorry, I'm sorry,' she whispered. She put a hand out. 'I should have helped you, Amber, I—'

Amber made a sound—'Uhh'—and pulled herself in tighter. Nina withdrew her hand.

Then Amber unfolded her body and eased herself upright. Her cut-off jeans looked stiff with dirt, her thighs soft and flat. Her head hung on her neck. She dragged her legs around until she was sitting on the edge of the bed. Still she didn't look at Nina. She scrubbed at her face with the back of one hand. The rash under her nose was scabbed. There were semicircles of dirt beneath her nails, dirt in the creases of her knuckles, dirt like grey ash worked into her pink tank top.

What was the look she gave Nina as she stood, tottered, caught hold of the bedhead? Before she rasped in another great breath and steadied herself and walked past her sister through the half-built kitchen to the open door and out? It wasn't blame. It wasn't resentment. It wasn't fear or gratitude or relief. None of those. Nina thought—and she couldn't be sure, because she couldn't make herself meet Amber's gaze directly for more than a second—that it might be a look of resignation.

Amber walked right out into the middle of the lawn and then she turned around. She was too far away for Nina to see her cracked lips and the chafed red skin at her wrists, the scab between her nose and mouth like a smear of raspberry jam. The way the veins snaked, ruined, in her long arms. The sun had come out and from this distance she looked tall and pale and luminous, and for a moment Nina allowed herself to imagine that her sister was in fact changed—that she'd been scoured, blasted, forced free.

Amber's legs bent like the legs of a foal, and she sank into a sitting position. She leaned forward and ran her hands in wide, sideways scoops over the grass. Meg walked out to her with a glass of water and she took it and drank and her long, stark throat showed. Meg said something but Amber did not respond. She dropped the glass to the ground and got back up. Leaving her sister standing there she walked to the car. She tugged at the handle of one of the rear doors, and when the door would not open she banged with her open palms at the window, fast and hard, and went on banging until the car's lights flashed and it made its neat, quick double *bip* sound—a city sound, a sound of control, misplaced here in the soupy air. Nina saw that Meg was holding out the key and had pressed the button. Amber got into the car and shut the door.

Meg walked to the steps, passing Nina with her eyes lowered, and Nina followed her, and without speaking the two of them went to their separate rooms to pack their bags.

Amber could not be convinced to get out of the car to shower or change, and because this made it feel wrong to allow herself such a luxury Nina also stayed in what she was wearing—the dirty summer dress. Meg's clothes and Meg herself might have been clean, but nothing could be done about the filthy sling. So they drove—Nina behind the wheel—to Cairns, a grimy, smelly, silent trio, to the burble and twang of local AM radio fading in and out.

They stopped at a petrol station to fill the car, and Meg bought sandwiches that none of them ate much of—although Meg watched like a hawk in the rear-view mirror to make sure that Amber did manage at least a bite—and milky weak coffee that made Nina feel sick.

At the airport, while Meg was at the ticket counter, Amber wordlessly carried her bag into the toilets and emerged wearing clean clothes. Nina, now able to, took her turn, changing precariously in a cubicle, stepping out of and into things while standing on her undone sandals.

Meg did not say anything about the price of the tickets, but she got them on the next flight. There was a two-hour wait. Amber pocketed her boarding pass and walked away. Meg and Nina sat a seat apart in the gate lounge and gazed at a screen on which local news stories played—a rodeo, a cattle competition, a choir chosen to perform at an international festival.

When the flight was called Amber did not appear. When almost everyone else had boarded Meg went looking for her. When the announcement had been made over the PA system— *'This is the final boarding call for Amber, Meg and Nina Atkins booked on flight DJ one-two-nine-six to Melbourne. Please proceed to gate three immediately,'* their names blaring out so bald and strange into all that glass and whiteness—Meg reappeared. She had Amber by the arm, and Amber was heavy-eyed, listing diagonally, and holding a plastic glass with red wine slopping out of it onto the floor. Behind them came hurrying a middle-aged woman in a black uniform, her crimson-dyed hair in a severe ponytail.

'Excuse me! Excuse me! Drinks can only be consumed in the bar!' the woman called.

Wine flew as Meg tried to take the glass from Amber. Nina could smell it.

'You can't bring that with you,' said Meg in a low voice. There was wine on her sling.

'Nuh, nuh, I wan' . . .' slurred Amber, and then, 'Oh!' as she lost her grip and the glass fell and bounced and rolled away.

'Thank you,' said the crimson-haired woman in a tired voice, and picked up the glass and walked off without a backward glance, leaving the spray of wine on the tiles.

'Come on,' said Meg to Amber. 'Time to get on the plane.'

Amber's eyes looked yellow. They stared at nothing.

Meg led her, lurchingly, past Nina and towards the doors, the waiting flight attendant. Nina began to follow.

'I'm sorry,' moaned Amber. 'I'm sorry, Meg.'

'That's okay, that's okay, shh, let's just get on the plane now. Got your boarding pass?' Meg worked her hand into the pocket of Amber's jeans and pulled out the crumpled slip.

The attendant looked at the boarding passes. Then she looked at Amber. Then she looked at Meg. 'Is, ah, is she okay?' she said.

'She's fine,' said Meg. 'I'm taking care of her. She'll be fine.'

The woman pursed her lips and narrowed her eyes. But she let them through.

At a desk, another attendant was calmly doing something with a phone. The PA crackled. 'Amber, Meg and Nina Atkins,' the other woman was saying into the phone, her words simultaneously booming out through the PA.

'Oh God,' called Meg from inside the boarding tunnel. 'We're right here, it's us, you idiot.'

Nina watched the first attendant's hand take her pass. Red nails. Gold ring.

Things like this happen all the time, thought Nina. All the time. And nobody even notices.

She followed her sisters into the tunnel. A blankness had come over her. She receded into it, away from whatever else might, if she let it, happen in her mind and body—which was something much too big and terrible to be allowed. Which was—okay, she knew what it was, and she couldn't let it be there because it was so big and terrible and rending that it would break her: it was the apparently impossible combination of love and disappointment.

III.

NINA'S DINNER AT THE THAI restaurant with the leather people and the beer and the crying and then the confrontation with Meg outside her house had been on a Wednesday night. On the Thursday Nina wore the tracksuit pants and Kennards top again (after sleeping in them), changing the lingerie underneath to a pair of red satin bikini briefs (gapingly too big) and a sheer pink bra with tiny embroidered polka dots (actually pretty nice and a good fit, although she did it up as tight as she could, and made the straps so short they hurt).

At work Ursula visited her in the scanner room—again—and told her that Meg had called—again—and Gwen now too, and asked—again—if she was okay.

'Thank you,' said Nina. And, 'Okay,' and, 'Yes, I'm fine.'

For lunch in the cafeteria she ate the remains of a chicken schnitzel and some fruit salad left by a woman from HR.

After work she did not go into the gardens over the road, but she didn't go home either—she caught the tram back through the city and got off at her usual stop, then instead of turning onto her street she went down a different street to a small local park that was mostly filled with tanbark and children's play equipment. She sat on the ground there, against a fence. People came and went, glancing warily in her direction. A toddler approached and his mother called to him and then hurried over and carried him away. An elderly man paused on the path and regarded Nina with open disapproval. Only the teens in their school uniforms, climbing like raucous giants all over the swings and slides, drinking Slurpees and eating Skittles and filming each other with their phones, ignored her.

She sat there for a long time. Things came, in her mind. Robert came. Robert's death, which after eighteen months still seemed unreal, even though—she was coming to realise, in a fumbling, raddled way—it had tilted the balance of things so sharply.

He'd died instantly and alone, driving headlong and fast into a tree on the side of a road near an art gallery in the Dandenongs. An autopsy showed that he'd had a heart attack, which had presumably caused him to drive off the road, but Nina couldn't help imagining it as a simple case of distraction. She imagined Robert, humming and adjusting his smudgy glasses, leaning to peer up through the far corner of the windscreen at the succulent blue of the mid-afternoon sky, or at some pleasingly downy rounds of cloud. Peering, leaning, exclaiming even, to himself, 'Just *look* at that!' Peering, leaning—a little too far. His hands on the wheel bearing, thoughtless ballast, to the right.

In any case, it was sudden and not intentional. In Nina's imagining of it—and Nina did not see Robert's body; only Gwen did, and afterwards gave an unusually direct and vehement instruction that her daughters were not to—there was no violence; it was joyous, *light*; and it was so like Robert, she'd thought, with a muffled and confusing anger, sitting in the church, to die like that. To just pop off with no warning. With his mind on other things. Whoops! As if the clouds, the sky, the exquisiteness of a particular colour, the glorious springing fleece of a particular cloud, were his actual exit—as if he disappeared himself into the delicious details of these things. How unfair this had seemed to Nina as she sat in the middle of the front pew. Beside her Amber wept in agonised jerks, wiping her face with her bare hands. Nobody gave her a tissue; Nina didn't have one and Meg was busy with Gwen, actually holding her together it would seem, around the shoulders, with her big arm.

Why was it unfair? Why was Nina angry, if that's what you'd call this semi-buried, difficult feeling? Nina didn't know, and she didn't want to think about it really, to uncover it fully, whatever it was. It just seemed to her, as Amber (who was thirty-one, for God's sake) sobbed wetly like a child, hair sticking to her face, and Meg with grim duty encircled Gwen so that she didn't just tumble into nothingness and leave them as well, that Robert had got out of something. That was all. Nina left it at that. Anyway, it was Meg who was really angry. Meg by then had been angry for a while.

It was getting later, cooler. The parents with toddlers were leaving the playground, pushing their pushers. One kid made a sound of protest, a low wail, resigned, almost formal. The tanbark smelled earthy, wormy. Nina considered the word *yearning*. She hated it, but it was the right word: she missed Robert with a dog-like yearning. Where was he? Why couldn't he be here, coming across the tanbark towards her, a button hanging from his jacket, emanating enjoyment, casting about, *appreciating* everything?

When he'd cut back his hours at the university in 2011 Robert had taken up baking. He began holding weekly Sunday brunches, which Nina and Amber and Meg were expected to attend—which they did attend, despite the ugliness that since the Sweetwater trip had crouched, compressed and darkly humming, between the three of them. Even Amber did her best, although she was always exempt, always forgiven, her absences, her inconsistencies expected.

It was at these events that Meg's anger rose, and went on rising. Because even though they were all alive and functioning in the world (more or less), even though they were convening for Sunday brunches, spending time together, they still did not seem to be a good enough family for her. Robert and Gwen, having never learned the true nature of the visit to Sweetwater, were going on with their ridiculous fiction that Amber was 'recovered' just because she'd turned from heroin to prescription drugs five years earlier. Robert and Gwen were wilfully ignoring the reality of Amber's ongoing not-okay-ness. Which was pretty hard to take. Although Nina might have settled for it. Would have, in fact. But what she might or might not have settled for didn't matter, because Meg was not going to settle. Still could not. Meg just could not leave things alone.

Every Sunday they went, Meg and Nina and (sometimes, mostly, but not always) Amber, to sit in the kitchen or in warmer weather outside at the heavy teak table with its unreliable chairs, and be presented by a smiling, floury Robert with sweet things from the oven.

Nina could not help feeling that a revision was being made, a sort of simulacrum offered. But then, wasn't her family always revealing itself to be not what she'd thought it was? (Gwen with her blue latex gloves, briskly rifling through Amber's drawers.) What had prompted this unexpected desire for regular together-ness on Robert's part? Was he aware that something had gone wrong between his daughters? Had he *intuited* this? Were these brunches intended to be a possible forum for reconciliation? It was hard to tell. Nina, three years on, growing colder, tanbark dust between her fingers, watching the teenagers gamely perform their rudeness and their jocularity at maximum volume, still didn't know. Robert intuiting much seemed unlikely. He was an outward person. Had been.

It was true, though, that never before had such formalised nurture existed in the Atkins household. There'd always been food, of course, and mealtimes, but these were everyday things, practical and forgettable, executed by Gwen with a view to endurance. Now Robert was having a go at nurture, coming at it with a beginner's zeal, not pacing himself at all—and here were these tables, these mornings, ceremonious, beautiful, with their smells of sugar, yeast and coffee, their splashes of early sun. Newspapers. The six-stacker CD player that Robert still found marvellous, loaded with Neil Young and Joni Mitchell and Nick Drake. Nasturtiums in a jar: pale stems furred with tiny bubbles, orange rag petals, lily-pad leaves. Cinnamon scrolls with deep sticky spirals, babka tipped from its ring tin, thunking onto the rack. Tarts, flans, grainy sweet almond paste, soft hot raisins with hoods of baked crust. Poached pear in translucent slices. Flecks of vanilla. Custards, glazes, syrups, whipped cream, flaking pastry, puffs of icing sugar, beads of honey.

Robert's pleasure verged on the ecstatic. He beamed, scattering crumbs, leaving buttery fingerprints on serving spoons, plates, chair backs, his glasses, the clean tablecloth that Gwen had put down. 'Try it with just a dob of cream,' he urged, and, 'Look, look!' as he lifted a slice of babka to show the silty folds of pale and dark brown, like something geological. Sugar crunched under his slippers as he tended to the oven, then the table, then the oven again. It was, Nina thought, as if he were painting, but with food and with their eating of it.

It could be said that the conflict, the scenes that regularly disrupted these brunches, were caused by Amber—Amber not showing up; Amber showing up extremely late, dry-lipped and yellow-eyed; Amber leaving early with a not-quite-audible excuse—but they weren't really. Really they were caused by Meg. Meg's response. Her rage, breaking out, avalanching.

Some of the teenagers were starting to leave now, swinging up their backpacks, turning at the street, still yelling to their friends. Nina eased out her legs, leaned her head against the fence. Her mind selected a brunch. It must have been winter, because there was daphne on the table. Underneath the sweet thread of the daphne and the almost tangible, almost edible scent of Robert's *pains au chocolat*, the back room of the Thornbury house smelled like it always had, like the ancient brown couch and the truly terrible carpet and that rug which had probably never been washed, but smelled also—newly, frighteningly—like a house in which old people lived, of a sort of unknowing, truly inveterate staleness.

Before Robert had even served the pastries Amber had left, making some bullshit excuse and banging the front door the way she always did, not angrily, just stupidly, carelessly, and Meg had jumped up and tried to catch her, almost running, causing the floorboards in the hallway to bounce—and then come back, weighty and slow and terrifying.

Robert, standing by the bench with the oven mitts on like a seal with a pair of dirty red flippers, said, 'Don't worry about it, darling. It's not for you to worry about.'

'I know!' shouted Meg, wearing her Face of Fury, crimson, with white around the mouth. 'I know that! I know it's not for me!'

'That's right,' said Robert. 'It's for us. It's not your problem.'

Oh God, thought Nina. Don't say that. Don't say anything.

Meg remained standing. She gripped the back of a chair and the table shuddered. There was clinking, a sliding of plates; the jar holding the sprig of daphne toppled and wet the tablecloth.

Gwen got up and crept past Robert. She began to do quiet things with the kettle and the teapot, her back turned.

Oh God, thought Nina. Don't try to hide.

Meg was either too furious to speak or trying to choose which grievance to start with. She shook her head, closed and opened her eyes, stared up at the ceiling, raised her hands as if imploring someone, some outside force, for help.

'How can you say that?' she cried at last. 'It's always been my problem! I've always been the only person who's tried to do anything about it! Where were you, back when she was fucking up? When she couldn't pass school? When she was so *lost*?' She noticed Gwen at the sink. 'You too, Mum. What were you doing to solve the problem? Making cups of tea?'

Nina fixed her eyes on the wet spot on the tablecloth, the tipped jar, which was rolling back and forth in the shockwaves from Meg's grip on the chair. The daphne sprig with its stem in the air, standing on the head of its flowers. She couldn't stand to see Robert's face, his wounded incomprehension. Gwen had not turned around.

Meg yanked the chair out and slammed herself into its seat. 'Don't you get it? We could have saved her then! Before it was too late! But you just, neither of you, could ever say no to her. You let her do whatever she wanted. You let her get lost! You *let* her become a junkie!'

'Now look, Meg,' said Robert.

Meg ignored him, or didn't hear. She was getting even louder. 'And what about her breakdown? What about all that? You knew it was because of what happened with that Emily kid, locking Bam in the—'

'Now look,' said Robert, taking off the oven mitts. 'No one actually saw—'

'It! Doesn't! Matter!' shouted Meg. 'It happened, and it happened because she was just *out there*, unsupervised, with all these people we didn't know. She was only fourteen!' She threw back her head and squeezed her eyes shut. 'I tried *so hard* to keep Bam away from that world, those drama people. She was too young. She needed supervising. But you two just would not help. You kept giving in. Why? Were you that scared of her? She was the child. You were the parents. It was *your job* to keep her safe.'

Meg opened her eyes and turned them on Robert. (Gwen still had her back turned.) Meg's chest heaved up and down.

Robert took up the tray of *pains au chocolat* from the bench. He brought it to the table. He selected a pastry and set it, tenderly, on a plate.

Oh no, thought Nina. Don't do that.

Robert slid the plate bearing the perfect golden whorl, its nub of chocolate still soft and glossy, towards Meg.

And with a howl of fury Meg snatched it up and threw it to the floor. She got out of her chair and grabbed her bag, and then she stomped from the house, slamming the front door very deliberately behind her.

Gwen brought the teapot over and put it down with care. She righted the daphne and its jar, and blotted up the spilled water with a napkin. 'You can't reason with Meg,' she said, 'when she gets like that.'

'What a waste,' said Robert, admiring the remaining *pains au chocolat* sadly. 'You'll have to take some with you, Neen.'

From their perturbed and mystified expressions Nina could guess at what her parents made of this and Meg's many other tantrums. Meg was, Robert and Gwen probably thought, too idealistic. And she didn't recognise all of the work they *had* done, the ways in which they had tried to help Amber. And, thought Nina—as she sat drinking her tea and not really listening to Robert talk about Yayoi Kusama and the notion of infinite space—they had. They had! Robert and Gwen had been there all along, trying. In the wrong way, and not enough, it was true—but perhaps they weren't capable of doing better, or more. They were good parents. But they were bad as well. They were both, and Nina could actually see that, and Meg could not, or perhaps could but didn't want to. Would not give in to seeing it. Would not stop wanting more from them.

And now, thought Nina, sitting alone on the cold ground in the dark park, Robert was dead and not here anymore to have a go at revising their family with pastries and to continue to take delight in almost everything. Robert doing these things was something that Nina had not valued—and now (her chin shook, there in the dark; her lips shook and drew down at the corners) she did, and it was too late. The brunches were over, and Robert was not here for Meg to blast with what seemed to have become her only family-fixing tool, her much-too-powerful fire hose of rage. Robert, who had been the only family member strong enough to withstand such a blasting. Gwen was just this sort of wisp, and Amber was as abject as ever, really. Meg was still bossy, but in an automatic kind of way, as if her heart was no longer in it. Maybe Meg had even given up. There was so little left of them all. And now Amber with this stupid NA thing, what chance could it possibly have? Nina sighed and got up. Could she not just have a rest from all this? She began to walk home.

The next morning—Friday—she changed the underwear for a pair of cream silk shorties that immediately began to crawl upwards as if determined to cut her in half, and a crimson bra that was much too small even with the straps at their longest and from the cups of which much of her breast tissue emerged like rising dough. She wore the Kennards top and tracksuit pants again, even though the pants now had grass stains and the top a ripe smell. Her hair when she brushed it felt thick with oil. She splashed her face and cleaned her teeth and blew her nose. She could smell herself, though—her body. She stood looking at the shower and the dry scrap of soap in its holder. There came the memory of what it felt like to be clean—a feeling like rinsed glass, like clear water—but she crushed it. Anyway, she'd packed the towels.

At work Ursula came to the doorway of the scanner room and said, 'Um, Nina?' but Nina pretended not to hear and Ursula went away again. At lunchtime she took over a table from two men in nurses' scrubs and ate their pizza crusts and drank the dregs of their cafe latte and green tea. She saw Sidney near the lifts doing things on her phone, and even though she was there for some time Nina didn't go over to her. In fact, she moved to a different table that was hidden behind a column. She felt tired. The lingerie cinched her brutally from every angle. Good, she thought.

After her shift that day she didn't get off the tram. She just stayed on as it went all the way to the end of the line and then all the way back to the other end, over and over again. At one point the driver got off and another driver got on. Five o'clock must have come because, going through the city, the tram got extremely crowded, although the seat beside Nina stayed empty—most of the time, anyway; sometimes someone sat in it, but they usually got up again not long afterwards. Then, as it passed into the suburbs of the inner and then not-so-inner south-east, the tram emptied. On the next pass back through the city it filled up once more, although not as much. Nina stayed on until it got dark outside. She was hungry and very thirsty and she needed to go to the toilet.

The dark room came to her. The pillow on the floor. The sheets crumpled at the foot of the mattress. The towel, the cloths and bucket. The tight ties. The compressed flesh.

She let the tram sway her. She kept her eyes closed. Sometimes she cried.

At last she got off at her stop and walked down the street. There were fresh letters in the mailbox; she ignored them and went inside.

On Saturday she woke early, as usual. The silk shorties were riding up in a dank, persistent ridge. Half asleep, she gave in and worked them off under the covers, together with the tracksuit pants. She undid the bra and wriggled out of it and lay looking through the bare window at the pink-grey air.

Meg on Wednesday night, running to block her on the path; Gwen's anxious, careful voice messages; Amber's calls and letters—none of this needed time and space to float into her mind; it was all there, right there, very close. The curtainless window didn't stop it from coming, and nor did the horrible undershorts, the tracksuit pants with their op shop odour, the hardness of the stripped room.

Nina cried for a while. Not the free-flowing leakage that had taken place in the Thai restaurant but a guttural dry sobbing, her face turned into the pillow.

There wasn't much point in getting up. She didn't have to go to work. When the crying was finished she lay very still. The muscles around her eyes felt as if they were stuck in a clenched position. Birds were calling outside, two of them it sounded like, whistling morosely back and forth. Then she heard the storm of parrots that she often saw on her way to work, hurtling into the big gum tree that stood in the middle of the roundabout at the end of her block, red and green and yellow. Come into the city in search of water, Viv said. Their calls were riotous, almost hysterical, a big round cloud of noise.

❦

She must have fallen back to sleep, because now she was waking into the white glare of daylight. Outside there were traffic sounds, the hum of a plane, a car door slamming. Nina closed her eyes again. Maybe she could sleep for the whole day, delete it, wake up tomorrow. Or at least just lie there. But she needed the toilet.

She was in the hallway wearing only the Kennards top when someone knocked on the door. It was the long, adamant knock of a person who has already been knocking for some time—and Nina realised that this was what had woken her, this sound. She stood, the cool side of a cardboard box against her thigh, her bladder swollen, her mind flitting. What if it was Meg? Or Amber?

The knocking came again, and something shifted in Nina's mind. It wasn't just Meg and Gwen and Amber that she didn't want to see. Even if this person knocking was Sidney, who dropped in sometimes on a weekend, maybe bringing Ellis in his bike-riding gear, with croissants, or if it was Viv in her overalls, with vegetables from her garden or her toolbox to fix things, the bathroom taps, the guttering—Nina didn't want to see them. She didn't want to see anybody. She'd crossed into another phase. She didn't want anyone to look at her, to speak to her, to require her to look or speak back. She wanted to hide completely, to bury herself.

This was not good. This was not just an interesting time—something was going quite seriously wrong. But the urge to hide was severe, and when the knocking came again, and Sidney's voice, calling, 'Nina? Hello? Nina? You home?' she turned and crept into the bathroom.

She sat on the toilet and let her urine out in as quiet a stream as she could, then wiped and did not flush. She went back into the hallway, which felt treacherously quiet. Sidney was not giving up. Nina could see, in the strip of light at the bottom of the front door, the shadows of feet.

'Nina? Hello? Nina, please open up.'

Nina tiptoed back into the bedroom and got back in the bed. The bundle of clothes at the bottom had gone cold, but the place where she'd been lying was still warm. The awful bra was there under the covers, sticking its underwires into her arm. She stared out at the view of the paling fence and the red-brick wall of the house next door. At last the knocking stopped.

She lay with her mind almost completely blank. After a while a kind of loose, sleepy relief began to rise. Here it was, the new phase. Submission was all that was required.

From outside, from the direction of the street, there came a rattle: the side gate. A thud, and then the sounds of the bolt scraping back and the gate opening and footsteps, and first Sidney's face and then Meg's appeared at the bedroom window.

There was a small amount of embarrassment at this, but mostly just a tired irritation.

'Nina,' said Meg through the glass. 'Go and open the door.' She looked towards the back of the house. 'What are all those eggshells doing there?'

Nina put the quilt over her face.

There was a brusque rapping. 'Nina!' came Meg's voice. 'I'm really worried about you. So is Mum, and Ursula at your work, and so is Sidney. We're here because we think you need help. Now go and open the door, please, and let us in.'

Nina began to laugh. She sat up in the bed. Her eyes were gritty. She felt hot and dry and dangerous. She called out, not looking at Meg or Sidney but staring straight ahead at the row of cupboard doors: 'Oh, so it's time to do an intervention on me now, is it, Meg? You going to fix me up, is that it? Get me all nice and fixed up like you did with Amber?'

Silence from the window. They were still there, though; she could see them out of the corner of her eye.

'Fuck off, Meg,' she shouted. 'And go away, please, Sidney.'

They just stayed there. Tap-tap-tap, on the glass. Tap-tap-tap.

'Nina.'

'Come on.'

'Open up.'

'Nina.'

This went on for some time. Nina lay with the covers over her head, and when she needed more air with the covers up to her chin, her head turned from the window. Waves of feeling moved through her. Dullness, irritation, humiliation, shame.

Every now and then she yelled, 'Leave me alone!' or 'Go away!' but this only stirred them to further tapping and calls.

Then they did go away. Quiet. No faces at the window. Nina waited for a while, then got up, went to the kitchen, bent over the sink and gulped water directly from the spout. She stood and listened to the water slosh in her stomach. Her legs got cold and she went back to the bedroom and put on the blue tracksuit pants that were still under the covers at the bottom of the bed. She didn't bother with underwear.

In the kitchen again she fried an egg, and it was when she opened the back door to get some rocket that she realised they'd tricked her. Meg was right there, and stuck her foot in the door as Nina tried to shut it. Nina looked down at Meg's ugly pink-and-blue sneaker with the door banging ineffectually against it and gave up.

'I'm fine,' she said, and went back to the stove and stood over it eating the egg. She heard them come into the room. She finished the egg and put the pan and the spatula in the sink but there didn't seem to be any point in washing them. When she turned around they were just standing there. Sidney was also wearing sneakers, but hers were black and looked like suede, sleek and fancy. She looked like a glam cat burglar in her black clothes and gold jewellery, her hair tied back. Her face was difficult to look at, though; when she did look at it, for a moment, Nina couldn't believe how tender and shocking her embarrassment was. Meg's face she didn't even go near. She kept her eyes on Meg's hands instead, which were gripped together at waist level.

Nina pulled out a chair and sat. 'I can't do it. I'm sorry,' she said to Meg's hands. 'The NA thing. So please stop asking me. And can you ask Mum and Amber to stop as well?'

'Okay,' said Meg's voice from above the hands, very quietly.

'It's just,' said Nina, and then, 'What did you say?'

'I said okay.' Meg sat down.

Sidney stayed standing, back against the wall.

Now Nina saw Meg's face. It was very still and very serious, and it seemed tired. Nina didn't feel embarrassed looking at Meg. What she felt—and it came on like a landslide—was a leaping sort of uncontrolled rage. Shit, came a distant thought, it's my turn.

'What's going on?' said Meg, in that careful, quiet voice.

Nina took hold of the edge of the table. She could hear the grinding of her own teeth. She shook her head.

'Please tell me,' said Meg.

'It won't work,' said Nina.

'What won't work?'

'What do you think?' Nina stared into Meg's eyes. The rage ran up her legs and down her arms. Her voice was like gravel being pushed through a sieve. 'NA. Amber. Don't you *know* it won't work?'

Meg didn't answer.

'Don't you?'

In the background Sidney murmured something and walked off in the direction of the back door.

'Meg?'

Meg raised her shoulders and dropped them. 'No. I don't know that. I can't predict the future.'

'Well don't you *suspect* that it won't work? Based on what's happened in the past?'

Meg shrugged again. 'I'm trying not to think about it that way.'

Nina sighed an enormous broken sigh. She put her face in her hands. Quickly, before another flare of the rage propelled her to shout unreasonable things, she said, 'Look. You do whatever you want, that's fine. But I need to stay away. I'm tired. I can't handle another disappointment. It'll kill me.'

There was a pause, marked only with the strained cadence of Nina's breaths, loud against her palms.

Then Meg said, 'I'm not here about Amber's NA, Nina. I'm here because I'm worried about *you*.'

Nina got to her feet, shoving her chair away. 'Oh God,' she cried, 'can't you see that it's the same thing? I was okay until this NA thing happened! I was fine! I had my life. I was just living, you know, doing the best I could. And then you all started hassling me and . . .'

'And what?'

'This.' Nina gestured at the boxes in the hall, the empty kitchen shelves, the pan in the sink. 'And this.' She ran her hands through the air either side of her face, then her body, the Kennards top, the tracksuit pants. 'I started doing all this stuff and I don't even know why, really, and now I can't . . . I don't know how . . . I can't get . . . back.'

Meg looked up at her. Then she too rose. 'What about a shower?' she said. 'Let's start with that. And then let's find some clean clothes—'

'No, no, no! Listen. Meg.' Nina was aware of a keenness, a peeled kind of sensation. She leaned over the table. 'I don't think . . . I don't even know if I want to go back. To how I was.'

Meg was getting brisk now. She went to the bathroom and looked in. 'Where're your towels?'

Nina followed her. 'They're packed. But I don't want a shower.'

Meg bent over the bath and put in the plug. 'Okay, a bath then.' She turned on the taps.

Nina turned them off again. Then she laughed.

Meg sat down on the rim of the bath, her chin tucked a bit, hands between her knees.

'You're just like Mum,' said Nina. 'Who cares about stupid things like having a bath? What kind of a way is that to spend your life?'

Her anger was strangely elevating. It was like the tail end of a night on ecstasy, a sort of burnt-out, reckless rapture.

Meg looked up at her. 'I think you'd feel a lot better if you got clean. Washed your hair. Put on some fresh clothes. Had some good food.'

'Whatever.' Nina went back into the kitchen.

There was, again, the sound of water running into the bath. Meg appeared in the doorway. 'Where will I find the towels?' She went towards the hallway, the rows of boxes.

Nina didn't answer. She was pacing, she realised, in the small space between the sink and the table. 'This is the thing,' she called to Meg, who was bent over a box. 'I don't think I can go back.'

Meg said something inaudible.

'Because that life'—Nina walked three steps to the sink, turned, walked three steps to the table—'was a shitty life.' She went to the sink again, turned on the tap and drank from it. When she turned around, with long wet drips soaking into the front of the Kennards top, she saw Meg going into the bathroom with some towels in her arms. 'Are you listening to me, Meg? I'm going to tell you about my life now.'

The sound of the water stopped. Meg appeared in the doorway.

'Are you listening?' said Nina again. 'I need you to listen.'

'I'll listen if you hop in the bath,' said Meg. 'Come on. You can talk to me while you have a bath.'

Nina laughed again. Classic Meg. 'This is funny,' she said as she went past her sister and into the bathroom again. 'Don't you think it's funny?'

'Clothes off,' said Meg.

Nina pulled the Kennards top over her head. It stank. She slid down the tracksuit pants and stepped out of them. She got into the bath. The water was hot and clear. She lay back and closed her eyes.

'Before you ask,' she said, 'I broke up with that guy a long time ago. The married one. So there's nothing really obviously *wrong*.' The elevation was still there, the recklessness. She rode it. Words came out, surprising her. 'It's like, I didn't know what I wanted, for such a long time, when I was young. And then I think I might have found out. I found these things, anyway, that seemed like they might be worth having. But I don't . . . have them anymore.'

'Mm.'

'And I can't blame Amber for everything.'

'Here.' A hard curved shape was placed into her hand: a cake of soap, new and smooth.

'I don't know what to do, Meg.'

'Mm.'

'I'm not all right.'

'It's okay. You don't need to make any decisions right now. Just wash yourself.'

Still with her eyes closed, Nina sat up a bit and rubbed the soap automatically under each arm.

'Meg?'

'Mm?'

'Do you think people can change?'

Nina opened her eyes.

Meg was kneeling on the floor beside the bath. She had the sleeves of her jumper pushed high up her arms. She was squirting a blob of Nina's shampoo into the palm of one of her hands. 'Put your head back,' she said.

Nina kept her head up. She looked into her sister's sad, tired face. 'Answer me.'

'Do I think people can change?'

'Yeah.'

'Of course I do.'

'You would say that.'

'Lie back. Get your hair wet.'

Nina slid down again, right down. Her eyes fell shut. Her ears filled and went dead. She could hear the soughing of her own breaths, fattened by the water. A pinprick pop. The glug of her pulse. Her limbs went loose. She was so tired. She allowed her mind to slow, and the recklessness eased. A thick ticking. Heat and blackness. And there, far, far away, behind everything else, deep in her consciousness, something tiny appeared, calling and waving to her. What was it? It wasn't a thought or even a memory. It was a *presence*. Very, very faint.

You have twenty-three new voice messages.

Three missed calls from: Amber.

Missed call from: Amber.

Two missed calls from: Amber.

Please read! written across the top of one of the envelopes that Sidney had tossed onto the kitchen table.

It was Amber. Amber, who Nina through decades of practice had become very good at not really noticing. Because this was what happened with someone like Amber. Someone who didn't just cause but *was* disappointment. Someone who had become a thing that you just had to withstand. Someone of whom it was necessary to have absolutely zero expectations. It reached the point where if you tried to even think about a person like that your mind, of its own accord, veered elsewhere.

Meg's hand was at the back of Nina's head, lifting it gently, insistently. The air broke fresh over Nina's ears. Meg's body was close, her forearm supporting Nina's head. Nina could smell wool and eucalyptus and ylang-ylang. Meg's fingers began to work the shampoo into her hair, rubbing firmly in circles all over her scalp. Nina kept her eyes closed.

They did keep surprising her, her family. Meg hadn't given up; Nina had got that wrong. Of course she hadn't. Even without Robert, here she was, bobbing up, over and over, trying to fix things and calling on Nina to play her part. And here, too, was Amber. Doing something new. Amber, who had never tried to change anything, never shown any resolve or persistence, who had only inflicted herself upon others, indiscriminately, involuntarily, her loveliness and her hideousness—here was Amber, *being intentional.* Nina could feel her own defences, how deep they were, how resistant. *It won't work. I can't handle another disappointment.* But there was also this novelty, this shocking thing: Amber calling to her, calling on and on, calling with determination, with constancy.

Am I ready? she wondered, lying curled in clean sheets, warm and clean herself, her belly full of the pizza that Sidney had brought. She was back in bed, back in her hard, empty room. But now Meg was on the other side of the wall, on the couch, under the chevron blanket, having found herself a spare pillow and more clean sheets in one of the boxes.

Was Nina ready for whatever was coming next? For what might be required of her? She didn't know. The truth was that it had felt like a relief to move away from them, her sisters, to only answer the occasional phone call, show up for Christmas lunch. It had felt like a long-awaited relief, to be more and more on her own. As if this was how her life was meant to be lived. It *was* a relief. It was certainly easier. Just as it had felt easier to give up art, to give up poetry and her students, and Luke, to quit the bookshop and the gallery and get the job at the hospital. That change had felt right—a scaling-down. Things had been steady, contained, there in the basement and the scanner room, those windowless dim places where it was just her.

And when the NA news came, when the phone calls started, and Amber's letters—it had all been too much, the thought of going back. Nina had lost something, some tolerance. Or her nerve. So she'd stayed away, and scaled things even further down—down and down, into ridiculousness. She saw herself, flapping up the ramp at work in the Dunlop Volleys, eating strangers' leftovers, having to be hauled, shaking, to her feet by poor Ursula in the sharp spring sunset, under the fluttering trees. Who did things like that? A crazy person?

'Am I crazy?' she'd whispered to Meg, in the bath.

'No,' Meg had whispered back. 'Not crazy. I think you're just scared.'

She was scared. Very scared. She didn't want to be here in this tiny corner. This hard and tiny corner. In this egg-eating, rocket-picking, smelly-clothes-from-a-garbage-bag-wearing, no-curtains, ugly bare life. Alone. Punishing herself with ill-fitting lingerie. But she didn't know how to get out. How to fix herself.

Even if Nina, as Meg put it, *showed up*, and even if Amber forgave her, and even if Amber got clean—and stayed clean— there would still be climate change, and the oppression of women and girls, and racism and war and illness and people just dying all of a sudden in car accidents, driving into trees. There would still be all of that.

Did Meg really believe that a bath and some shampoo, and clean clothes and a good dinner, and falling asleep in fresh sheets with your big sister just there on the other side of the wall was *anything at all*, in the grand scheme of things?

Well, here was the thing. Yes. Evidently Meg did.

Do you think, Amber had said, in the watery darkness of the verandah, in the smothering clamour of the rain, in the most despairing voice that Nina had ever heard, *that I haven't tried a hundred times to beat this?* The same Amber who was, at the age of thirty-three, trying again.

Nina did a lot of walking around, in the weeks that followed. She tried, because backsliding felt so terribly close, to keep things—to keep herself—light. Just showering and dressing in her own clothes, her old underwear, which Meg had unpacked and returned to the cupboards, and eating what Meg—who was dropping in every day and putting things in the fridge and pantry—called 'proper food', just doing that felt like a lot. There was a kind of sick bubble inside her that she worried was going to burst at any moment, and send her back.

She walked the streets of her suburb. She passed fences frothing with jasmine and sucked in the rich air like a smoker with a cigarette just off a long-haul flight. She approached a woody shrub that stuck straight up, erupting at its top into coarse clumps of small leaves and quills of yellow flowers. A wattlebird hung upside down in it, probing, its beak evilly curved, its red wattles like genitals, its head sleek, its feathers scalloped. A cat ran out to her from a driveway, its white paws a blur, its tail thrilling upwards. It rippled against her legs and she stopped to pat it, thinking of Robert.

Everywhere she saw rubbish. Torn plastic bags, McDonald's wrappers, the crooked skirts of Slurpee lids impaled on long fat Slurpee straws, a once-pink sock on the road, flattened and grey. Everywhere she saw flowers. Wisteria, lilac, the studs of yellow daisies, native irises pushing from their casings, grevillea, alyssum, wallflowers and poppies, purple convolvulus in lazy drapes, flutters of weed-flowers above the tide of grass in the vacant block, lemony yellow and pink. And she could hardly miss the people. Girls in twos and threes, wearing leggings and cropped t-shirts that were glaring clean, smelling of expensive laundry powder, phones in their hands. Thick-necked bodybuilders easing themselves from behind the wheels of their Commodores outside the twenty-four-hour gym, holding lightly their big soft bags. The woman from the shopping centre's florist eating her lunch at an outdoor table, the end of a pink ribbon hanging from the pocket of her blue apron.

People, rubbish, flowers. And bricks and timber posts and streetlights and ropy lumps in the pavement and gum trees and dogs and children and the whizz of bicycle tyres, a weak afternoon moon very high up, the wavery bright reflection of the council swimming pool against the brick wall, over the brick fence. And the trains going through as she walked on the bike path, the flash of light on their metal, the flicking of their windows.

She took two weeks off work and she walked every day and didn't do much else apart from the showering and the dressing and the eating, and the acceptance of Meg's care.

('Did you have breakfast?'

'It's only nine o'clock, Meg, but yes, I did.'

'What did you have?')

She was grateful, really, even if the whole business so often felt like a tussle, and made her behave like a teenager. She was immensely, unspeakably grateful.

Each night she fell into bed exhausted and slept blackly until morning. Meg had put the curtains back up and so the first thing to do every day was to open them, and let in the light, and look up at the sky.

The bubble shrank. Some days it seemed to have disappeared entirely and she was able to slow down. Then it would swell back up, badly, and she would have to skip off again, trying to outrun it.

She was tired almost all the time. She felt like a piece of floating cloth—impossibly light, transparent almost—through which everything obliviously passed, thing after thing, leaving small traces.

Mostly she was pretty sure that she didn't have what it was going to take, what would be required of her. Meg appeared then—in real life, or in her head, annoyingly persistent, dragging her up. *Don't worry about that for now.* Okay, Nina thought. Okay. And she walked and walked, and let things pass through her, let the traces be left. And she got stronger.

She went to see Gwen and was struck all over again by the order, the lack of Robert. The immaculate white walls of the townhouse's interior. Only one painting in the kitchen–living area, from Robert's garden chair series: orange curved plastic and rusted metal against melted-looking grass. The floor—timber boards of artificial-seeming evenness and colour, with a satin finish—was spotless, the furniture new and strange. A low couch in pale grey, all rectangles, a wall-hung flatscreen TV, a sideboard with a vase of proteas and nothing else. Everywhere surfaces. Not one pile of papers or laundry or books.

'This place still seems so . . . new,' said Nina.

'I don't think I'll ever get used to it,' said Gwen.

By the door hung Gwen's bushwalking jacket and hat.

'Have you been on any good walks lately?' said Nina. 'Are you still going with your group?'

'Yes. A couple have dropped off. Liz, and Gillian. We're all getting old. But I've been going with Amber too. Her idea.'

They sat either side of one end of the kitchen's long, shining bench and drank tea and ate small quiches that Nina had brought, goat's cheese and spinach.

'What's it like, walking with Amber?'

'Fast.' Gwen's lips pursed with a held-in smile. For a moment she darted her eyes, brown and shiny, to meet Nina's.

A fat surge of need came upon Nina. 'Oh no,' she said.

'What is it?'

Nina's heart was racing. She looked down at her food. Her voice came out high and choked. 'Mum, I didn't help her. Something happened, a terrible thing, and I didn't help her; I ran away instead.'

'Neen.' Gwen got up and came around the bench, behind Nina. Her embrace was bony but surprisingly firm.

Nina stiffened, she couldn't help it, but Gwen didn't let go. Staying close, smelling dry and powdery and a little bit like an old lady, she rubbed Nina's arms and touched her hair. She spread her fingers over Nina's shoulders and pressed them down. 'Relax,' she whispered.

Nina tried to.

Gwen's fingertips kneaded the hard muscles across Nina's upper back. 'We all blame ourselves; it's what happens,' her voice said, right in Nina's ear. 'But I've said it before, and I'll say it again: I'm your mother and I get to tell you, you are not to blame for anything. And you must believe me.'

Nina did not remember Gwen having ever said this before. Had she? Perhaps she had. Perhaps Nina had not been able to hear her, over everything else.

After the meal, when Nina took the dishes to the sink, she saw a pamphlet stuck to the fridge: *Families Living with Addiction: The three Cs.*

She read the lines, with their vigorously asserted key words: *We didn't CAUSE it, we can't CURE it, we can't CONTROL it.*

'Do you believe in this?' she said. She touched the edge of the paper. 'This thing? The three Cs?'

Gwen was still sitting at the bench. She took a while to answer. 'Not really,' she said. 'Sometimes I still think I caused it. Or I could have stopped it from happening. If I'd done some things differently. If I'd been, I don't know, *better.*'

'Why have you got it on the fridge then? Are you *trying* to believe it?'

Gwen did one of her soft, breathy laughs. She straightened her back. Her face was slightly flushed, and she blinked and darted her eyes. Looking downwards she said quickly, in her shy voice, 'Mostly, Nina, I just believe in love.'

Then Gwen took Nina out into the small, tidy courtyard, to a tidy raised bed of peas.

'Look,' she said.

The vines tumbled upwards. Their white flowers shone. At the ends of their branches thinner stems made searching curls into the air. Gwen bent forward and put her fragile hands into the mess of them. Her eyes were closed. She was smiling.

One thing that Nina could do, one day soon, was go onto the university website and look at the positions coming up for the next semester, for casual tutors.

Another thing would be to wash all that lingerie, and hang it from the Hills hoist in the middle of the backyard. She'd do it on a weekend, when the weather was warmer, and perhaps she'd invite people to come in the evening and they would sit under the hanging rows of lace and satin. And she'd say, 'Take what you like.'

Who would come? Meg. There were bras big enough for Meg, and there were the boxer short things—they might be her style. Gwen. Why not? Gwen would blush and blink and smile her slow smile when Sidney chose something—a camisole of pale blue silk, perhaps—and made her take it. Of course Sidney would be there, getting that green bra after all. Sidney, and Ellis, smiling, in his shorts, with his bike-rider's calves.

Maybe Nina would invite Ursula. Maybe Ursula would bring Ros, and they could confer over the lingerie, Ros's fake nails clashing as she tried to read the tags. They would drink prosecco, probably, and bring a bag of chips. And there would be Viv in one of her tie-dyed singlets, with her purple cotton overalls and her health sandals, and a stubbie of beer.

And would Amber be there? Would Amber come?

She might. And then Nina would have to worry about whether or not to serve booze.

Amber might come and do her Casual Act and she—Nina—wouldn't be able to stand it.

Or Amber might say that she would come and then not come, which would be worse.

There were any number of things to worry about. Any thought of Amber, any interaction with her, would have a kind of glowing aura of worry around it. Was there some way to remove this?

Probably not.

Might it thin, though, in time? With exposure? As they kept on seeing each other?

If Amber came she would almost certainly take all the best lingerie, before anyone else got a chance. She would snatch things down and stuff them in her bag without even checking if the sizes were right, just going for the nicest colours, the best fabrics, the prettiest trims. It would be hard not to laugh at her standing there in the heavy gold light, against the purple shadows, with her concentrating face and her hunched shoulders, packing away like one of those chipmunks you see on the internet stuffing tissues into its cheeks.

It would be best to laugh. Although Nina might not want to. She might feel annoyed. There wasn't much to be done about that.

Anyway, Amber might not come. The important thing was to invite her, and to do the thing anyway, whether or not she showed up.

The others would come. That was something to rely on.

❧

But before any of that could happen, there had to be something else.

Nina, standing outside the church hall on a windy and cold evening in November, saw the last of the sun in the branches of a row of ragged sprouting spring shrubs, their small new leaves round and folded like the ears of just-born animals, almost too tender, too pink, almost ugly but not quite.

Nina, standing outside the church hall in clean clothes that were her own, in her own cotton underwear that fitted, with clean hair smelling of ylang-ylang, felt strange and damp, unsheathed.

Nina, walking up and down beside the spiked metal fence, near the open gate, saw through the tall churchy window with its pointy top the flat white light of an energy-saving globe, an internal wall painted a dreary beige, a mission-brown doorframe, and thought: Commitment is to everything—to ugliness, to boredom, to frustration, to acute discomfort. To disappointment. She took a deep breath of the evening air and willed herself not to run.

Nina, standing—cold now, her feet cold in her nice ankle boots, her hands in the pockets of her jacket—by the open gate, smelled dank cement and cigarette butts and the wet leaves of the shrubs, sharply alive.

Nina, shivering now and realising that she had timed things badly, that arriving early and having to wait was a mistake, paced back and forth outside the spiked fence, away from the gate, back to the gate, away and back, away and back.

And then went just a little further down the narrow side street with its rows of cars. And then was walking fast, almost running, away. Twin shabby terrace houses, garbage bins, a chained bike. A car park with a side row of gum trees, their roots bumping up the black asphalt, bending the painted lines. A tall apartment building with balconies—pot plants, clothes racks, chairs. The watery evening sky, one faint star.

And then stopped. Breathing hard. Perhaps crying a bit. And stood with folded arms and a stinging nose and a hurting throat.

And turned around.

And walked back.

And Nina—rushing now, because she could see people emerging from the side door, from the mission-brown entrance, crossing the cement yard and going out the open gate—reached the spiky fence and thought with a lurch, What if I don't recognise her?

Nina, blinking hard, stood by the gate and stared intently as people came through it.

A man with a scary face and a small head, short dark hair, a big round body in a light grey tracksuit.

A woman with nice clothes, car keys in hand. Pink lipstick.

A woman with a crazy grey mullet, making chewing motions, carrying a plastic bag.

A man in a flannel shirt and jeans, with a bald head and wire-framed glasses pushed on top of it. A neck tattoo, *BELIEVE*. Walking with a gliding motion.

A woman in a big khaki jacket with fake-fur trim around its hood, moving fast, head down. Jeans. Sneakers. Hair tied back. Thin. Broken. Ruined. A person to feel sorry for, to be afraid of, to avoid if at all possible. A person with toxic energy. A person with poor impulse control. A person who left wreckages, trails of ruin.

A person whose life was not even halfway finished. A person who was here, now, who had been at a meeting, who had sat through that meeting.

Nina stepped forward.

Amber looked up, and saw her.

ACKNOWLEDGMENTS

THIS BOOK WAS WRITTEN ON the unceded lands of the Wurundjeri Woi Wurrung people of the Kulin Nation, the Bunurong people, the Dharug people and the Kuku Yalanji people, and the author pays her respects to Elders past, present and emerging. Always was, always will be Aboriginal land.

Many thanks to Jane Palfreyman, Jane Novak, Ali Lavau, Christa Munns, and Amy Sambrooke and Veechi Stuart at Varuna The National Writers' House, Jacky Winter Gardens, Ashley Hay, Helen Garner, Tegan Bennett Daylight, Kate Ryan, Louisa Syme, Rachel Power, Claudia Murray-White, and Mick Turner.